DC LEAGUE OF SUPERPETS

THE GREAT MXY-UP

DC LEAGUE OF SUPER-PETS

THE GREAT MXY-UP

WRITTEN BY Heath Corson

ILLUSTRATED BY Bobby Timony

COLORS BY Jeremy Lawson

LETTERS BY Wes Abbott

Jim Chadwick Editor
Courtney Jordan Assistant Editor
Steve Cook Design Director – Books
Amie Brockway-Metcalf Publication Design
Sandy Alonzo Publication Production

Marie Javins Editor-in-Chief, DC Comics

Anne DePies Senior VP – General Manager
Jim Lee Publisher & Chief Creative Officer
Don Falletti VP – Manufacturing Operations & Workflow Management
Lawrence Ganem VP – Talent Services
Alison Gill Senior VP – Manufacturing & Operations
Jeffrey Kaufman VP – Editorial Strategy & Programming
Nick J. Napolitano VP – Manufacturing Administration & Design
Nancy Spears VP – Revenue

MIX
Paper from
responsible sources
FSC® C002589

Library of Congress Cataloging-in-Publication Data

Names. Corson, Heath. writer. | Timony, Bobby, illustrator. | Lawson,
    Jeremy (Cartoonist). colourist. | Abbott, Wes, letterer.
Title: DC League of Super-Pets : the great mxy-up / written by Heath Corson
    ; illustrated by Bobby Timony : colors by Jeremy Lawson : letters by Wes
    Abbott.
Other titles: Great mxy-up
Description: Burbank, CA : DC Comics, [2022] | "Superman created by Jerry
    Siegel and Joe Shuster, by special arrangement with the Jerry Siegel
    family" | Audience: Ages 8-12 | Audience: Grades 4-6 | Summary: "There
    is nothing the Super-Pets love more than spending time with their
    heroes, but are finding it difficult to be taken seriously as members of
    the team when their humans just don't understand them. When Mr. Mxyzptlk
    (a magical imp from the fifth dimension) arrives in Metropolis with a
    plan to wreak a little chaos and destruction, the Justice League are
    caught in his trap! The Super-Pets will need to come up with a plan to
    prevent Mxy's mischief from destroying the city-while somehow trying to
    rescue their human counterparts. The only problem is, they may need to
    recruit their greatest enemy in order to defeat him. DC League of
    Super-Pets: The Great Mxy-Up picks up immediately from where the movie
    leaves off!"-- Provided by publisher.
Identifiers: LCCN 2022000286 | ISBN 9781779509925 (trade paperback)
Subjects: CYAC: Graphic novels. | Superheroes--Fiction. | Pets--Fiction. |
    LCGFT: Superhero comics. | Funny animal comics. | Graphic novels.
Classification: LCC PZ7.7.C6736 Dc 2022 | DDC 741.5/973--dc23/eng/20220131
LC record available at https://lccn.loc.gov/2022000286

DEDICATION

Moosie
Tucker
Jasmine
Phineas
Petey
Missy
Dewey
Sammy, aka Princess Kittyface
Perkins
Peanut
Chelsea
Filthy the Rat
Nellie
Huckleberry Finch
Hector

We the creative team of this graphic novel would like to dedicate
this book to our own super-pets, past and present.
Here's to all the loving inspiration you gave us with your companionship.
Though some days we struggled to do this book with you,
we certainly couldn't have done it without you.

TABLE OF CONTENTS

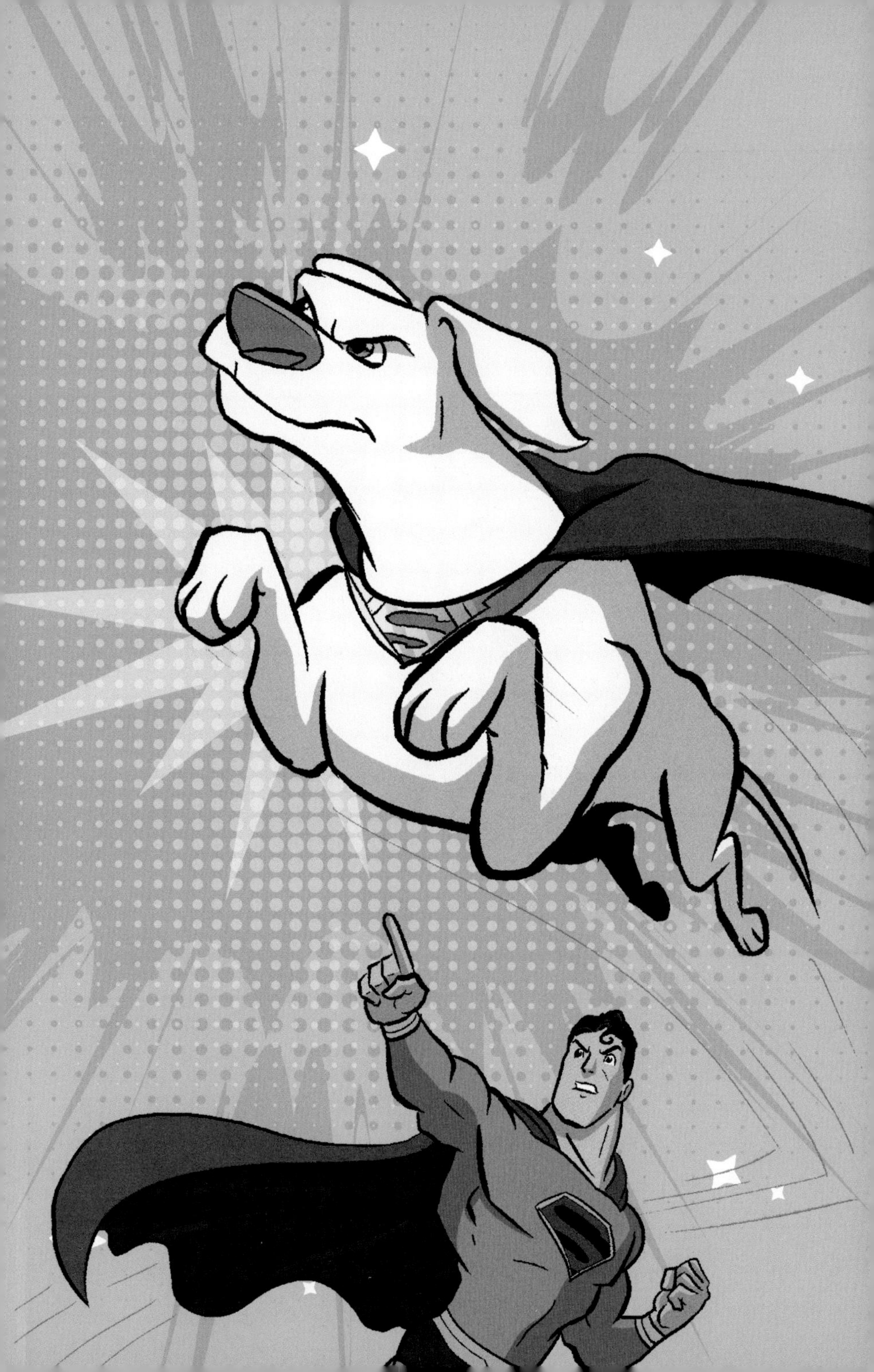

CHAPTER 1
No Pets Allowed

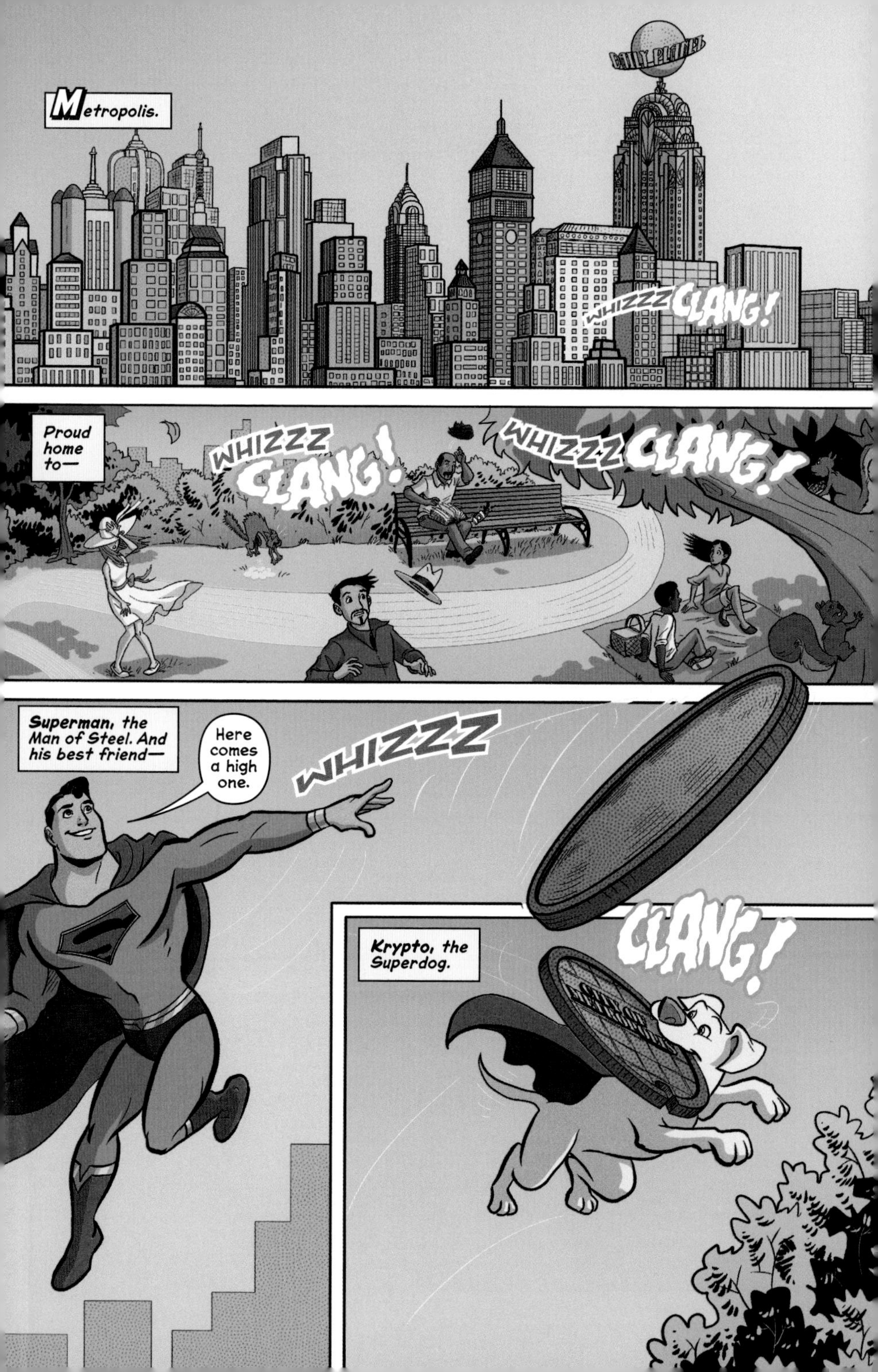
Metropolis.
DAILY PLANET
WHIZZZ CLANG!
Proud home to—
WHIZZZ CLANG!
WHIZZZ CLANG!
Superman, the Man of Steel. And his best friend—
Here comes a high one.
WHIZZZ
CLANG!
Krypto, the Superdog.

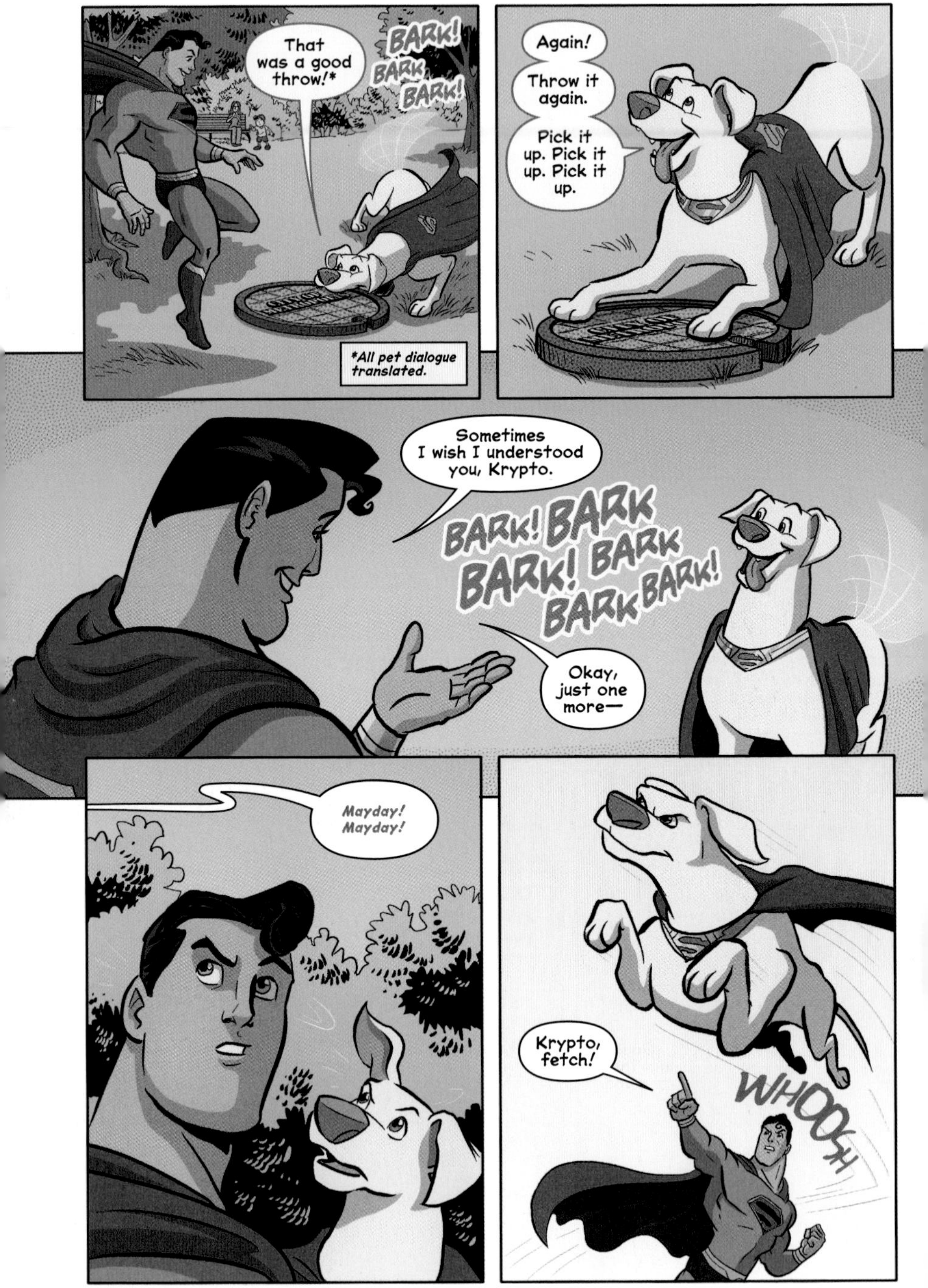
That was a good throw!*
BARK! BARK BARK!
*All pet dialogue translated.
Again!
Throw it again.
Pick it up. Pick it up. Pick it up.
Sometimes I wish I understood you, Krypto.
BARK! BARK BARK! BARK BARK BARK!
Okay, just one more—
Mayday! Mayday!
Krypto, fetch!
WHOOSH

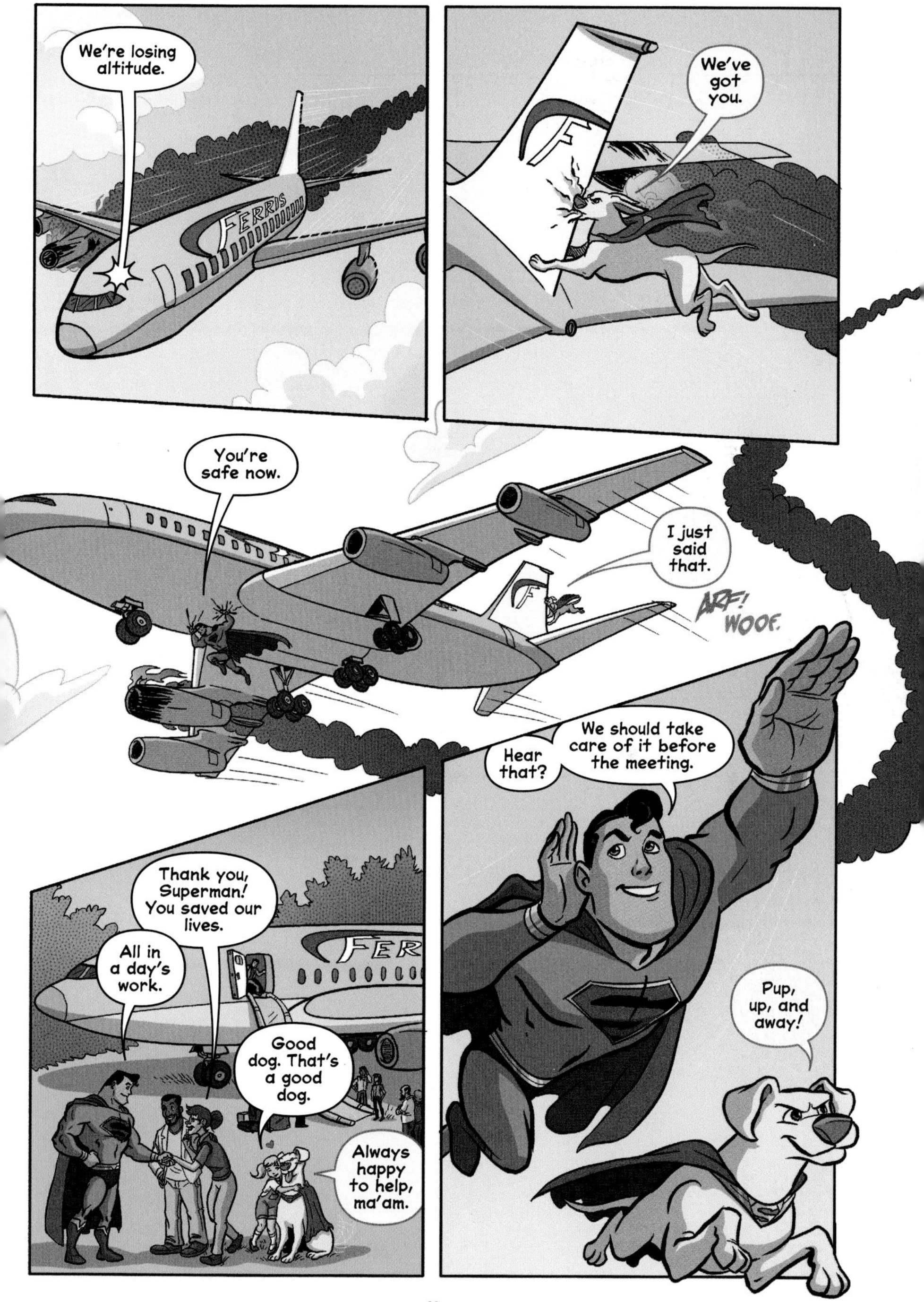
We're losing altitude.
We've got you.
You're safe now.
I just said that.
ARF! WOOF.
Hear that?
We should take care of it before the meeting.
Thank you, Superman! You saved our lives.
All in a day's work.
Good dog. That's a good dog.
Always happy to help, ma'am.
Pup, up, and away!

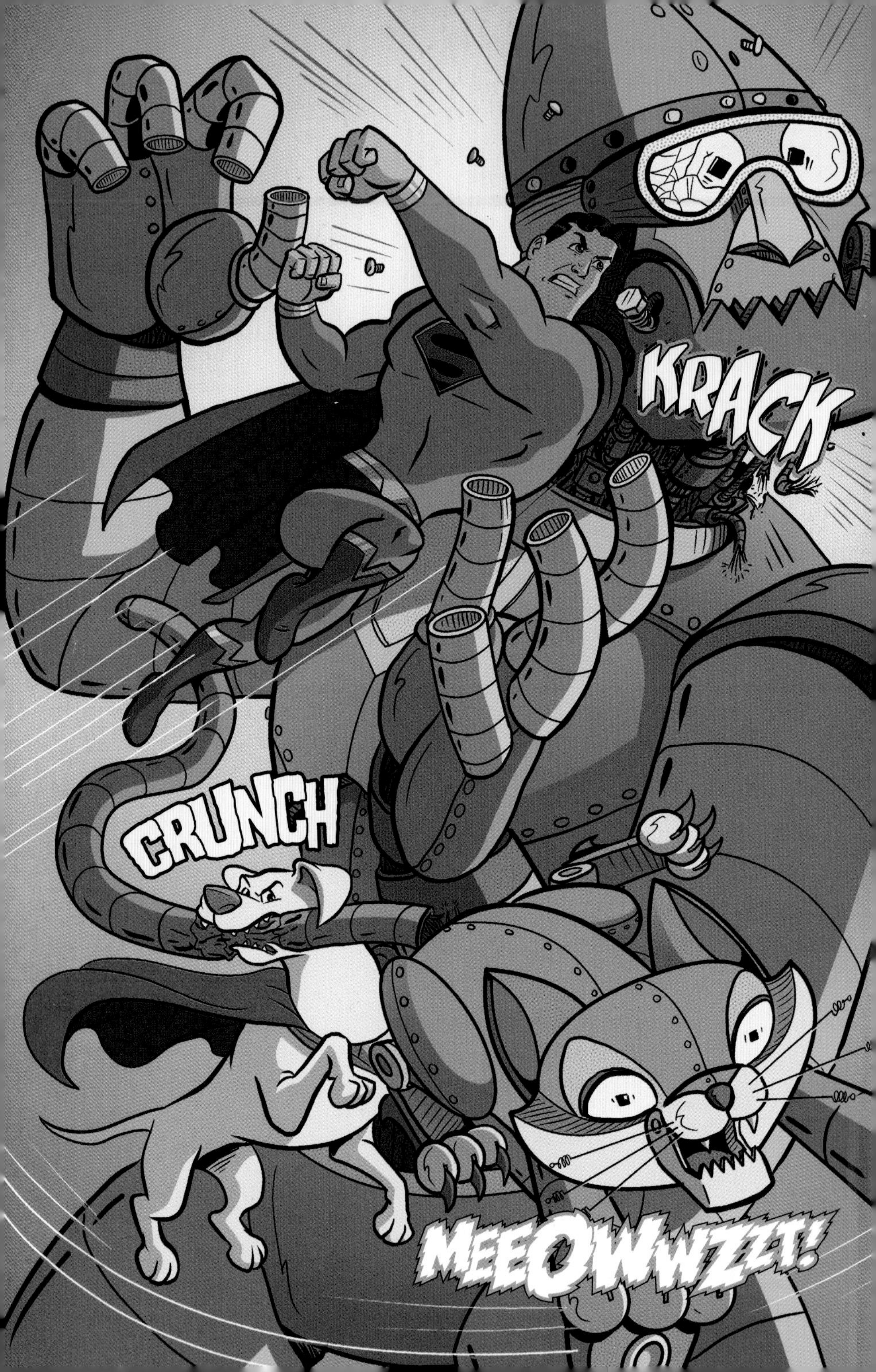
KRACK
CRUNCH
MEEOWWZZZT!

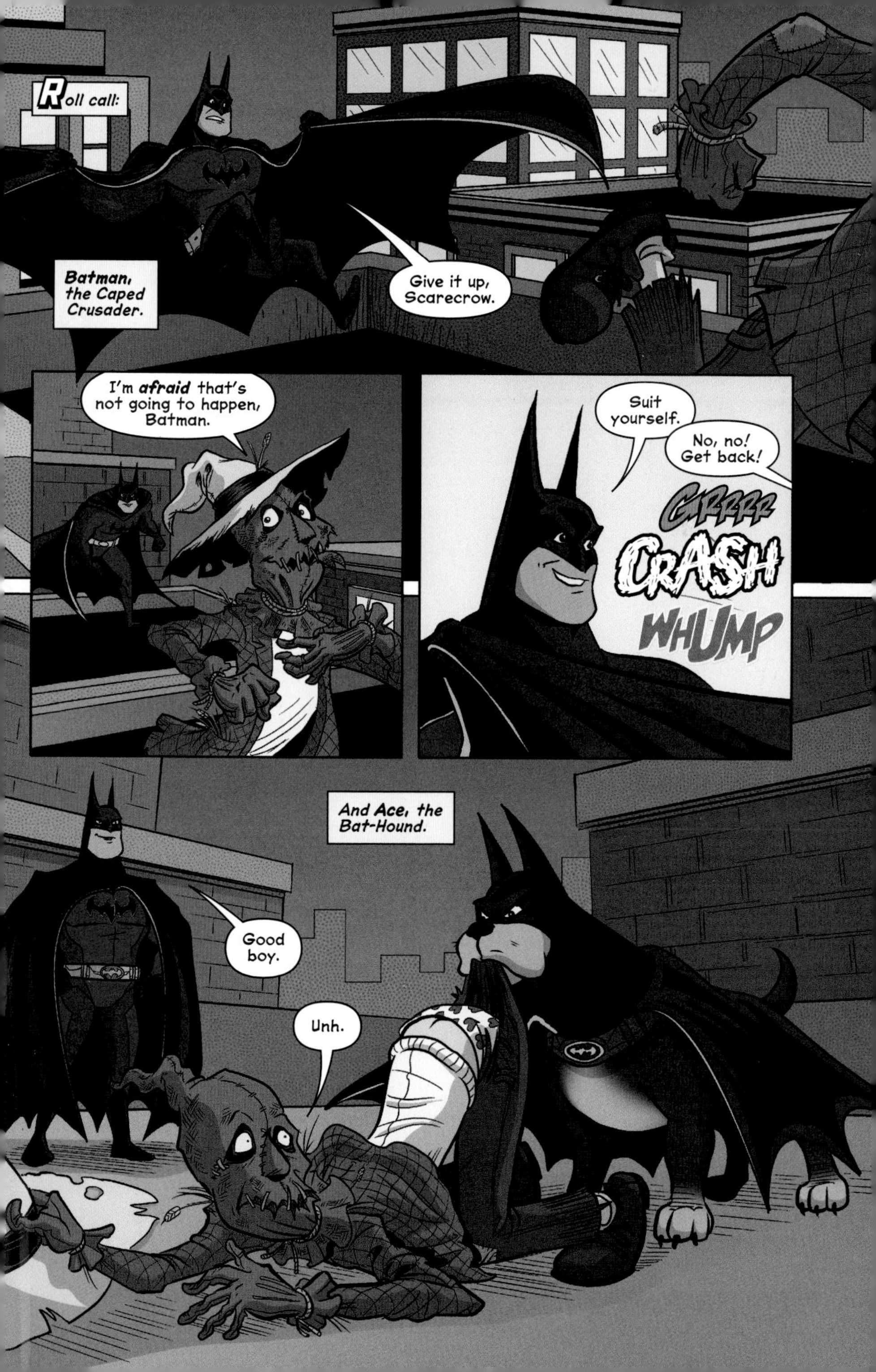
Roll call:
Batman, the Caped Crusader.
Give it up, Scarecrow.
I'm **afraid** that's not going to happen, Batman.
Suit yourself.
No, no! Get back!
GRRRR
CRASH
WHUMP
And Ace, the Bat-Hound.
Good boy.
Unh.

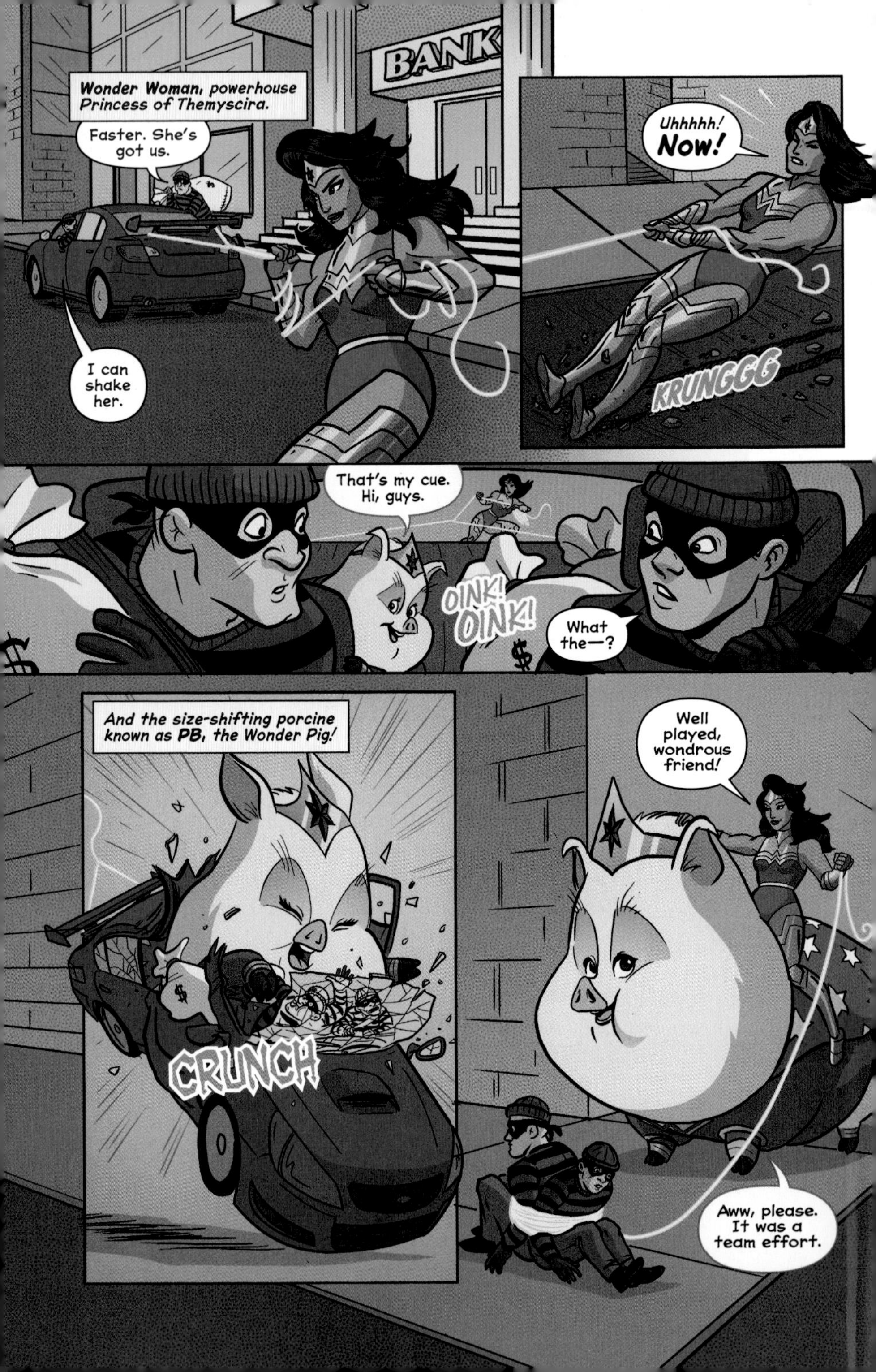
BANK
Wonder Woman, powerhouse Princess of Themyscira.
Faster. She's got us.
I can shake her.
Uhhhhh! Now!
KRUNGGG
That's my cue. Hi, guys.
OINK! OINK!
What the—?
And the size-shifting porcine known as PB, the Wonder Pig!
CRUNCH
Well played, wondrous friend!
Aww, please. It was a team effort.

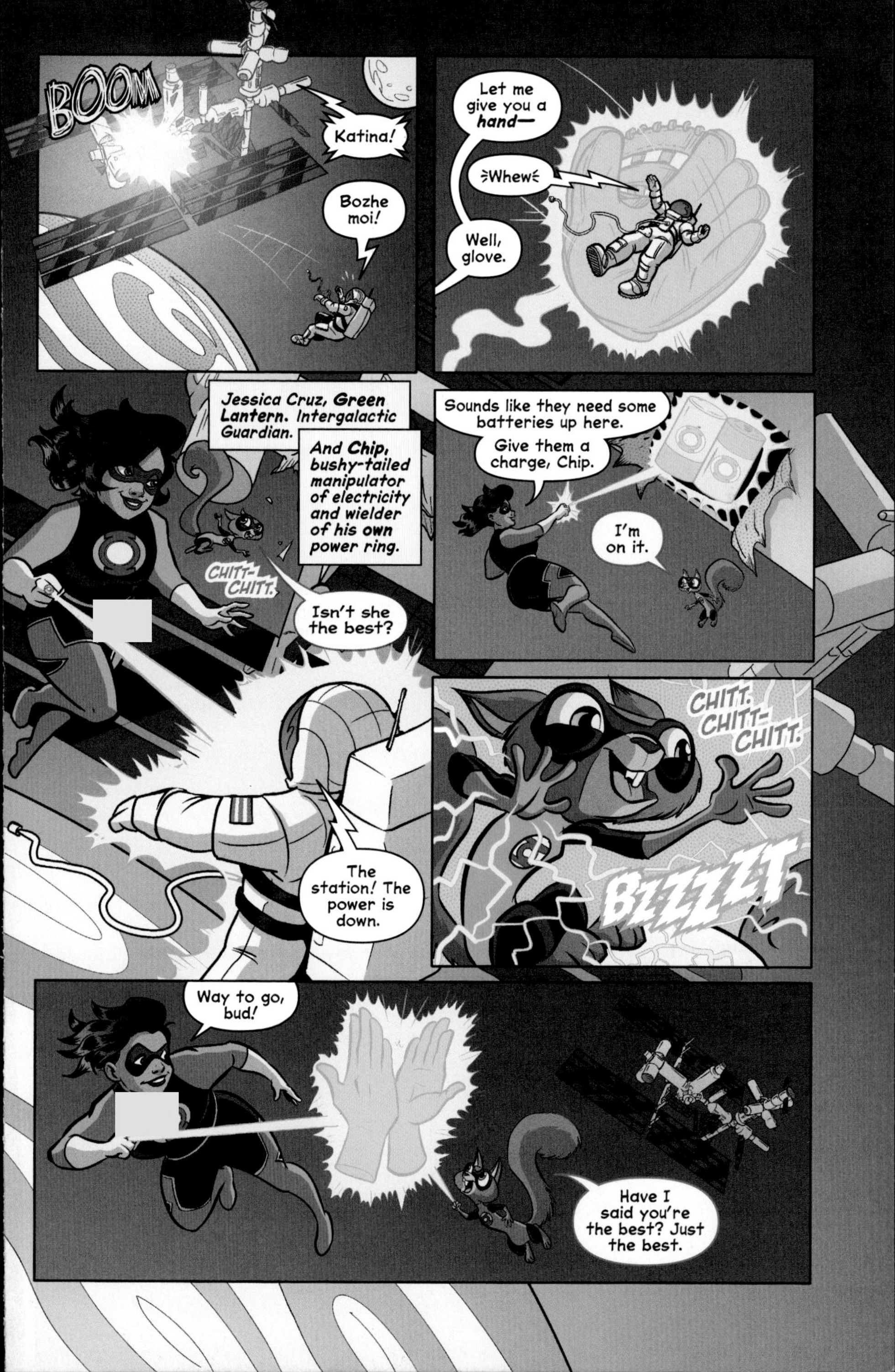

BOOM
Katina!
Bozhe moi!
Let me give you a hand—
Whew
Well, glove.
Jessica Cruz, Green Lantern. Intergalactic Guardian.
And Chip, bushy-tailed manipulator of electricity and wielder of his own power ring.
CHITT-CHITT.
Isn't she the best?
The station! The power is down.
Sounds like they need some batteries up here.
Give them a charge, Chip.
I'm on it.
CHITT. CHITT-CHITT.
BZZZZT
Way to go, bud!
Have I said you're the best? Just the best.

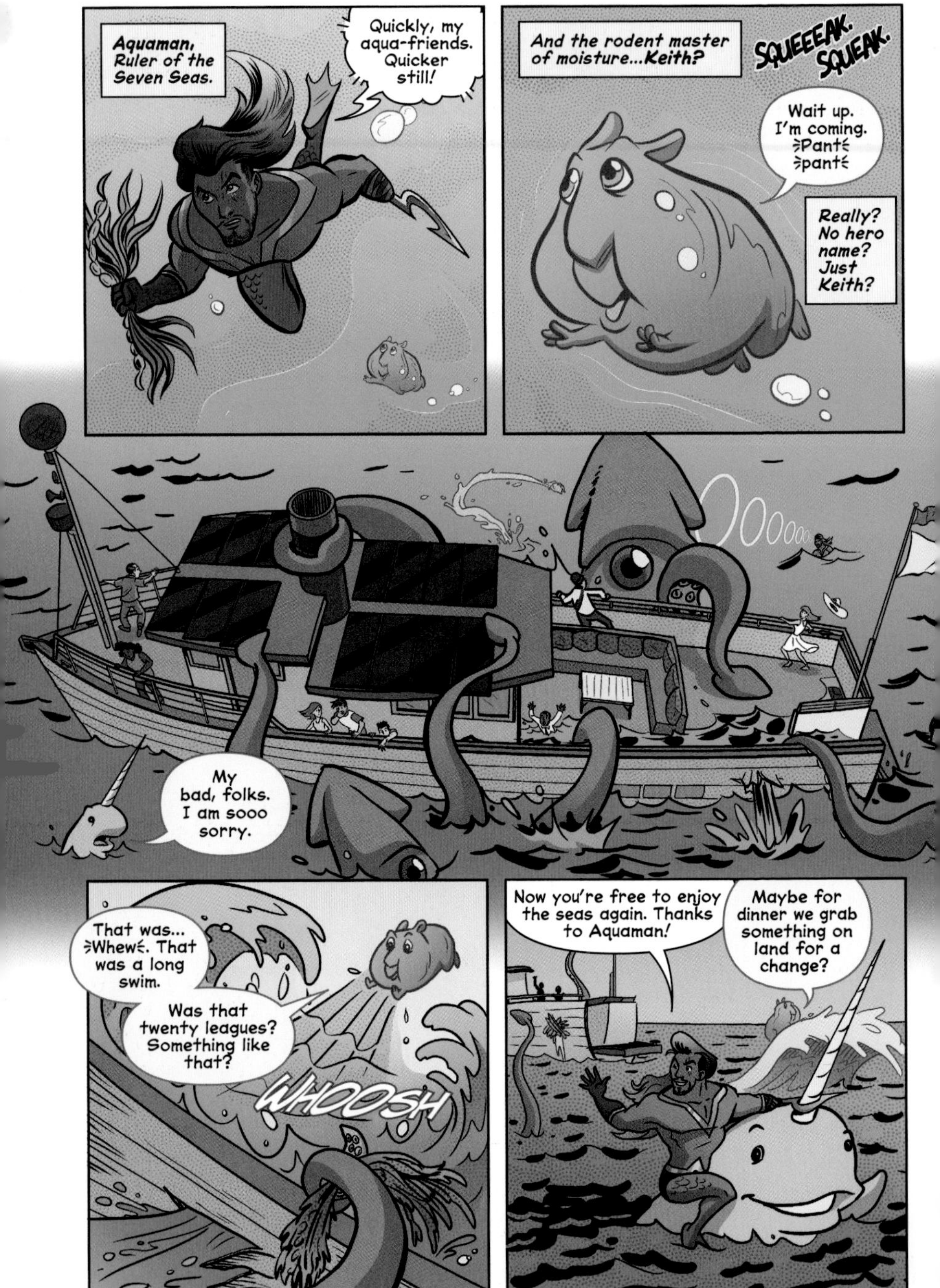
Aquaman, Ruler of the Seven Seas.
Quickly, my aqua-friends. Quicker still!
And the rodent master of moisture...Keith?
SQUEEEAK. SQUEAK.
Wait up. I'm coming. ≥Pant≤ ≥pant≤
Really? No hero name? Just Keith?
OOOooo
My bad, folks. I am sooo sorry.
That was... ≥Whew≤. That was a long swim.
Was that twenty leagues? Something like that?
WHOOSH
Now you're free to enjoy the seas again. Thanks to Aquaman!
Maybe for dinner we grab something on land for a change?

Cyborg, the cybernetic man.

Danger! Critical systems compromised.

Yep, there's your problem, General.

Looks like that virus overheated the quantum locator.

I think my guy can reroute it.

SW-EEAK SW-EEEAK

And Mark, the fuzzy flambé.

Who also apparently doesn't have a super nom de plume.

Cool your servos. I'll find it.

TSSSS TSSSS

wer on ading...

* Power on
* Loading...

All systems operational!

Oh, thank goodness.

There you are, General. Good as new.

And FYI, "password1234" is *not* a secure password.

SW-EEEAK

17

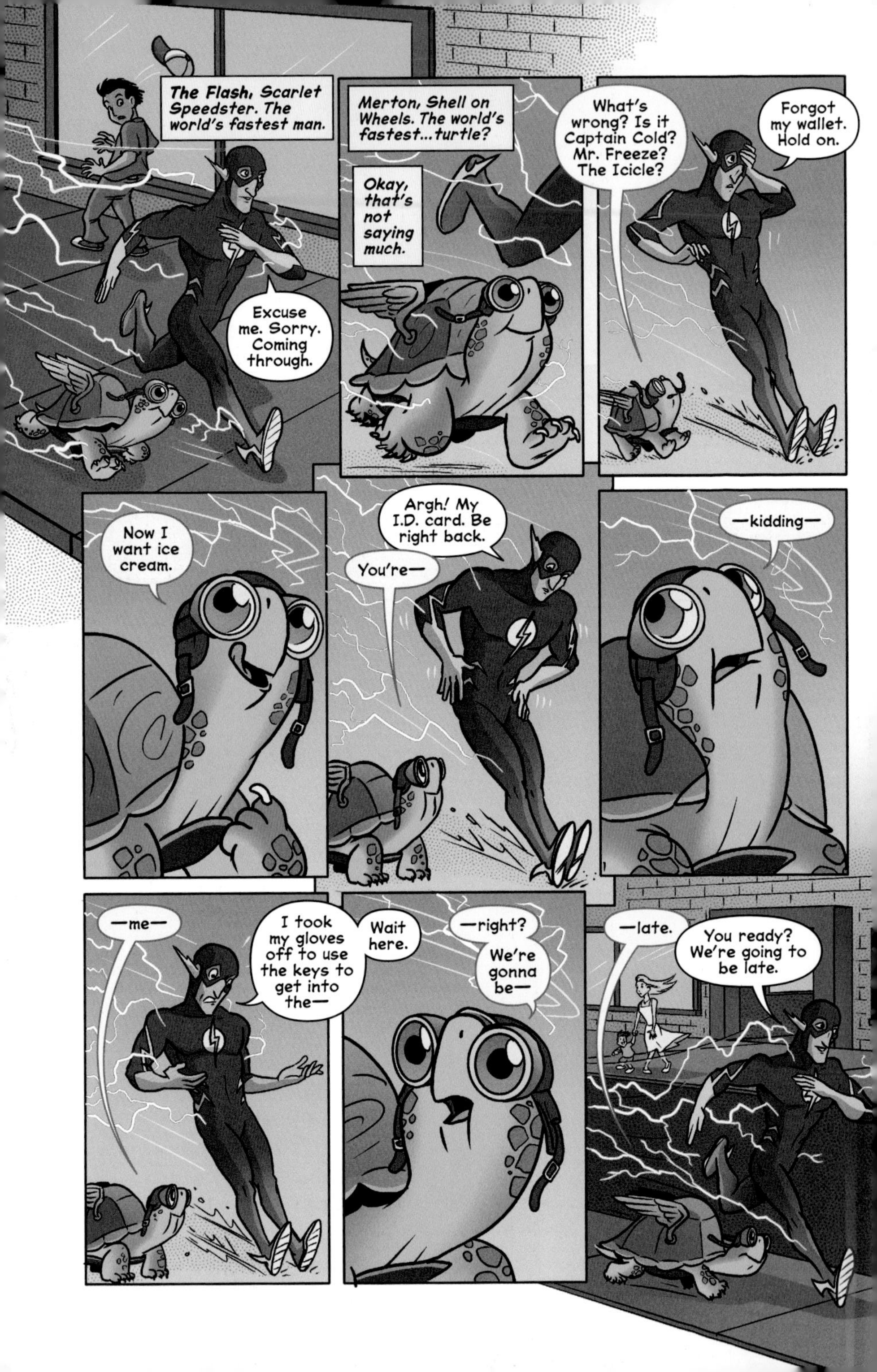
The Flash, Scarlet Speedster. The world's fastest man.
Excuse me. Sorry. Coming through.
Merton, Shell on Wheels. The world's fastest...turtle?
Okay, that's not saying much.
What's wrong? Is it Captain Cold? Mr. Freeze? The Icicle?
Forgot my wallet. Hold on.
Now I want ice cream.
Argh! My I.D. card. Be right back.
You're—
—kidding—
—me—
I took my gloves off to use the keys to get into the—
Wait here.
—right?
We're gonna be—
—late.
You ready? We're going to be late.

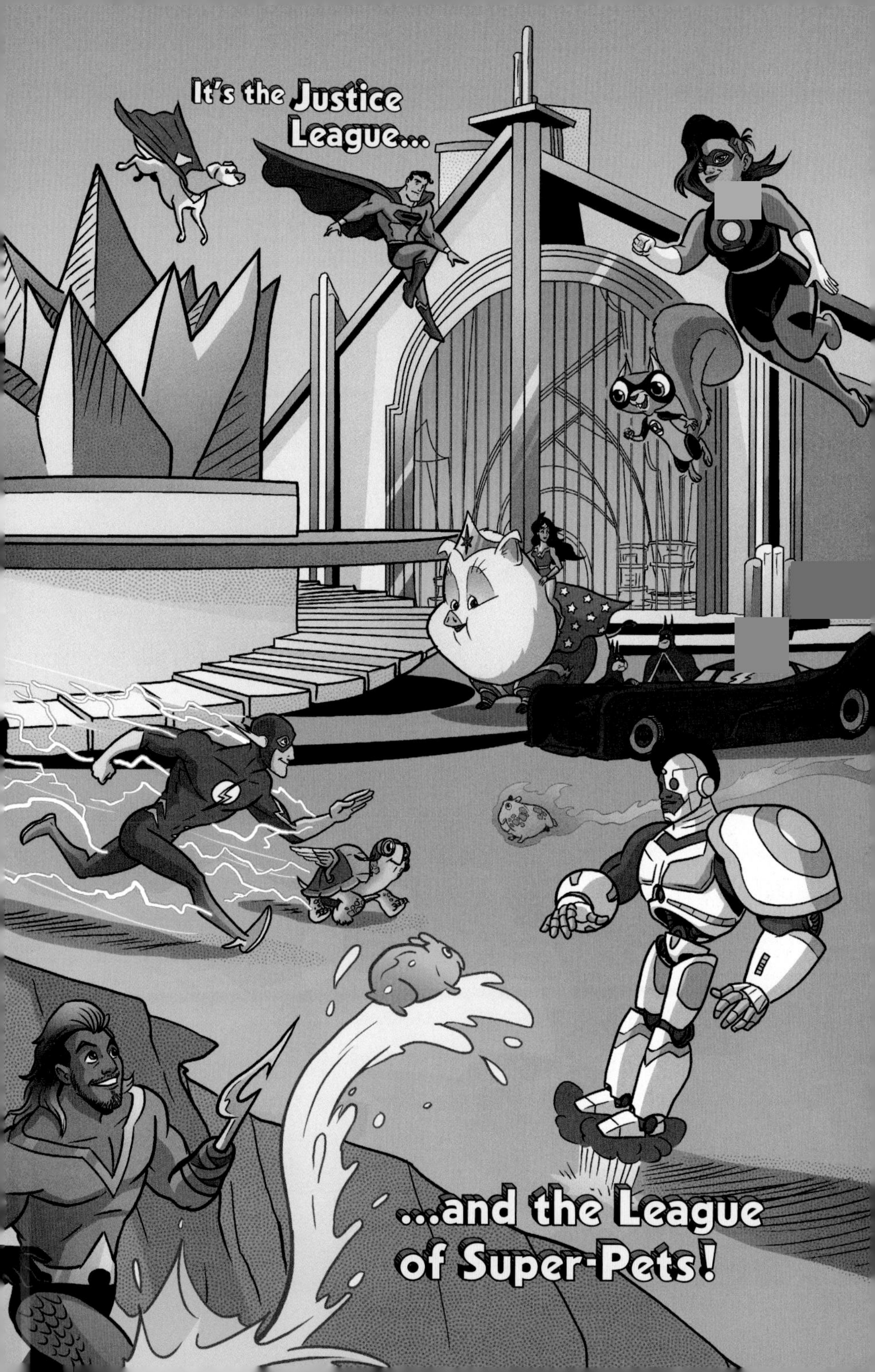
It's the Justice League...
...and the League of Super-Pets!

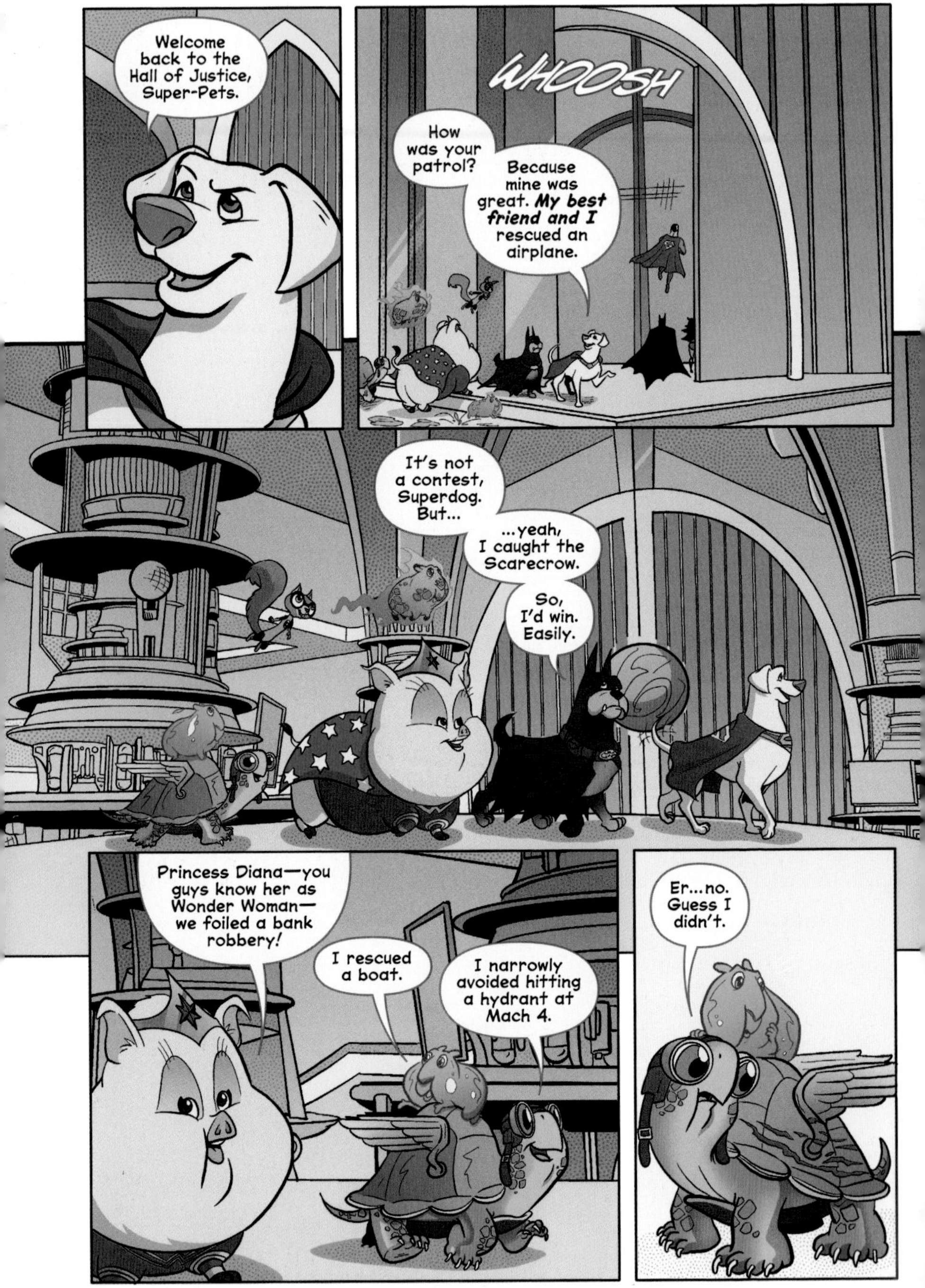

Welcome back to the Hall of Justice, Super-Pets.
WHOOSH
How was your patrol?
Because mine was great. ***My best friend and I*** rescued an airplane.
It's not a contest, Superdog. But...
...yeah, I caught the Scarecrow.
So, I'd win. Easily.
Princess Diana—you guys know her as Wonder Woman—we foiled a bank robbery!
I rescued a boat.
I narrowly avoided hitting a hydrant at Mach 4.
Er...no. Guess I didn't.

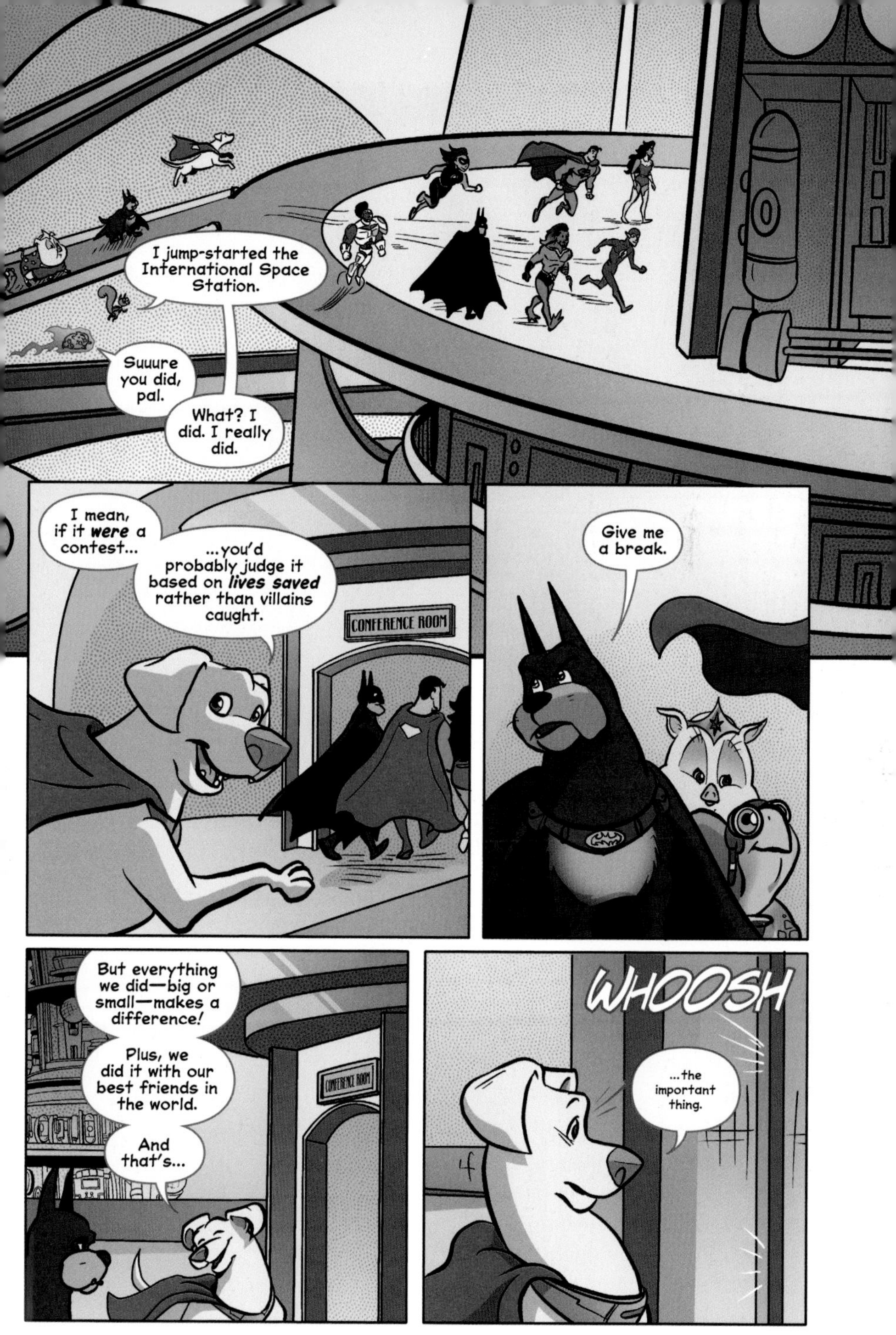
I jump-started the International Space Station.
Suuure you did, pal.
What? I did. I really did.
I mean, if it **were** a contest...
...you'd probably judge it based on **lives saved** rather than villains caught.
CONFERENCE ROOM
Give me a break.
But everything we did—big or small—makes a difference!
Plus, we did it with our best friends in the world.
And that's...
CONFERENCE ROOM
WHOOSH
...the important thing.

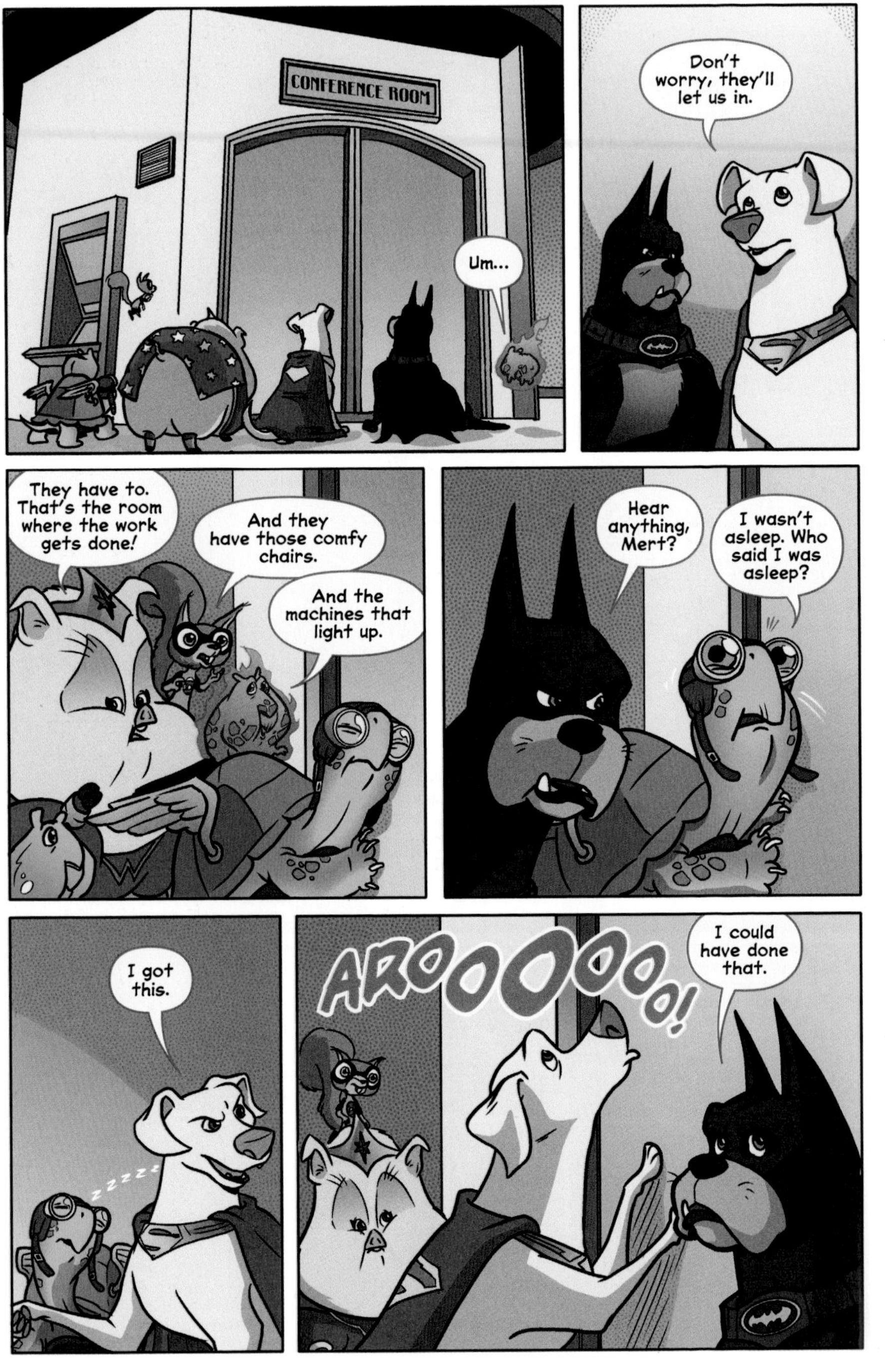
CONFERENCE ROOM
Um...
Don't worry, they'll let us in.
They have to. That's the room where the work gets done!
And they have those comfy chairs.
And the machines that light up.
Hear anything, Mert?
I wasn't asleep. Who said I was asleep?
I got this.
ZZZZZ
AROOOOOo!
I could have done that.

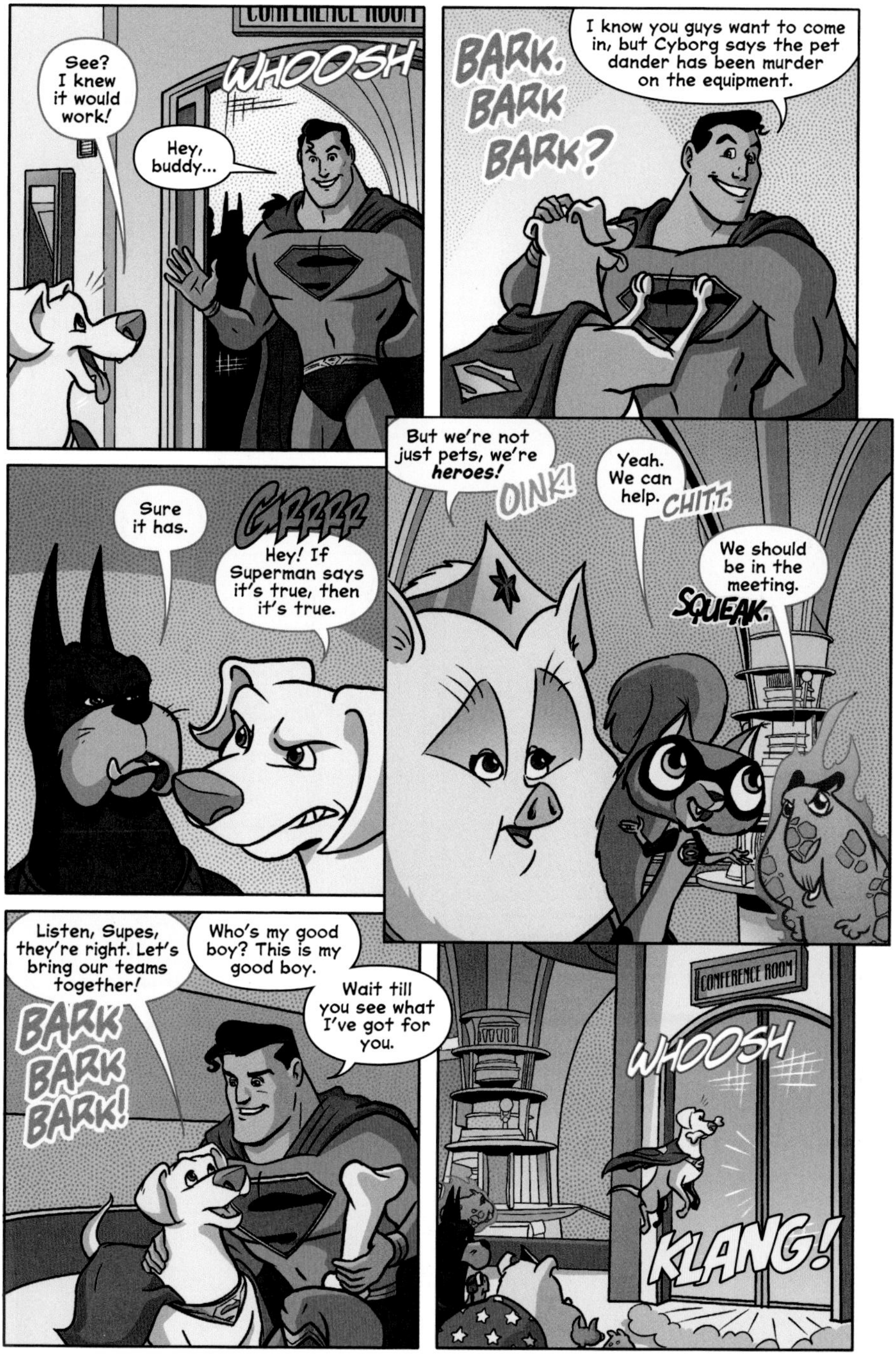
CONFERENCE ROOM
See? I knew it would work!
WHOOSH
Hey, buddy...
BARK. BARK BARK BARK?
I know you guys want to come in, but Cyborg says the pet dander has been murder on the equipment.
Sure it has.
GRRRR
Hey! If Superman says it's true, then it's true.
But we're not just pets, we're *heroes!*
OINK!
Yeah. We can help.
CHITT.
We should be in the meeting.
SQUEAK.
Listen, Supes, they're right. Let's bring our teams together!
BARK BARK BARK!
Who's my good boy? This is my good boy.
Wait till you see what I've got for you.
CONFERENCE ROOM
WHOOSH
KLANG!

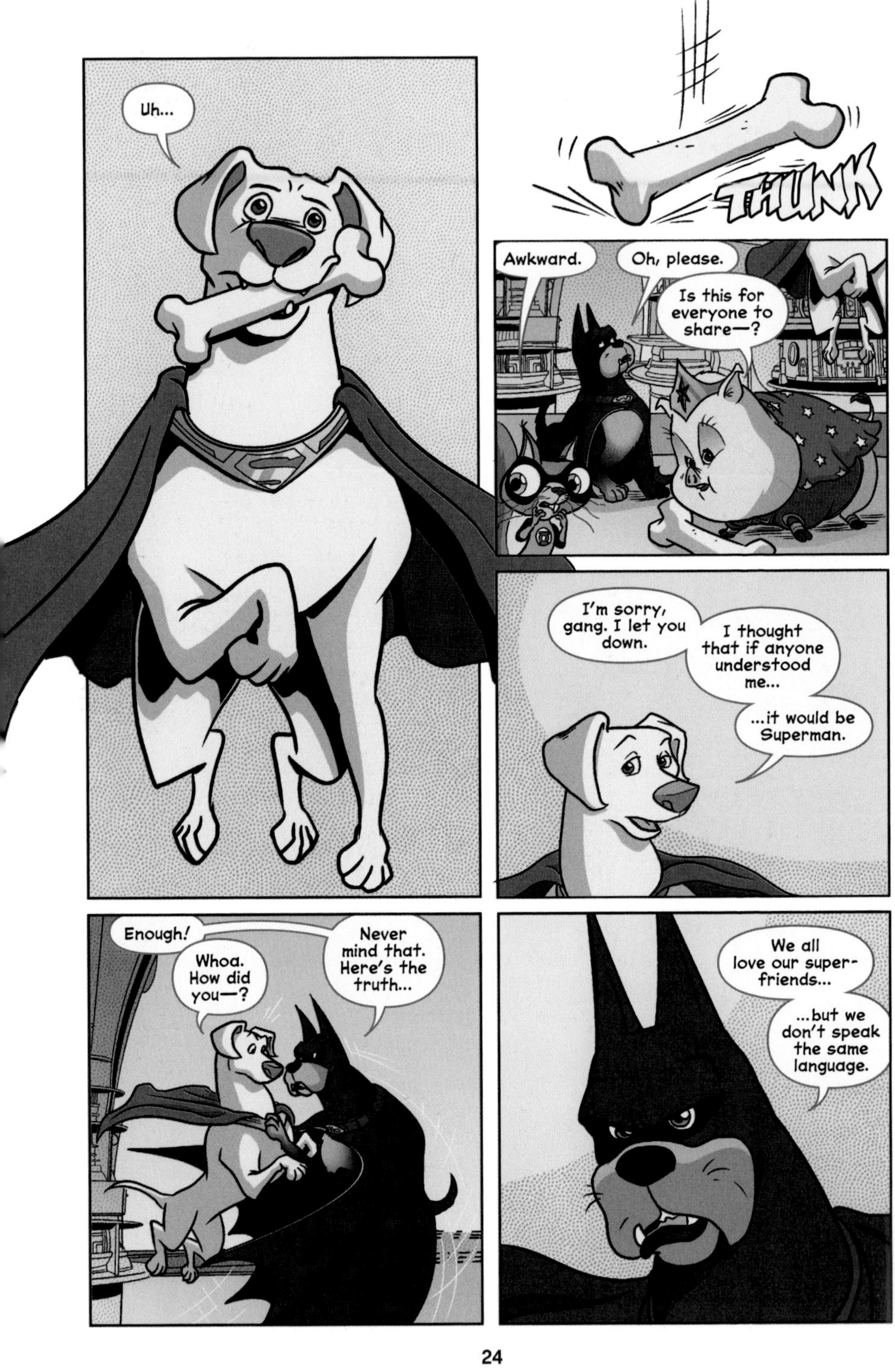
Uh...
THUNK
Awkward.
Oh, please.
Is this for everyone to share—?
I'm sorry, gang. I let you down.
I thought that if anyone understood me...
...it would be Superman.
Enough!
Whoa. How did you—?
Never mind that. Here's the truth...
We all love our super-friends...
...but we don't speak the same language.

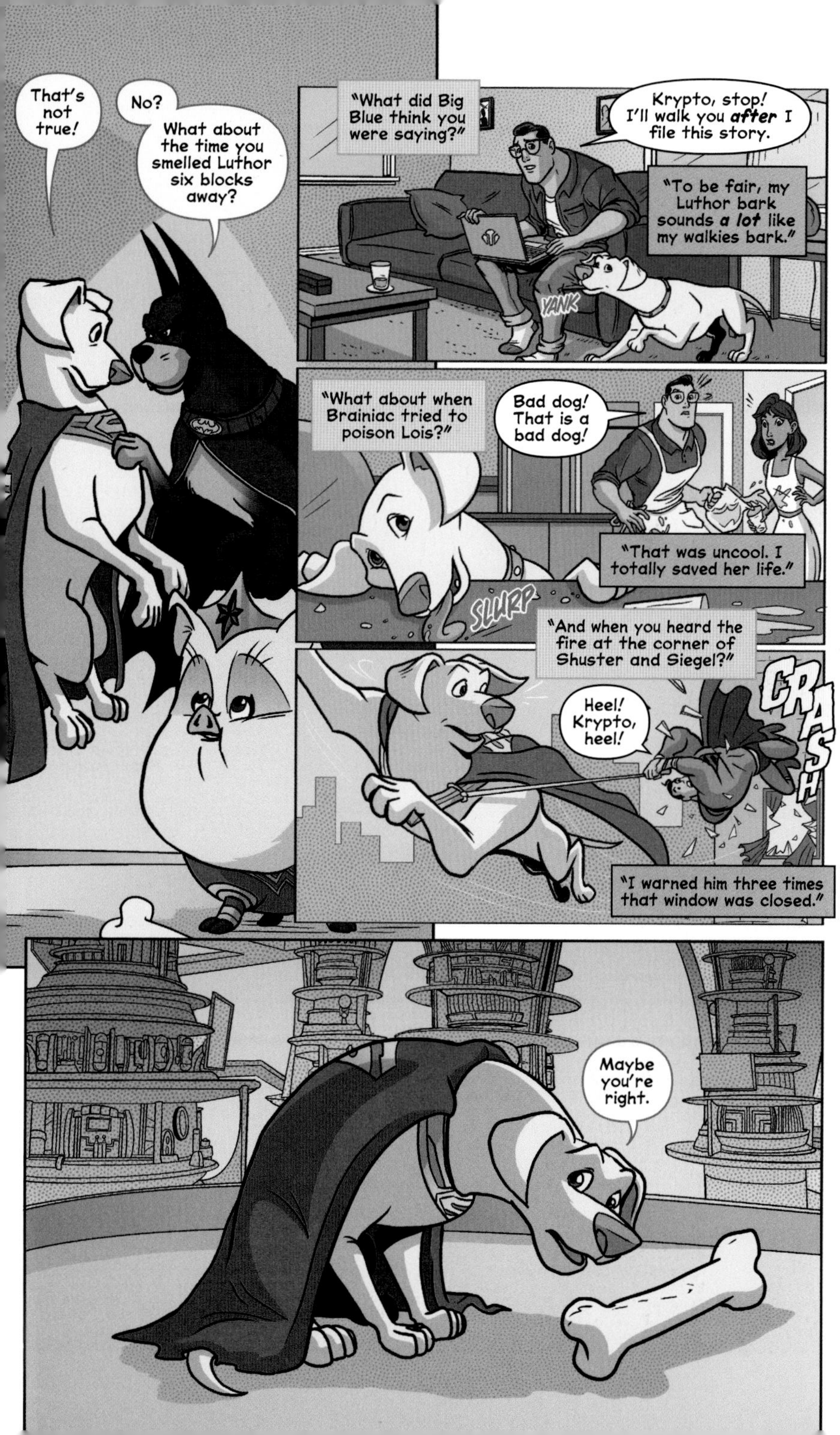

That's not true!
No?
What about the time you smelled Luthor six blocks away?
"What did Big Blue think you were saying?"
Krypto, stop! I'll walk you **after** I file this story.
"To be fair, my Luthor bark sounds **a lot** like my walkies bark."
YANK
"What about when Brainiac tried to poison Lois?"
Bad dog! That is a bad dog!
"That was uncool. I totally saved her life."
SLURP
"And when you heard the fire at the corner of Shuster and Siegel?"
Heel! Krypto, heel!
CRASH
"I warned him three times that window was closed."
Maybe you're right.

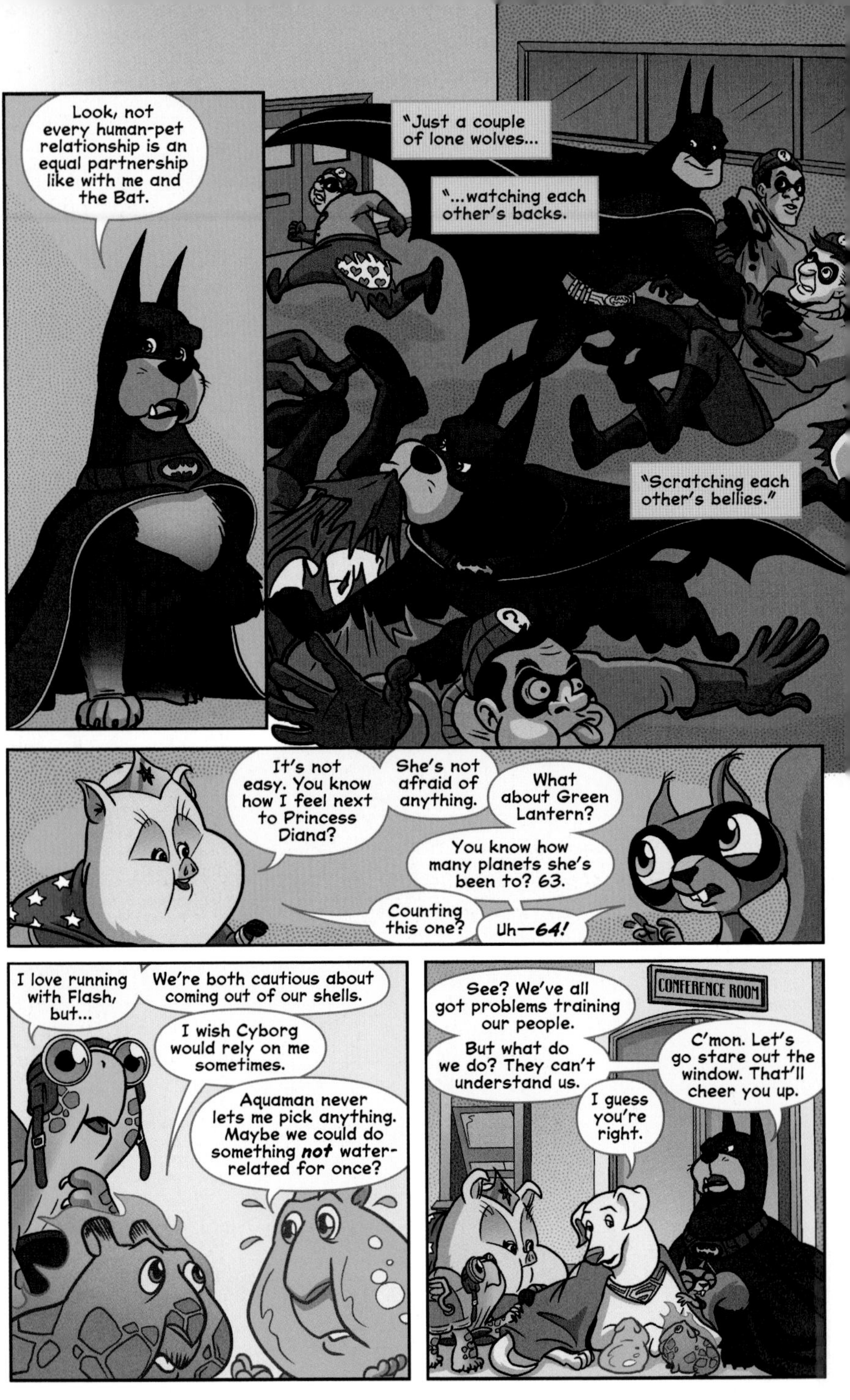

Look, not every human-pet relationship is an equal partnership like with me and the Bat.
"Just a couple of lone wolves...
"...watching each other's backs.
"Scratching each other's bellies."
It's not easy. You know how I feel next to Princess Diana?
She's not afraid of anything.
What about Green Lantern?
You know how many planets she's been to? 63.
Counting this one?
Uh—**64!**
I love running with Flash, but...
We're both cautious about coming out of our shells.
I wish Cyborg would rely on me sometimes.
Aquaman never lets me pick anything. Maybe we could do something ***not*** water-related for once?
CONFERENCE ROOM
See? We've all got problems training our people.
But what do we do? They can't understand us.
C'mon. Let's go stare out the window. That'll cheer you up.
I guess you're right.

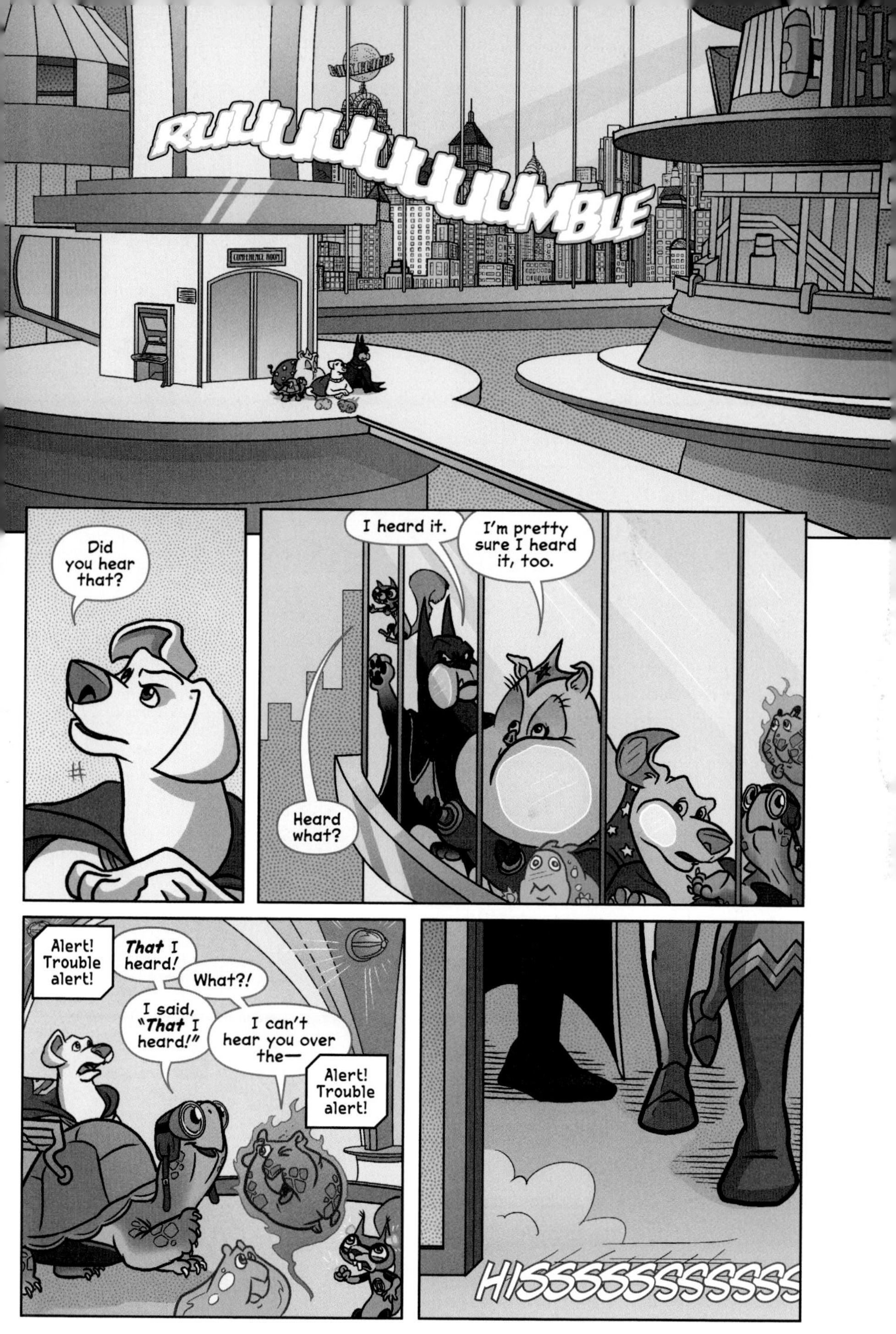
RUUUUUUUUMBLE
CONFERENCE ROOM
Did you hear that?
I heard it.
I'm pretty sure I heard it, too.
Heard what?
Alert! Trouble alert!
That I heard!
What?!
I said, "***That*** I heard!"
I can't hear you over the—
Alert! Trouble alert!
HISSSSSSSSSSS

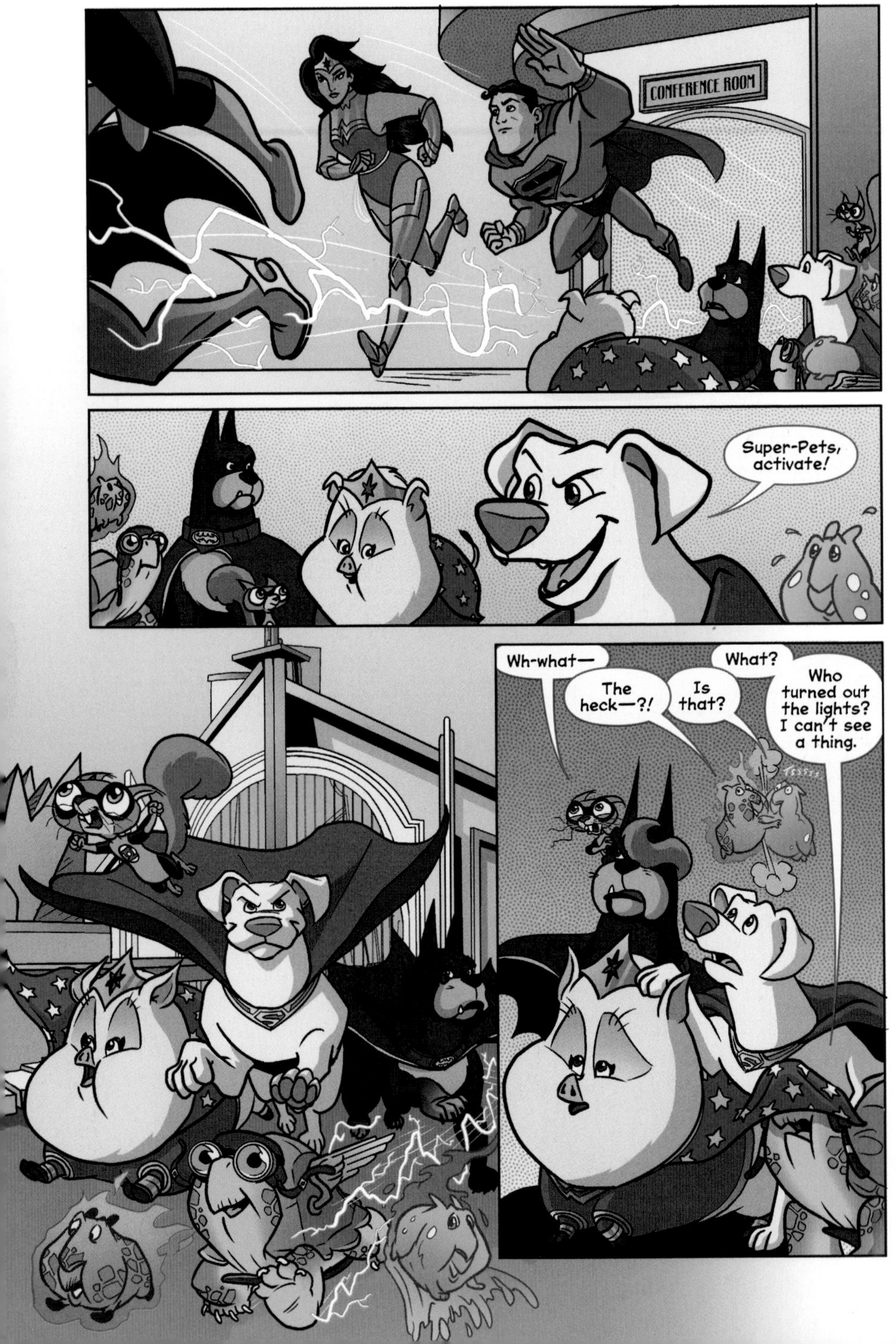
CONFERENCE ROOM
Super-Pets, activate!
Wh-what—
The heck—?!
Is that?
What?
Who turned out the lights? I can't see a thing.

CHAPTER 2
The Thing That Ate Metropolis

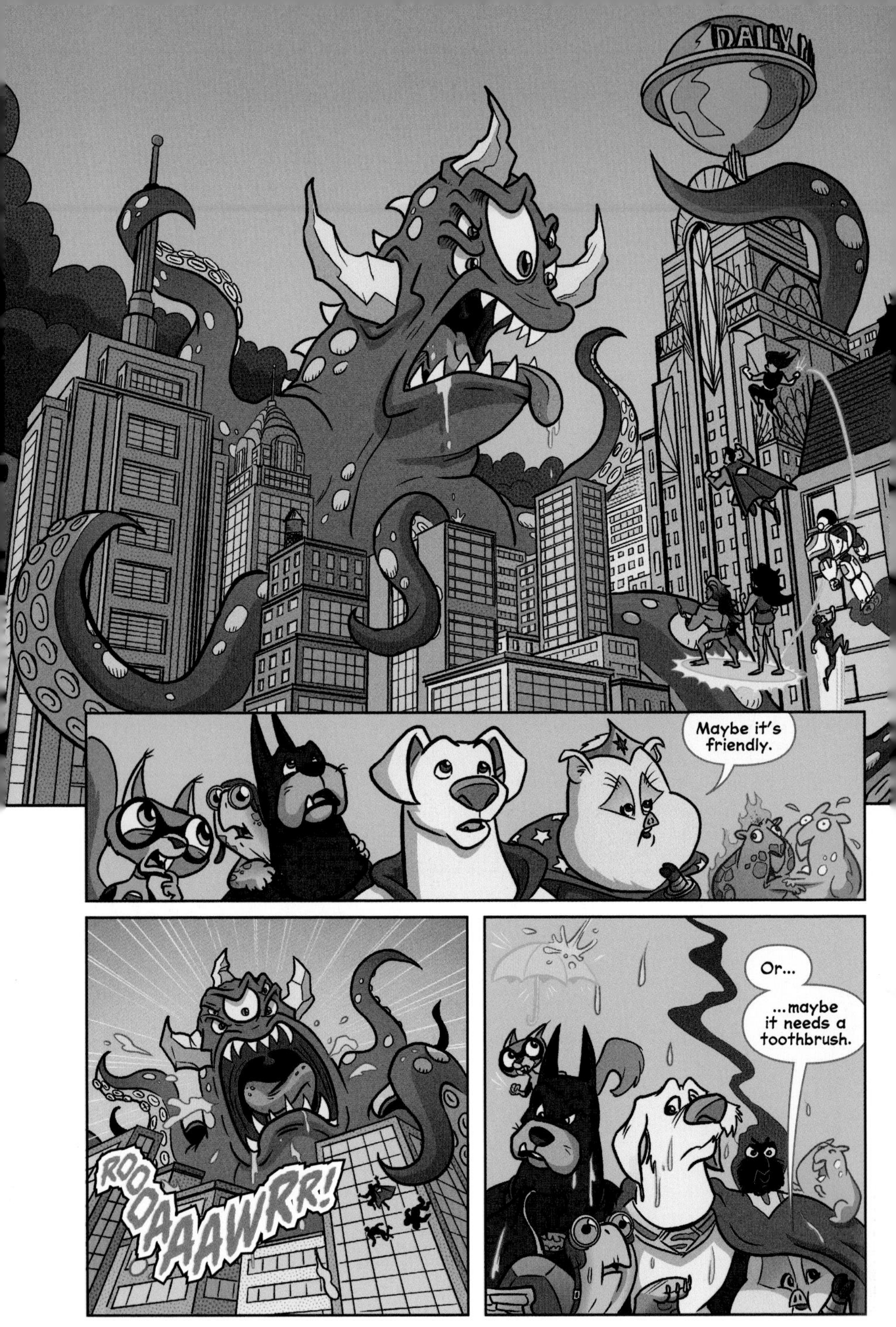
DAILY
Maybe it's friendly.
ROOOAAAWRR!
Or...
...maybe it needs a toothbrush.

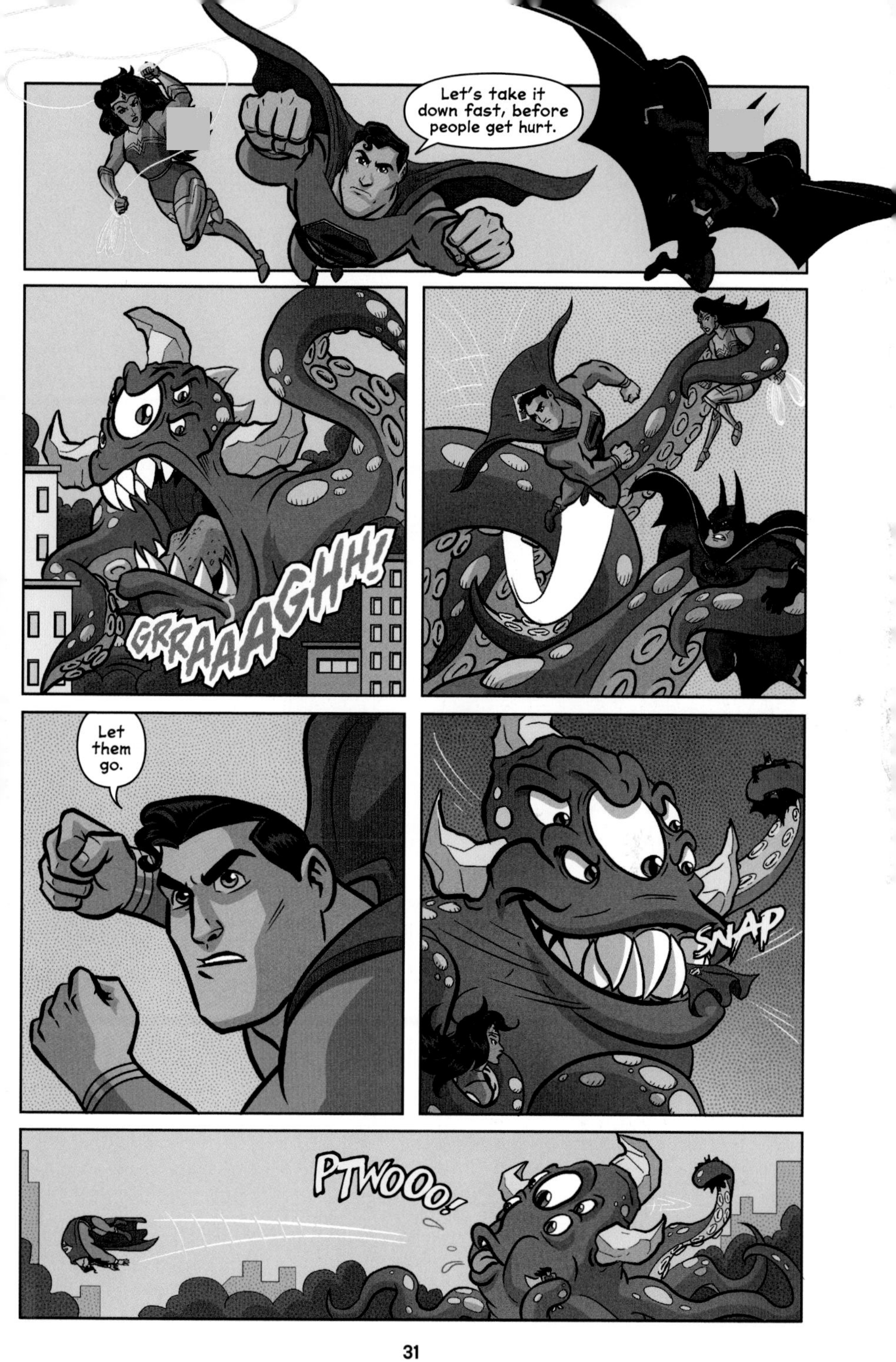

Let's take it down fast, before people get hurt.
GRRAAAGHH!
Let them go.
SNAP
PTWOOOo!

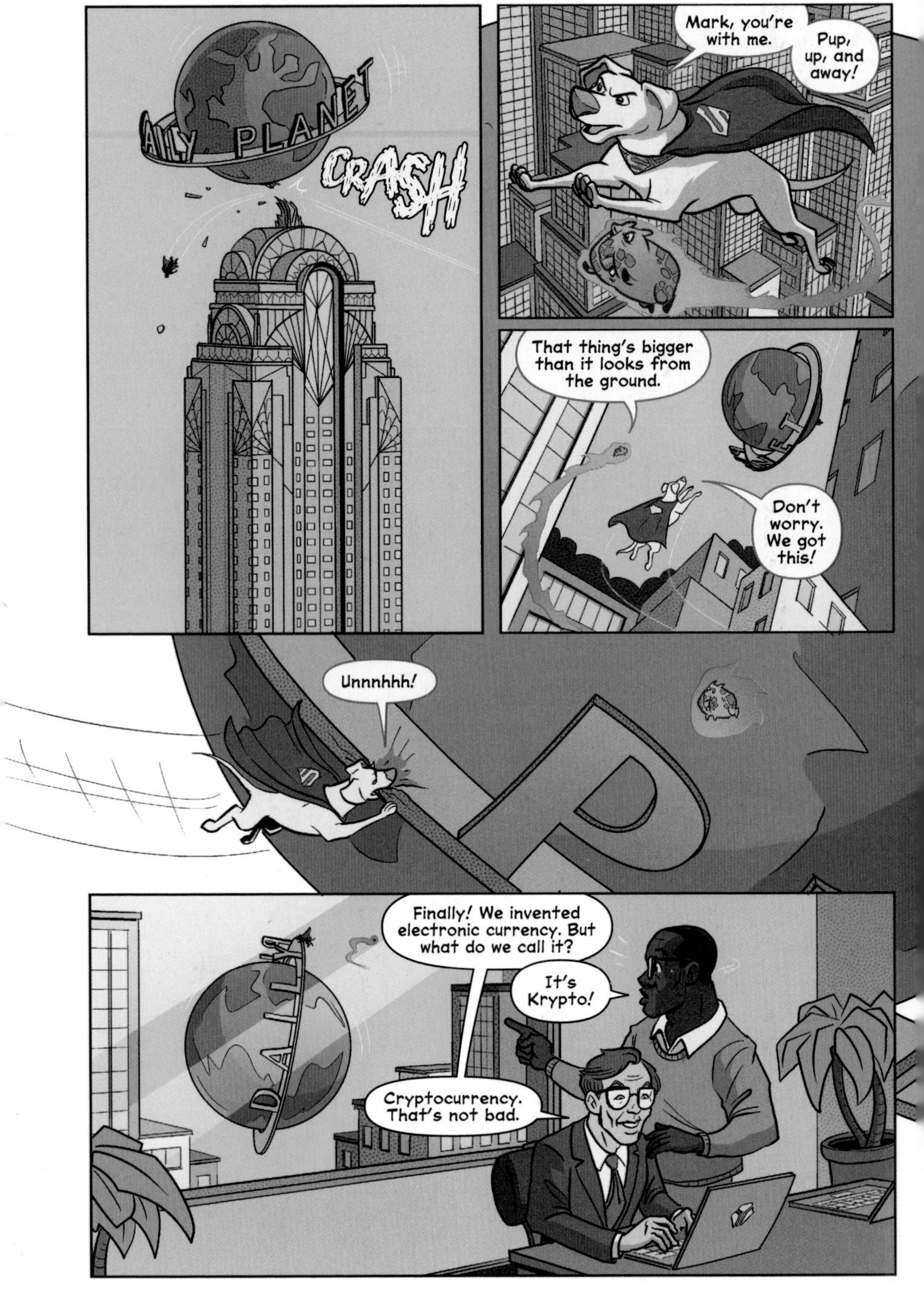
DAILY PLANET
CRASH
Mark, you're with me.
Pup, up, and away!
That thing's bigger than it looks from the ground.
Don't worry. We got this!
Unnnhhh!
Finally! We invented electronic currency. But what do we call it?
It's Krypto!
Cryptocurrency. That's not bad.

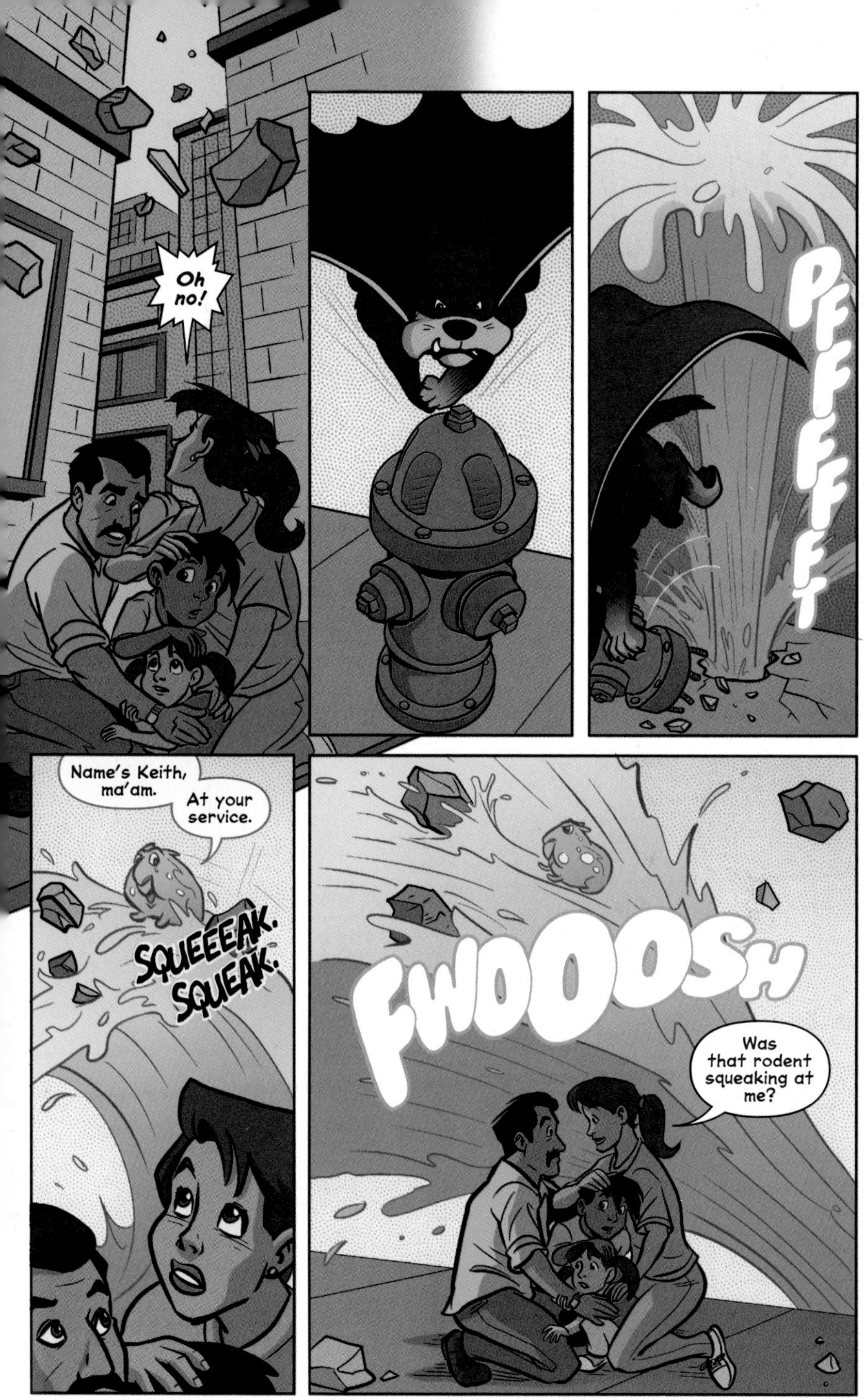
Oh no!
PFFFFFT
Name's Keith, ma'am.
At your service.
SQUEEEAK. SQUEAK.
FWOOOSH
Was that rodent squeaking at me?

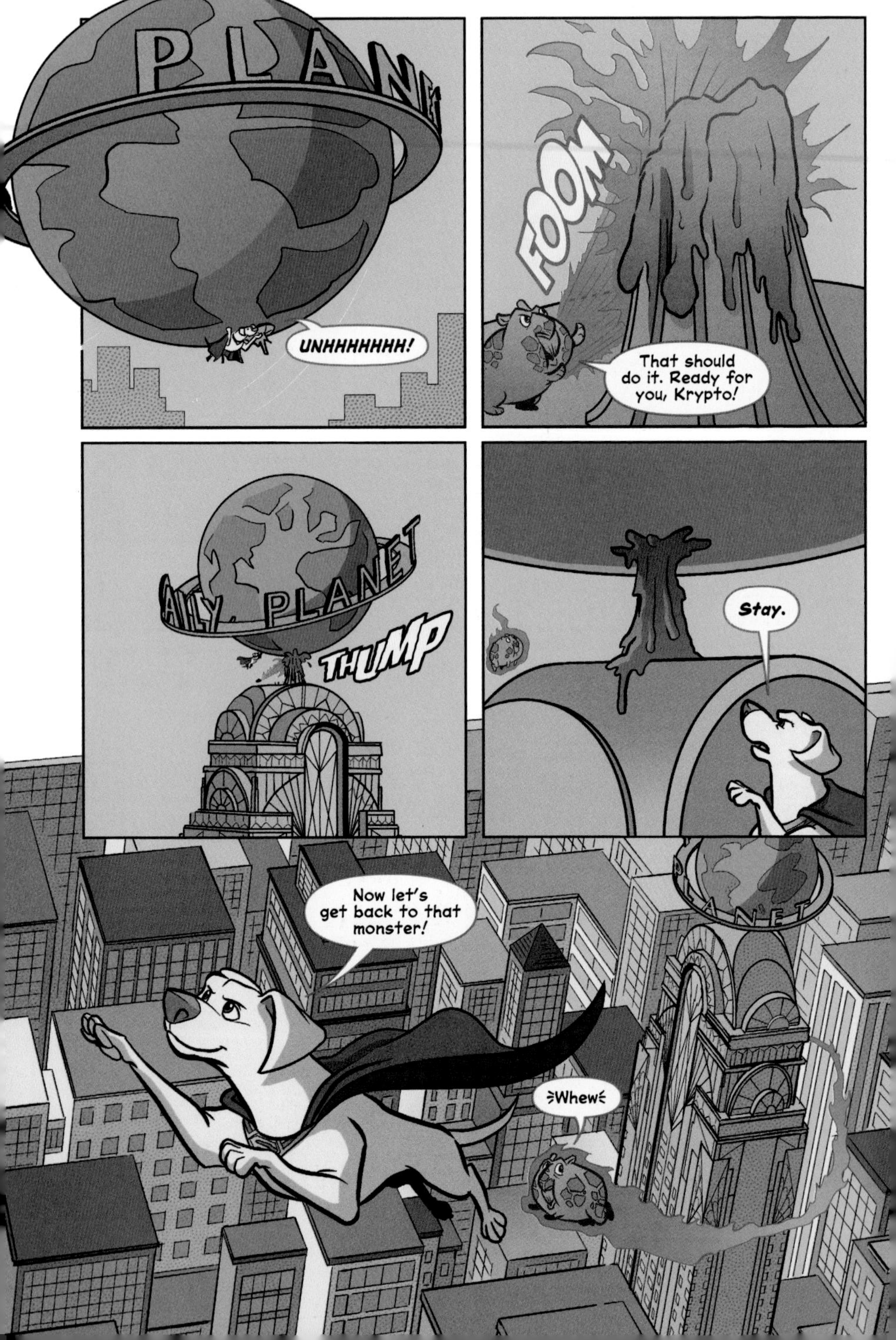
PLANET
UNHHHHHHH!
FOOM!
That should do it. Ready for you, Krypto!
DAILY PLANET
THUMP
Stay.
Now let's get back to that monster!
PLANET
Whew

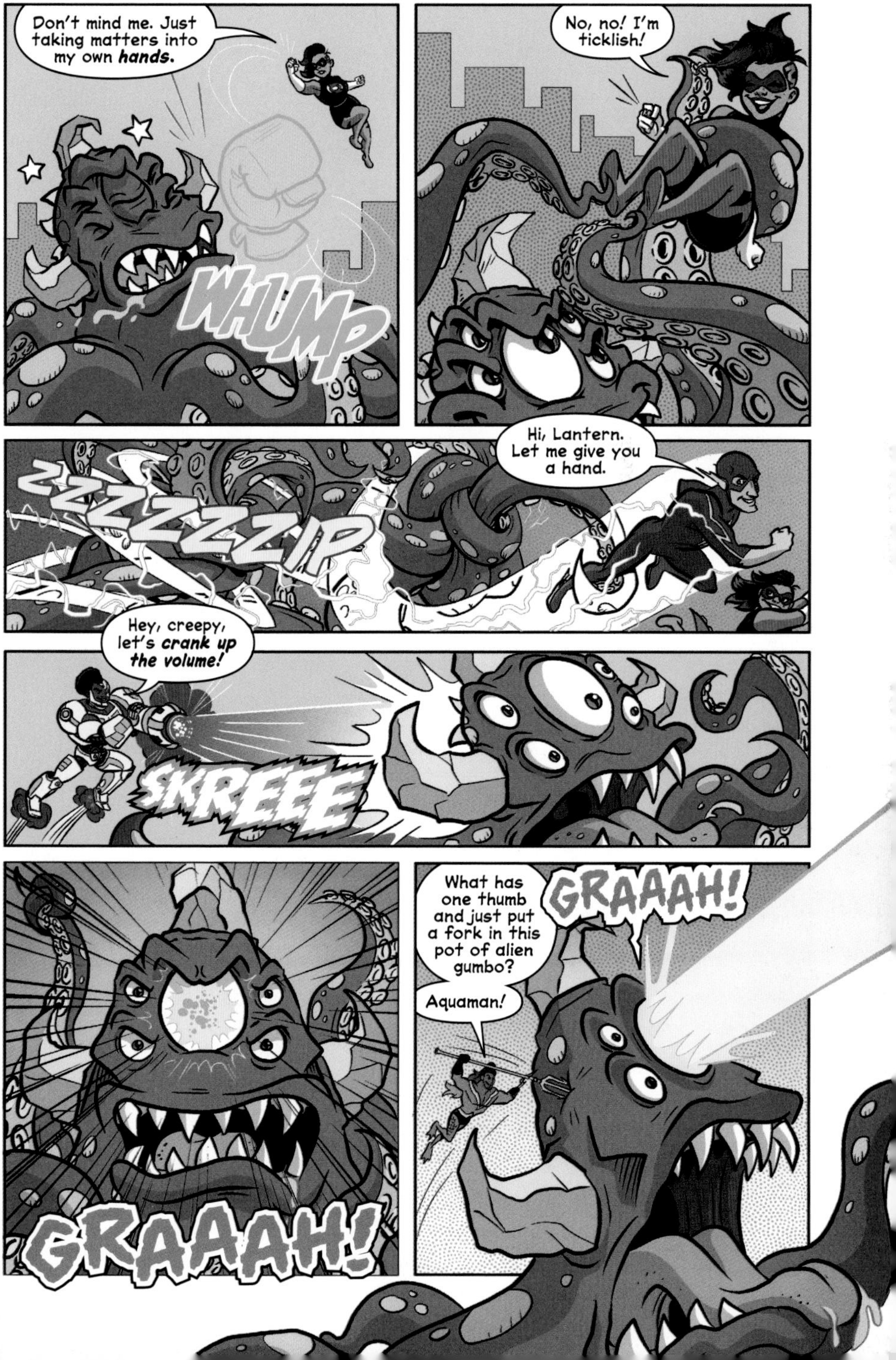
Don't mind me. Just taking matters into my own **hands.**
WHUMP
No, no! I'm ticklish!
Hi, Lantern. Let me give you a hand.
ZZZZZZZIP
Hey, creepy, let's **crank up the volume!**
SKREEE
GRAAAH!
What has one thumb and just put a fork in this pot of alien gumbo?
Aquaman!
GRAAAH!

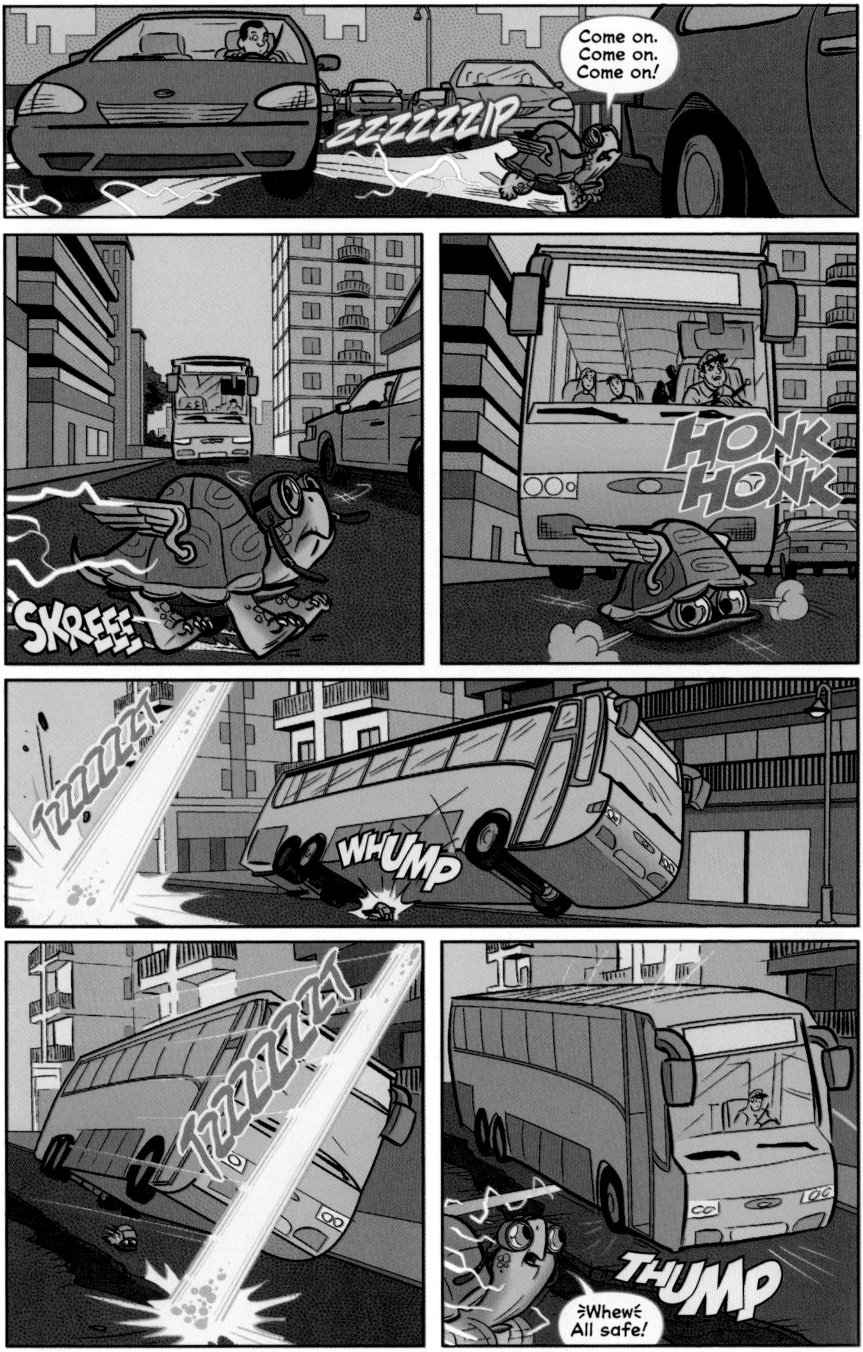
Come on. Come on. Come on!
ZZZZZZZIP
SKREEE
HONK HONK
WHUMP
THUMP
Whew All safe!

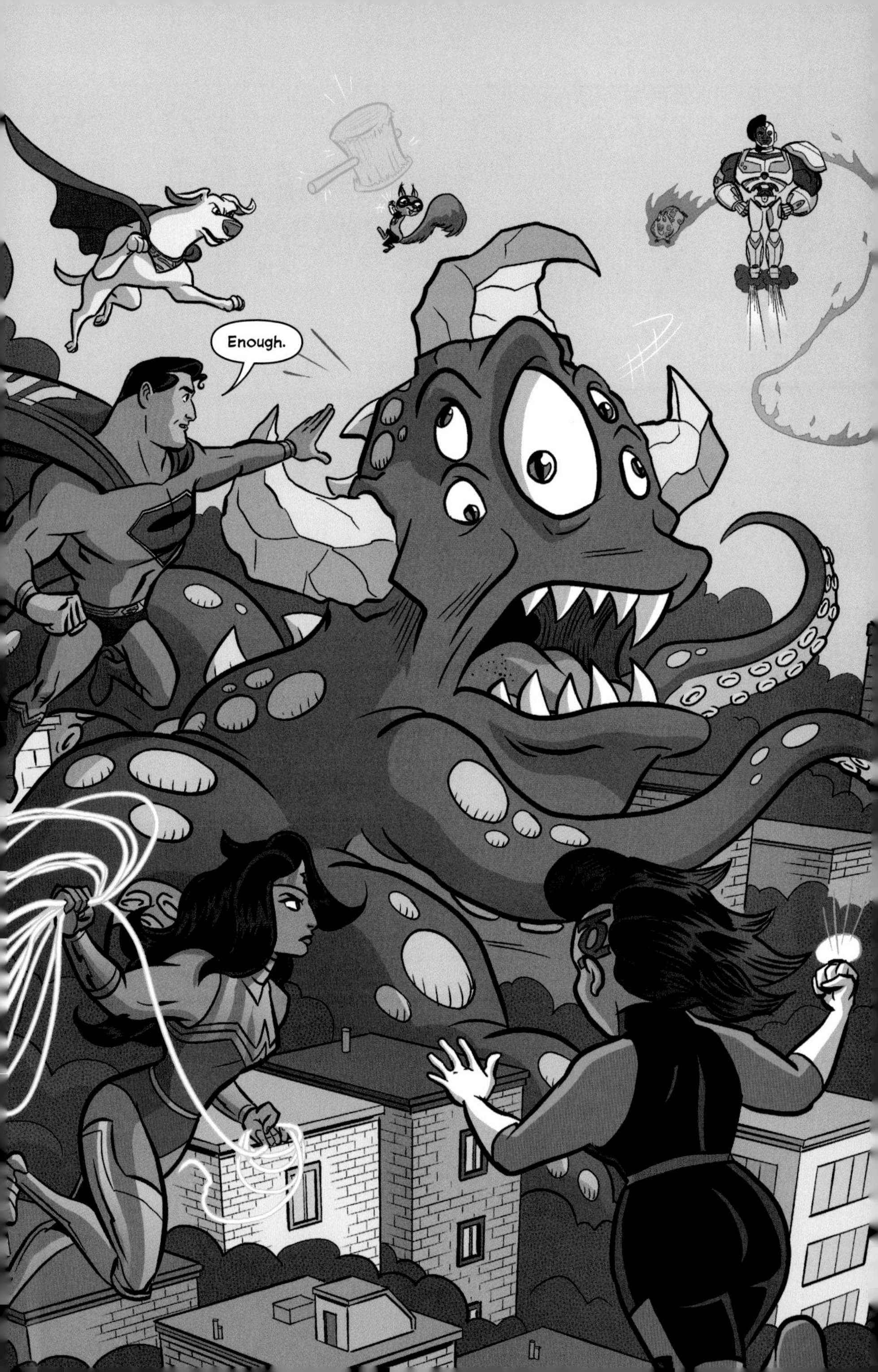
Enough.

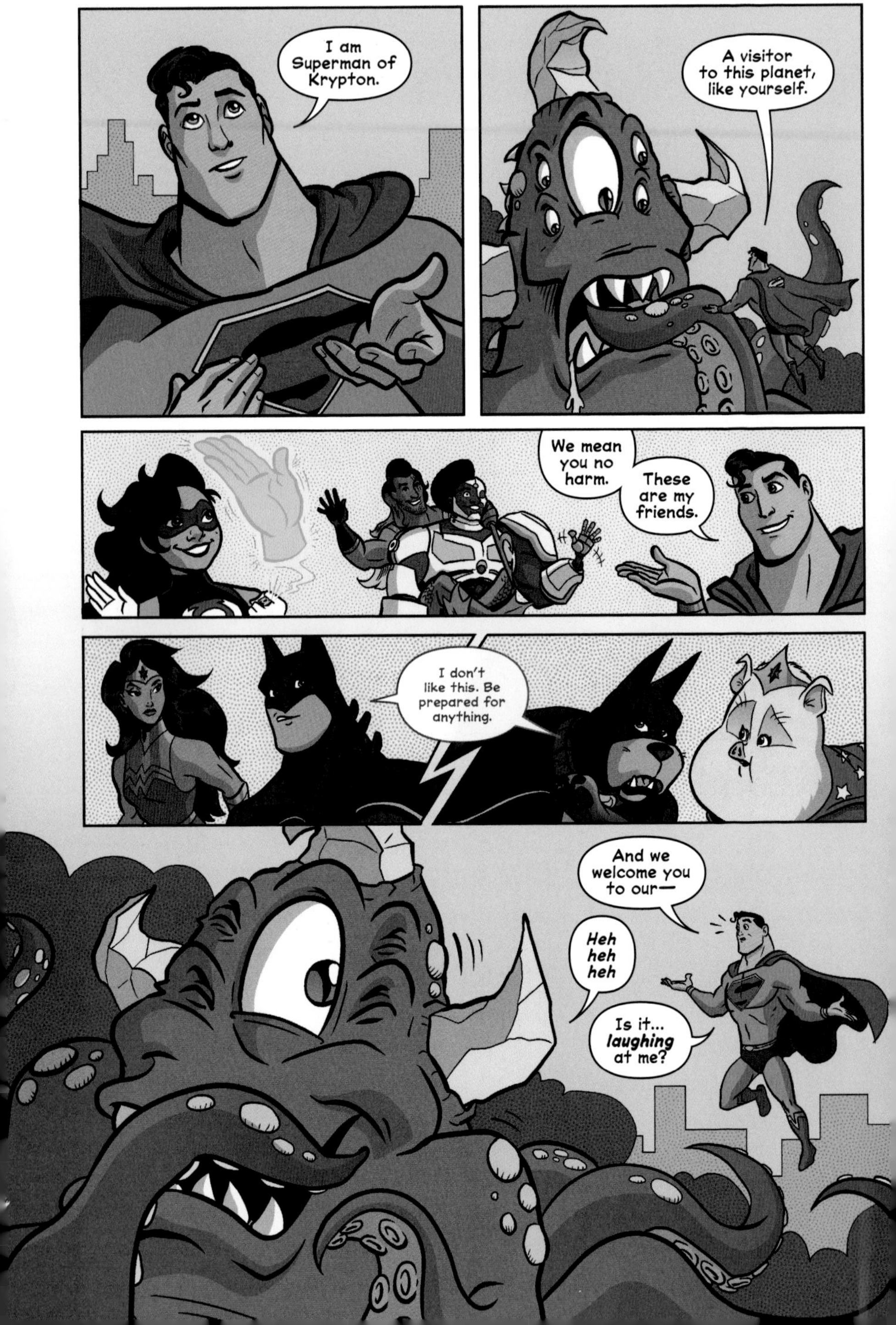

I am Superman of Krypton.
A visitor to this planet, like yourself.
We mean you no harm.
These are my friends.
I don't like this. Be prepared for anything.
And we welcome you to our—
Heh heh heh
Is it... ***laughing*** at me?

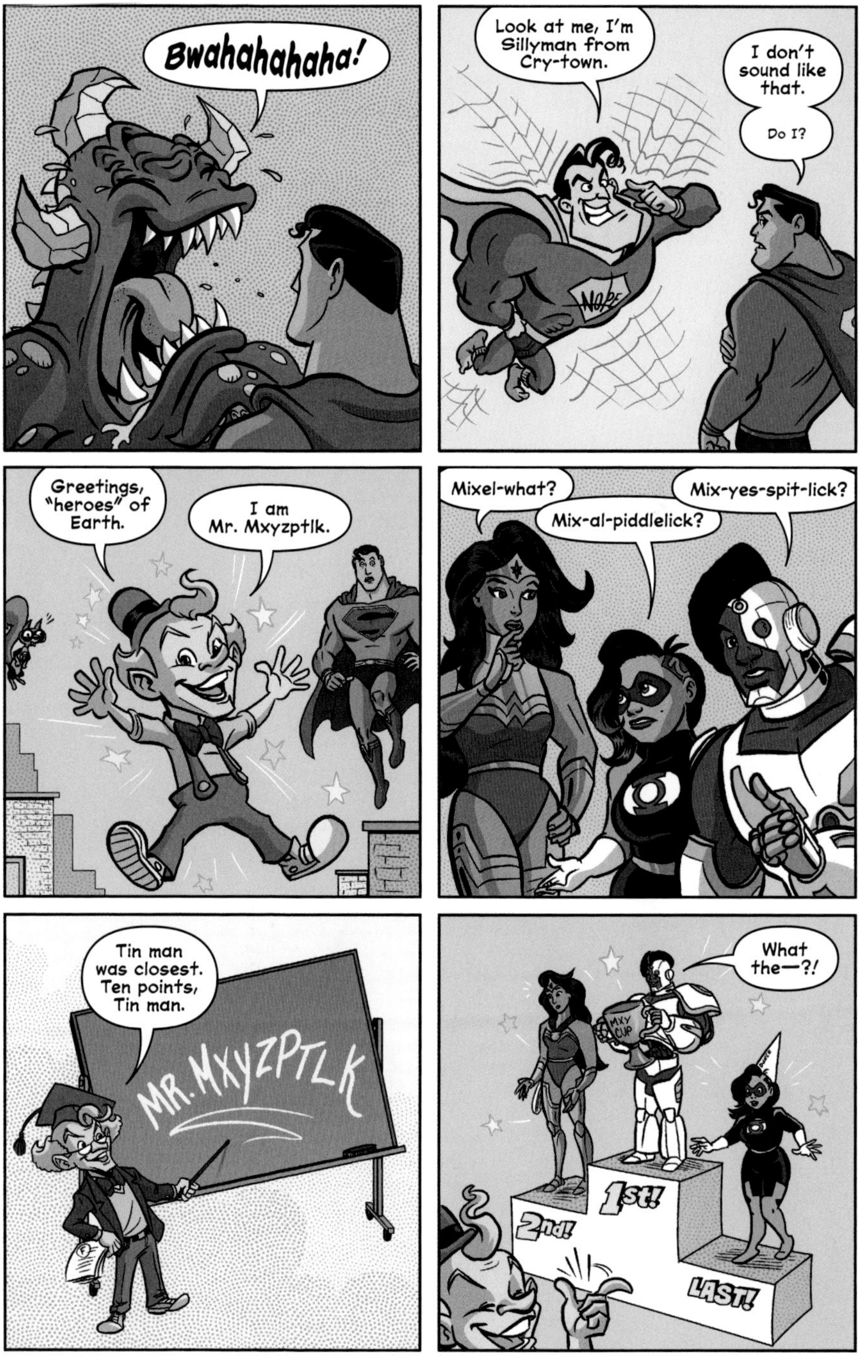
Bwahahahaha!
Look at me, I'm Sillyman from Cry-town.
NOPE
I don't sound like that.
Do I?
Greetings, "heroes" of Earth.
I am Mr. Mxyzptlk.
Mixel-what?
Mix-al-piddlelick?
Mix-yes-spit-lick?
Tin man was closest. Ten points, Tin man.
MR. MXYZPTLK
What the—?!
MXY CUP
1st!
2nd!
LAST!

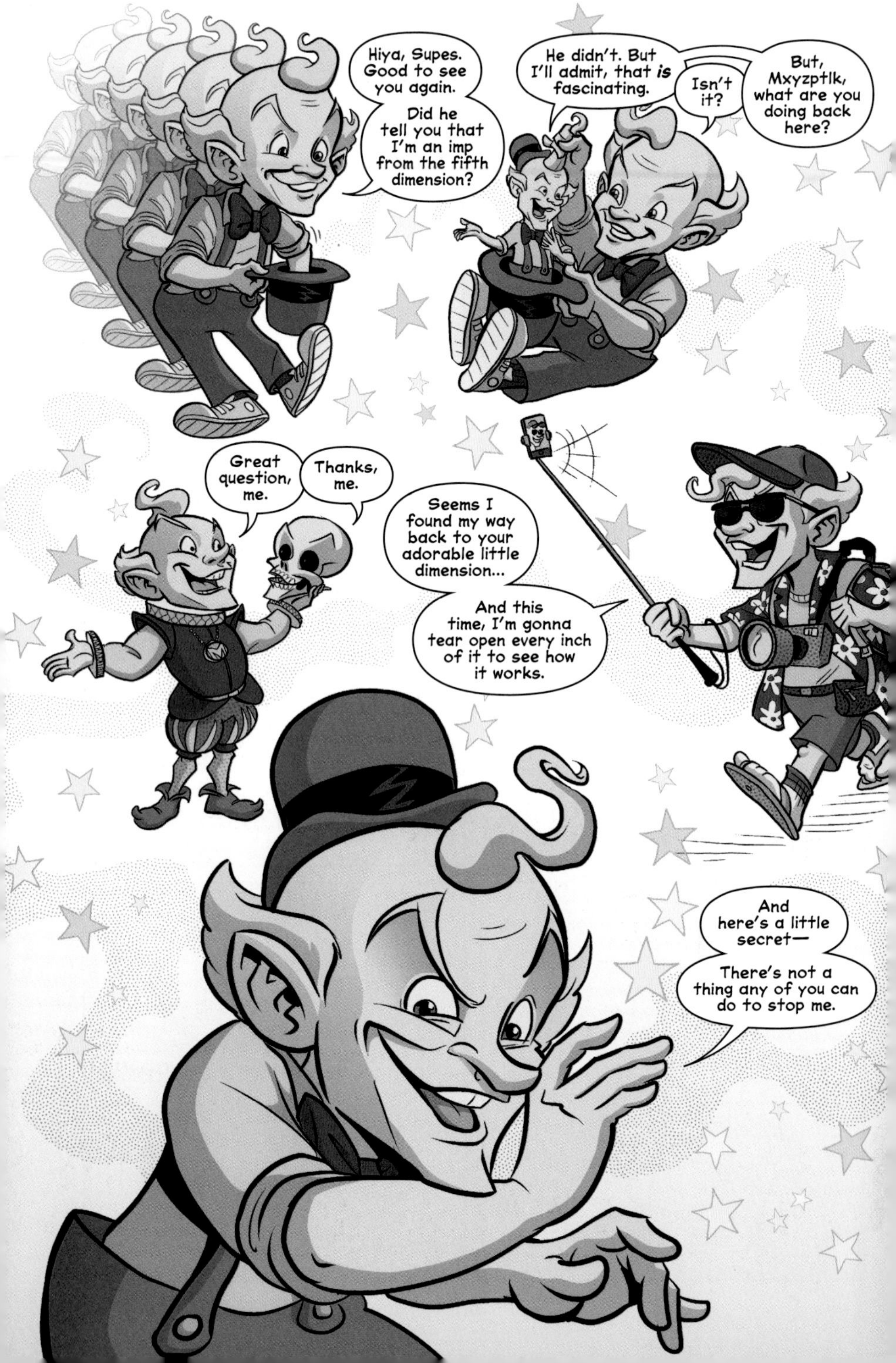
Hiya, Supes. Good to see you again.
Did he tell you that I'm an imp from the fifth dimension?
He didn't. But I'll admit, that **is** fascinating.
Isn't it?
But, Mxyzptlk, what are you doing back here?
Great question, me.
Thanks, me.
Seems I found my way back to your adorable little dimension...
And this time, I'm gonna tear open every inch of it to see how it works.
And here's a little secret—
There's not a thing any of you can do to stop me.

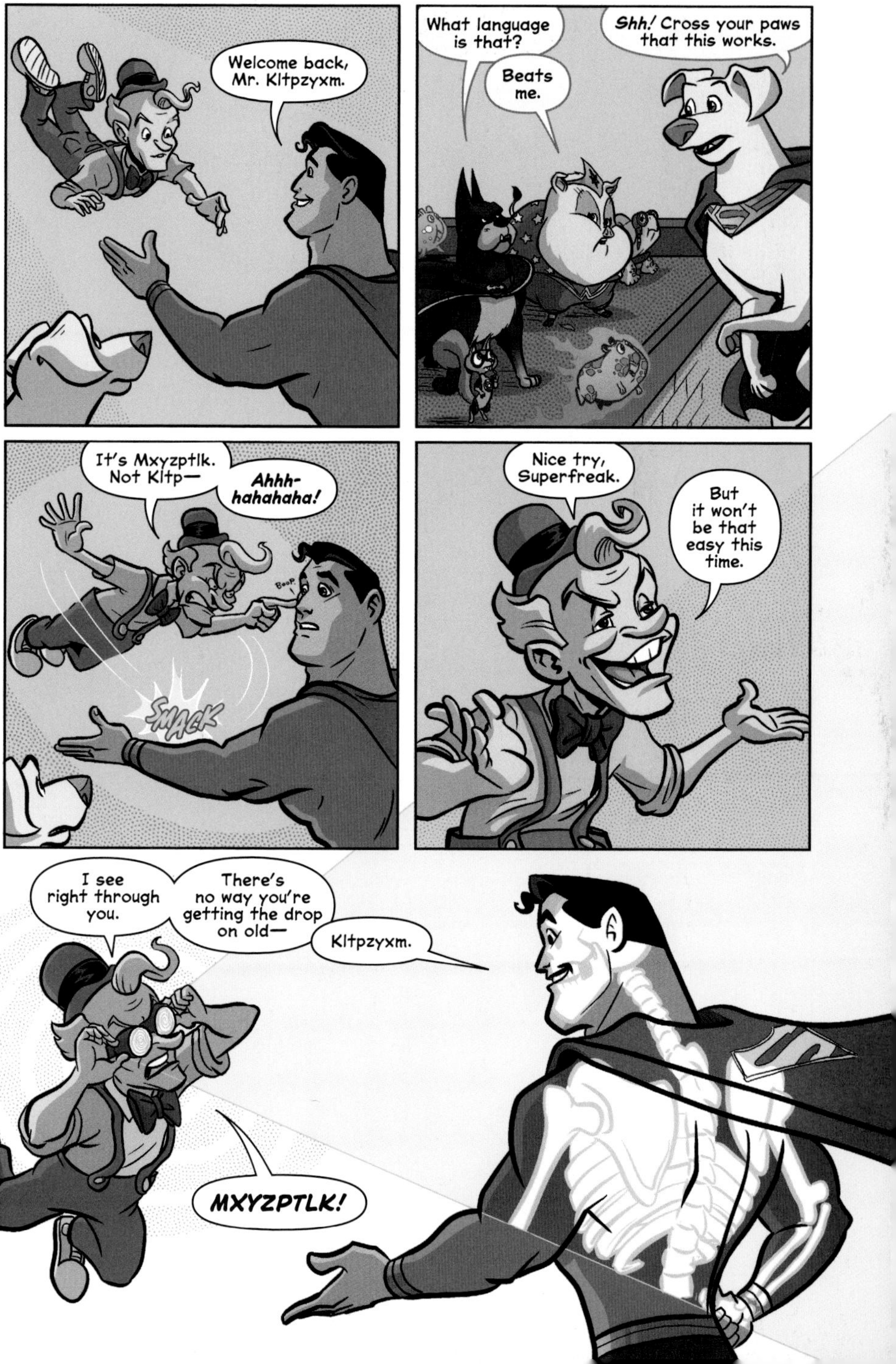
Welcome back, Mr. Kltpzyxm.
What language is that?
Beats me.
Shh! Cross your paws that this works.
It's Mxyzptlk. Not Kltp—
Ahhh-hahahaha!
BOOP.
SMACK
Nice try, Superfreak.
But it won't be that easy this time.
I see right through you.
There's no way you're getting the drop on old—
Kltpzyxm.
MXYZPTLK!

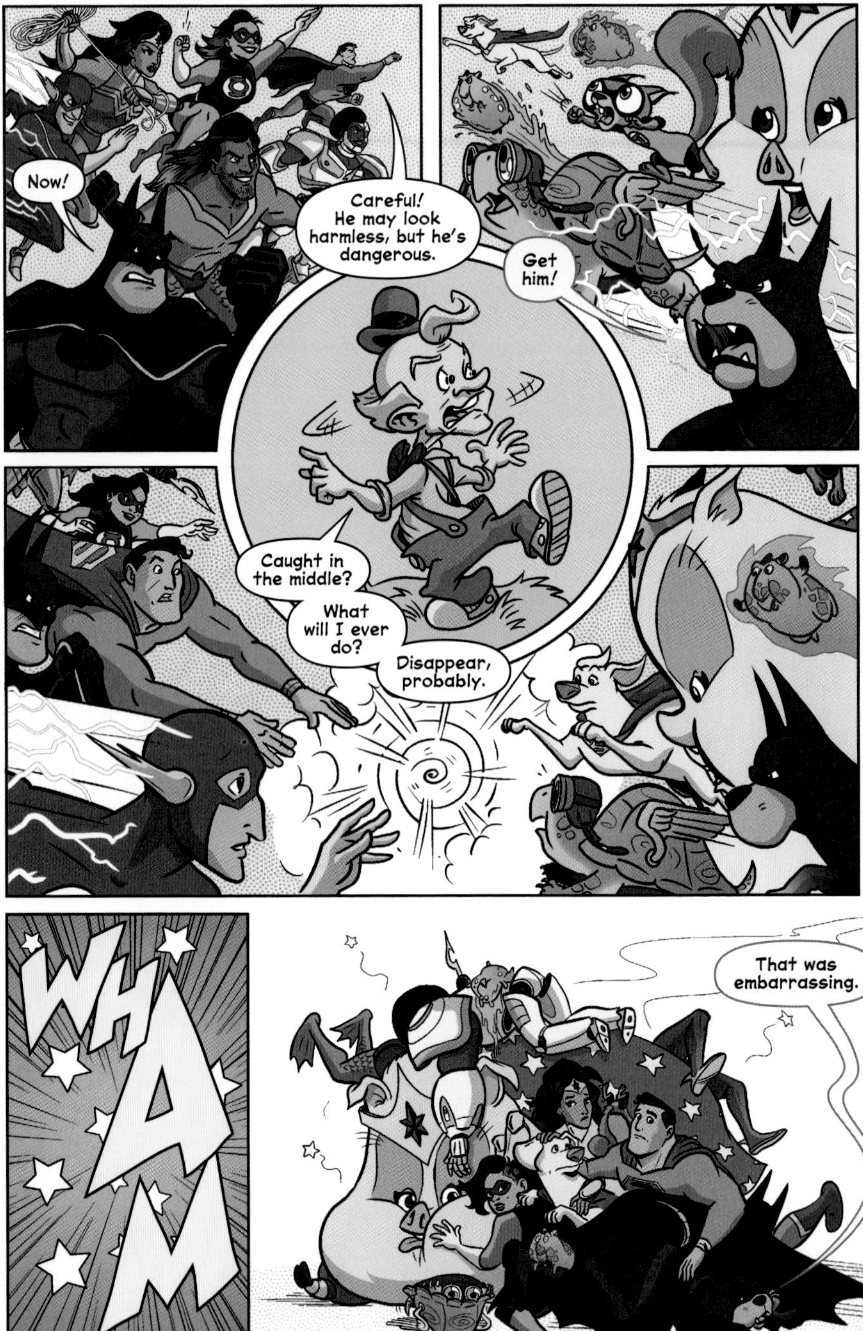
Now!
Careful! He may look harmless, but he's dangerous.
Get him!
Caught in the middle?
What will I ever do?
Disappear, probably.
WHAM
That was embarrassing.

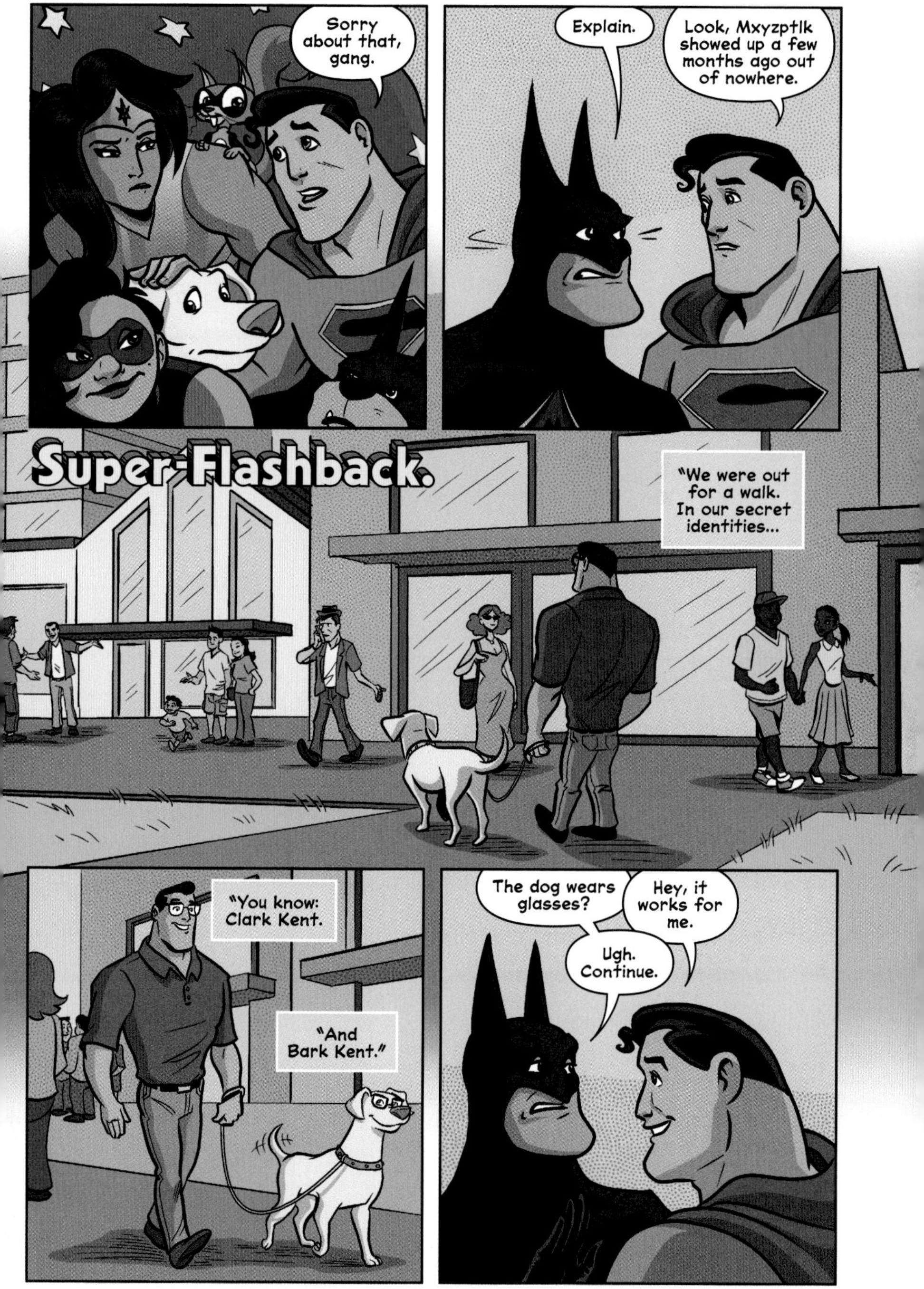
Sorry about that, gang.
Explain.
Look, Mxyzptlk showed up a few months ago out of nowhere.
Super-Flashback.
"We were out for a walk. In our secret identities...
"You know: Clark Kent.
"And Bark Kent."
The dog wears glasses?
Hey, it works for me.
Ugh. Continue.

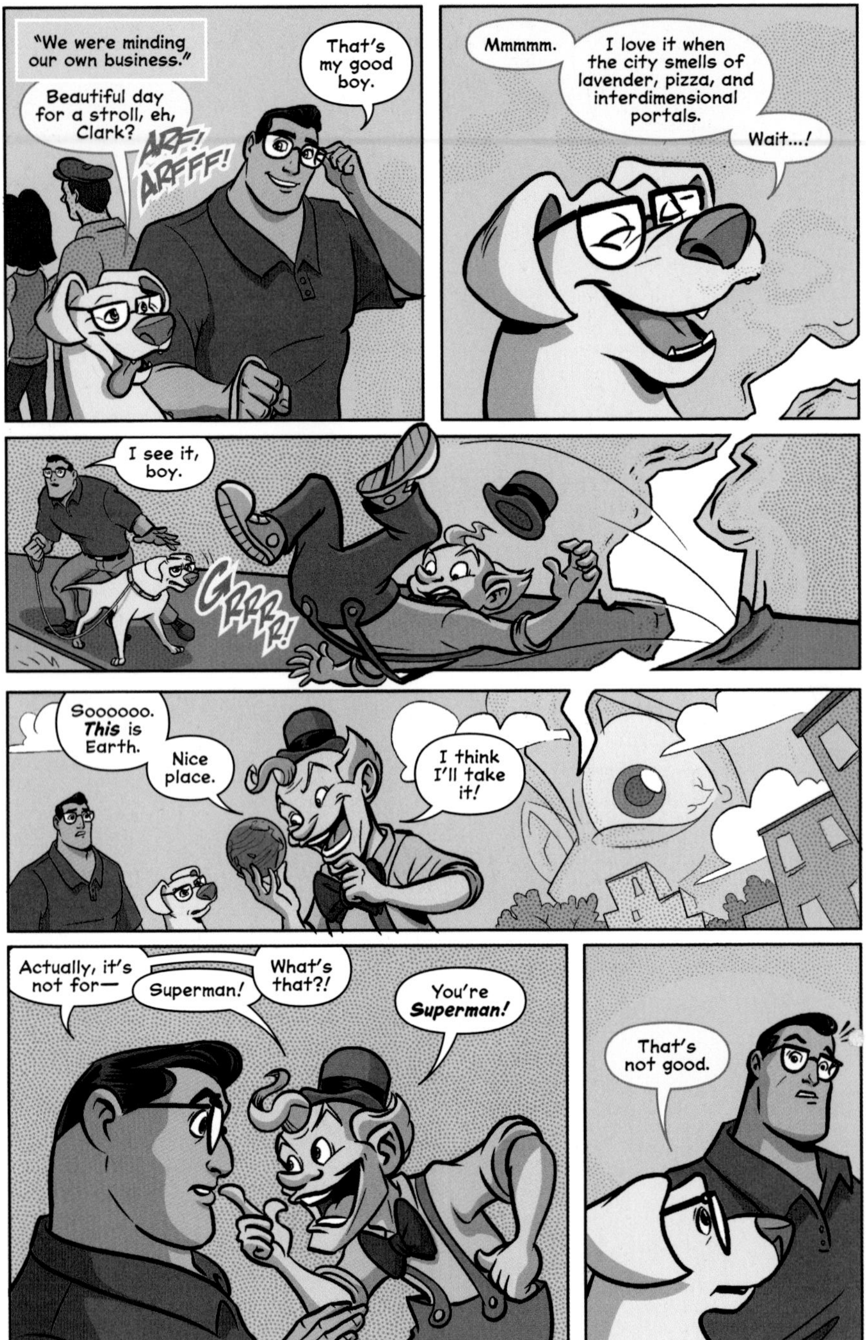
"We were minding our own business."
Beautiful day for a stroll, eh, Clark?
ARF! ARFFF!
That's my good boy.
Mmmmm.
I love it when the city smells of lavender, pizza, and interdimensional portals.
Wait...!
I see it, boy.
GRRRR!
Soooooo. *This* is Earth.
Nice place.
I think I'll take it!
Actually, it's not for—
Superman!
What's that?!
You're *Superman!*
That's not good.

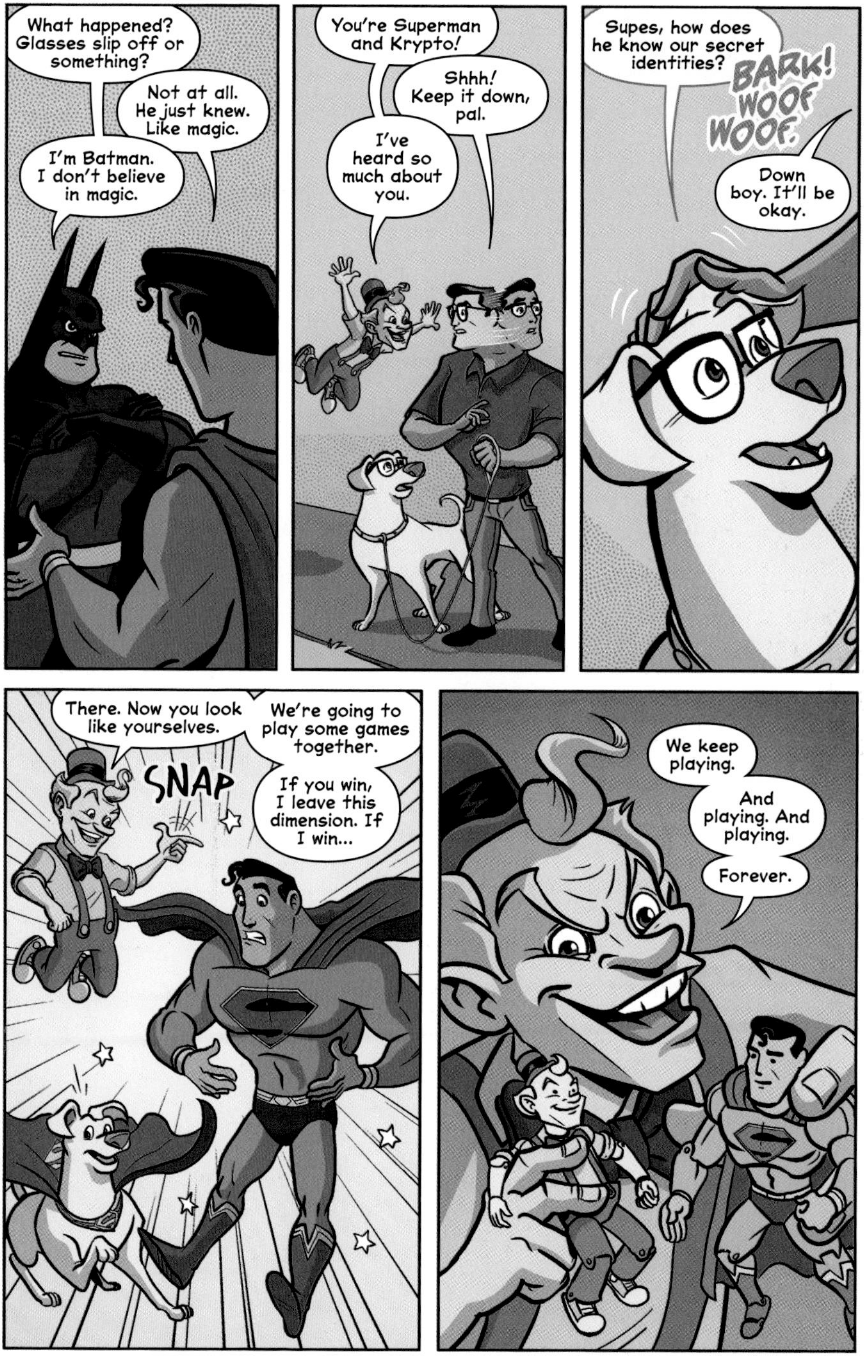
What happened? Glasses slip off or something?
Not at all. He just knew. Like magic.
I'm Batman. I don't believe in magic.
You're Superman and Krypto!
Shhh! Keep it down, pal.
I've heard so much about you.
Supes, how does he know our secret identities?
BARK! WOOF WOOF.
Down boy. It'll be okay.
There. Now you look like yourselves.
SNAP
We're going to play some games together.
If you win, I leave this dimension. If I win...
We keep playing.
And playing. And playing.
Forever.

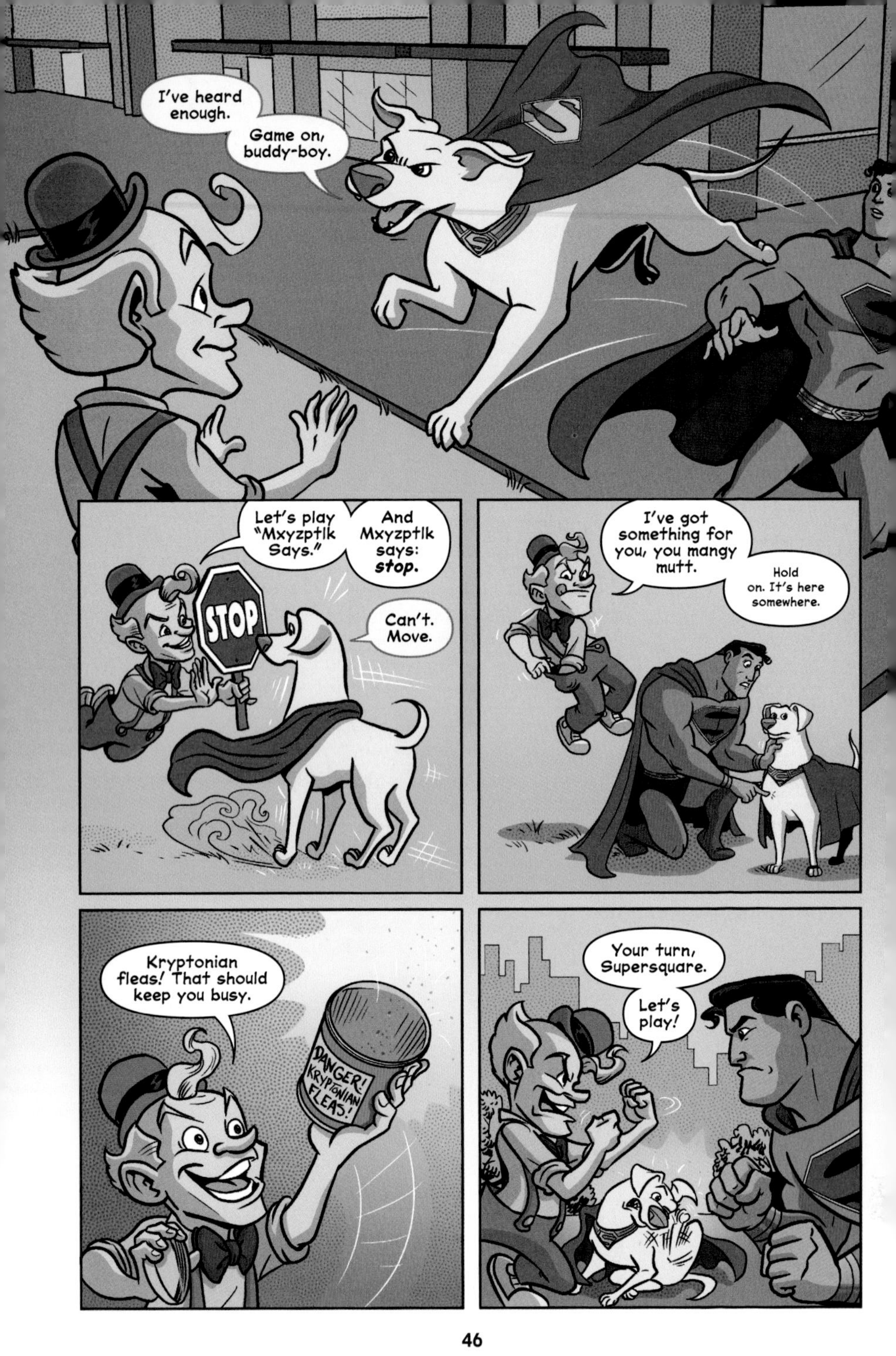
I've heard enough.
Game on, buddy-boy.
Let's play "Mxyzptlk Says."
And Mxyzptlk says: **stop.**
STOP
Can't. Move.
I've got something for you, you mangy mutt.
Hold on. It's here somewhere.
Kryptonian fleas! That should keep you busy.
DANGER! KRYPTONIAN FLEAS!
Your turn, Supersquare.
Let's play!

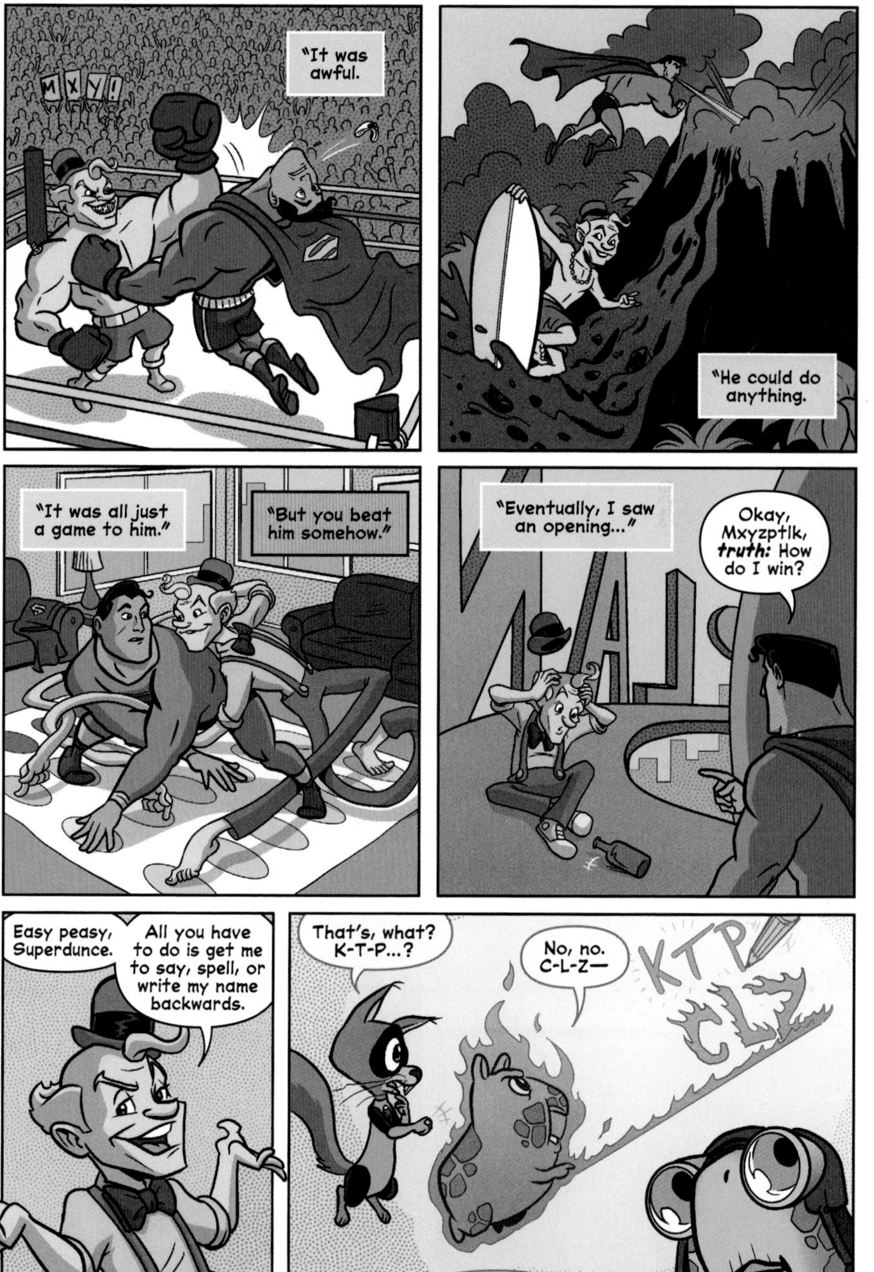
MXY!
"It was awful.
"He could do anything.
"It was all just a game to him."
"But you beat him somehow."
"Eventually, I saw an opening..."
Okay, Mxyzptlk, ***truth:*** How do I win?
Easy peasy, Superdunce.
All you have to do is get me to say, spell, or write my name backwards.
That's, what? K-T-P...?
No, no. C-L-Z—
KTP
CLZ
I can't spell it forward, never mind ***backwards.***

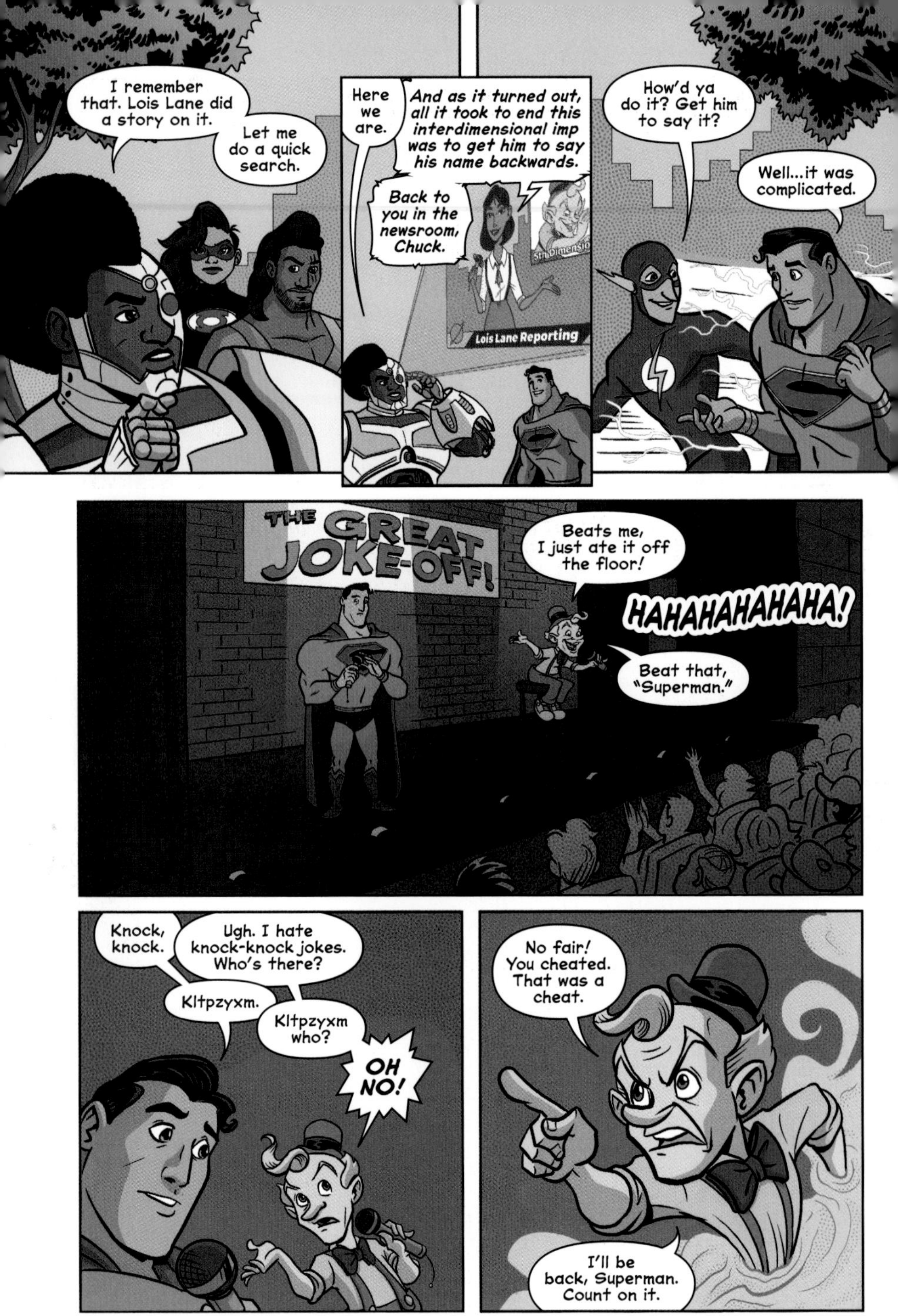

I remember that. Lois Lane did a story on it.
Let me do a quick search.
Here we are.
And as it turned out, all it took to end this interdimensional imp was to get him to say his name backwards.
Back to you in the newsroom, Chuck.
Lois Lane Reporting
How'd ya do it? Get him to say it?
Well...it was complicated.
THE GREAT JOKE-OFF!
Beats me, I just ate it off the floor!
HAHAHAHAHAHA!
Beat that, "Superman."
Knock, knock.
Ugh. I hate knock-knock jokes. Who's there?
Kltpzyxm.
Kltpzyxm who?
OH NO!
No fair! You cheated. That was a cheat.
I'll be back, Superman. Count on it.

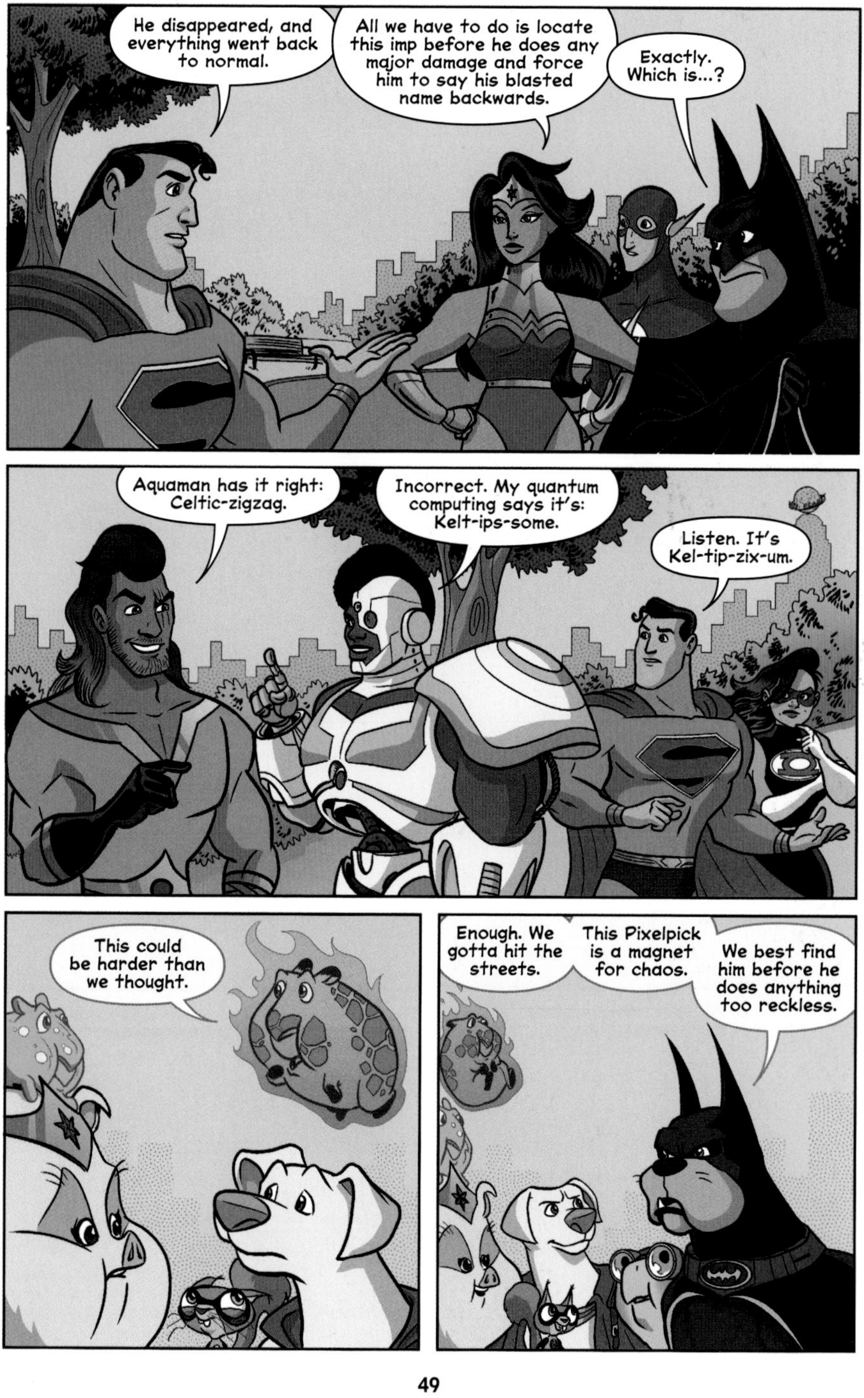
He disappeared, and everything went back to normal.
All we have to do is locate this imp before he does any major damage and force him to say his blasted name backwards.
Exactly. Which is...?
Aquaman has it right: Celtic-zigzag.
Incorrect. My quantum computing says it's: Kelt-ips-some.
Listen. It's Kel-tip-zix-um.
This could be harder than we thought.
Enough. We gotta hit the streets.
This Pixelpick is a magnet for chaos.
We best find him before he does anything too reckless.

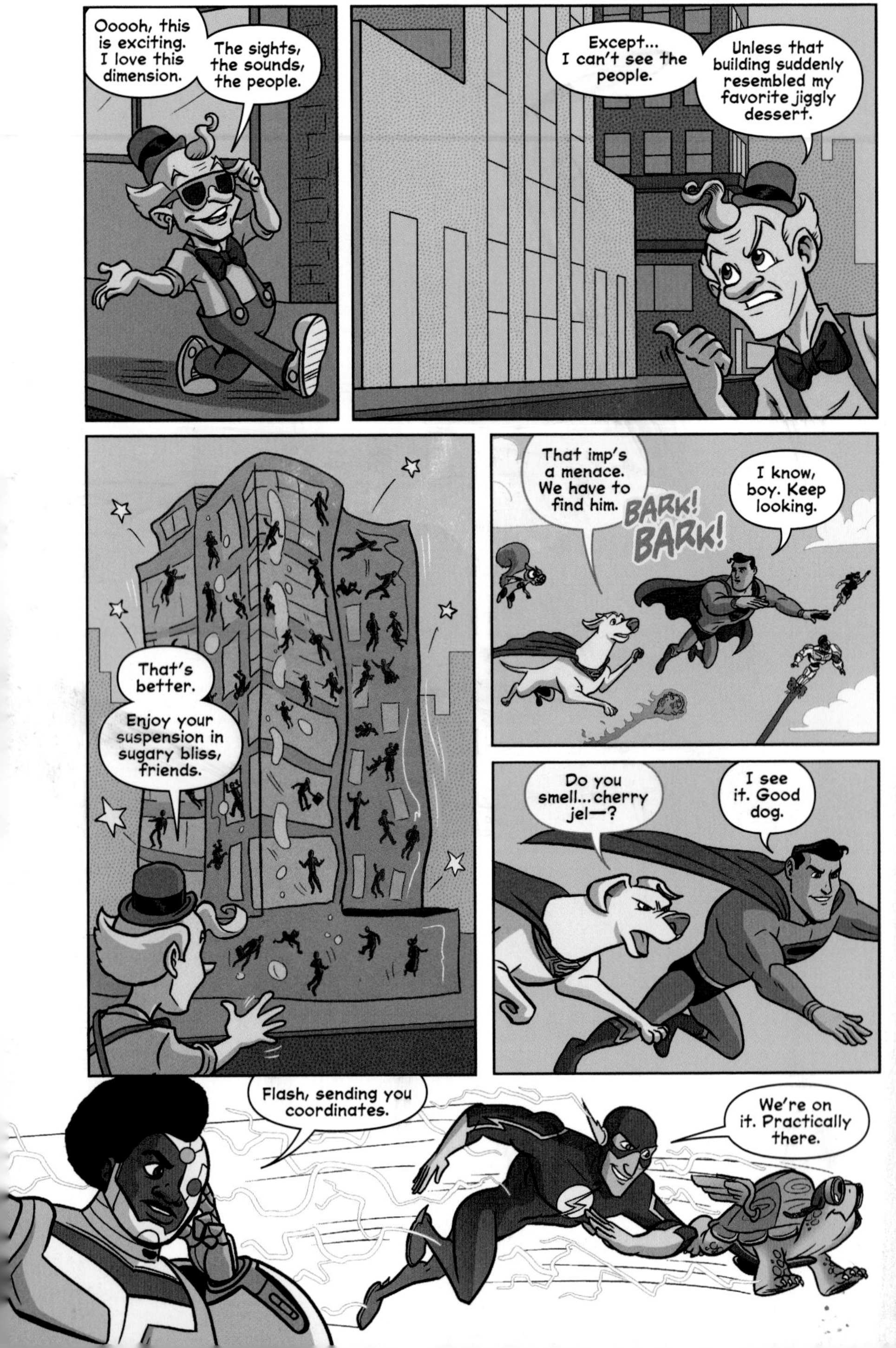

Ooooh, this is exciting. I love this dimension.
The sights, the sounds, the people.
Except... I can't see the people.
Unless that building suddenly resembled my favorite jiggly dessert.
That's better.
Enjoy your suspension in sugary bliss, friends.
That imp's a menace. We have to find him.
BARK! BARK!
I know, boy. Keep looking.
Do you smell... cherry jel—?
I see it. Good dog.
Flash, sending you coordinates.
We're on it. Practically there.

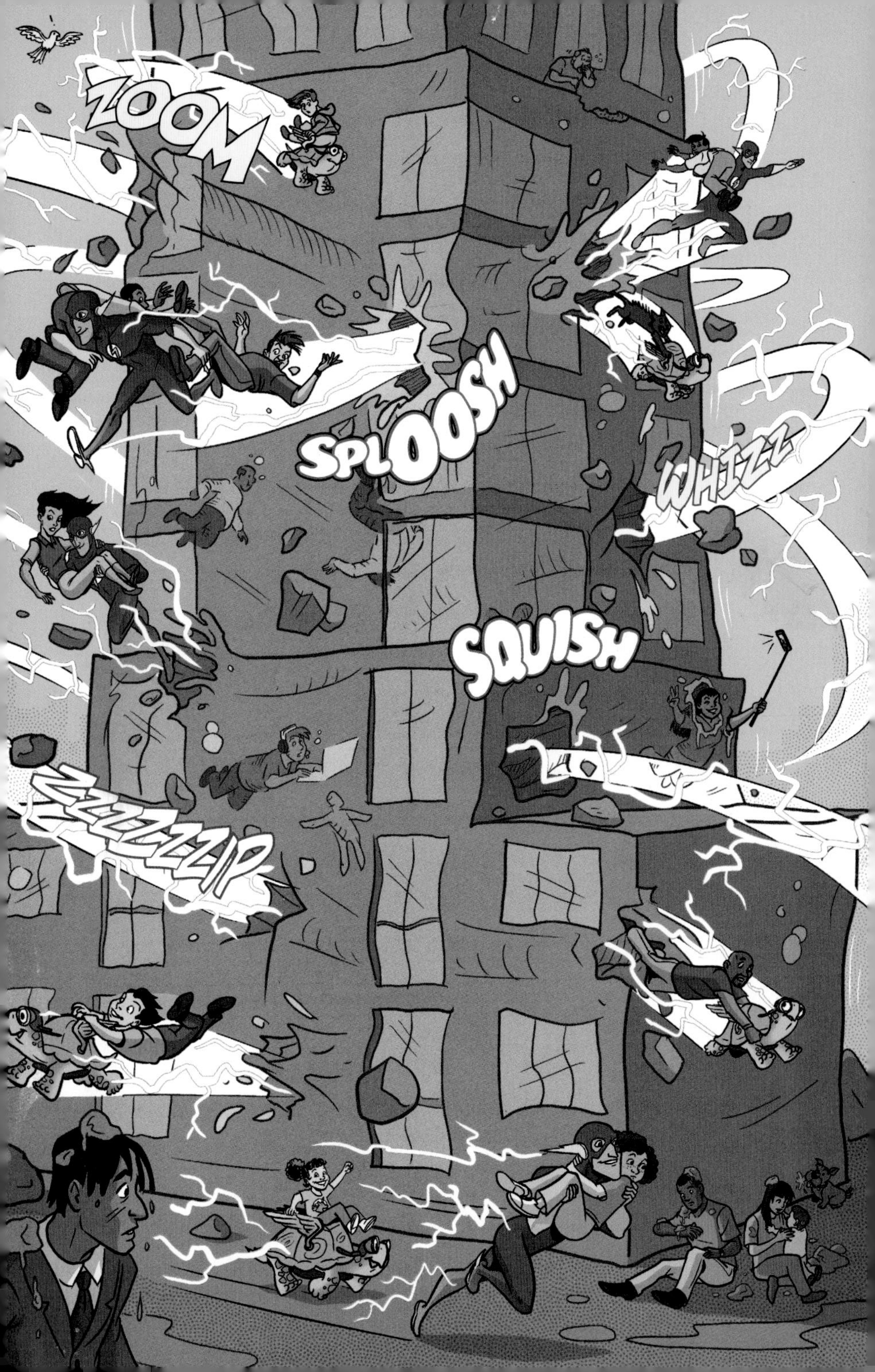
ZOOM
SPLOOSH
WHIZZ
SQUISH
ZZZZZZIP

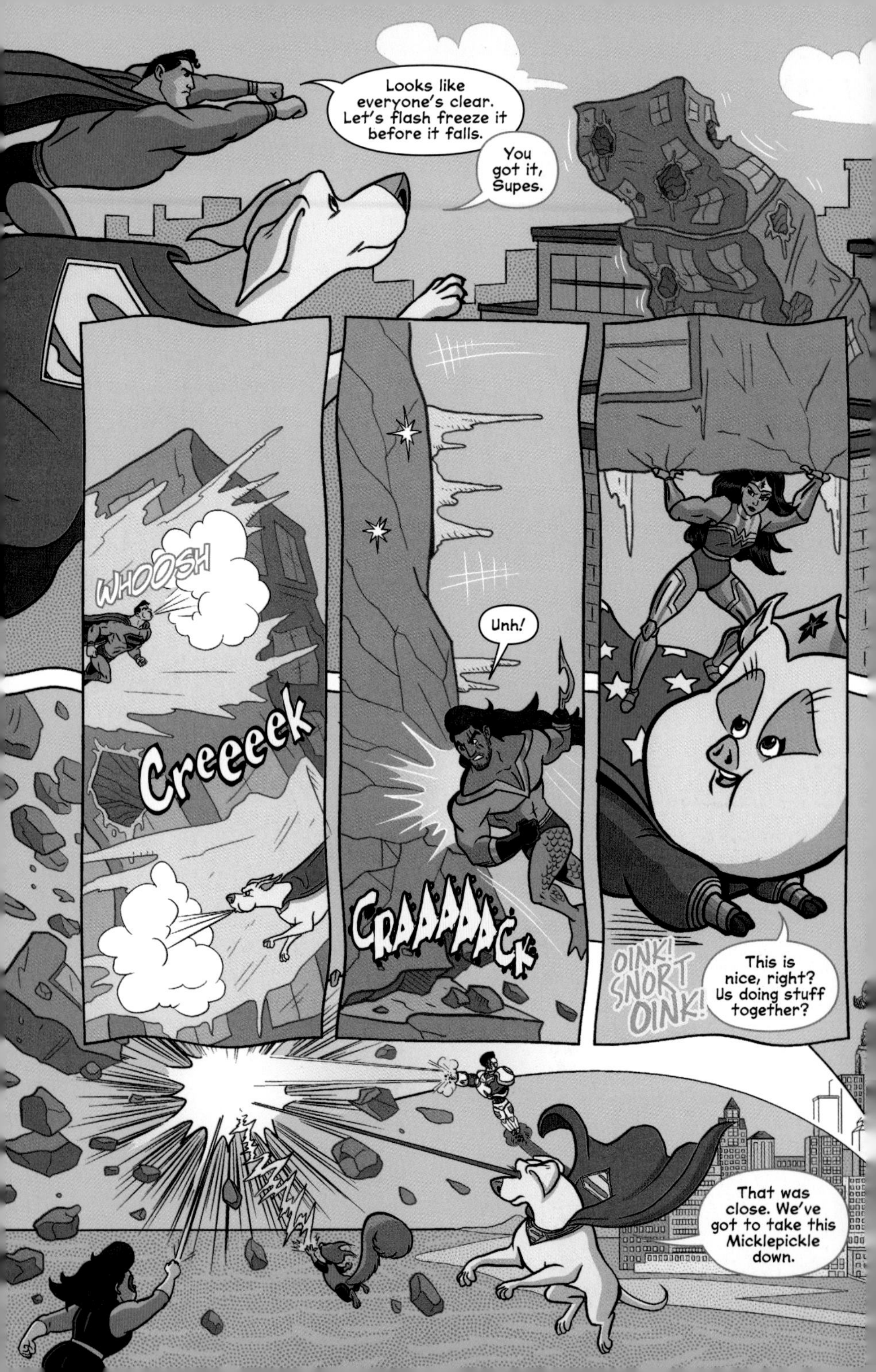
Looks like everyone's clear. Let's flash freeze it before it falls.
You got it, Supes.
WHOOSH
Creeeek
Unh!
CRAAAAACK
OINK! SNORT OINK!
This is nice, right? Us doing stuff together?
That was close. We've got to take this Micklepickle down.

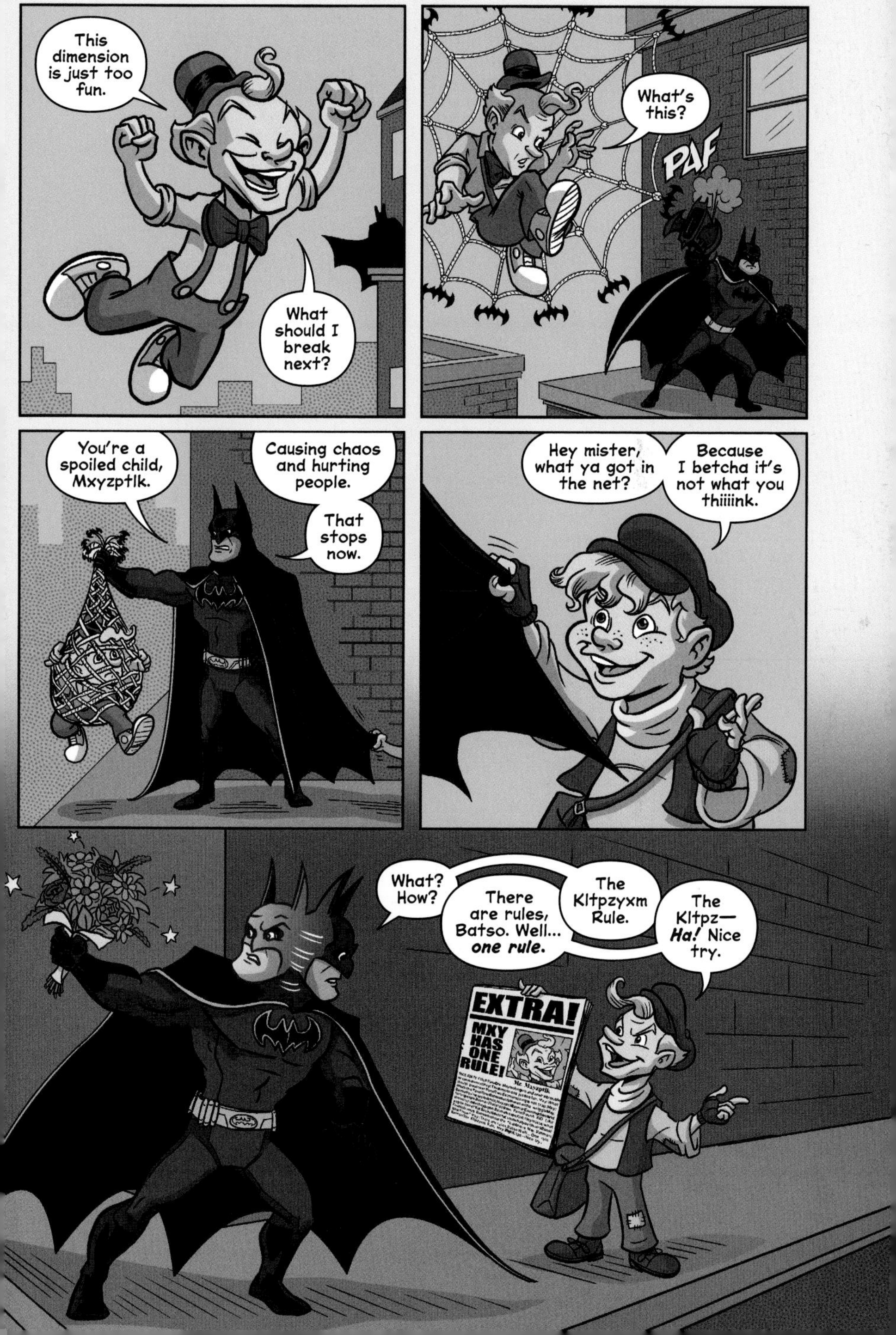
This dimension is just too fun.
What should I break next?
What's this?
PAF
You're a spoiled child, Mxyzptlk.
Causing chaos and hurting people.
That stops now.
Hey mister, what ya got in the net?
Because I betcha it's not what you thiiiink.
What? How?
There are rules, Batso. Well... ***one rule.***
The Kltpzyxm Rule.
The Kltpz—***Ha!*** Nice try.
EXTRA!
MXY HAS ONE RULE!

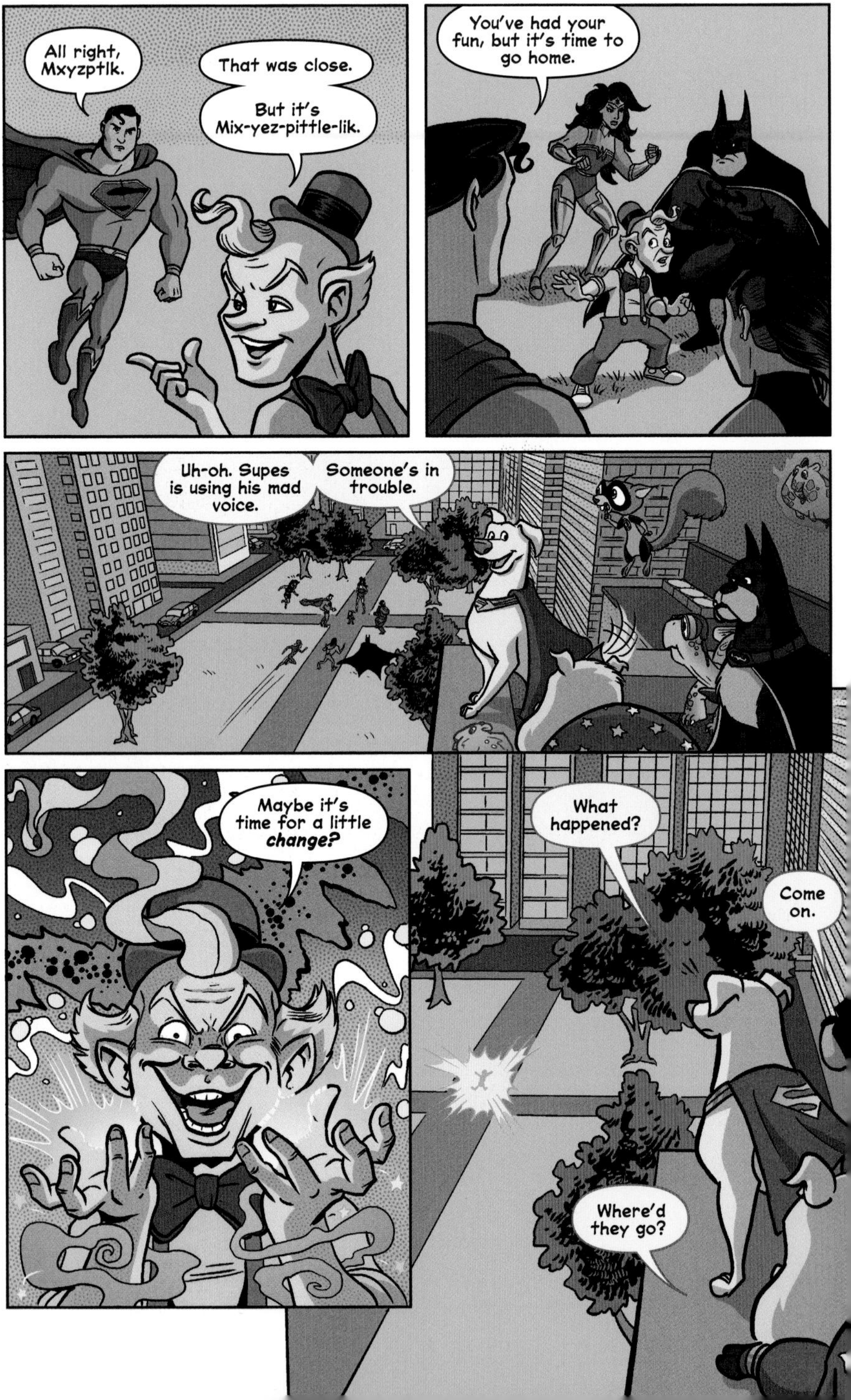
All right, Mxyzptlk.
That was close.
But it's Mix-yez-pittle-lik.
You've had your fun, but it's time to go home.
Uh-oh. Supes is using his mad voice.
Someone's in trouble.
Maybe it's time for a little *change?*
What happened?
Come on.
Where'd they go?

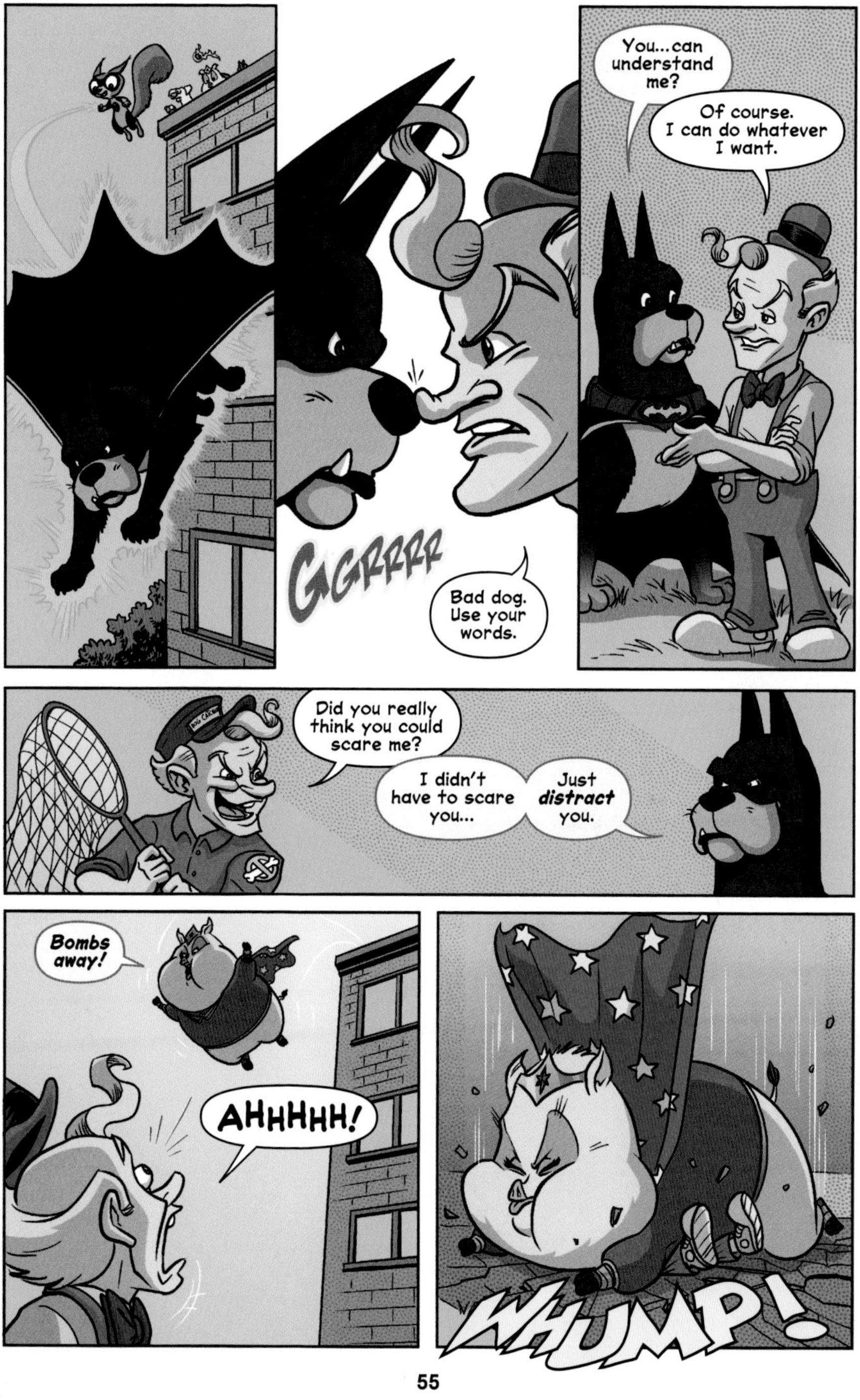

GGRRRR
Bad dog. Use your words.
You...can understand me?
Of course. I can do whatever I want.
Did you really think you could scare me?
I didn't have to scare you...
Just *distract* you.
Bombs away!
AHHHHH!
WHUMP!

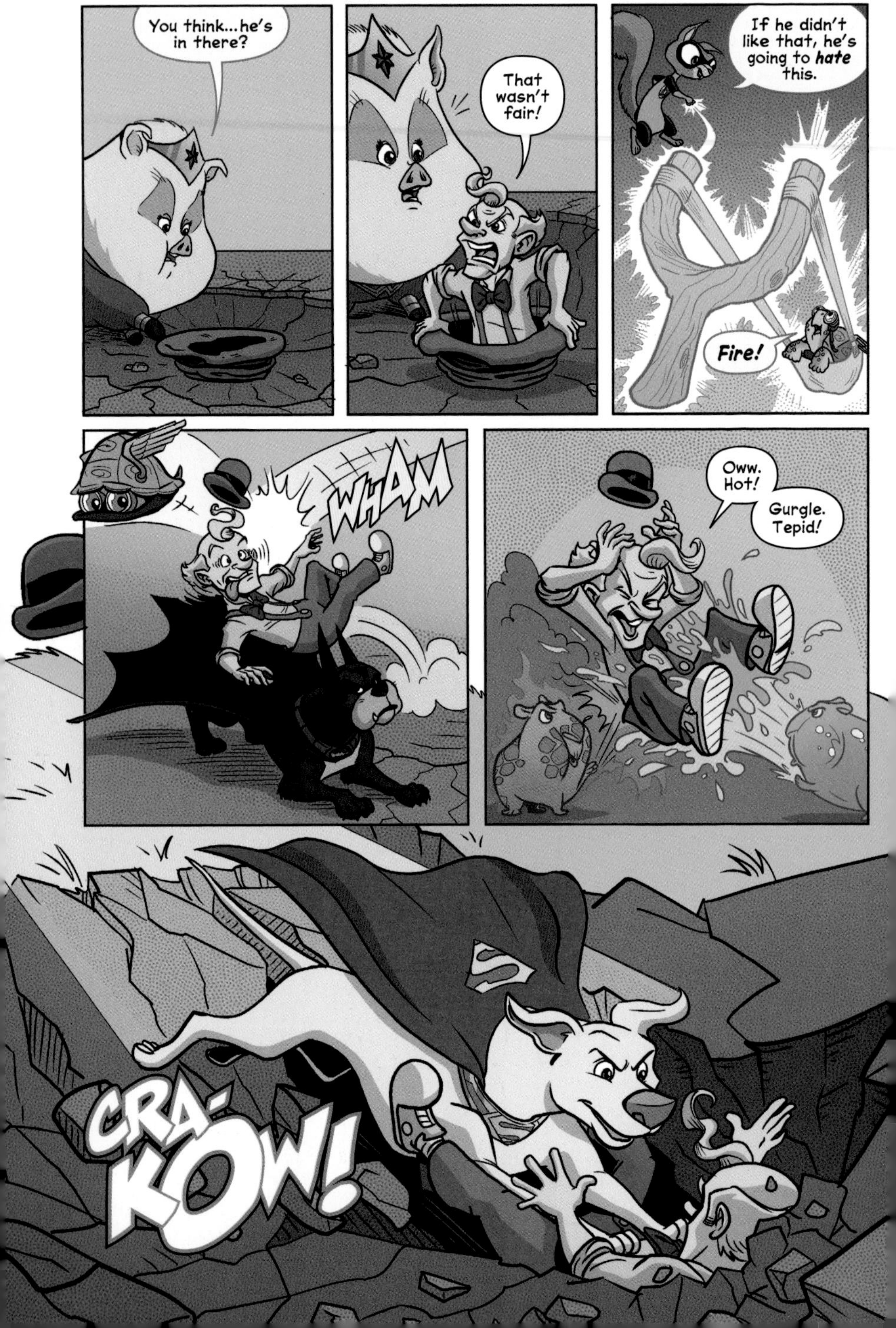
You think...he's in there?
That wasn't fair!
If he didn't like that, he's going to **hate** this.
Fire!
WHAM
Oww. Hot!
Gurgle. Tepid!
CRA-KOW!

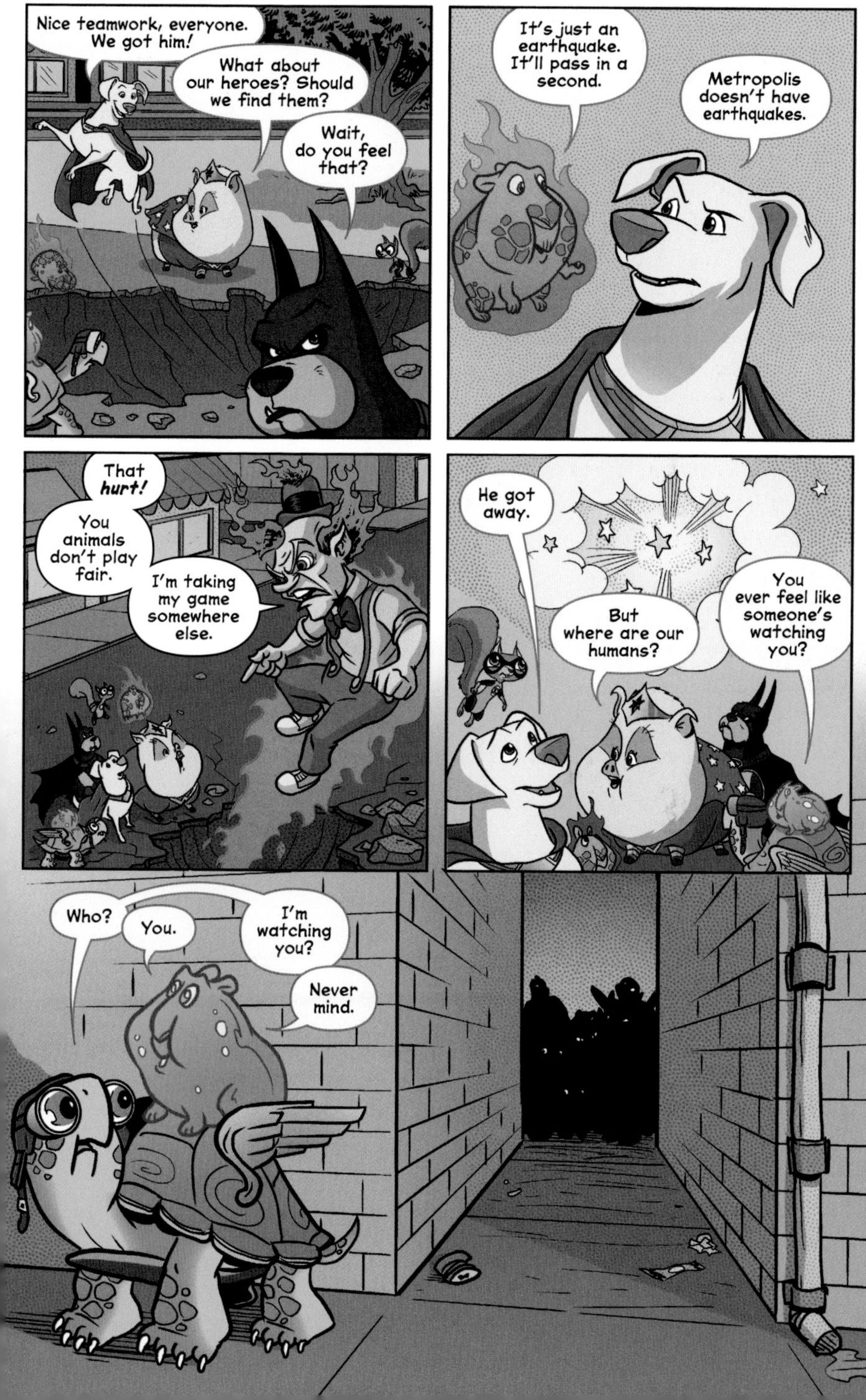

Nice teamwork, everyone. We got him!
What about our heroes? Should we find them?
Wait, do you feel that?
It's just an earthquake. It'll pass in a second.
Metropolis doesn't have earthquakes.
That *hurt!*
You animals don't play fair.
I'm taking my game somewhere else.
He got away.
But where are our humans?
You ever feel like someone's watching you?
Who?
You.
I'm watching you?
Never mind.

CHAPTER 3
Unleashed!

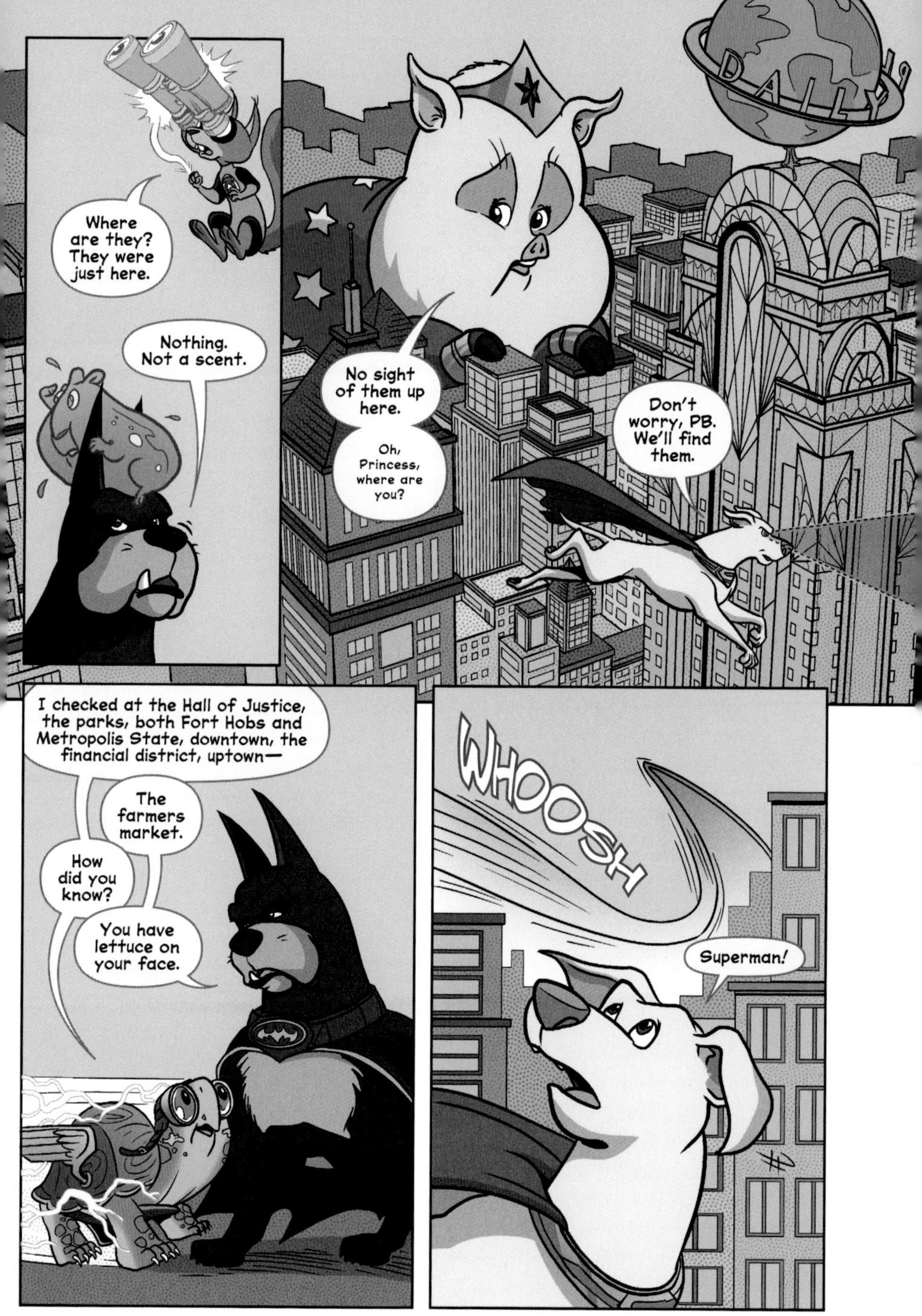
Where are they? They were just here.
Nothing. Not a scent.
No sight of them up here.
Oh, Princess, where are you?
Don't worry, PB. We'll find them.
I checked at the Hall of Justice, the parks, both Fort Hobs and Metropolis State, downtown, the financial district, uptown—
The farmers market.
How did you know?
You have lettuce on your face.
WHOOSH
Superman!

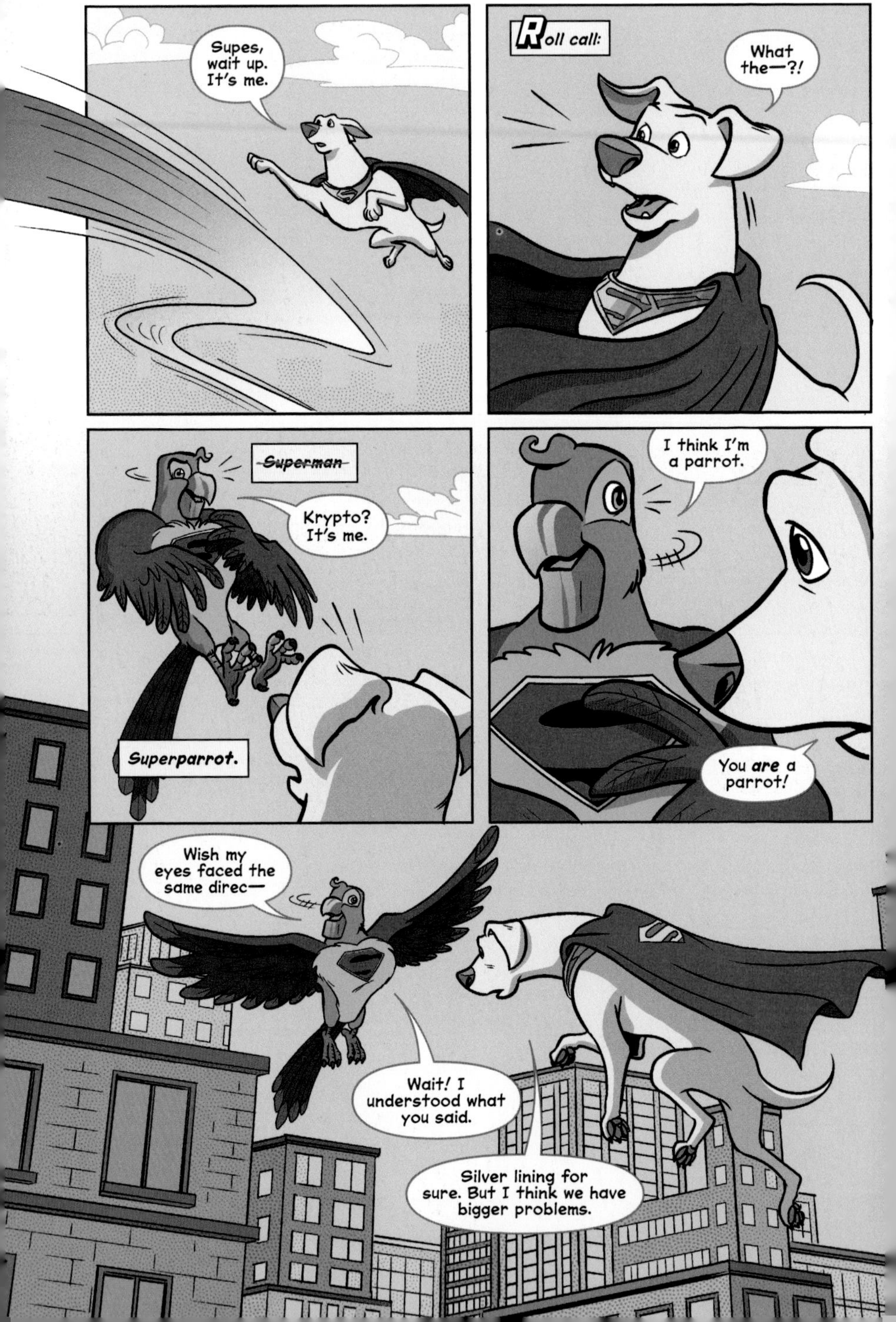
Supes, wait up. It's me.
Roll call:
What the—?!
~~Superman~~
Krypto? It's me.
Superparrot.
I think I'm a parrot.
You *are* a parrot!
Wish my eyes faced the same direc—
Wait! I understood what you said.
Silver lining for sure. But I think we have bigger problems.

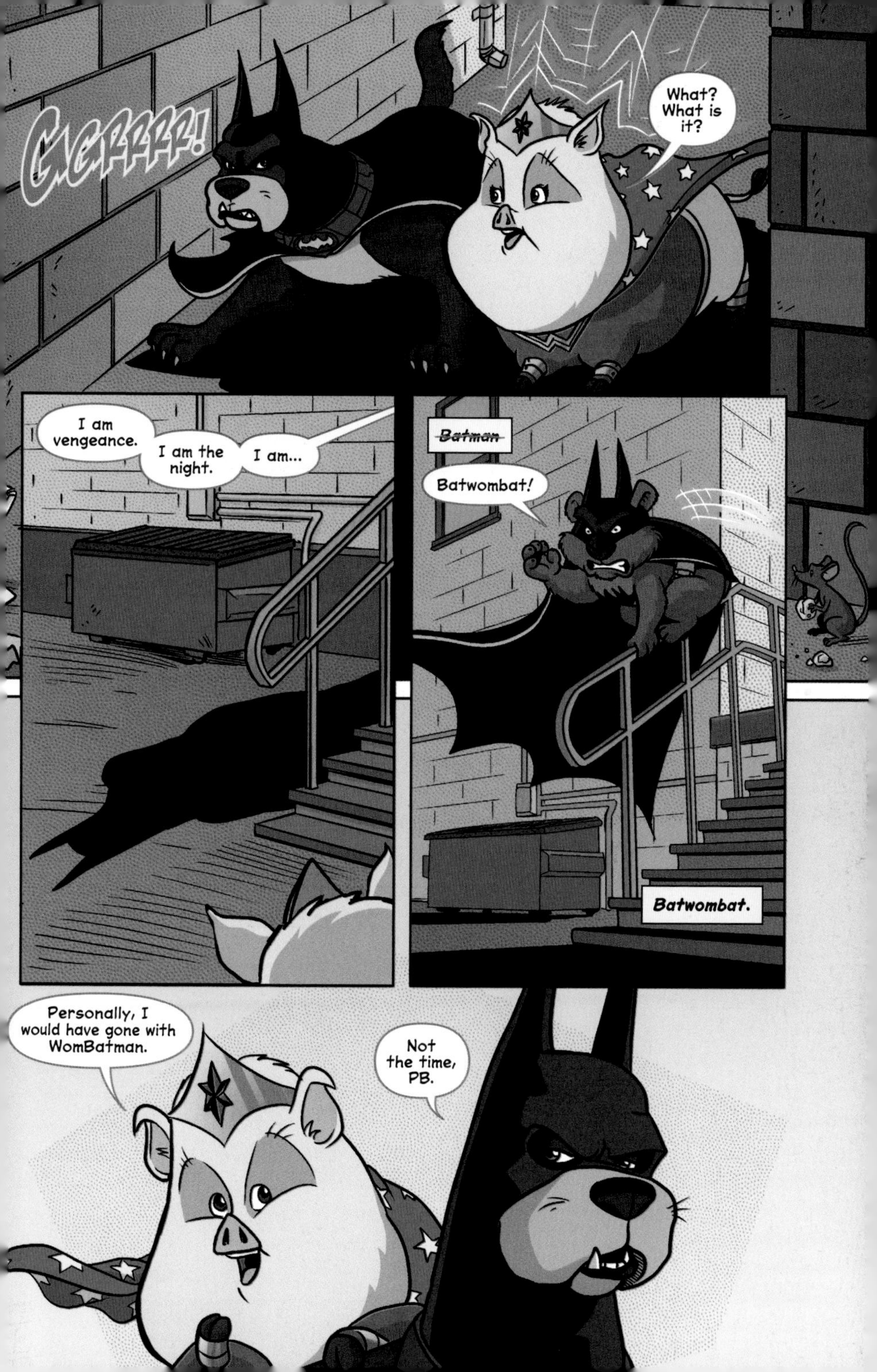
GRRRR!
What? What is it?
I am vengeance.
I am the night.
I am...
Batman
Batwombat!
Batwombat.
Personally, I would have gone with WomBatman.
Not the time, PB.

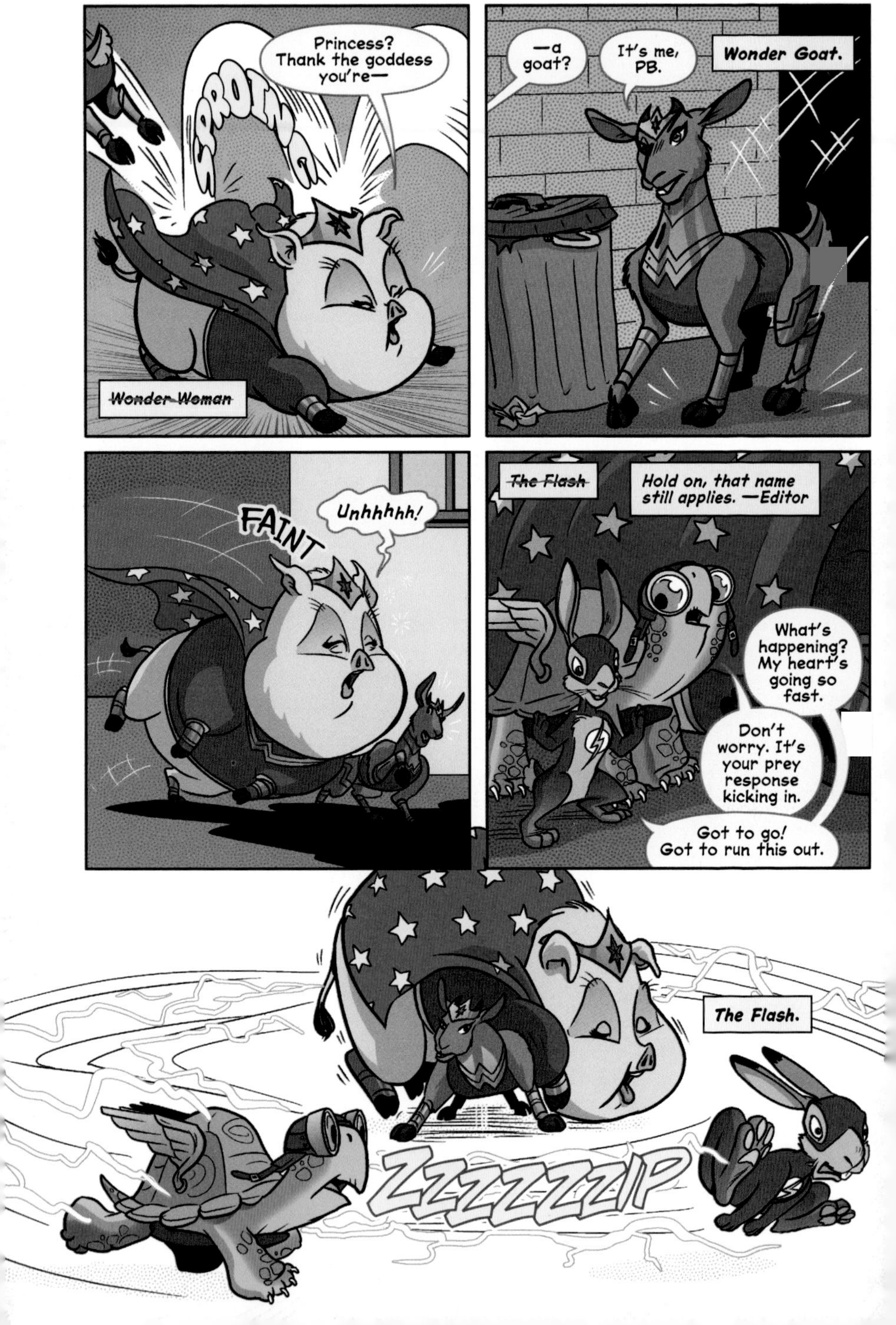
Princess? Thank the goddess you're—
SPROING
Wonder Woman
Wonder Goat.
It's me, PB.
—a goat?
FAINT
Unhhhhh!
The Flash
Hold on, that name still applies. —Editor
What's happening? My heart's going so fast.
Don't worry. It's your prey response kicking in.
Got to go! Got to run this out.
The Flash.
ZZZZZZZIP

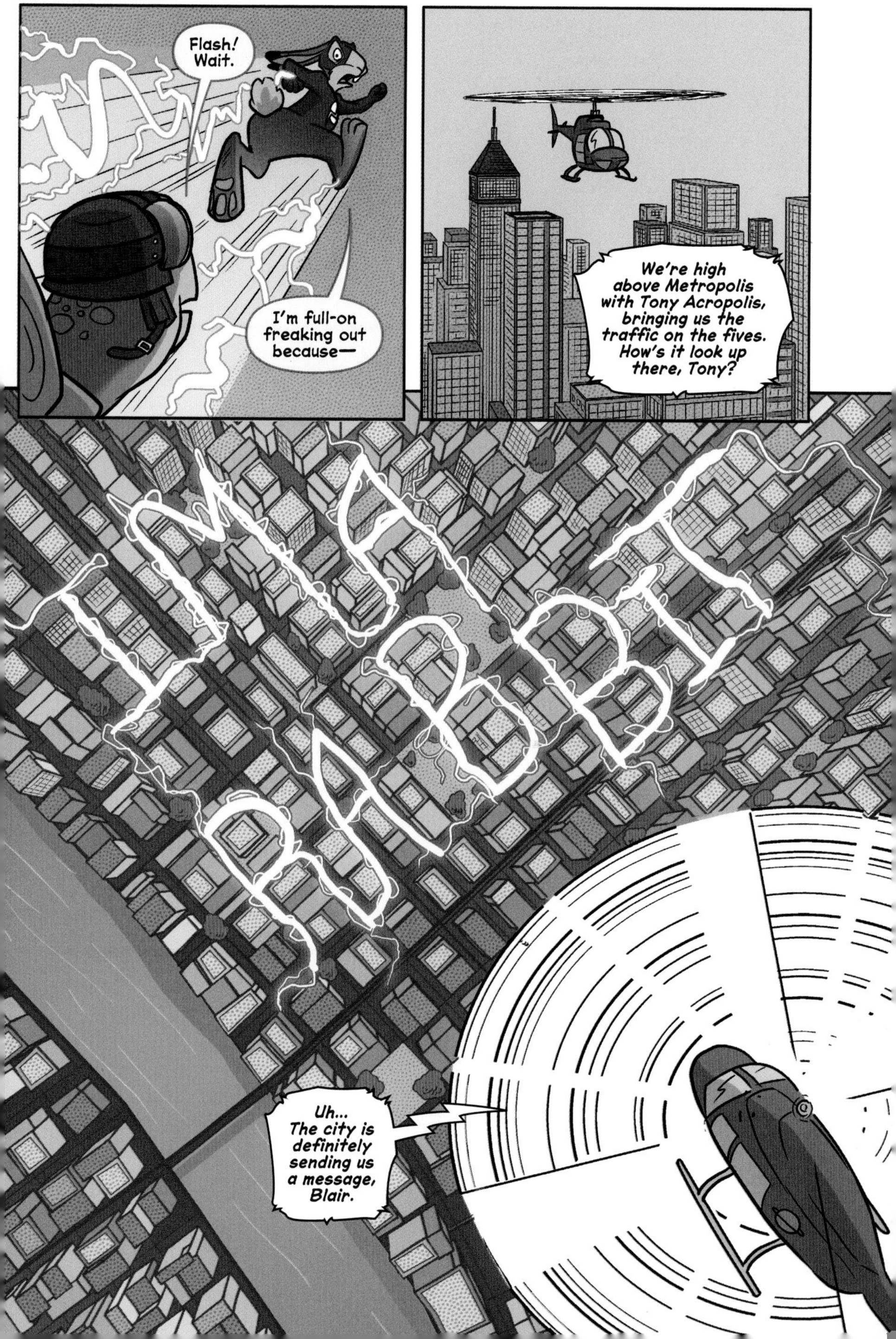
Flash! Wait.
I'm full-on freaking out because—
We're high above Metropolis with Tony Acropolis, bringing us the traffic on the fives. How's it look up there, Tony?
IM A RABBIT
Uh... The city is definitely sending us a message, Blair.

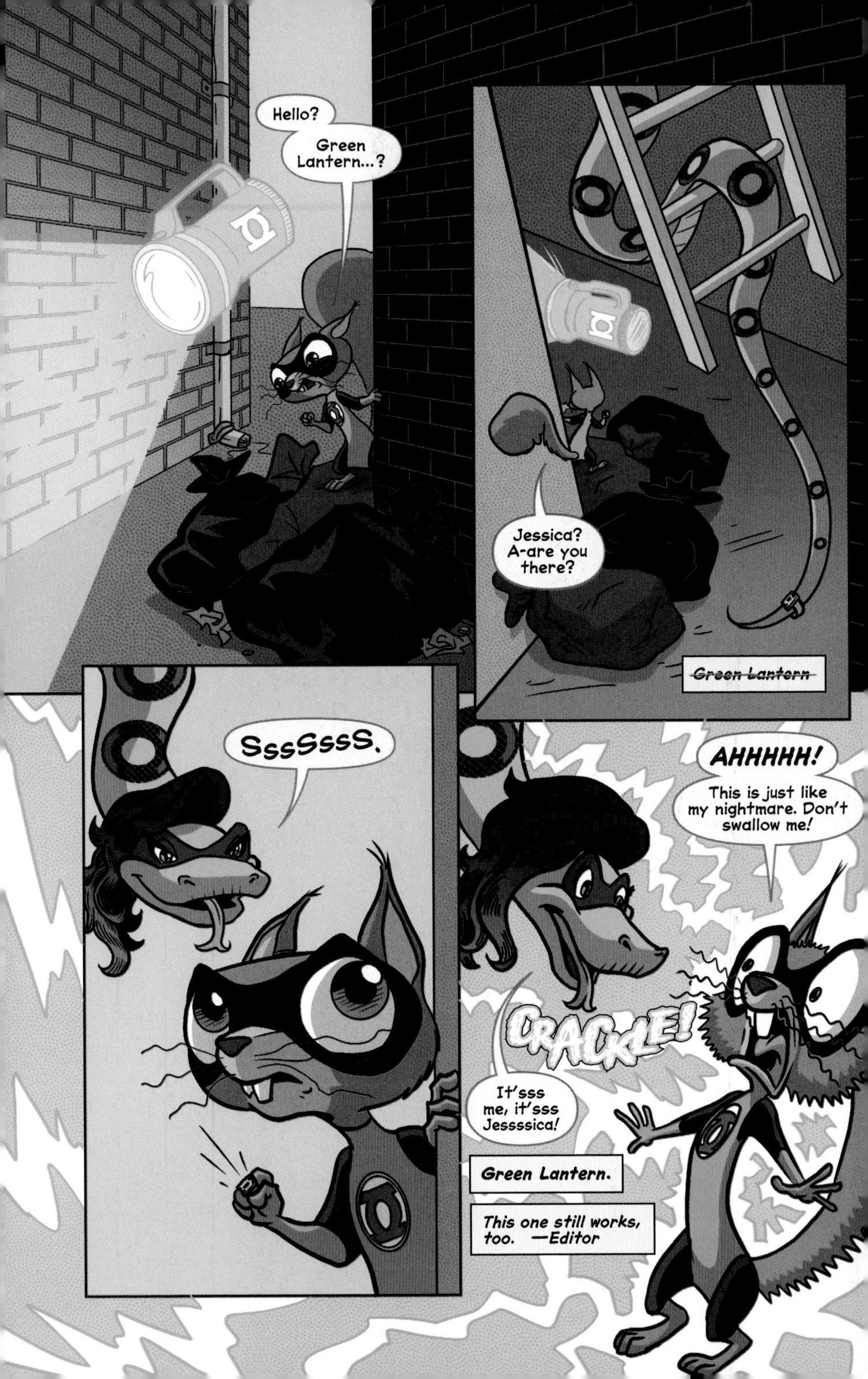
Hello?
Green Lantern...?
Jessica? A-are you there?
Green Lantern
SssSssS.
AHHHHH!
This is just like my nightmare. Don't swallow me!
CRACKLE!
It'sss me, it'sss Jesssica!
Green Lantern.
This one still works, too. —Editor

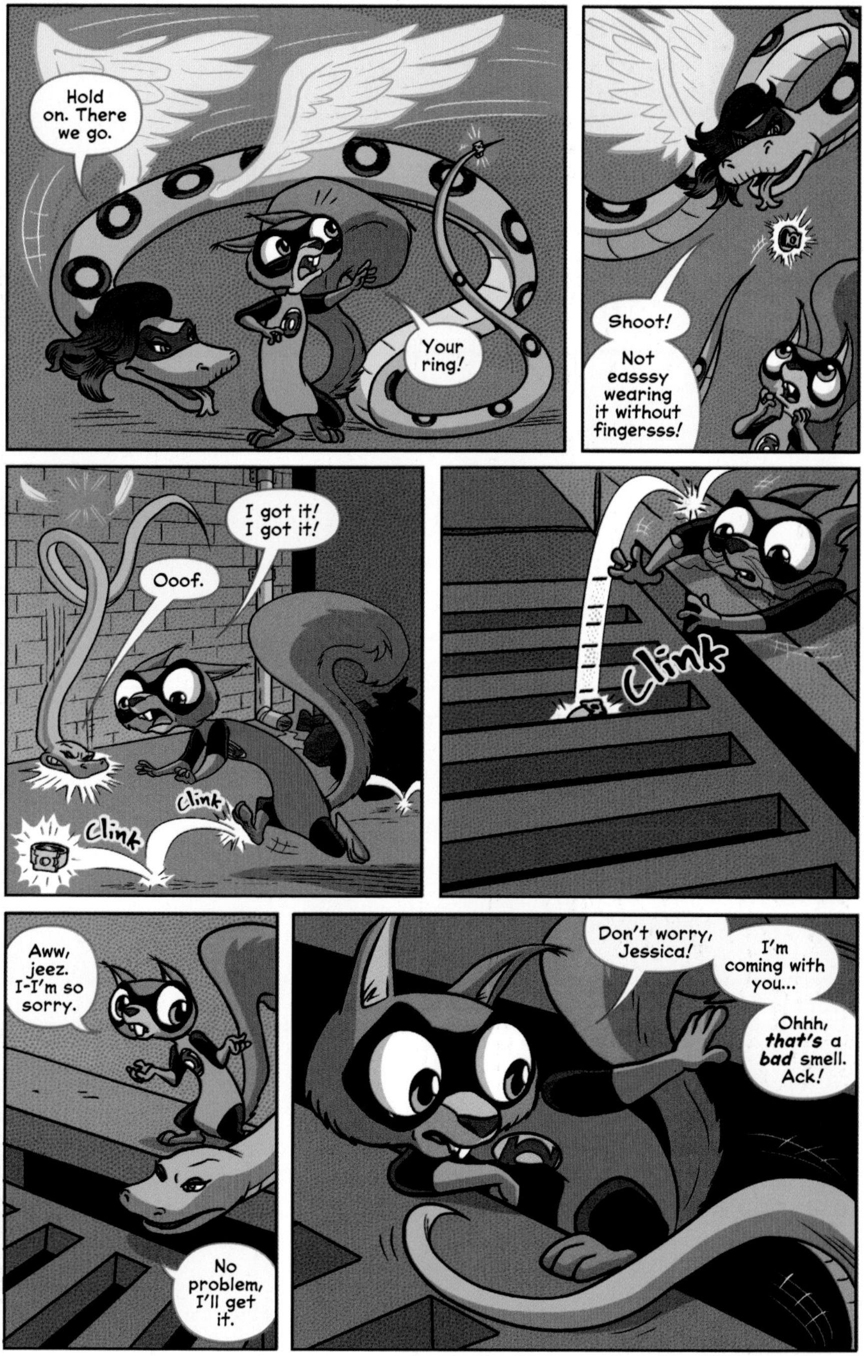
Hold on. There we go.
Your ring!
Shoot!
Not easssy wearing it without fingersss!
I got it! I got it!
Ooof.
Clink
Clink
Clink
Aww, jeez. I-I'm so sorry.
No problem, I'll get it.
Don't worry, Jessica!
I'm coming with you...
Ohhh, *that's* a *bad* smell. Ack!

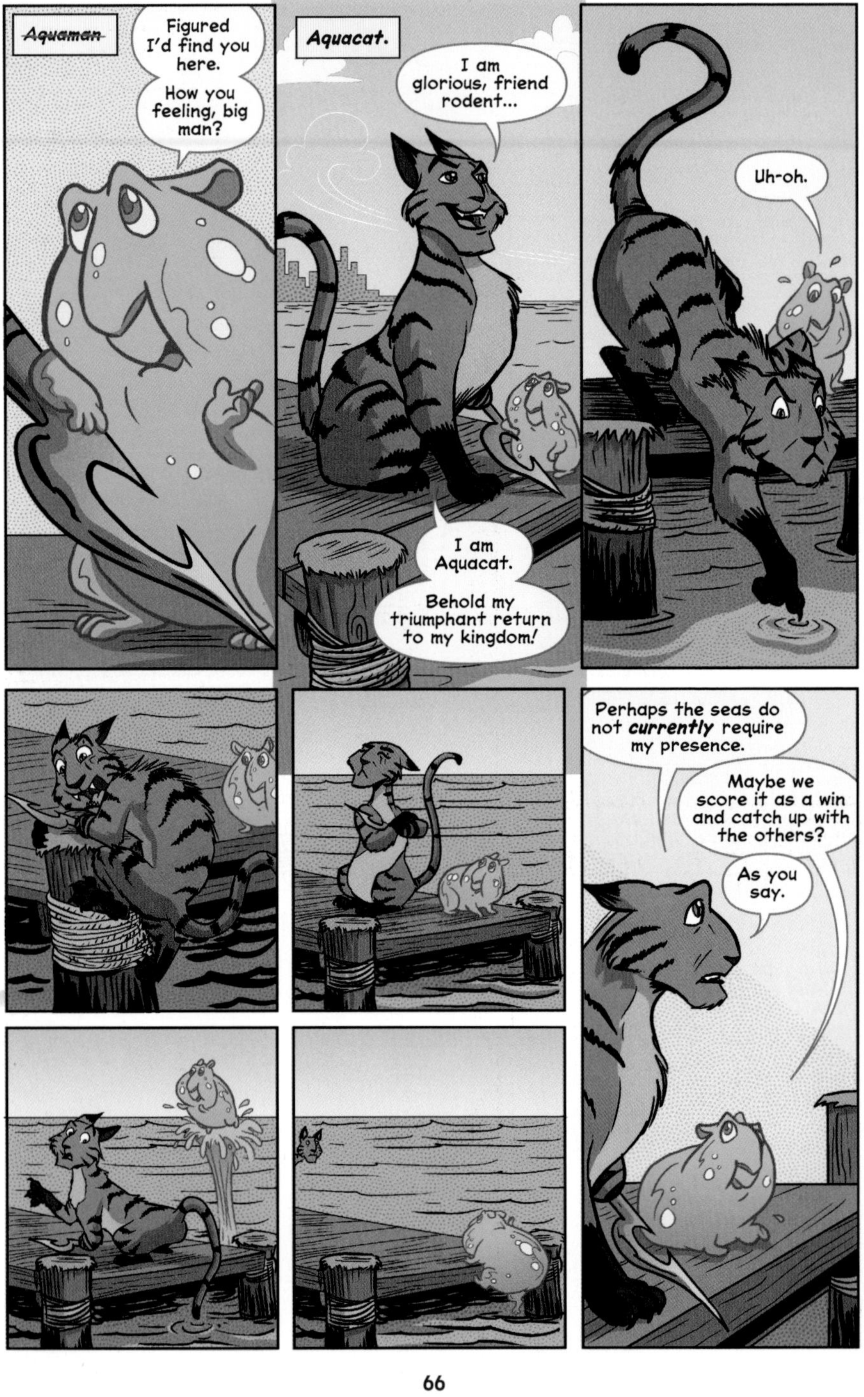
~~Aquaman~~
Figured I'd find you here.
How you feeling, big man?
Aquacat.
I am glorious, friend rodent...
I am Aquacat.
Behold my triumphant return to my kingdom!
Uh-oh.
Perhaps the seas do not ***currently*** require my presence.
Maybe we score it as a win and catch up with the others?
As you say.

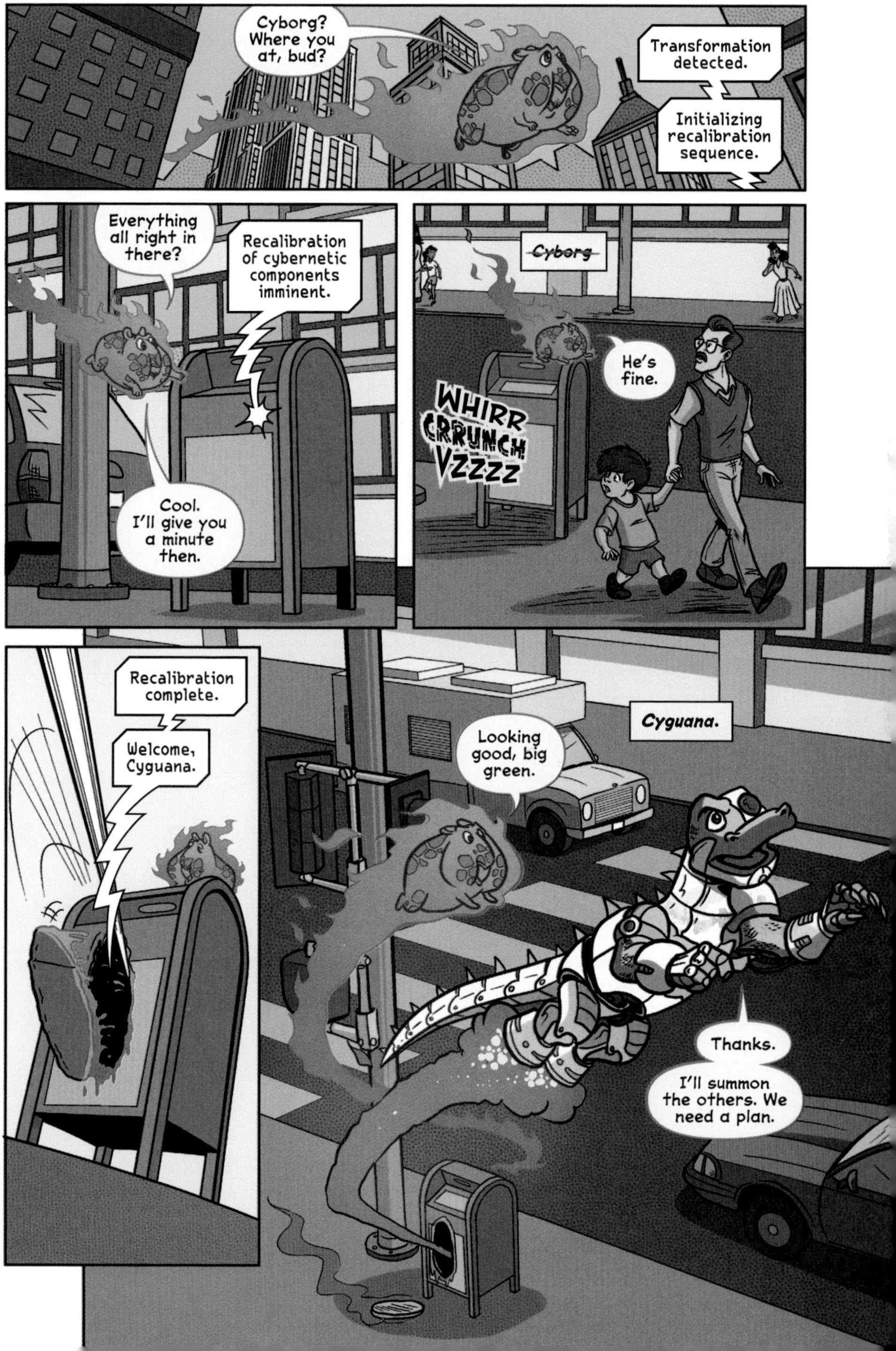
Cyborg? Where you at, bud?
Transformation detected.
Initializing recalibration sequence.
Everything all right in there?
Recalibration of cybernetic components imminent.
Cool. I'll give you a minute then.
Cyborg
He's fine.
WHIRR CRRUNCH VZZZZ
Recalibration complete.
Welcome, Cyguana.
Cyguana.
Looking good, big green.
Thanks.
I'll summon the others. We need a plan.

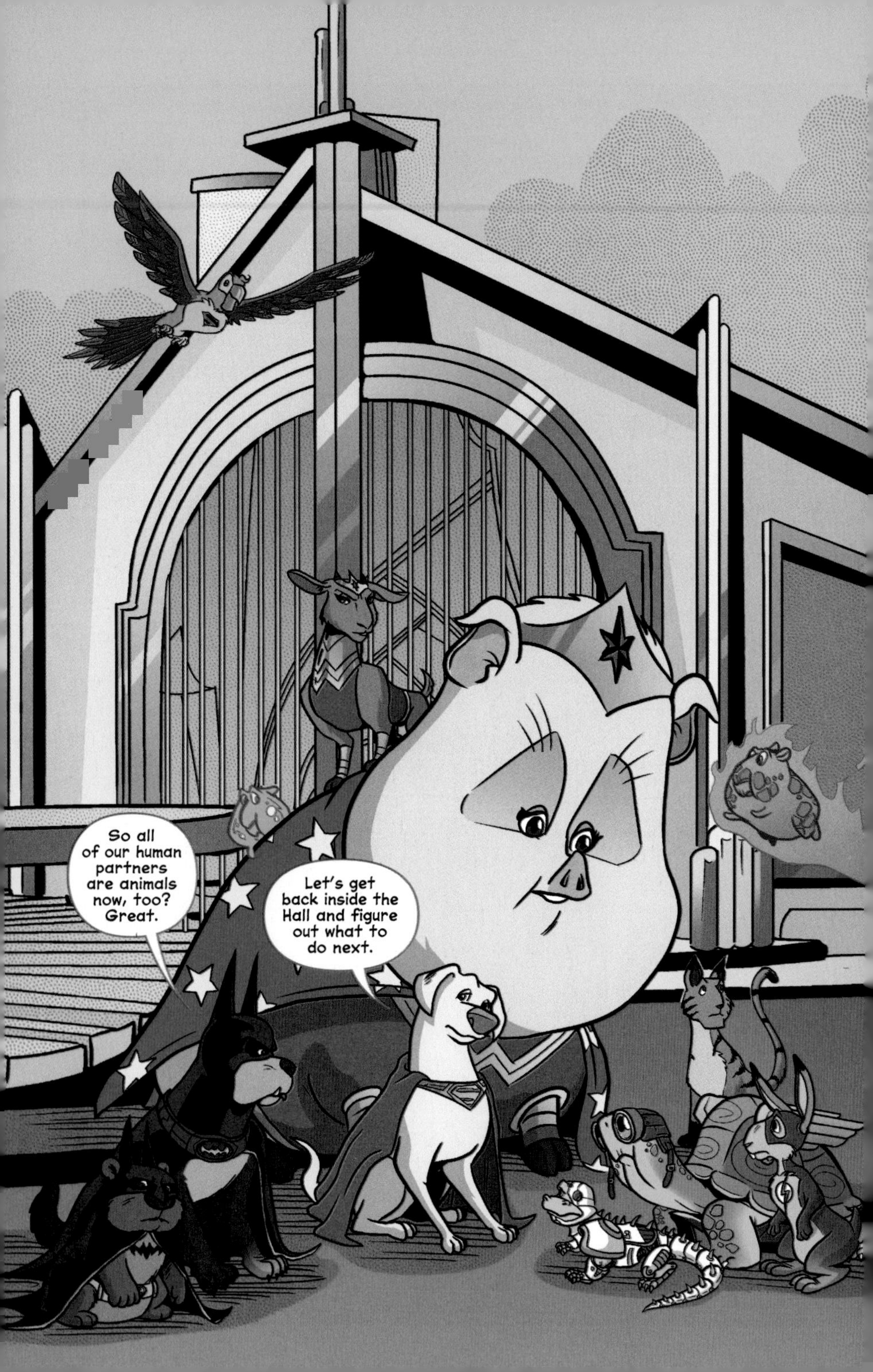
So all of our human partners are animals now, too? Great.
Let's get back inside the Hall and figure out what to do next.

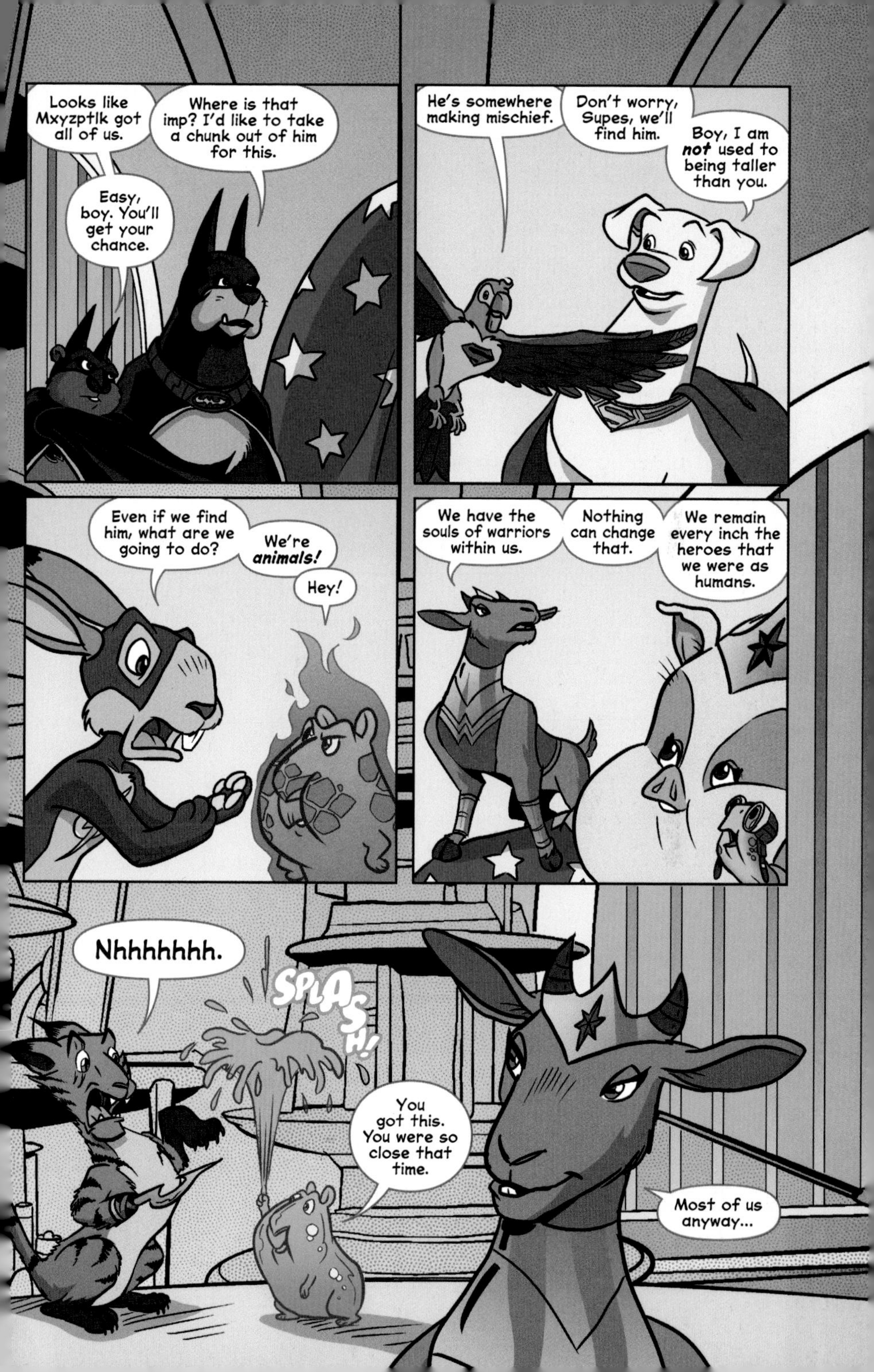
Looks like Mxyzptlk got all of us.
Where is that imp? I'd like to take a chunk out of him for this.
Easy, boy. You'll get your chance.
He's somewhere making mischief.
Don't worry, Supes, we'll find him.
Boy, I am *not* used to being taller than you.
Even if we find him, what are we going to do?
We're *animals!*
Hey!
We have the souls of warriors within us.
Nothing can change that.
We remain every inch the heroes that we were as humans.
Nhhhhhhh.
SPLASH!
You got this. You were so close that time.
Most of us anyway...

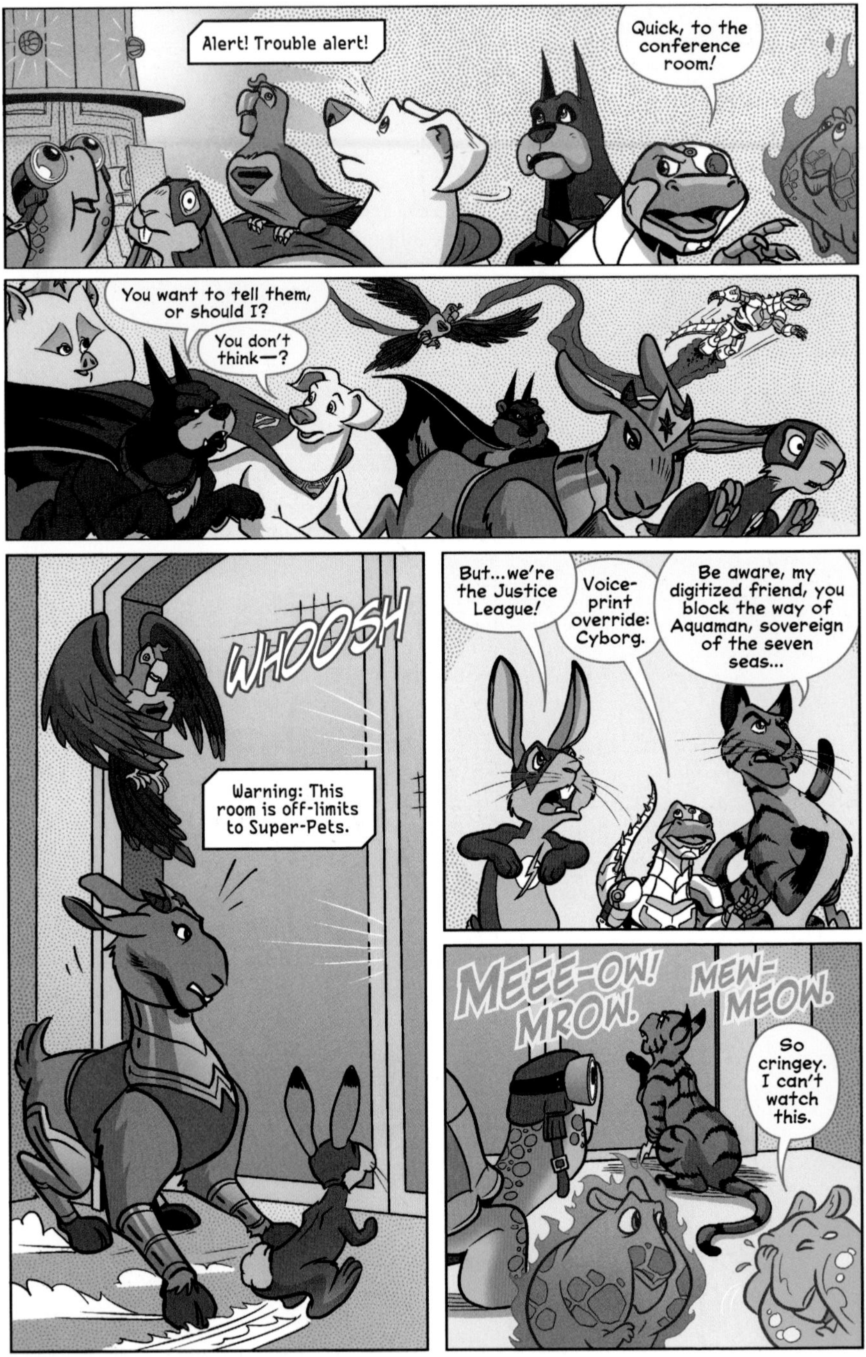

Alert! Trouble alert!
Quick, to the conference room!
You want to tell them, or should I?
You don't think—?
WHOOSH
Warning: This room is off-limits to Super-Pets.
But...we're the Justice League!
Voice-print override: Cyborg.
Be aware, my digitized friend, you block the way of Aquaman, sovereign of the seven seas...
MEEE-OW! MROW.
MEW-MEOW.
So cringey. I can't watch this.

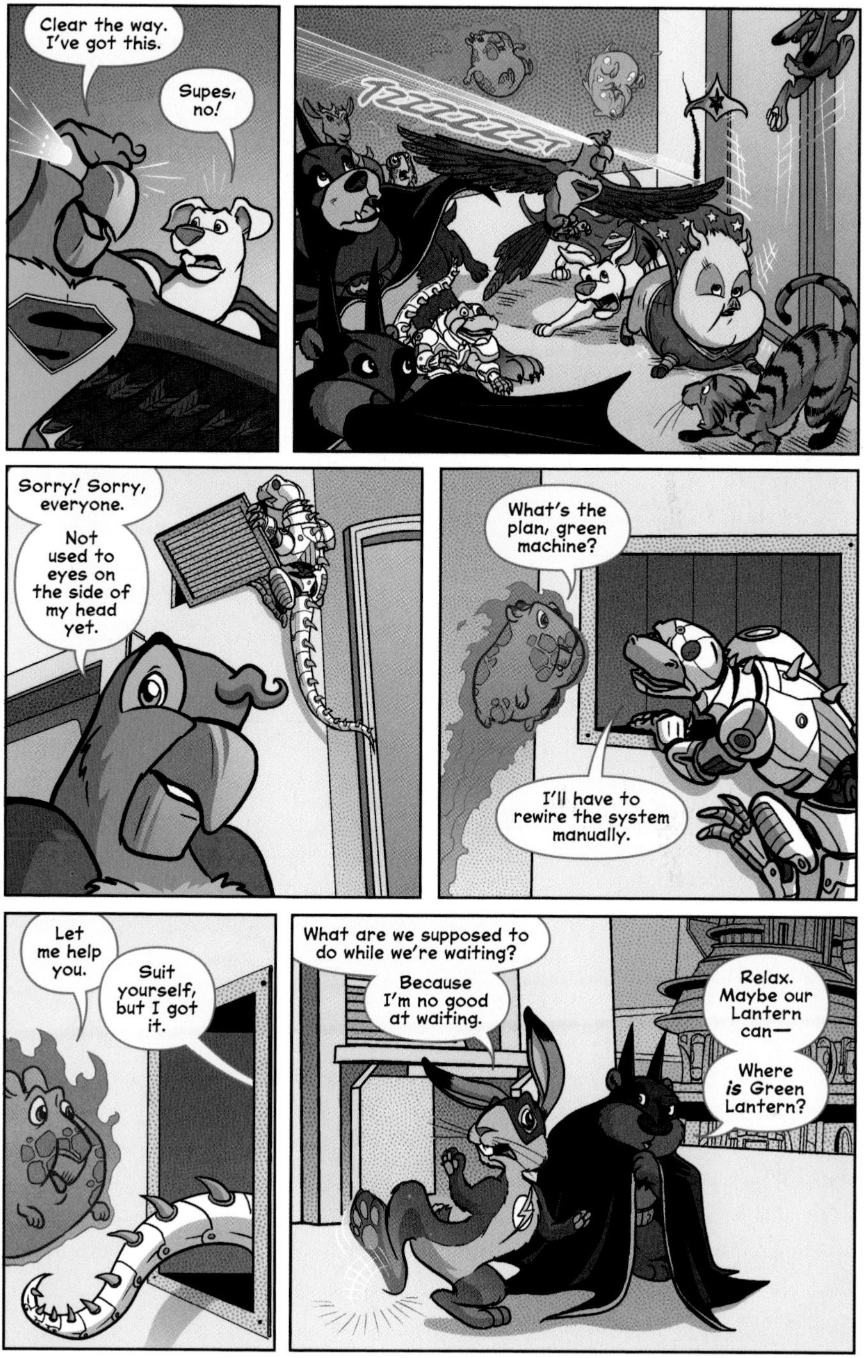
Clear the way. I've got this.
Supes, no!
TZZZZZZT
Sorry! Sorry, everyone.
Not used to eyes on the side of my head yet.
What's the plan, green machine?
I'll have to rewire the system manually.
Let me help you.
Suit yourself, but I got it.
What are we supposed to do while we're waiting?
Because I'm no good at waiting.
Relax. Maybe our Lantern can—
Where *is* Green Lantern?

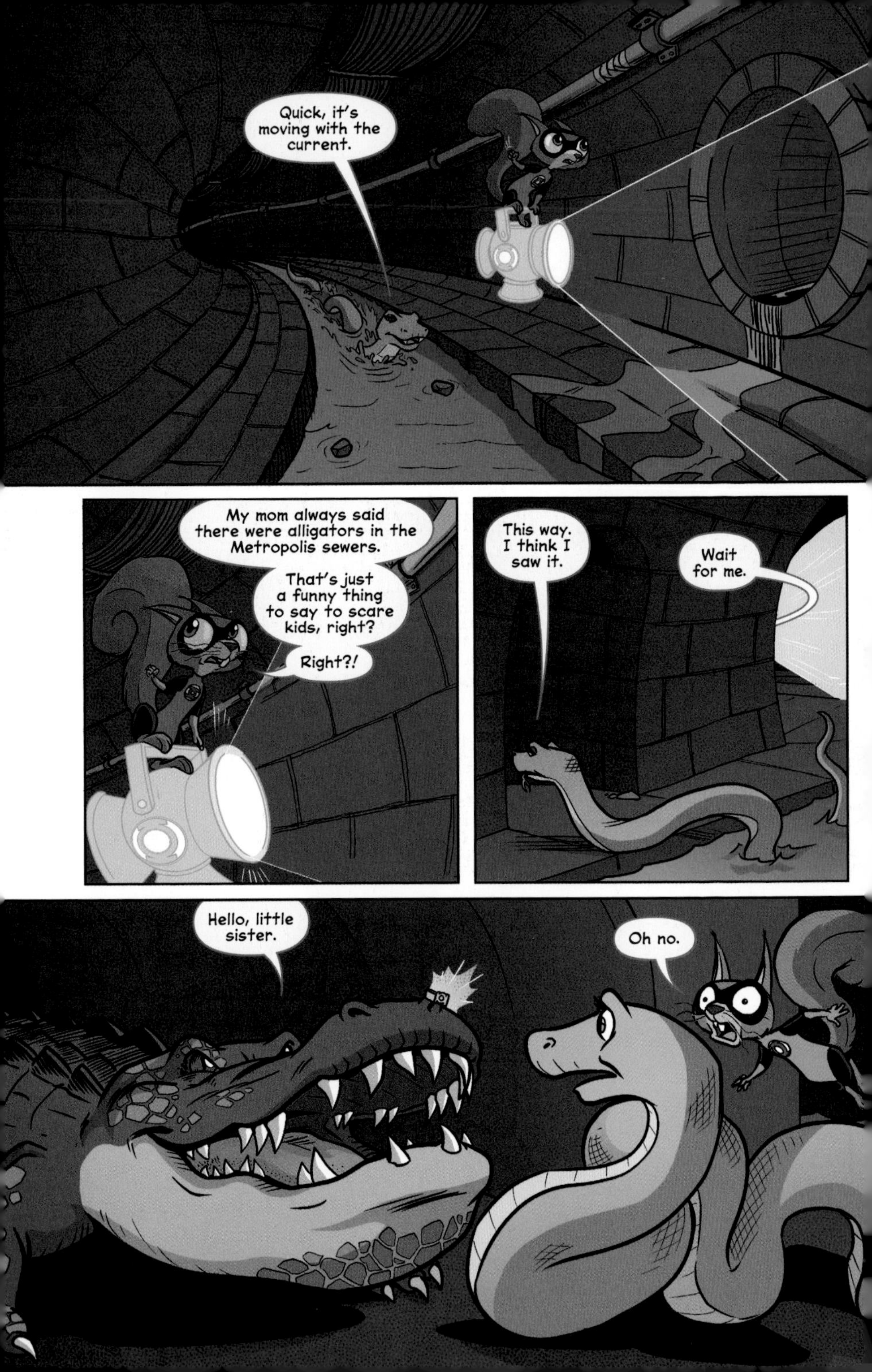
Quick, it's moving with the current.
My mom always said there were alligators in the Metropolis sewers.
That's just a funny thing to say to scare kids, right?
Right?!
This way. I think I saw it.
Wait for me.
Hello, little sister.
Oh no.

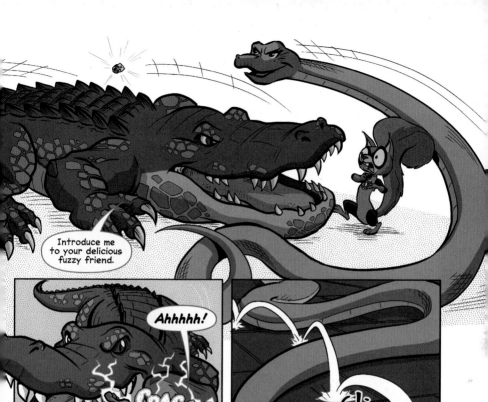

Introduce me to your delicious fuzzy friend.

Ahhhhh!

CRACKLE

Clink

What a snack you are.

Gulp!

I—I'm *not* eaten?

What happened?

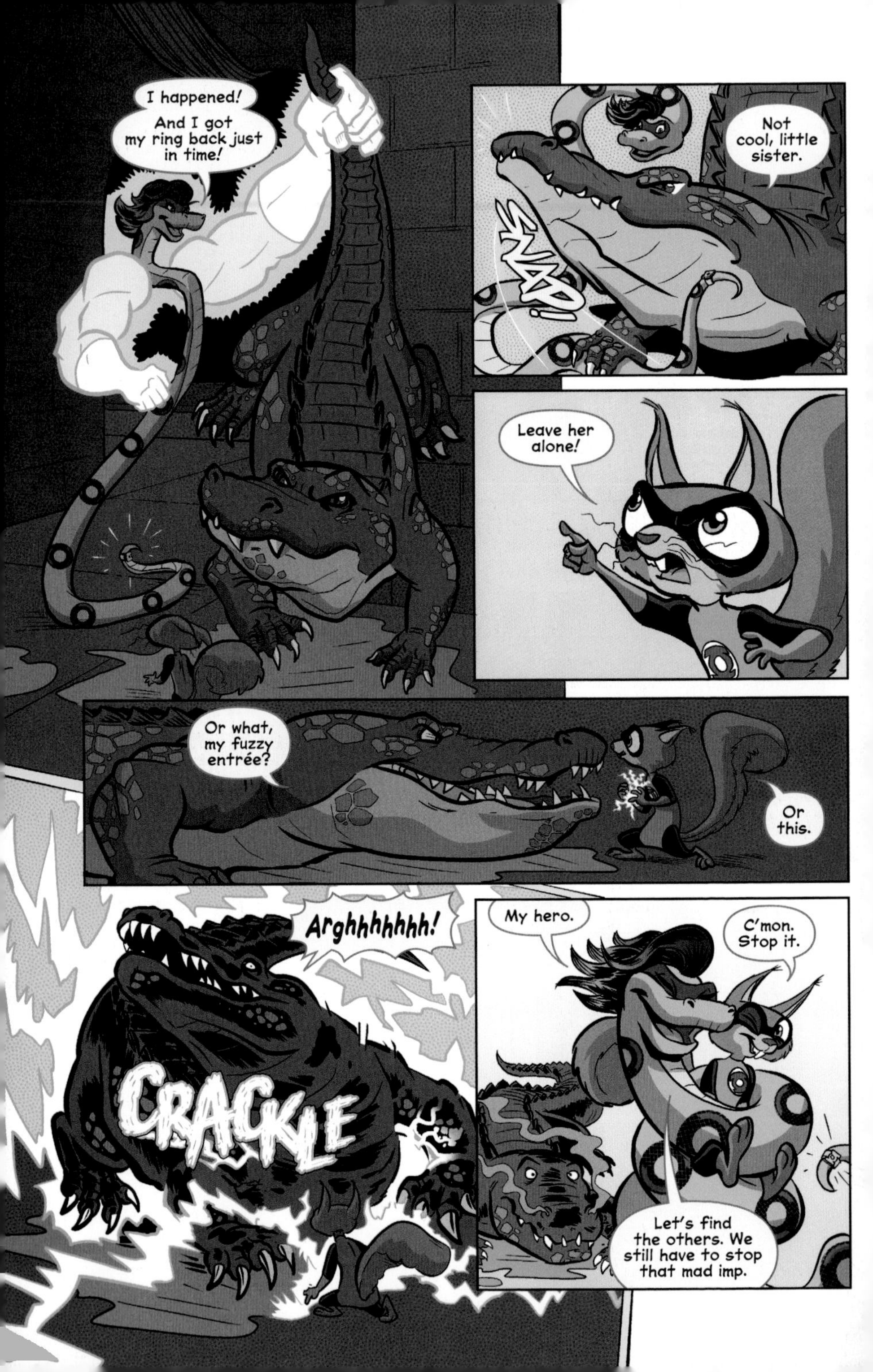
I happened!
And I got my ring back just in time!
Not cool, little sister.
SNAP!
Leave her alone!
Or what, my fuzzy entrée?
Or this.
Arghhhhhhh!
CRACKLE
My hero.
C'mon. Stop it.
Let's find the others. We still have to stop that mad imp.

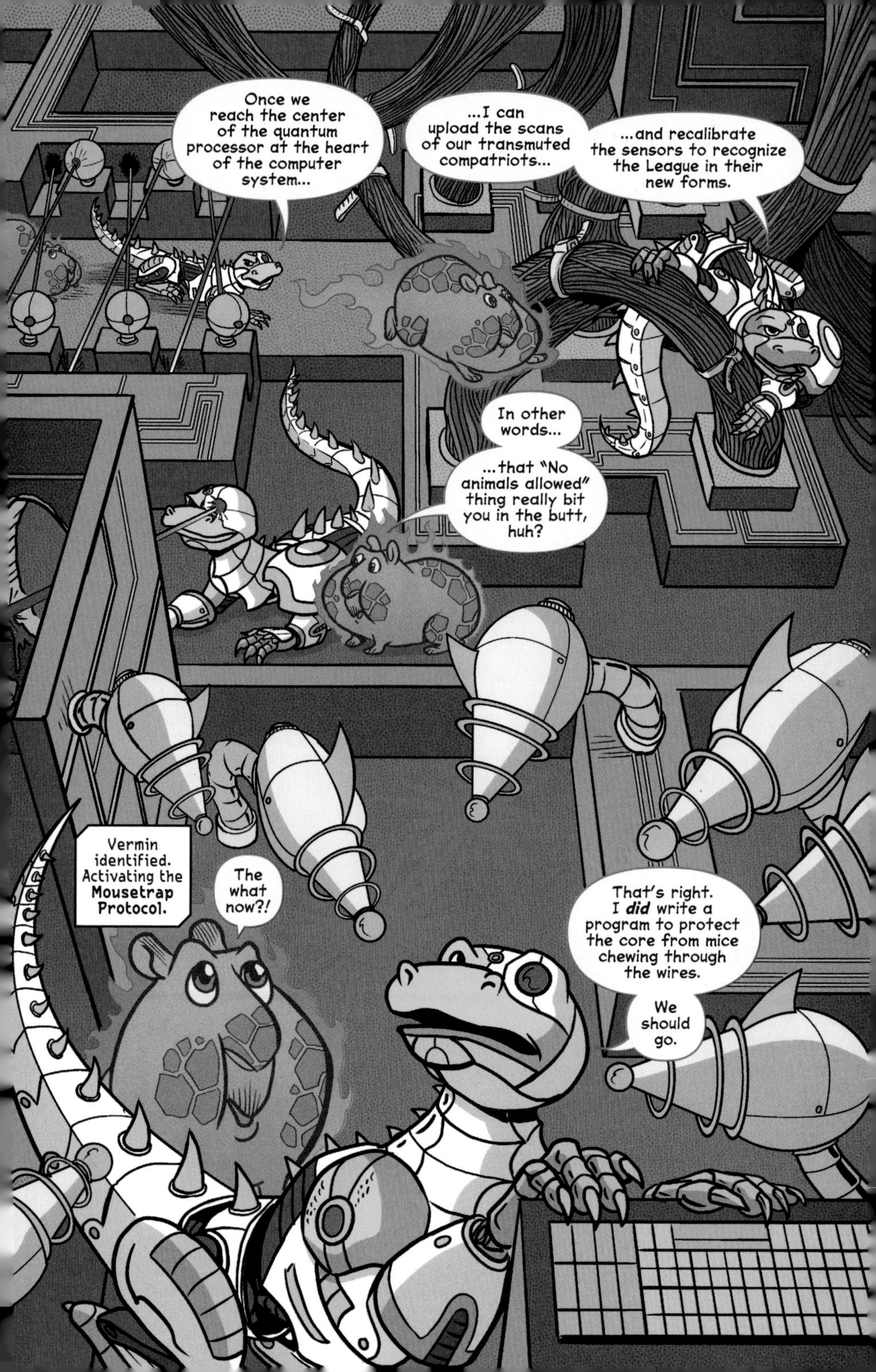
Once we reach the center of the quantum processor at the heart of the computer system...
...I can upload the scans of our transmuted compatriots...
...and recalibrate the sensors to recognize the League in their new forms.
In other words...
...that "No animals allowed" thing really bit you in the butt, huh?
Vermin identified. Activating the Mousetrap Protocol.
The what now?!
That's right. I did write a program to protect the core from mice chewing through the wires.
We should go.

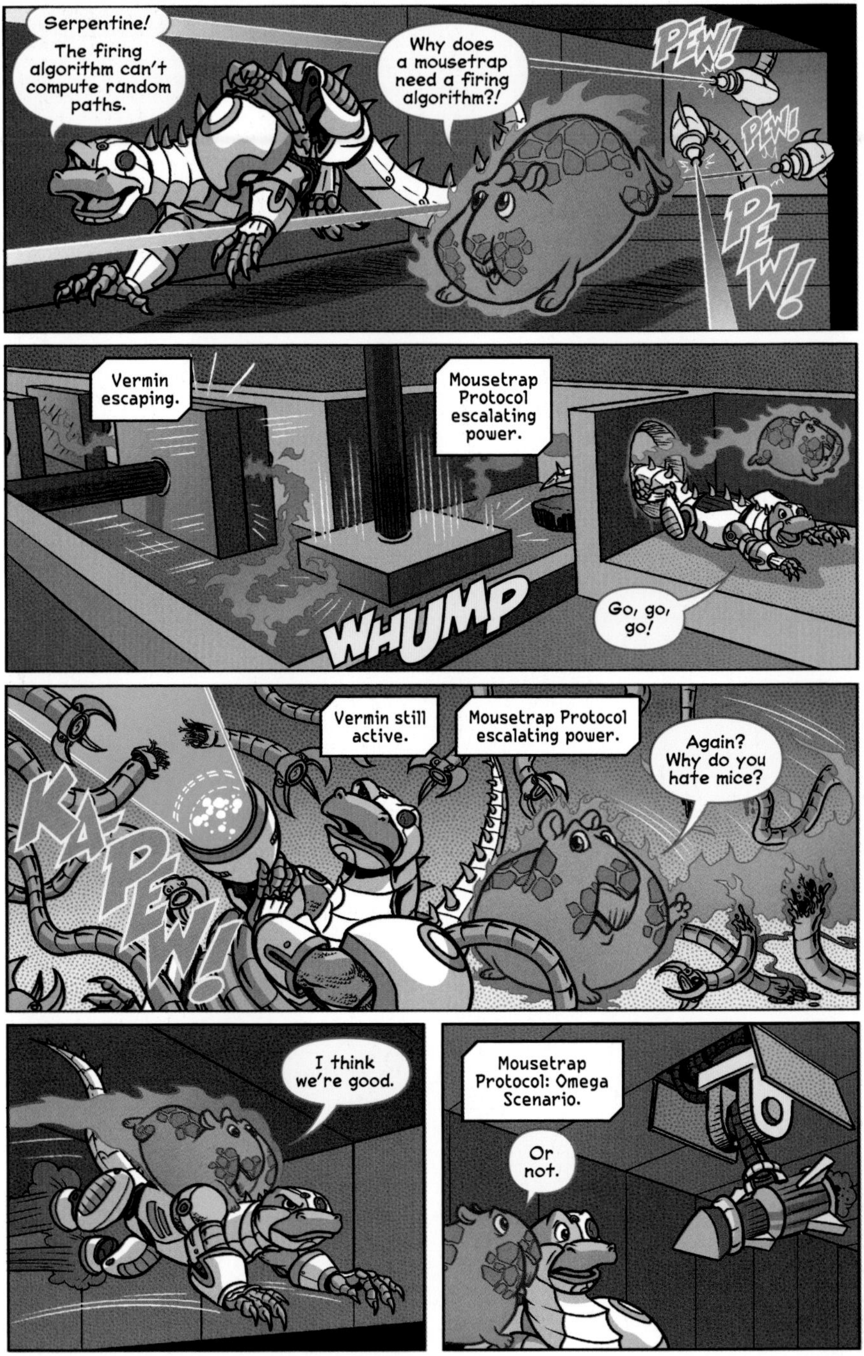
Serpentine!
The firing algorithm can't compute random paths.
Why does a mousetrap need a firing algorithm?!
PEW!
PEW!
PEW!
Vermin escaping.
Mousetrap Protocol escalating power.
WHUMP
Go, go, go!
Vermin still active.
Mousetrap Protocol escalating power.
Again? Why do you hate mice?
KA-PEW!
I think we're good.
Mousetrap Protocol: Omega Scenario.
Or not.

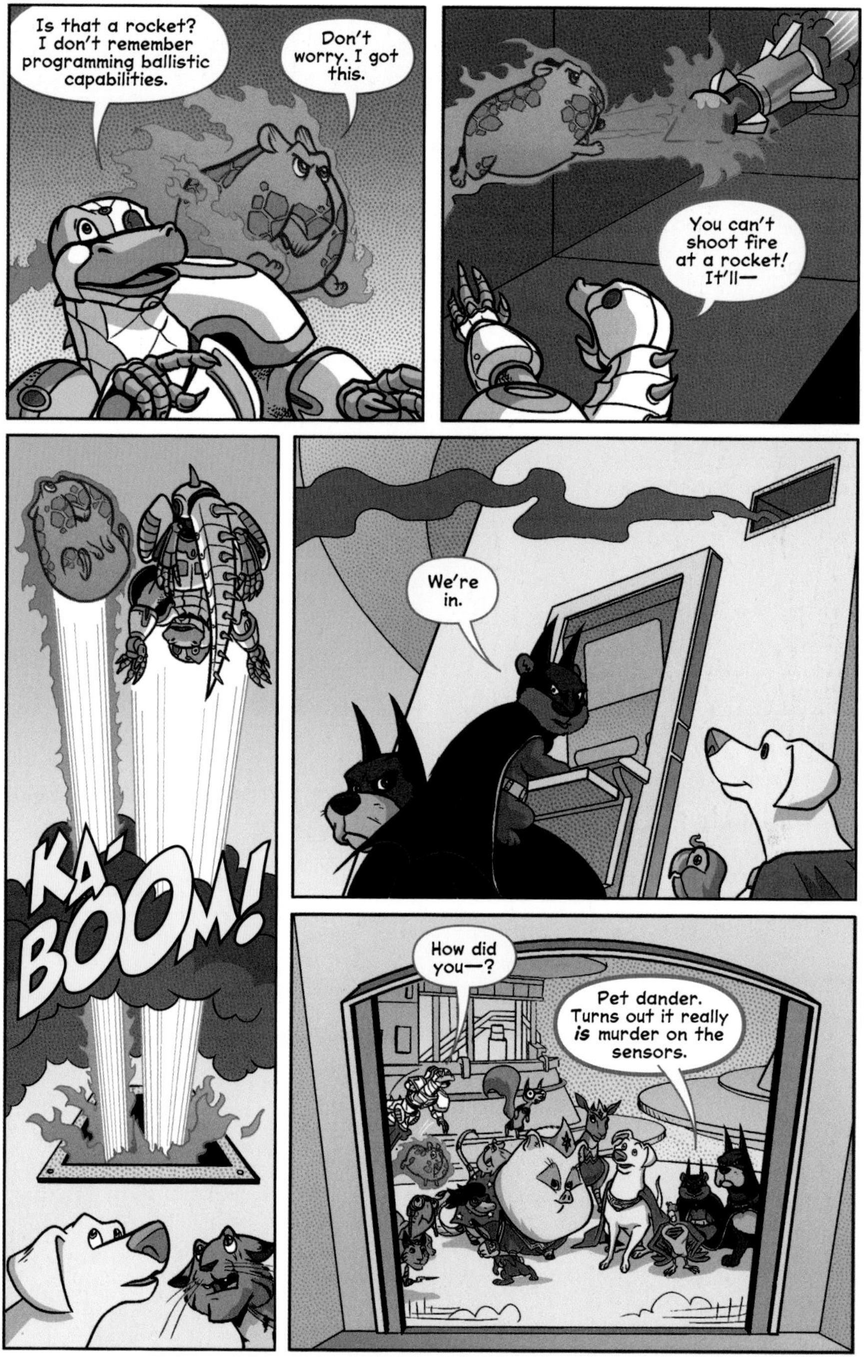
Is that a rocket? I don't remember programming ballistic capabilities.
Don't worry. I got this.
You can't shoot fire at a rocket! It'll—
KA-BOOM!
We're in.
How did you—?
Pet dander. Turns out it really *is* murder on the sensors.

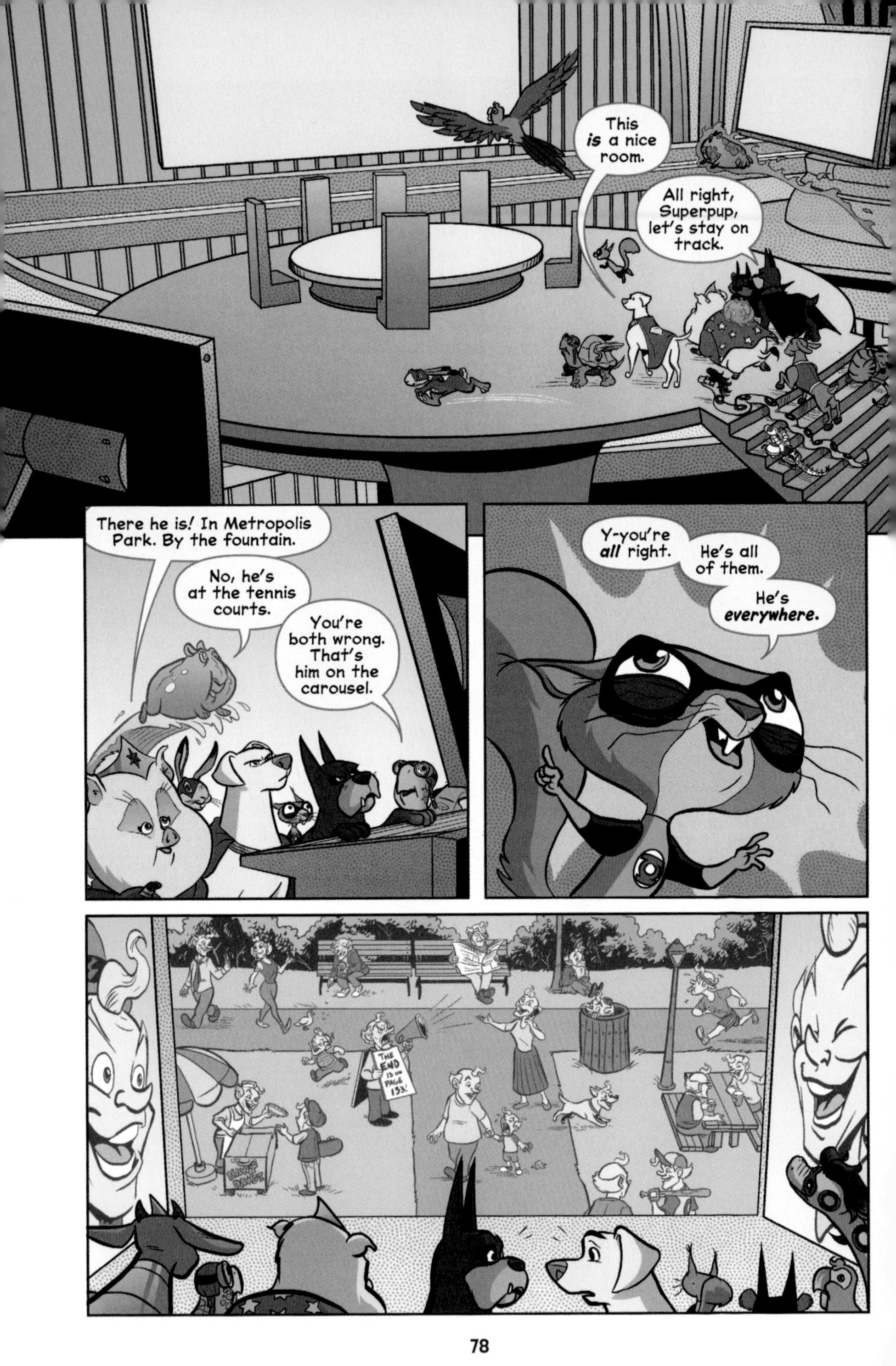
This *is* a nice room.
All right, Superpup, let's stay on track.
There he is! In Metropolis Park. By the fountain.
No, he's at the tennis courts.
You're both wrong. That's him on the carousel.
Y-you're *all* right.
He's all of them.
He's *everywhere*.
THE END IS ON PAGE 133!

CHAPTER 4
Hounded by
the Bark Side

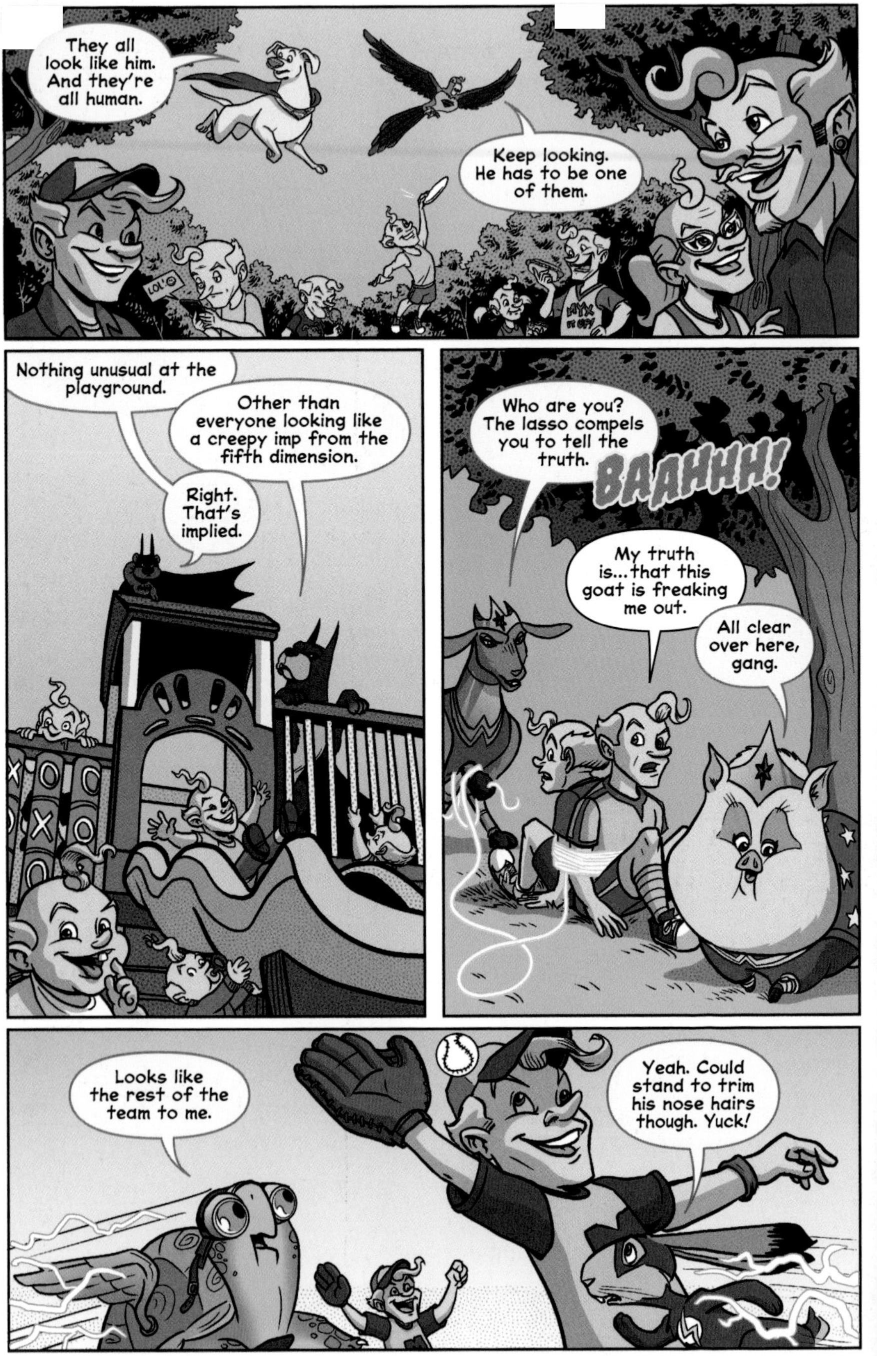
They all look like him. And they're all human.
Keep looking. He has to be one of them.
LOL
Nothing unusual at the playground.
Other than everyone looking like a creepy imp from the fifth dimension.
Right. That's implied.
Who are you? The lasso compels you to tell the truth.
BAAHHH!
My truth is...that this goat is freaking me out.
All clear over here, gang.
Looks like the rest of the team to me.
Yeah. Could stand to trim his nose hairs though. Yuck!

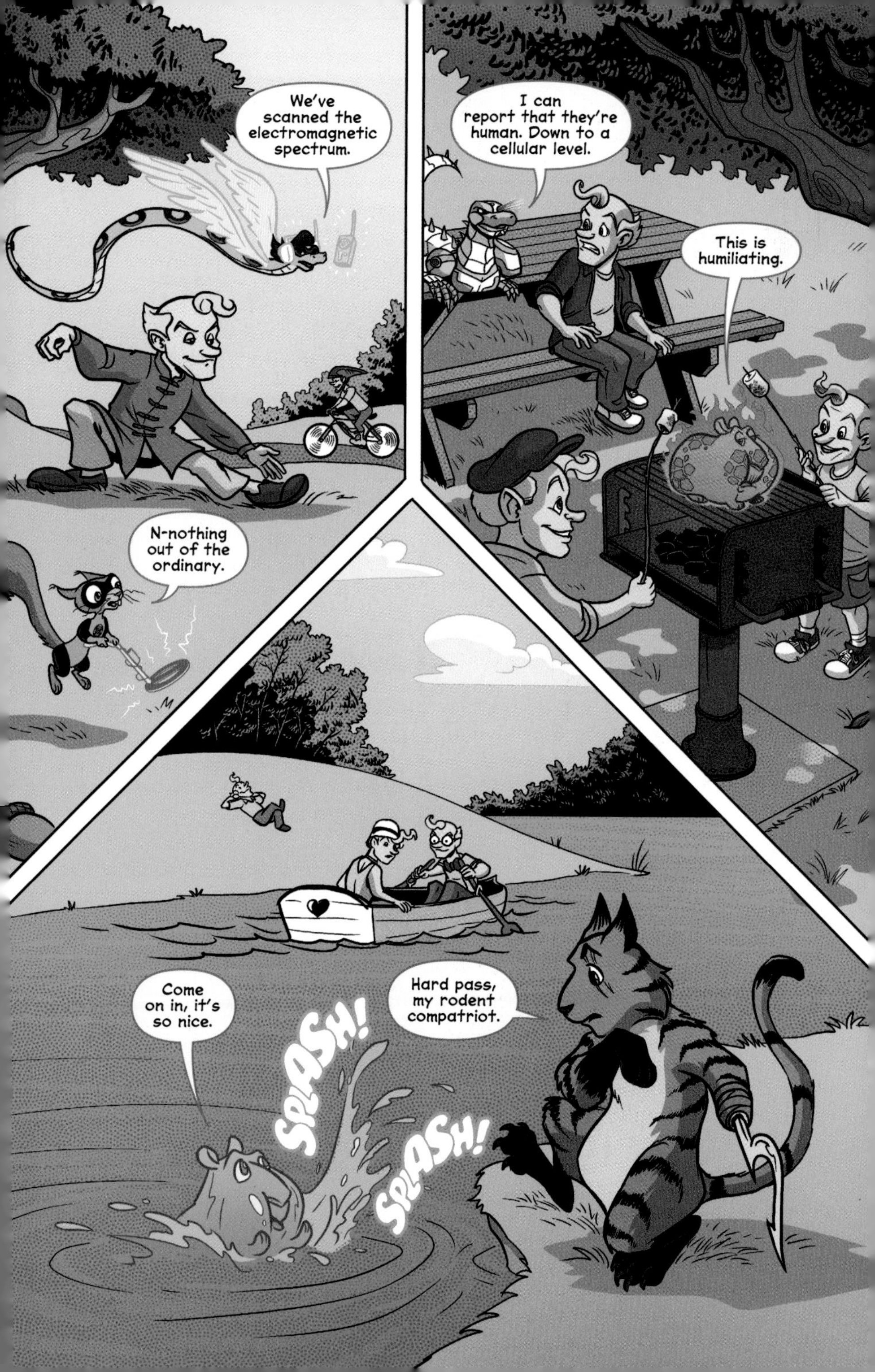
We've scanned the electromagnetic spectrum.
N-nothing out of the ordinary.
I can report that they're human. Down to a cellular level.
This is humiliating.
Come on in, it's so nice.
Hard pass, my rodent compatriot.
SPLASH!
SPLASH!

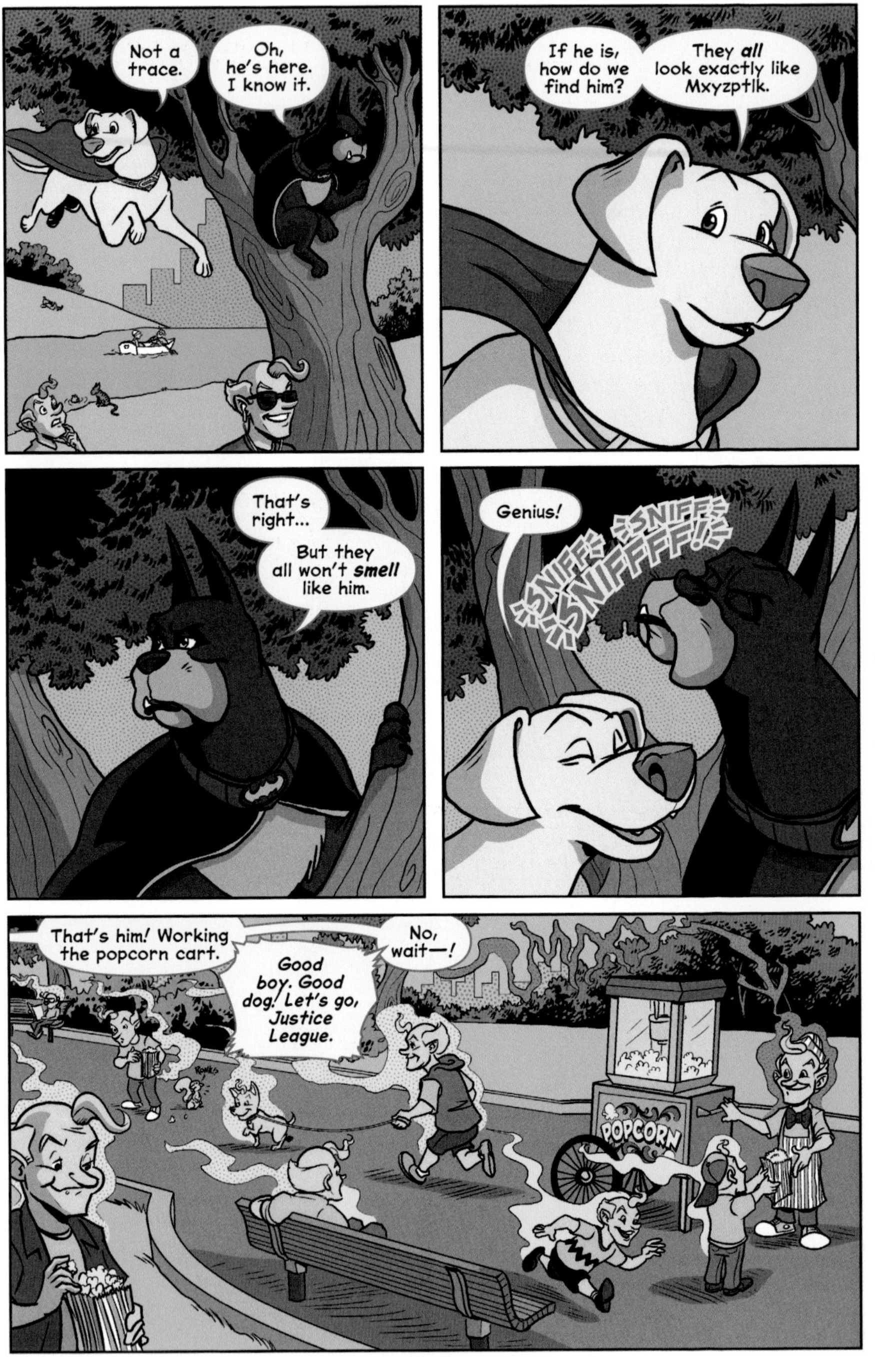
Not a trace.
Oh, he's here. I know it.
If he is, how do we find him?
They *all* look exactly like Mxyzptlk.
That's right...
But they all won't ***smell*** like him.
Genius!
SNIFF SNIFF SNIFFFF!
That's him! Working the popcorn cart.
No, wait—!
Good boy. Good dog. Let's go, Justice League.
POPCORN

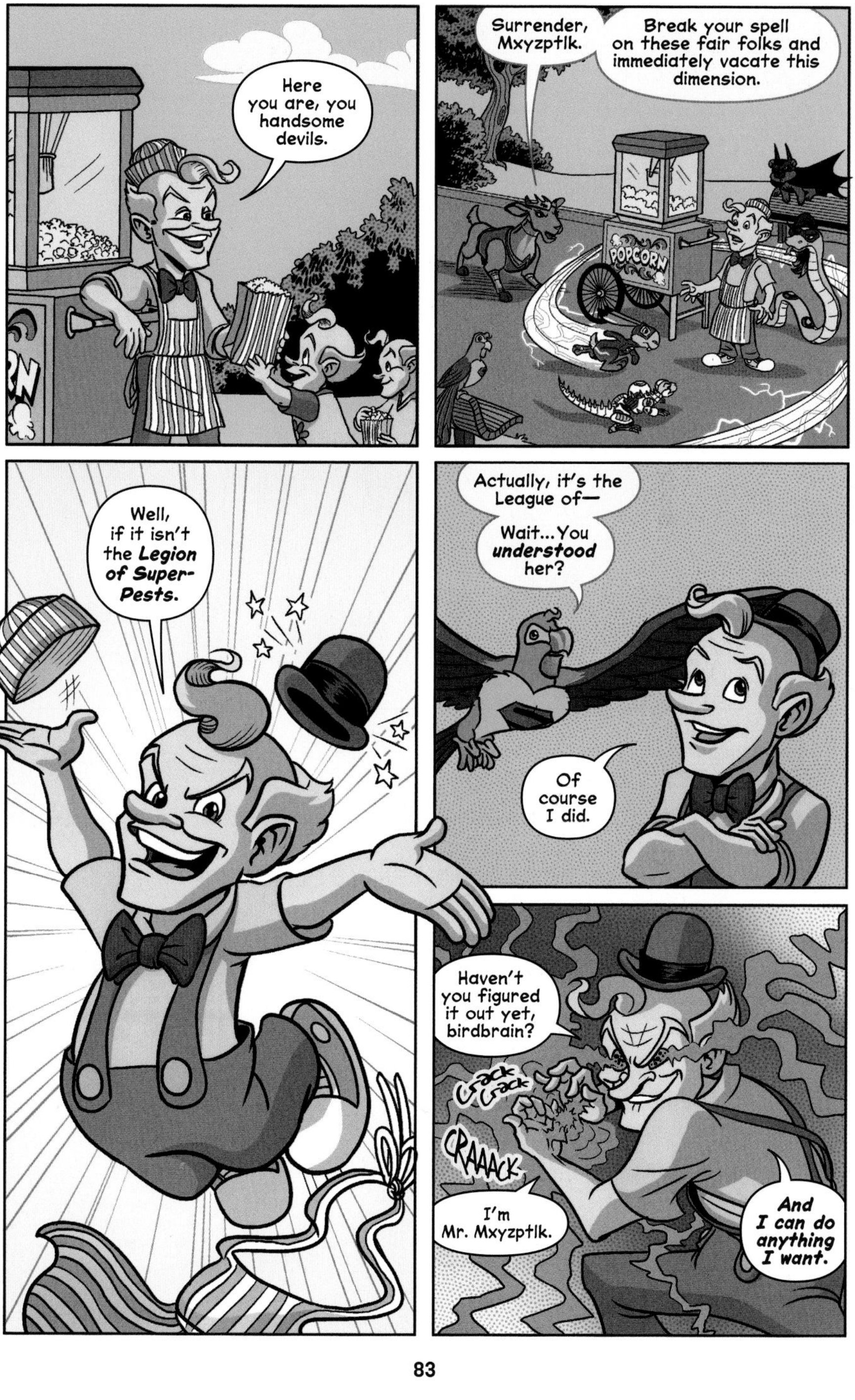
Here you are, you handsome devils.
Surrender, Mxyzptlk.
Break your spell on these fair folks and immediately vacate this dimension.
POPCORN
Well, if it isn't the *Legion of Super-Pests.*
Actually, it's the League of—
Wait...You *understood* her?
Of course I did.
Haven't you figured it out yet, birdbrain?
CRACK CRACK
CRAAACK
I'm Mr. Mxyzptlk.
And I can do anything I want.

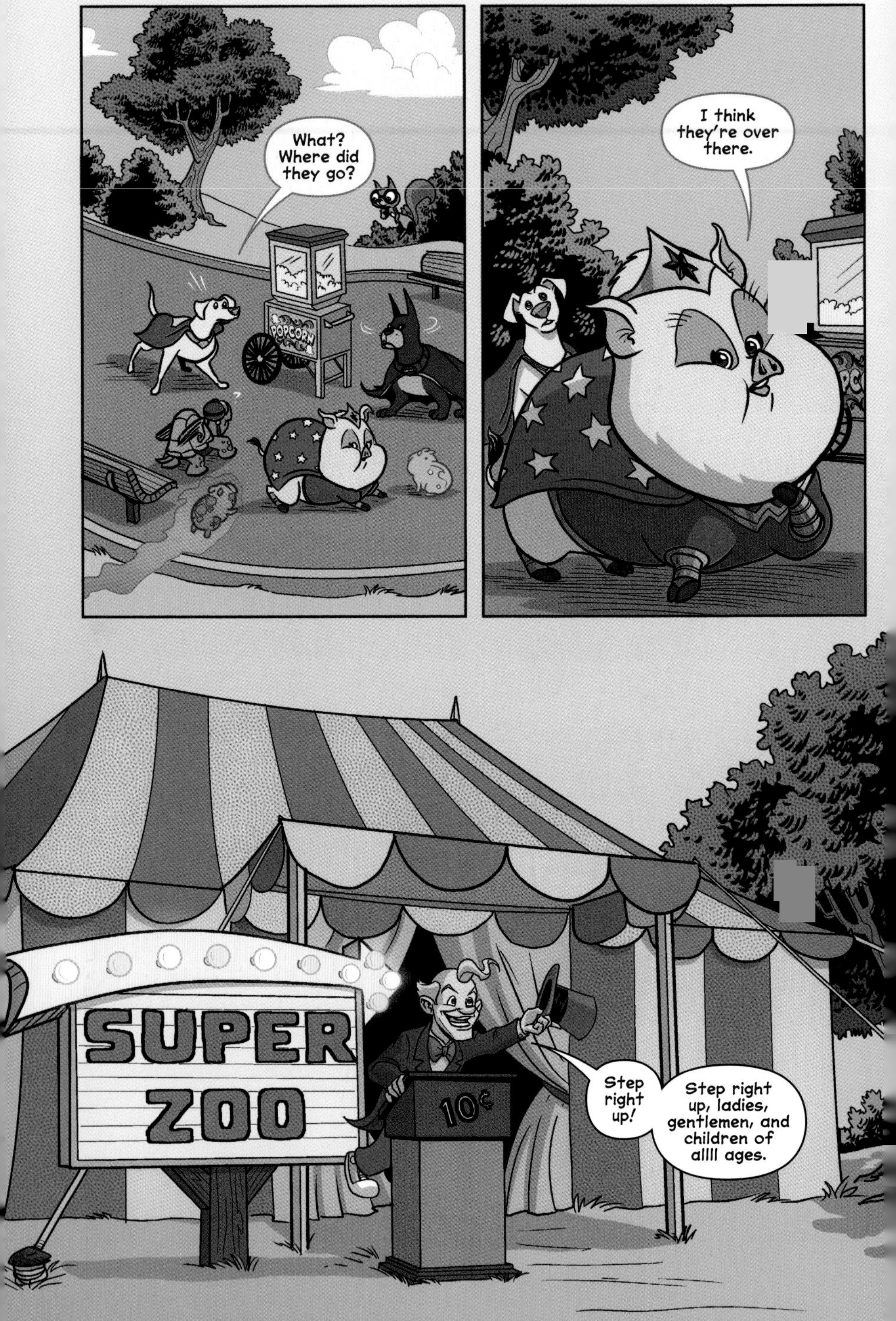
What? Where did they go?
POPCORN
I think they're over there.
SUPER ZOO
10¢
Step right up!
Step right up, ladies, gentlemen, and children of allll ages.

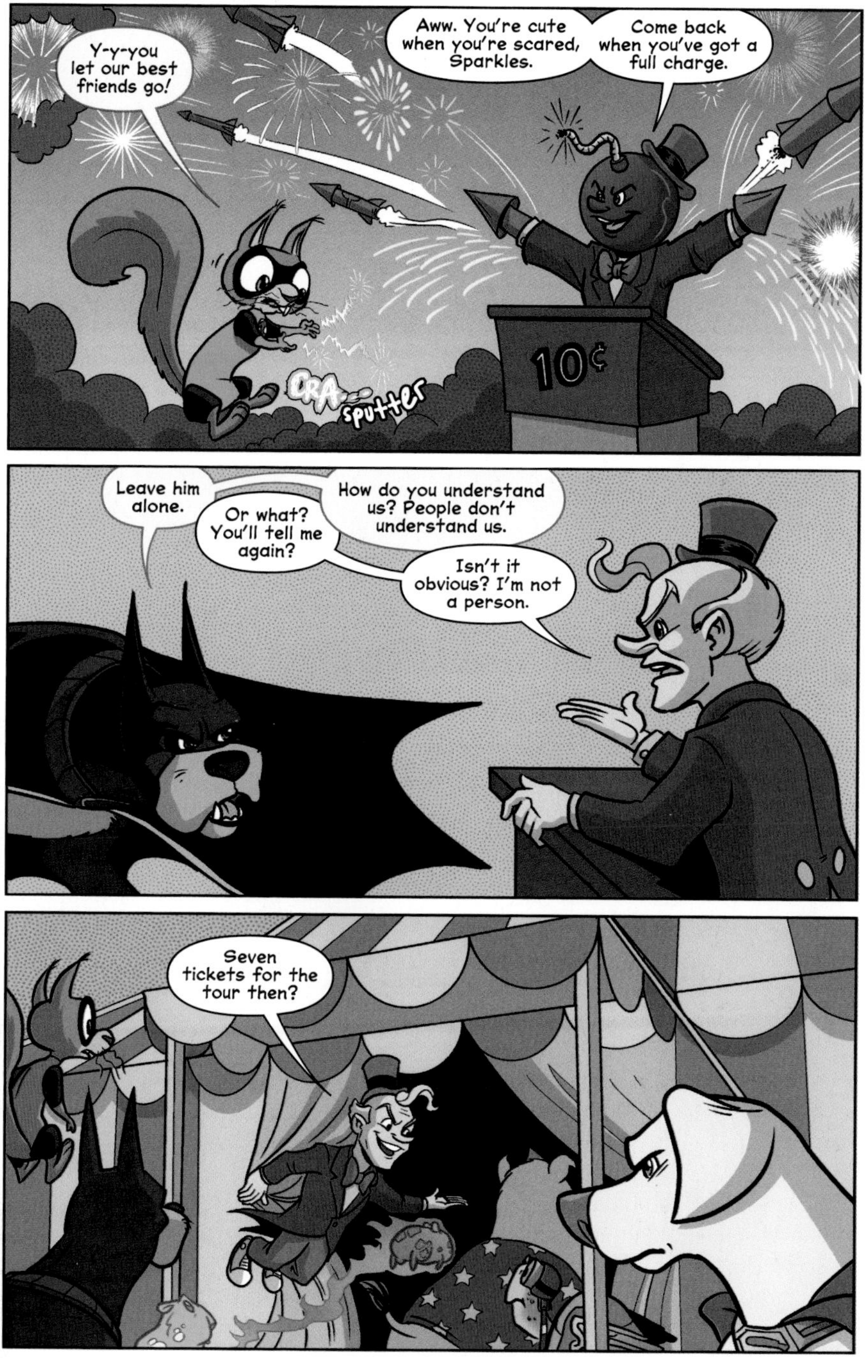
Y-y-you let our best friends go!
Aww. You're cute when you're scared, Sparkles.
Come back when you've got a full charge.
10¢
CRA-
sputter
Leave him alone.
Or what? You'll tell me again?
How do you understand us? People don't understand us.
Isn't it obvious? I'm not a person.
Seven tickets for the tour then?

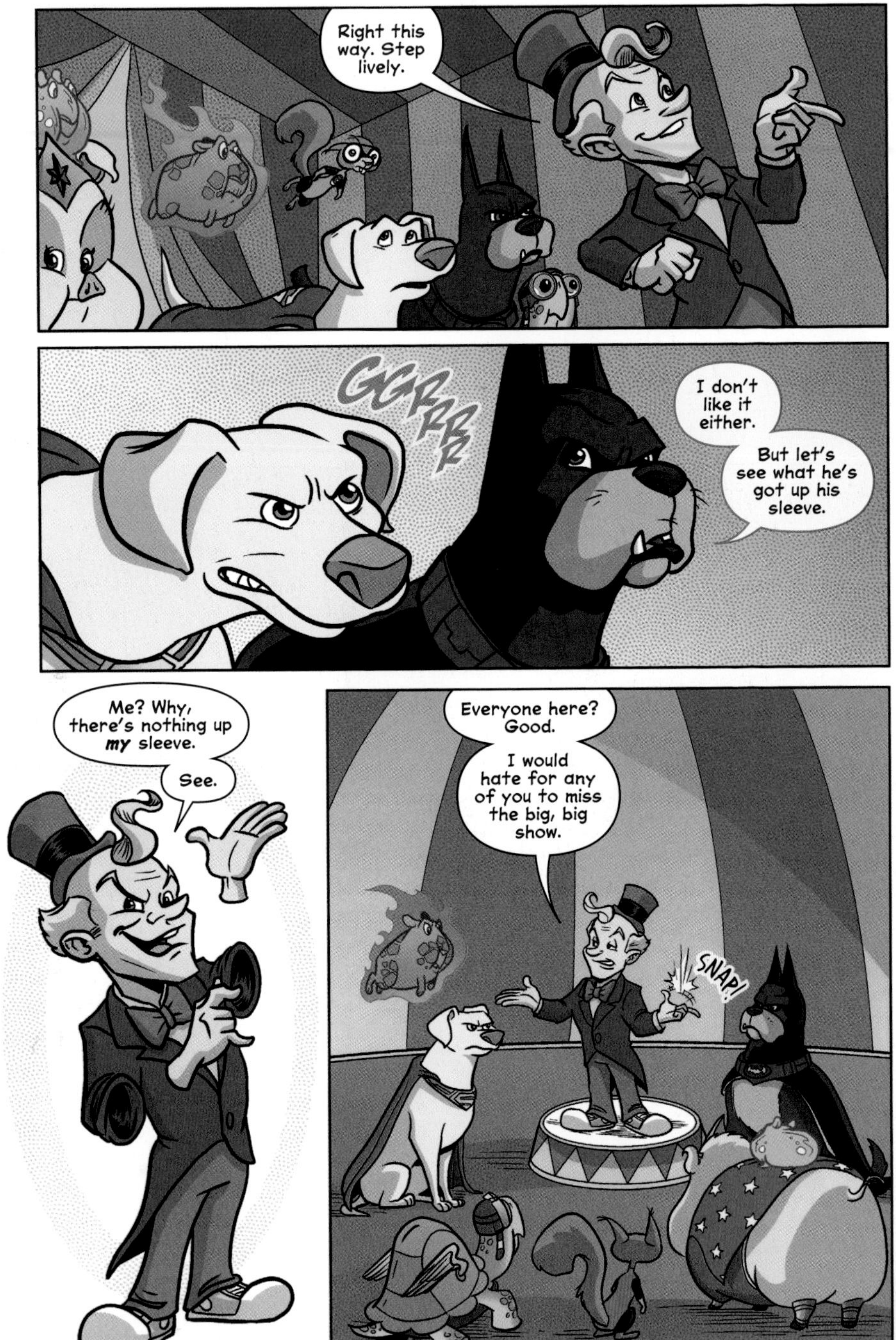
Right this way. Step lively.
GGRRRR
I don't like it either.
But let's see what he's got up his sleeve.
Me? Why, there's nothing up *my* sleeve.
See.
Everyone here? Good.
I would hate for any of you to miss the big, big show.
SNAP!

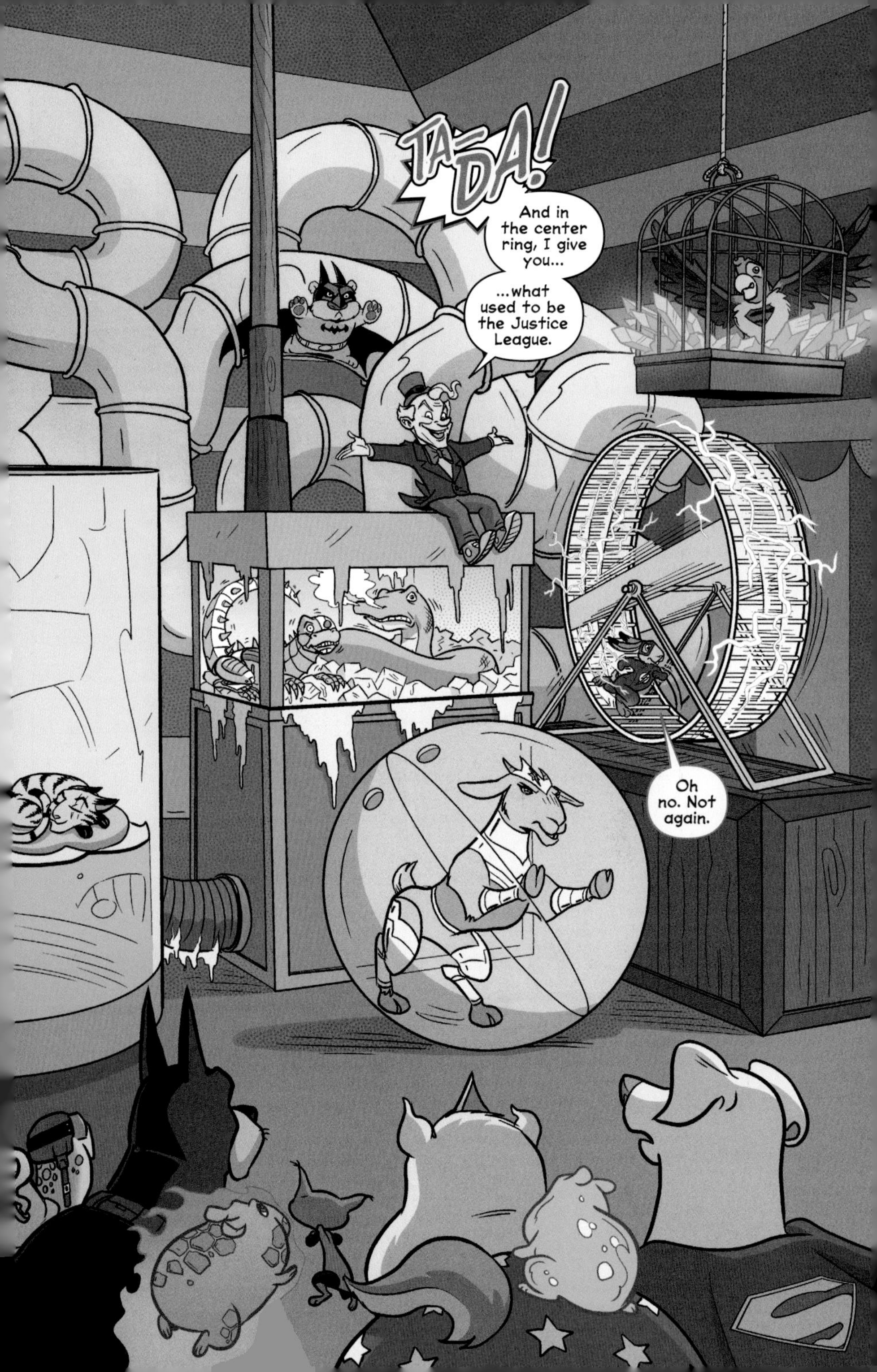
TA-DA!
And in the center ring, I give you...
...what used to be the Justice League.
Oh no. Not again.

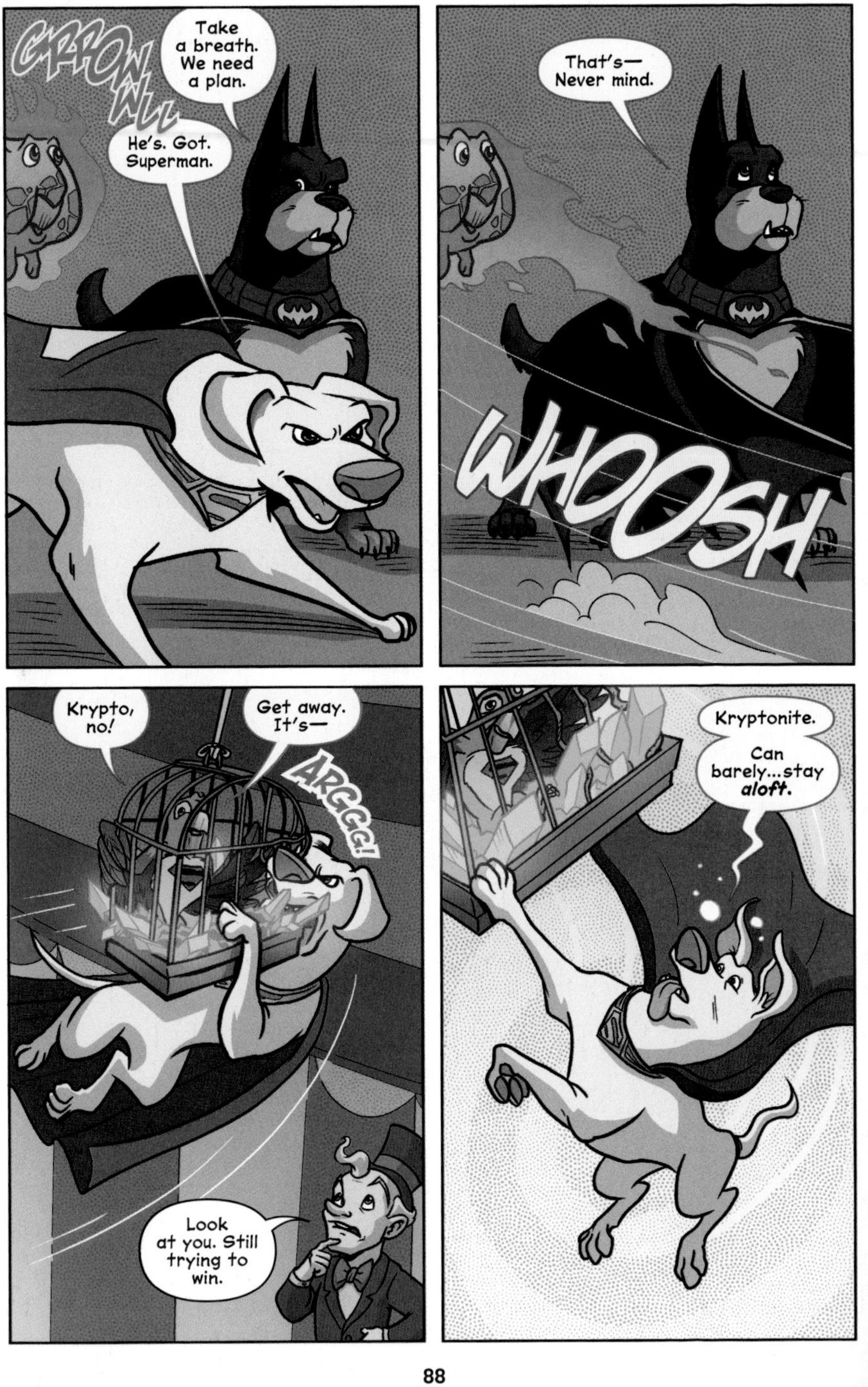
GRROWWLL
Take a breath. We need a plan.
He's. Got. Superman.
That's— Never mind.
WHOOSH
Krypto, no!
Get away. It's—
ARGGG!
Look at you. Still trying to win.
Kryptonite.
Can barely...stay *aloft.*

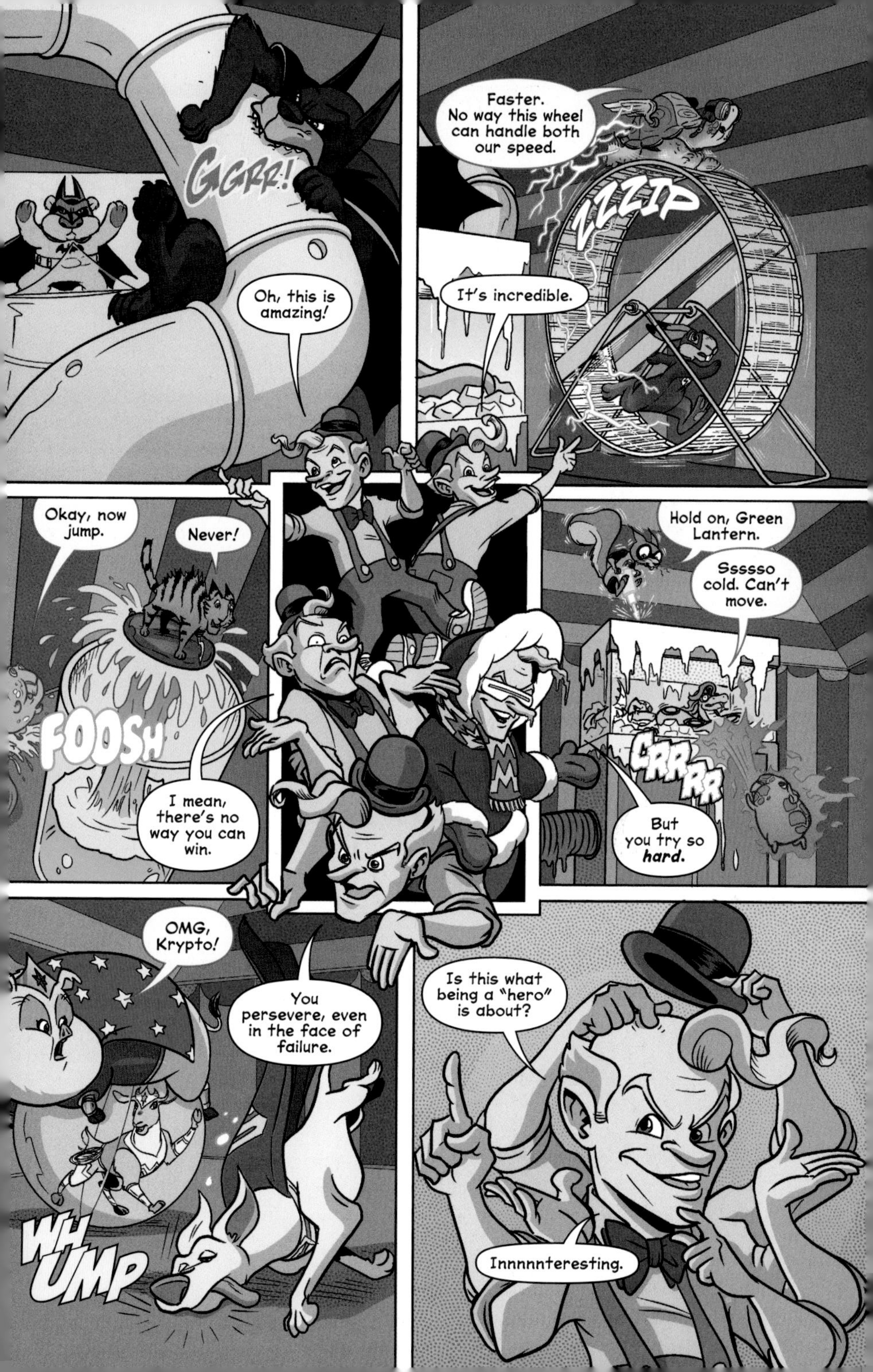
GGRR!
Oh, this is amazing!
Faster. No way this wheel can handle both our speed.
ZZZIP
It's incredible.
Okay, now jump.
Never!
FOOSH
I mean, there's no way you can win.
Hold on, Green Lantern.
Ssssso cold. Can't move.
CRRRR
But you try so ***hard.***
OMG, Krypto!
You persevere, even in the face of failure.
WHUMP
Is this what being a "hero" is about?
Innnnnteresting.

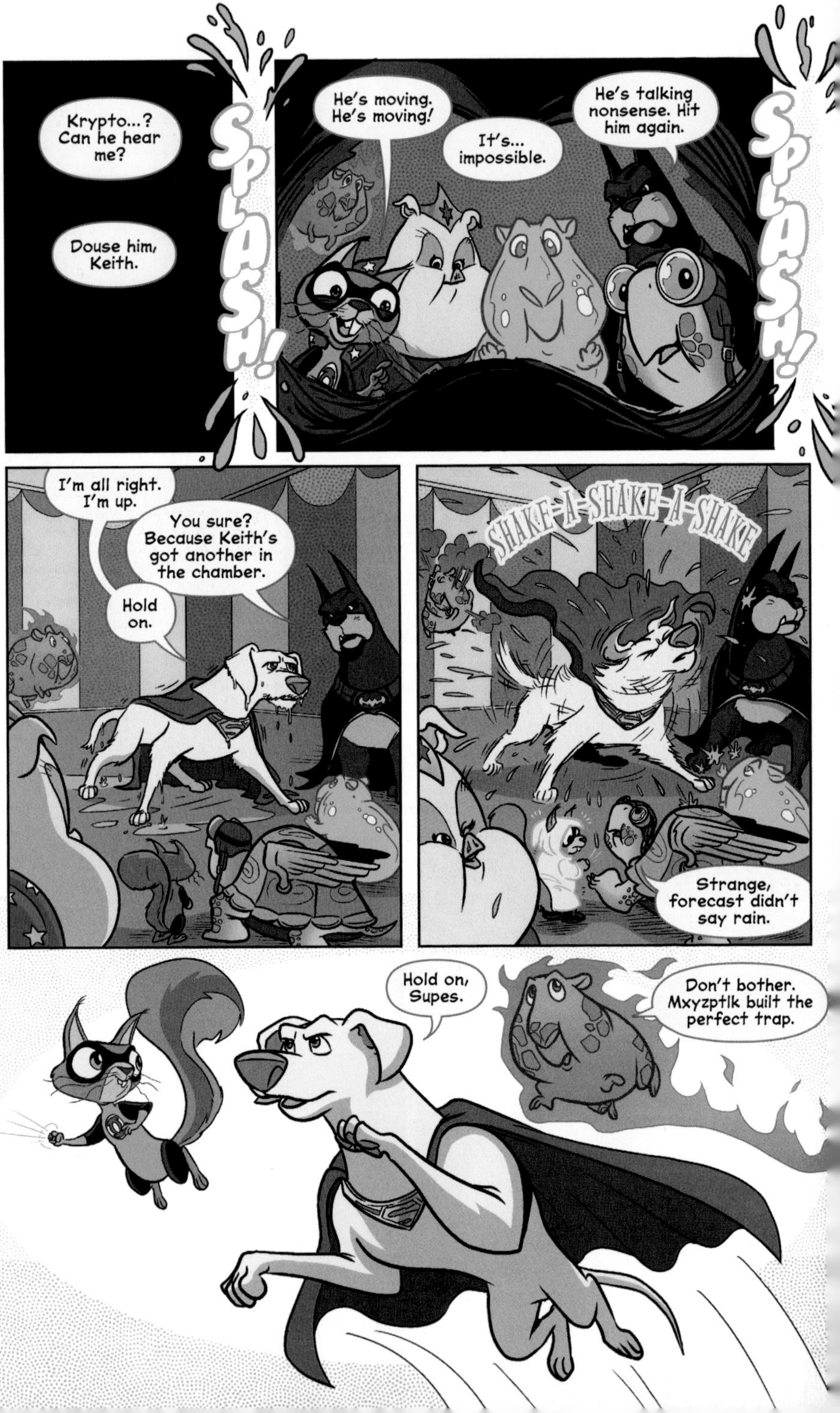
Krypto...? Can he hear me?
Douse him, Keith.
SPLASH!
He's moving. He's moving!
It's... impossible.
He's talking nonsense. Hit him again.
SPLASH!
I'm all right. I'm up.
You sure? Because Keith's got another in the chamber.
Hold on.
SHAKE-A-SHAKE-A-SHAKE
Strange, forecast didn't say rain.
Hold on, Supes.
Don't bother. Mxyzptlk built the perfect trap.

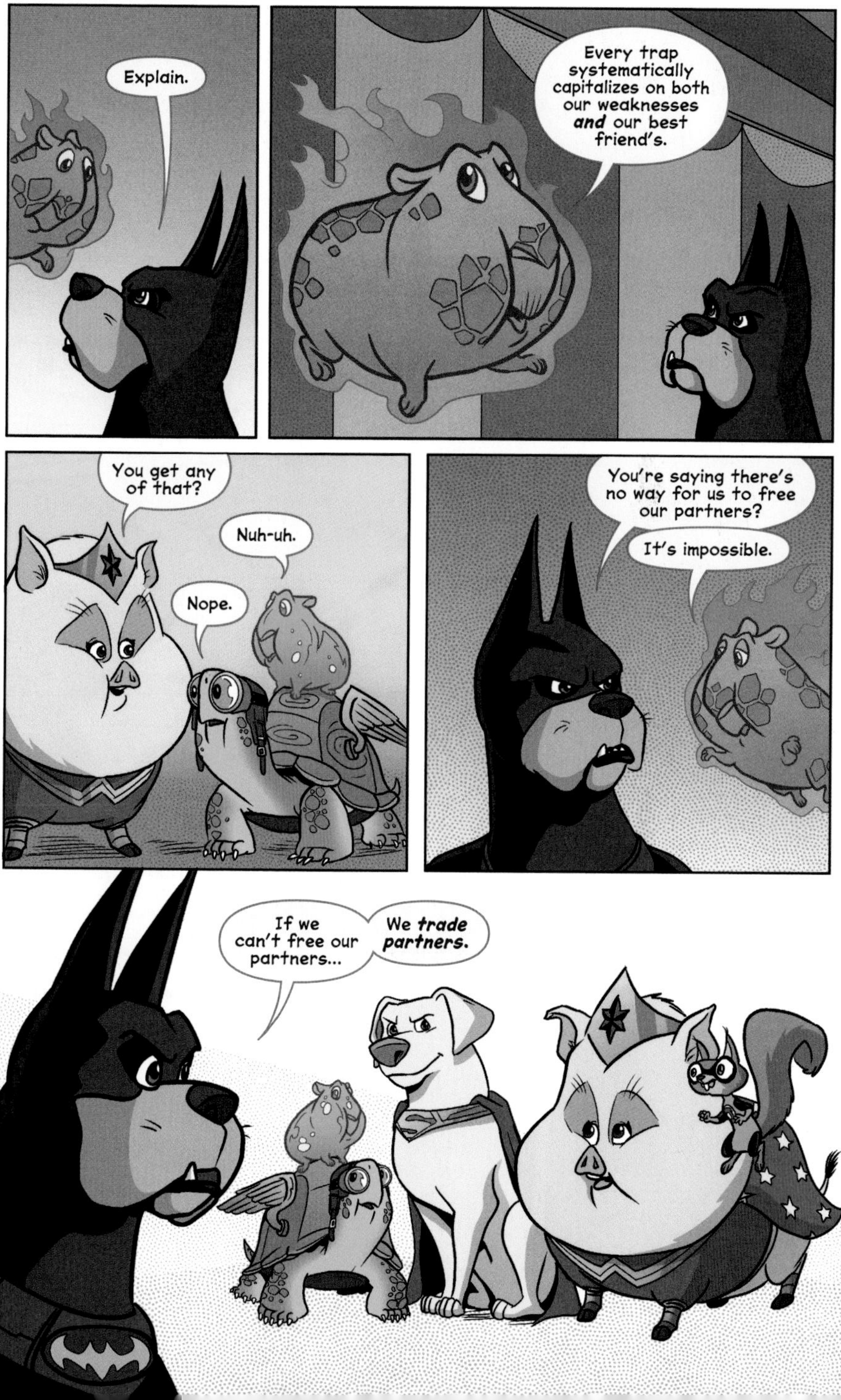

Explain.
Every trap systematically capitalizes on both our weaknesses *and* our best friend's.
You get any of that?
Nuh-uh.
Nope.
You're saying there's no way for us to free our partners?
It's impossible.
If we can't free our partners...
We *trade partners.*

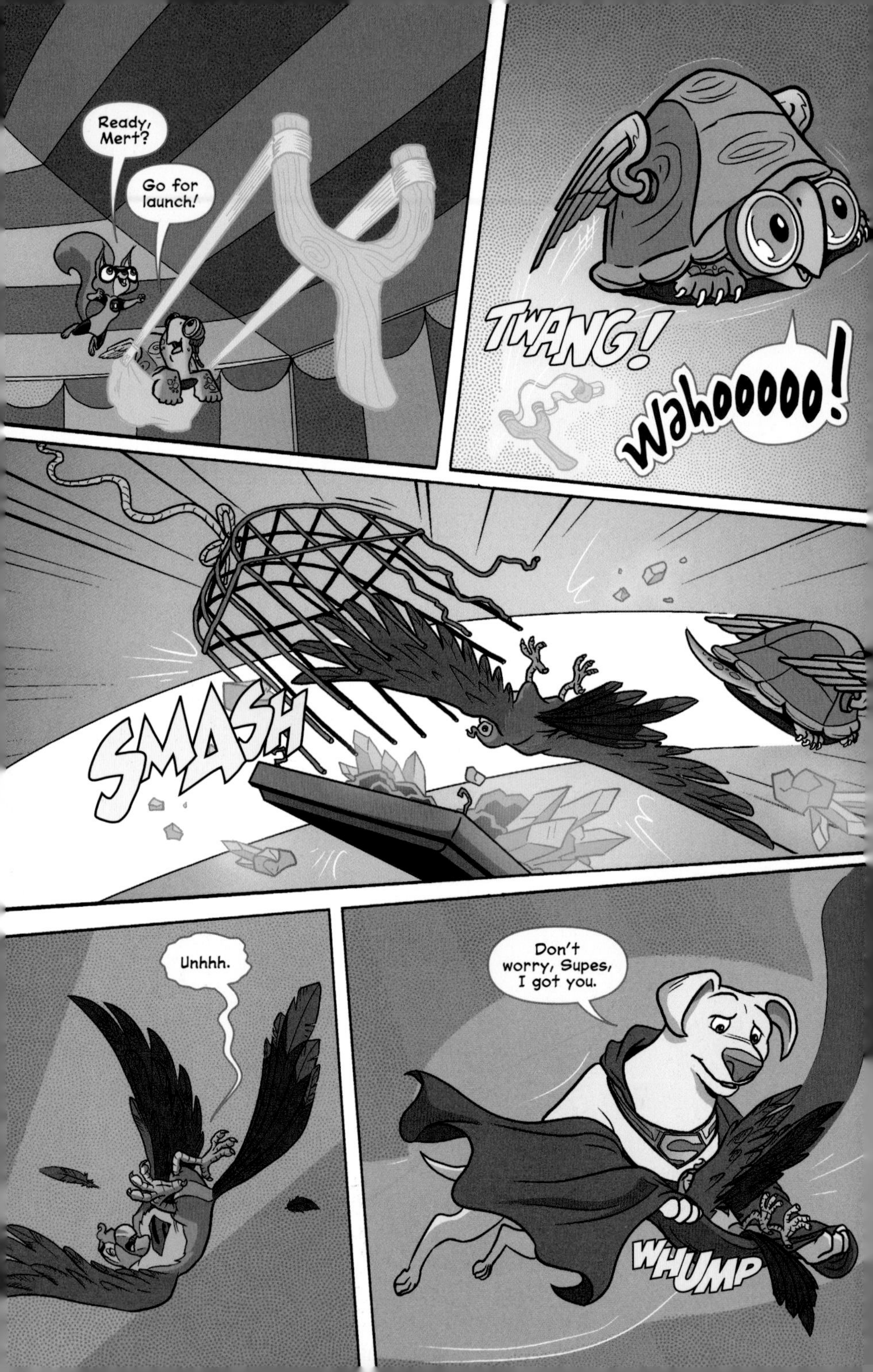
Ready, Mert?
Go for launch!
TWANG!
Wahoooooo!
SMASH
Unhhh.
Don't worry, Supes, I got you.
WHUMP

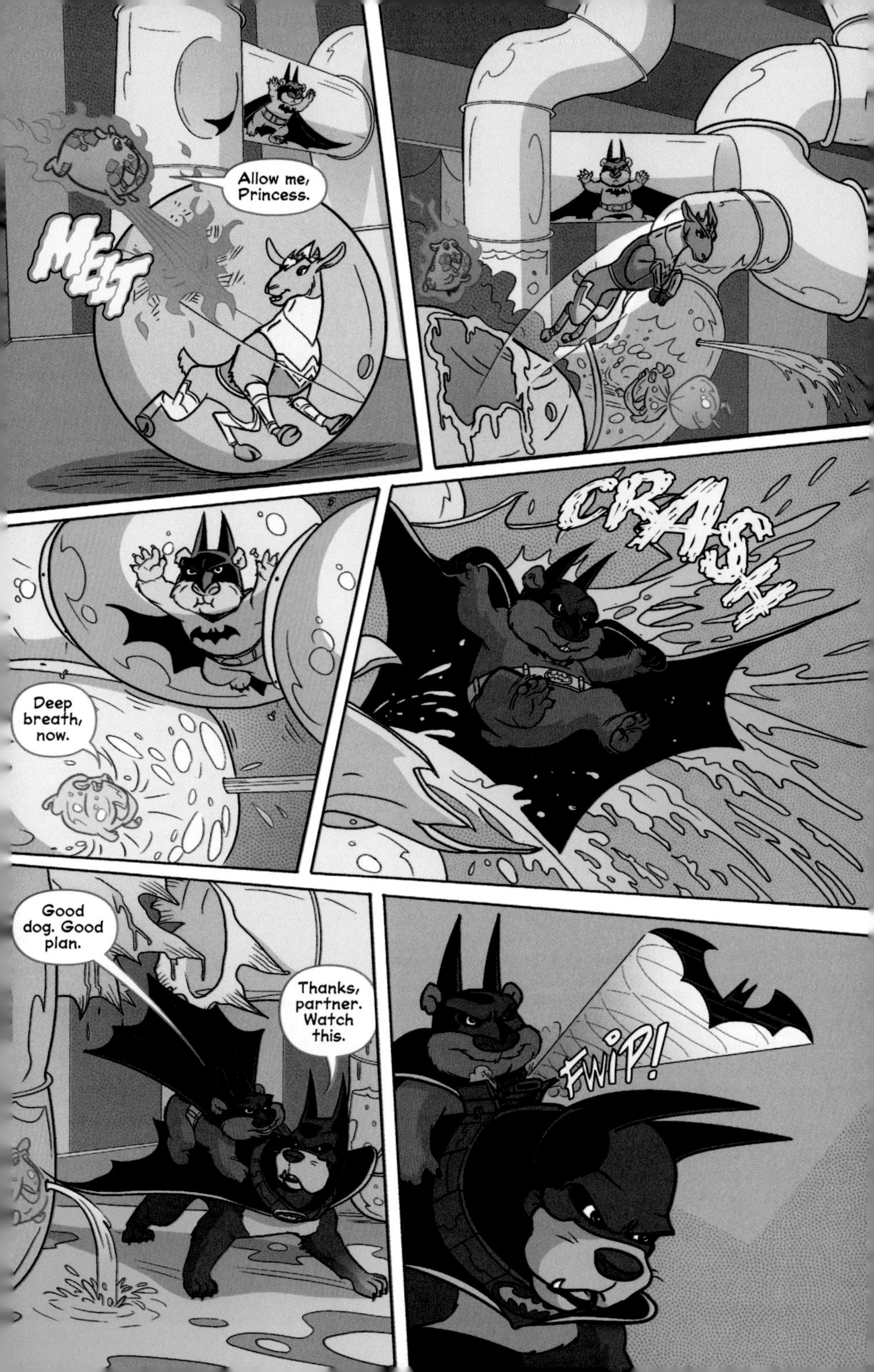
Allow me, Princess.
MELT
Deep breath, now.
CRASH
Good dog. Good plan.
Thanks, partner. Watch this.
FWIP!

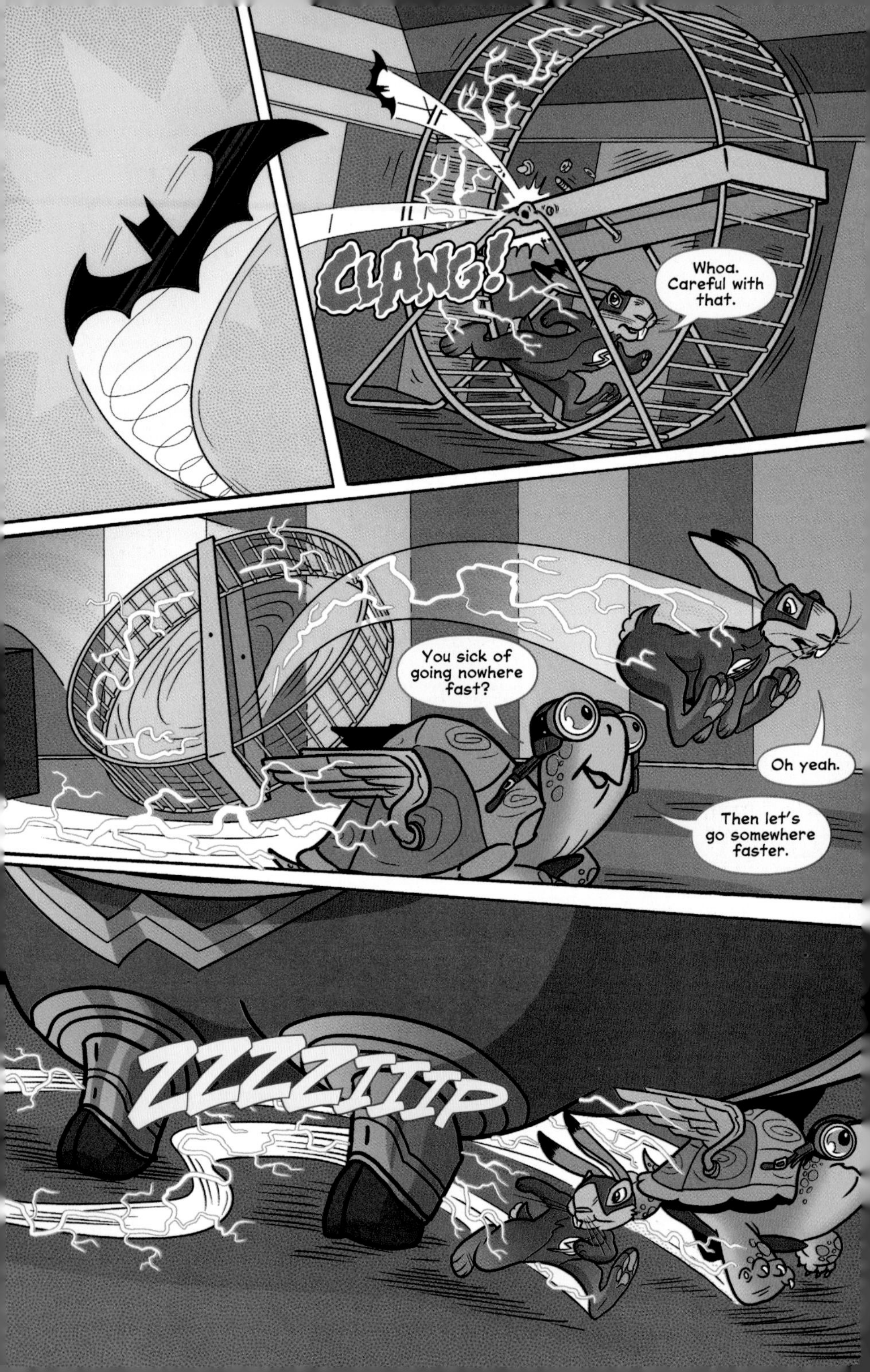
CLANG!
Whoa. Careful with that.
You sick of going nowhere fast?
Oh yeah.
Then let's go somewhere faster.
ZZZZIIIP

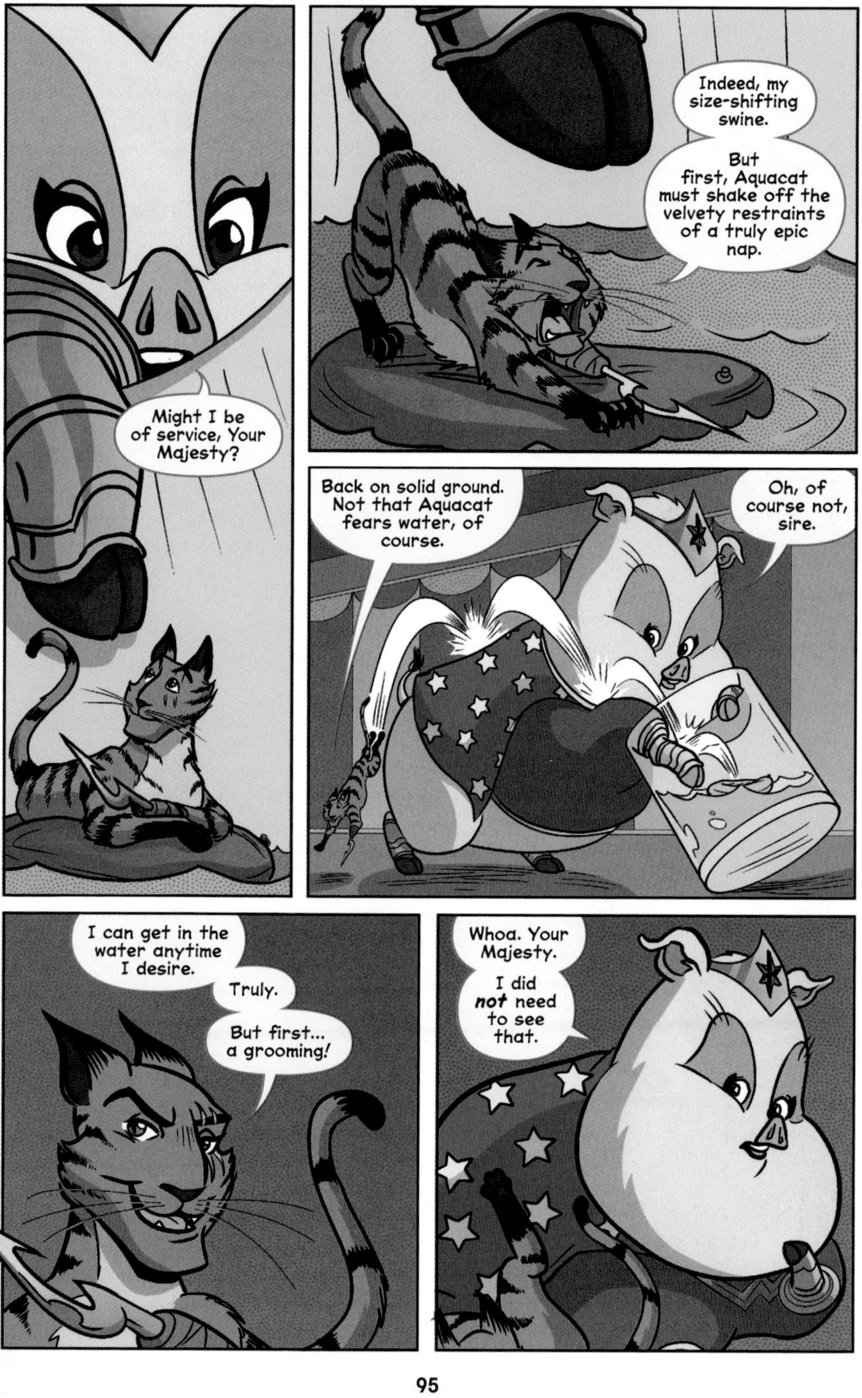
Might I be of service, Your Majesty?
Indeed, my size-shifting swine.
But first, Aquacat must shake off the velvety restraints of a truly epic nap.
Back on solid ground. Not that Aquacat fears water, of course.
Oh, of course not, sire.
I can get in the water anytime I desire.
Truly.
But first... a grooming!
Whoa. Your Majesty.
I did **not** need to see that.

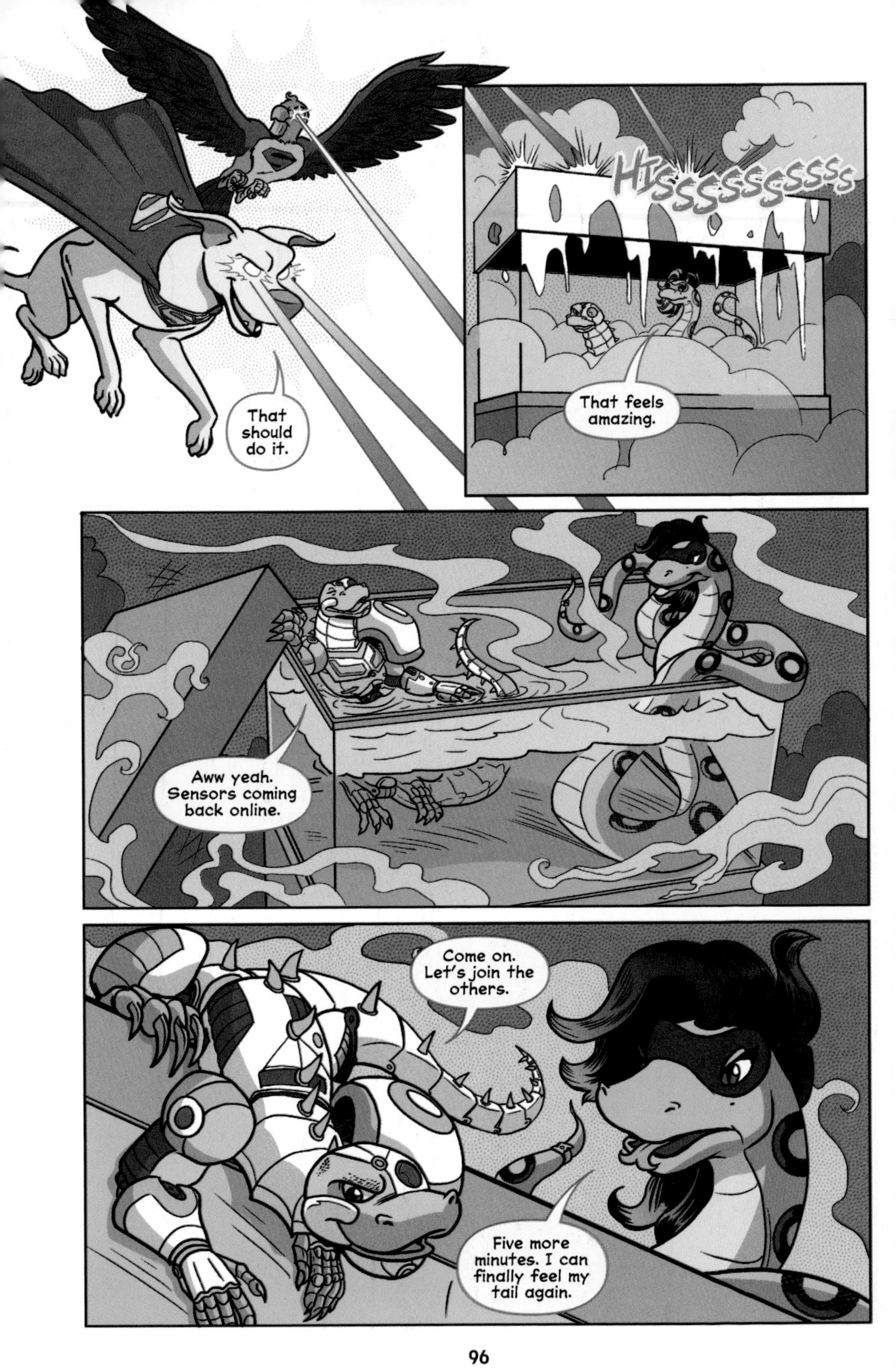
That should do it.
HISSSSSSSSSS
That feels amazing.
Aww yeah. Sensors coming back online.
Come on. Let's join the others.
Five more minutes. I can finally feel my tail again.

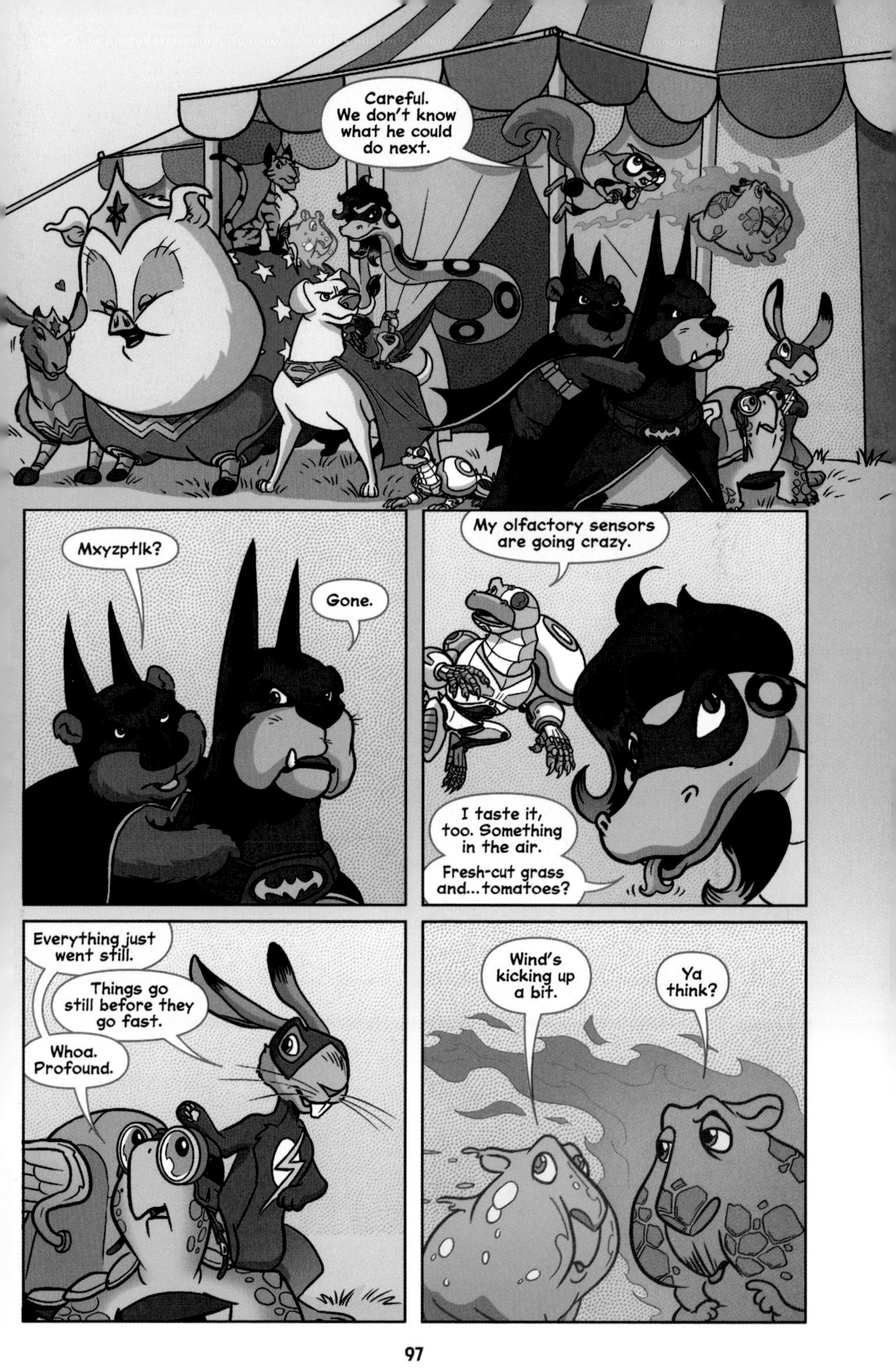

Careful. We don't know what he could do next.
Mxyzptlk?
Gone.
My olfactory sensors are going crazy.
I taste it, too. Something in the air.
Fresh-cut grass and...tomatoes?
Everything just went still.
Things go still before they go fast.
Whoa. Profound.
Wind's kicking up a bit.
Ya think?

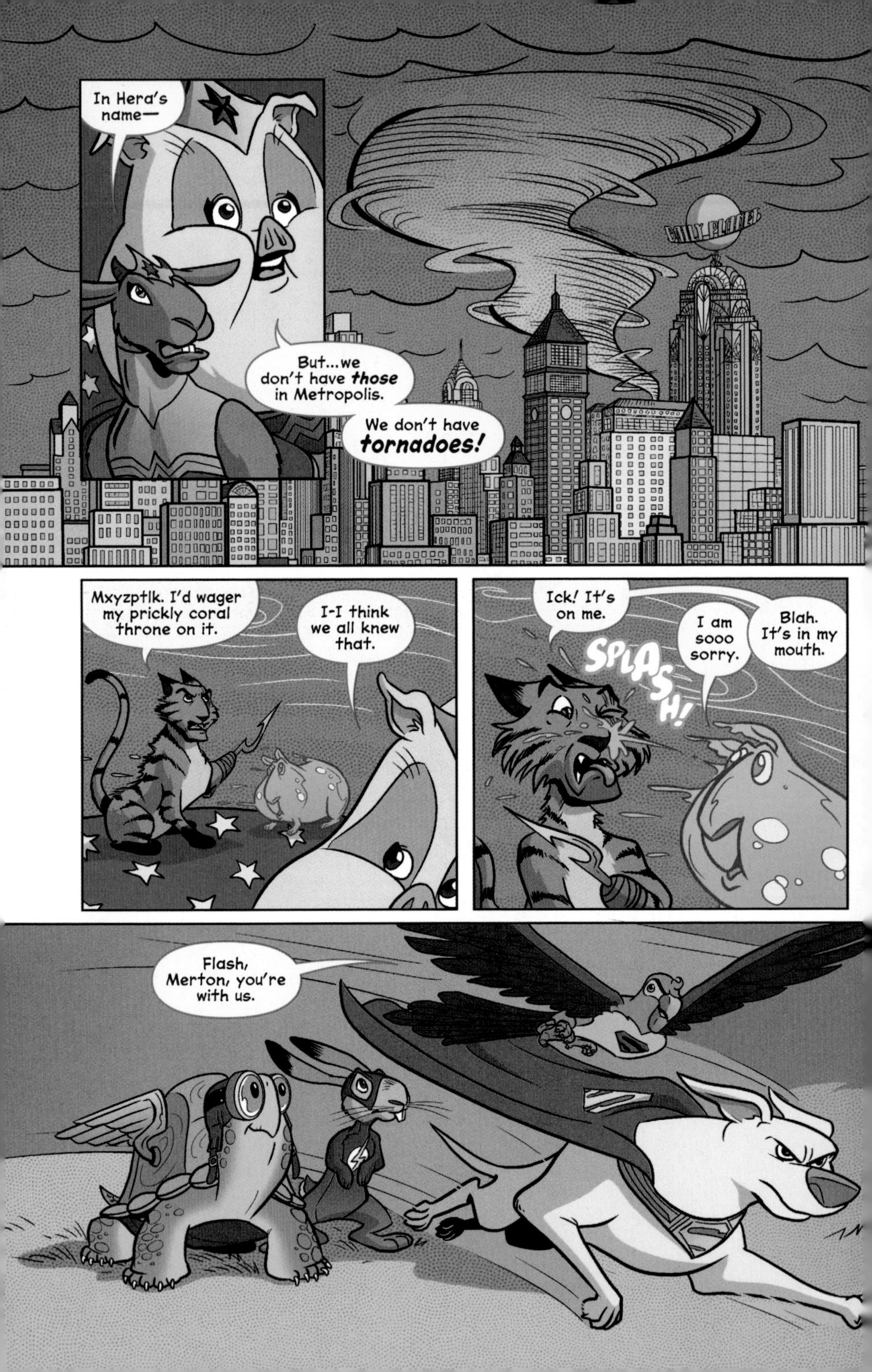
In Hera's name—
But...we don't have *those* in Metropolis.
We don't have **tornadoes!**
DAILY PLANET
Mxyzptlk. I'd wager my prickly coral throne on it.
I-I think we all knew that.
Ick! It's on me.
SPLASH!
I am sooo sorry.
Blah. It's in my mouth.
Flash, Merton, you're with us.

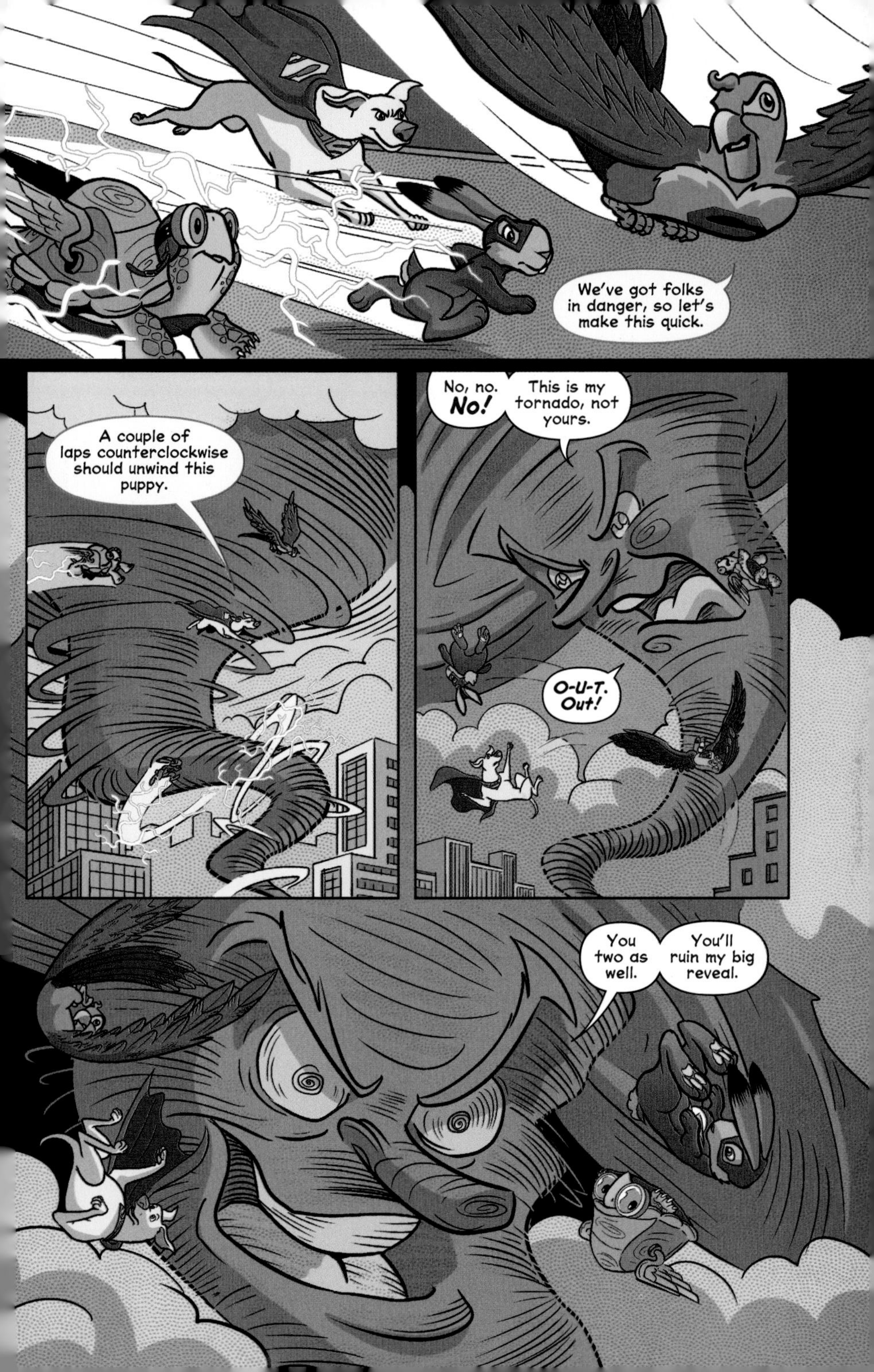
We've got folks in danger, so let's make this quick.
A couple of laps counterclockwise should unwind this puppy.
No, no. No!
This is my tornado, not yours.
O-U-T. Out!
You two as well.
You'll ruin my big reveal.

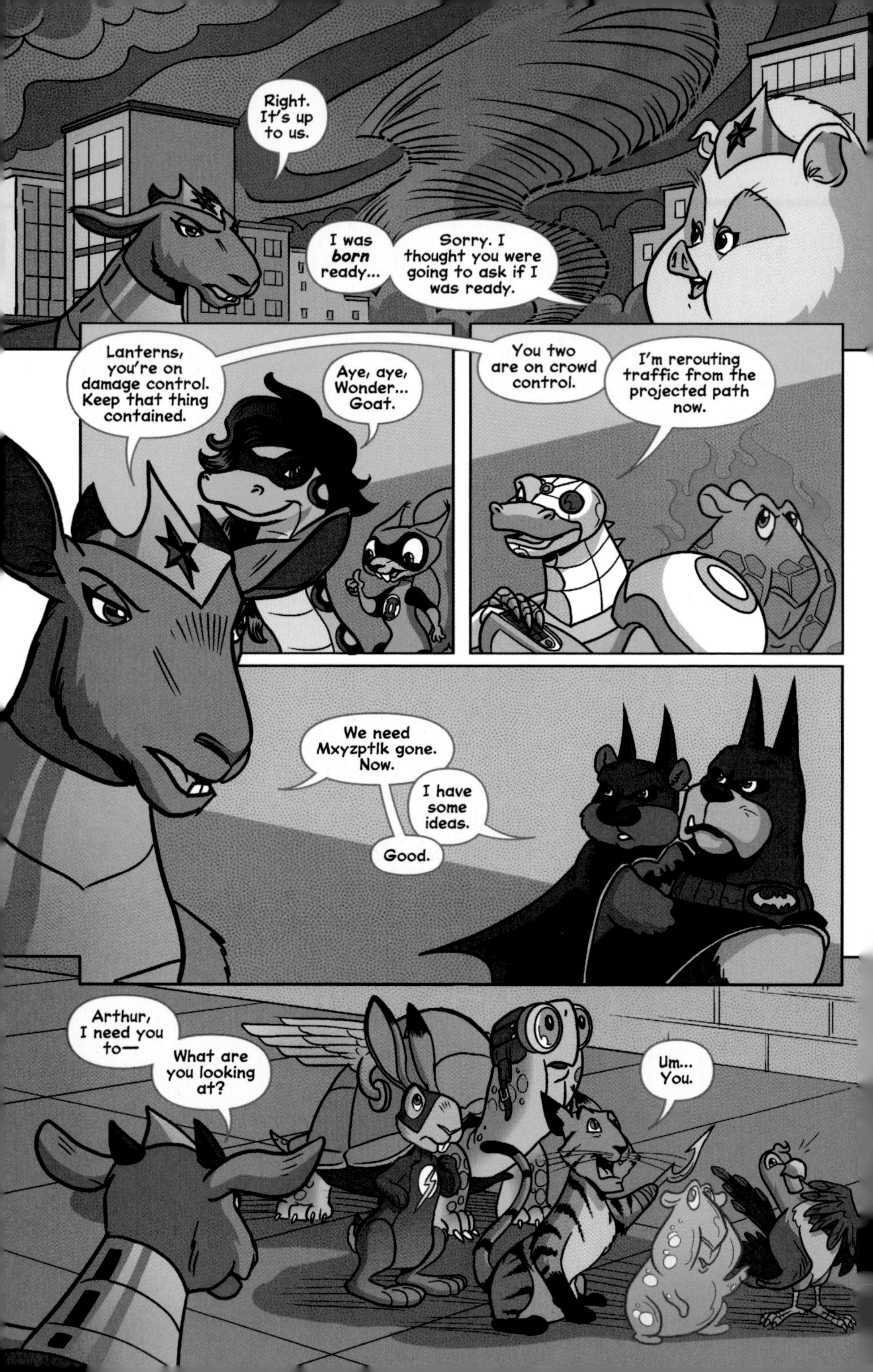
Right. It's up to us.
I was *born* ready...
Sorry. I thought you were going to ask if I was ready.
Lanterns, you're on damage control. Keep that thing contained.
Aye, aye, Wonder... Goat.
You two are on crowd control.
I'm rerouting traffic from the projected path now.
We need Mxyzptlk gone. Now.
I have some ideas.
Good.
Arthur, I need you to—
What are you looking at?
Um... You.

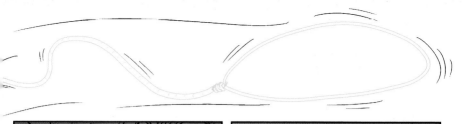

Fear not, mortals, your champion is here to save you.

TWANG!

I will vanquish this violent vortex for you, my Metropolitans.

Begone, foul winds. Blow no more, sayeth the woman of wonder.

You're welcome. You're *all* welcome.

You're my hero, Wonder Woman!

Yes, bathe me in your golden adoration.

I am your *hero!*

CHAPTER 5
False Scents
of Security

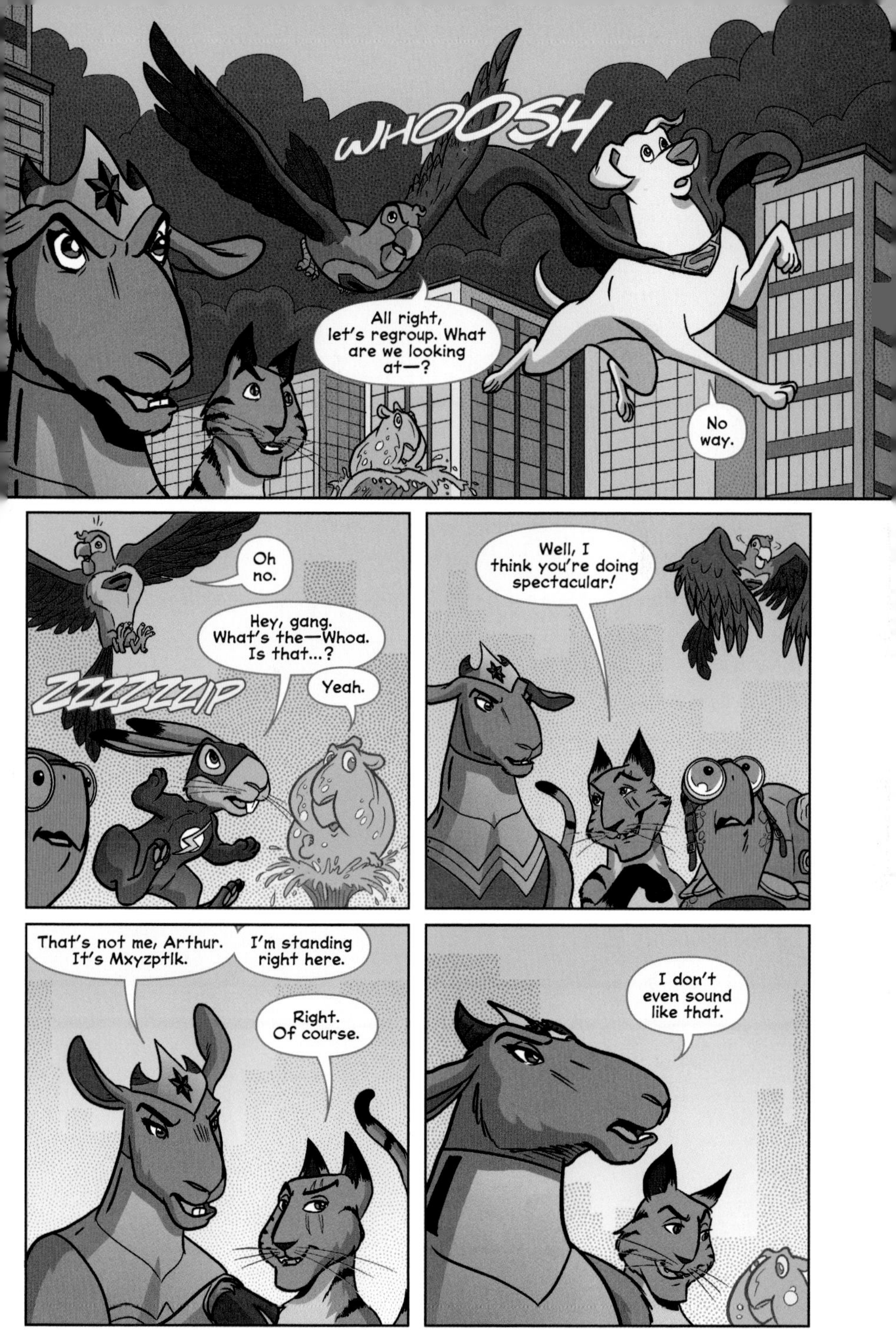
WHOOSH
All right, let's regroup. What are we looking at—?
No way.
Oh no.
Hey, gang. What's the—Whoa. Is that...?
ZZZZZZZIP
Yeah.
Well, I think you're doing spectacular!
That's not me, Arthur. It's Mxyzptlk.
I'm standing right here.
Right. Of course.
I don't even sound like that.

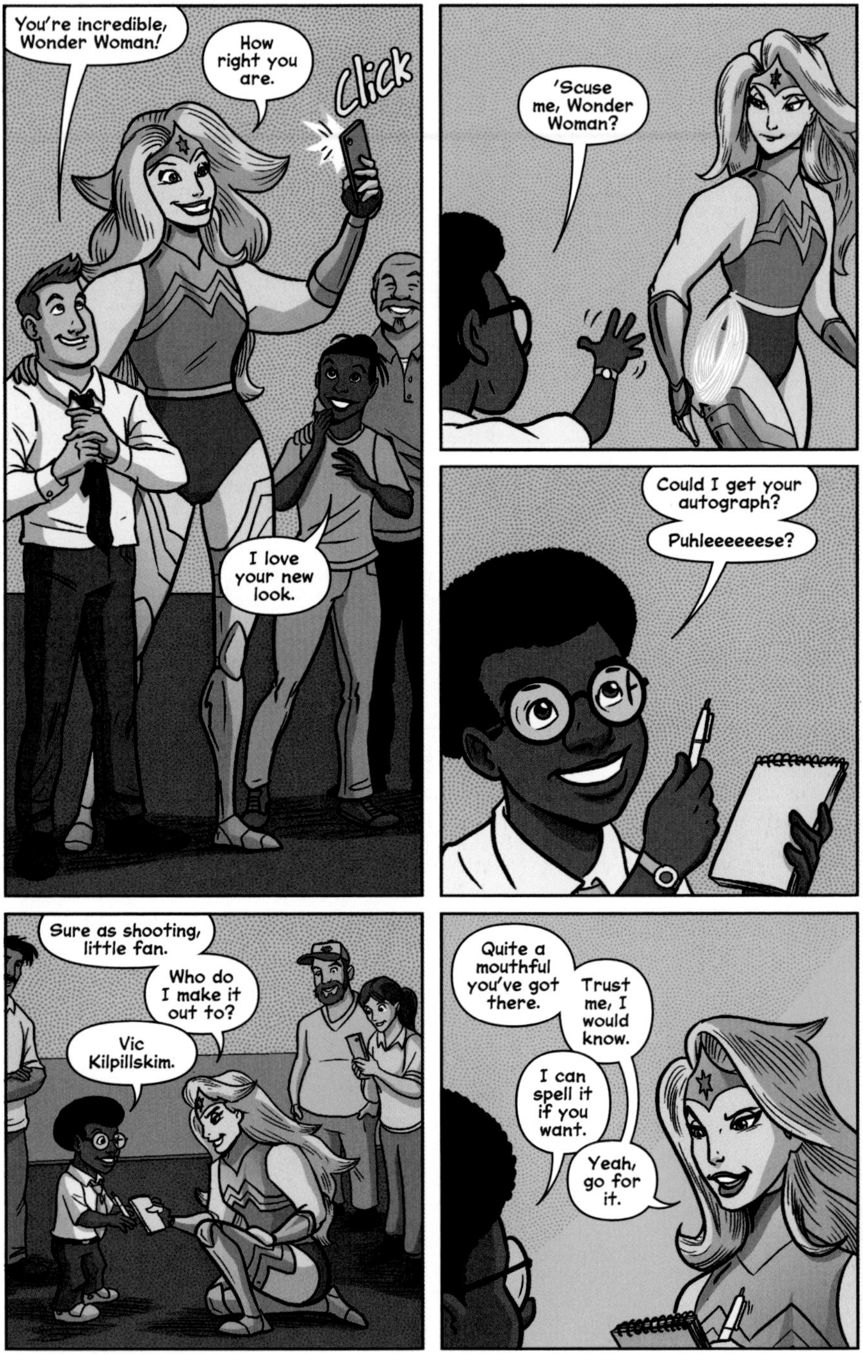

You're incredible, Wonder Woman!
How right you are.
Click
I love your new look.
'Scuse me, Wonder Woman?
Could I get your autograph?
Puhleeeeeese?
Sure as shooting, little fan.
Who do I make it out to?
Vic Kilpillskim.
Quite a mouthful you've got there.
Trust me, I would know.
I can spell it if you want.
Yeah, go for it.

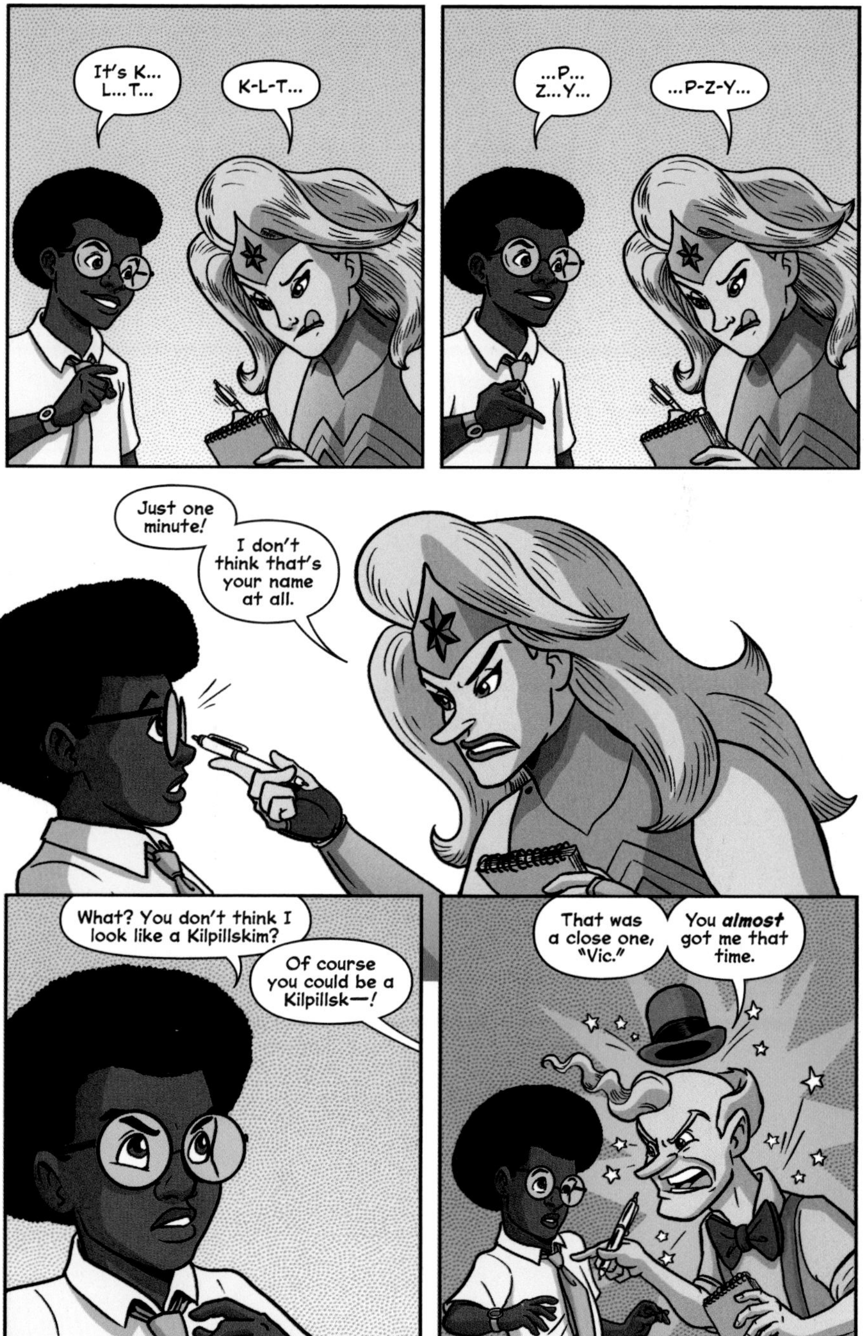
It's K...
L...T...
K-L-T...
...P...
Z...Y...
...P-Z-Y...
Just one minute!
I don't think that's your name at all.
What? You don't think I look like a Kilpillskim?
Of course you could be a Kilpillsk—!
That was a close one, "Vic."
You *almost* got me that time.

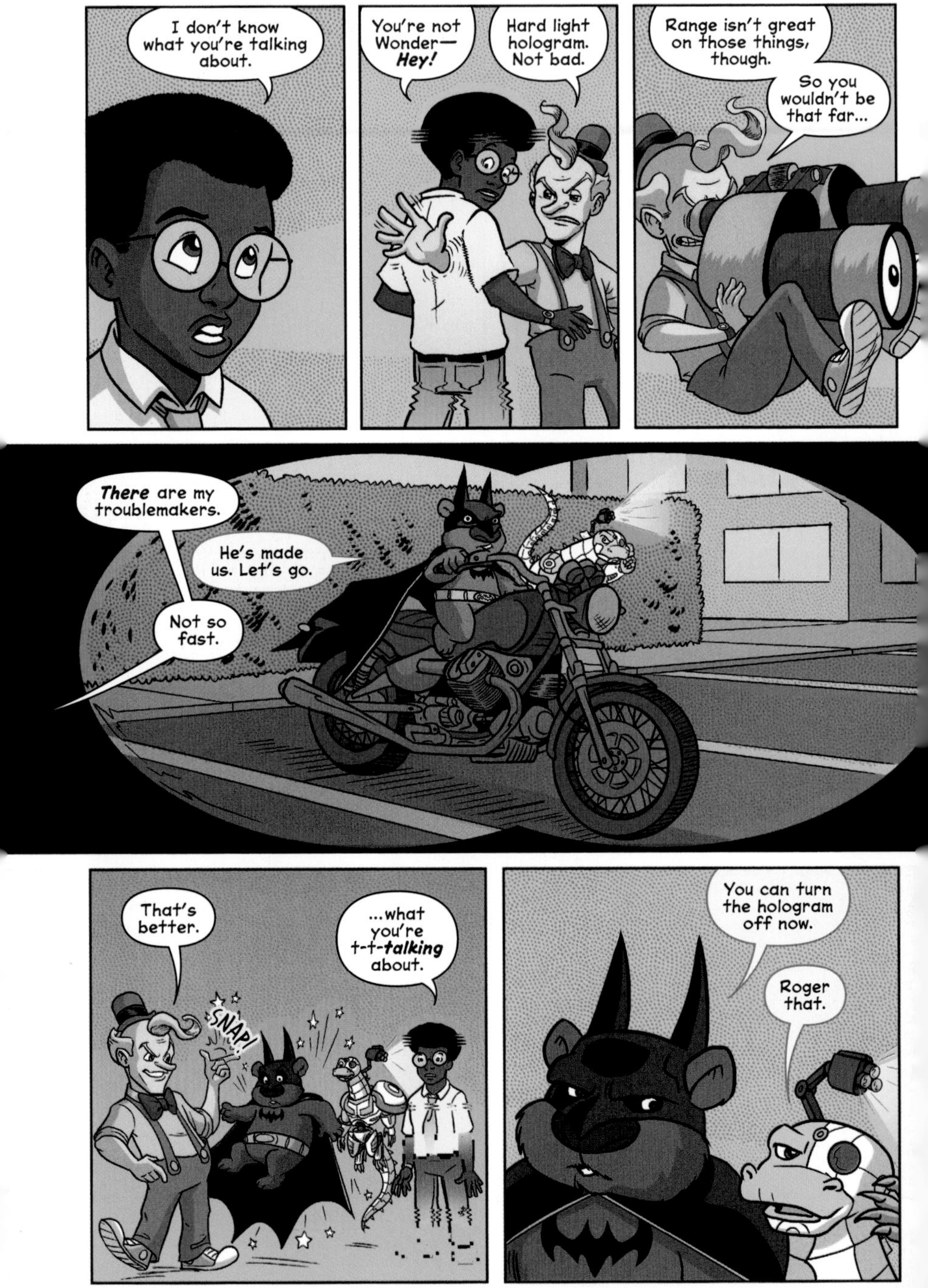
I don't know what you're talking about.
You're not Wonder— *Hey!*
Hard light hologram. Not bad.
Range isn't great on those things, though.
So you wouldn't be that far...
There are my troublemakers.
He's made us. Let's go.
Not so fast.
That's better.
SNAP!
...what you're t-t-*talking* about.
You can turn the hologram off now.
Roger that.

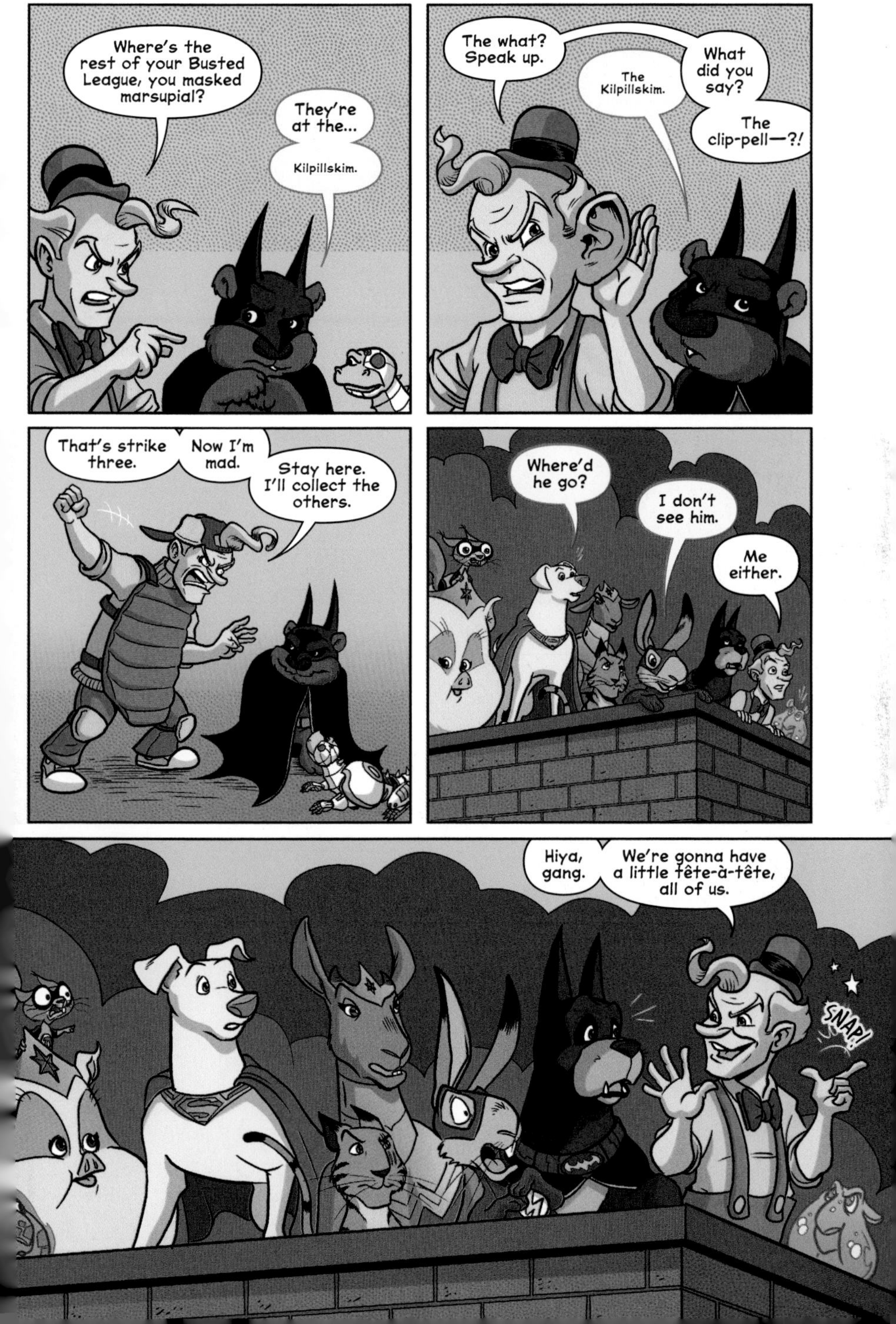

Where's the rest of your Busted League, you masked marsupial?
They're at the...
Kilpillskim.
The what? Speak up.
The Kilpillskim.
What did you say?
The clip-pell—?!
That's strike three.
Now I'm mad.
Stay here. I'll collect the others.
Where'd he go?
I don't see him.
Me either.
Hiya, gang.
We're gonna have a little tête-à-tête, all of us.
SNAP!

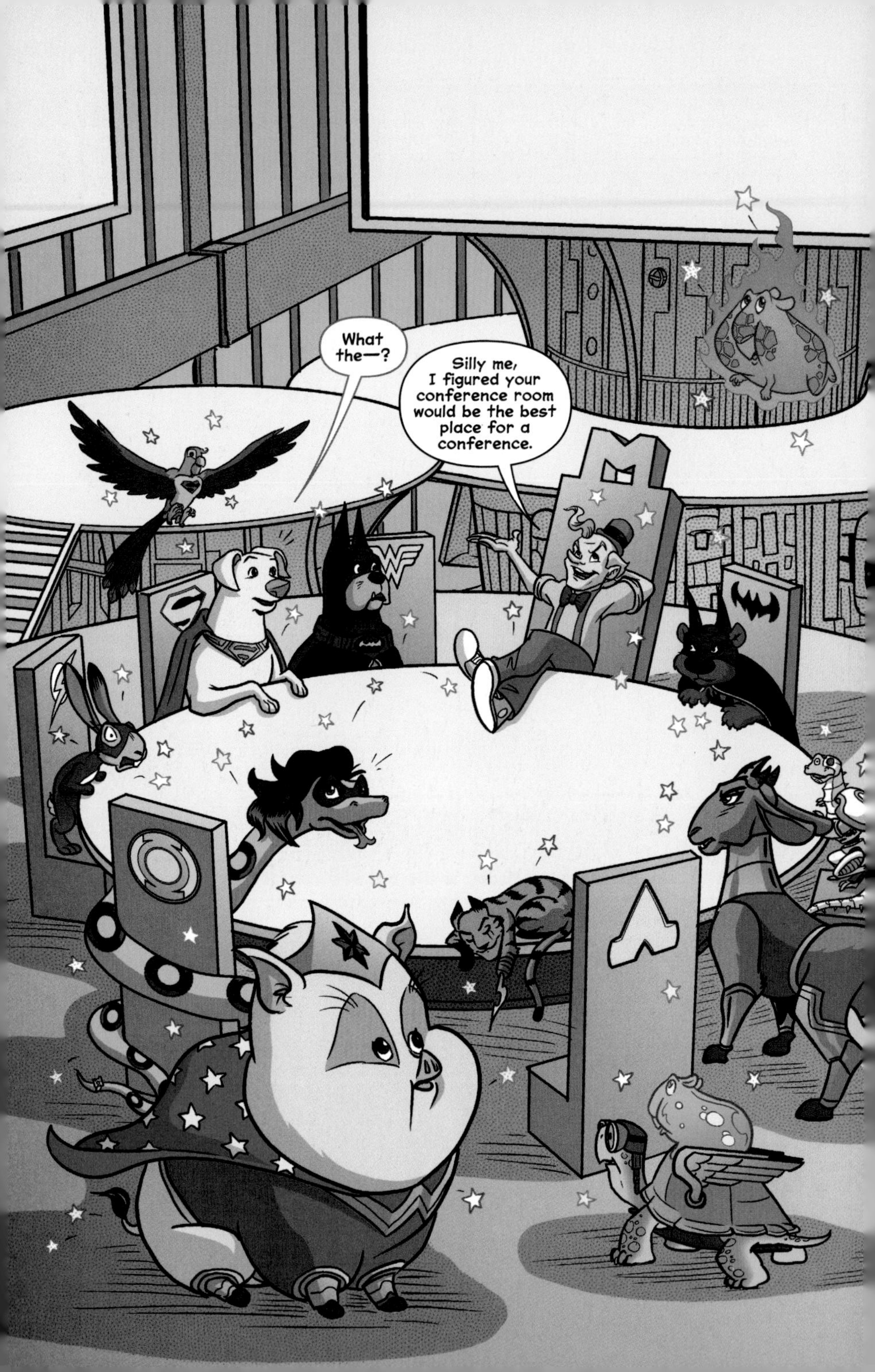
What the—?
Silly me, I figured your conference room would be the best place for a conference.

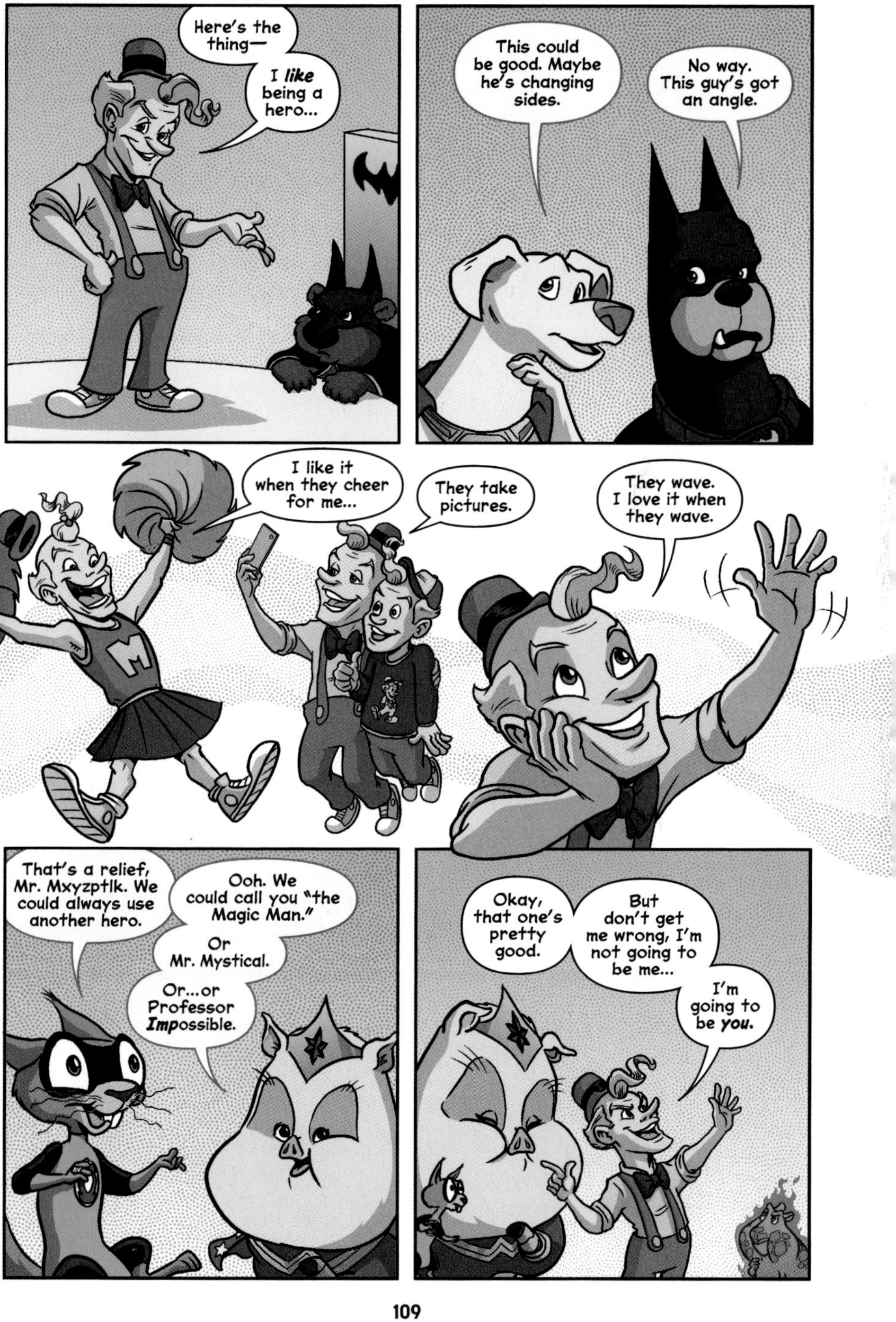

Here's the thing—
I *like* being a hero...
This could be good. Maybe he's changing sides.
No way. This guy's got an angle.
I like it when they cheer for me...
They take pictures.
They wave. I love it when they wave.
That's a relief, Mr. Mxyzptlk. We could always use another hero.
Ooh. We could call you "the Magic Man."
Or Mr. Mystical.
Or...or Professor *Imp*ossible.
Okay, that one's pretty good.
But don't get me wrong, I'm not going to be me...
I'm going to be *you*.

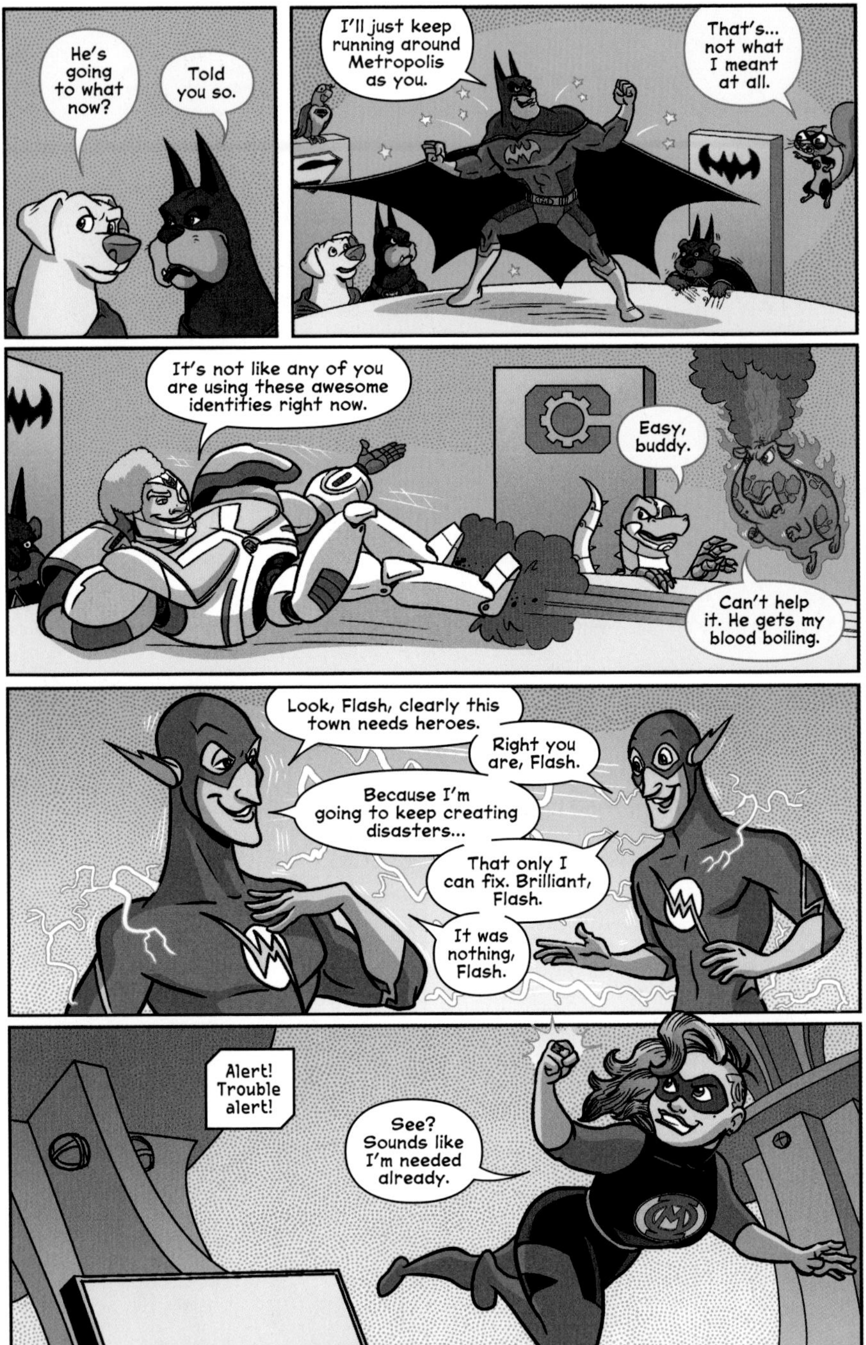
He's going to what now?
Told you so.
I'll just keep running around Metropolis as you.
That's... not what I meant at all.
It's not like any of you are using these awesome identities right now.
Easy, buddy.
Can't help it. He gets my blood boiling.
Look, Flash, clearly this town needs heroes.
Right you are, Flash.
Because I'm going to keep creating disasters...
That only I can fix. Brilliant, Flash.
It was nothing, Flash.
Alert! Trouble alert!
See? Sounds like I'm needed already.

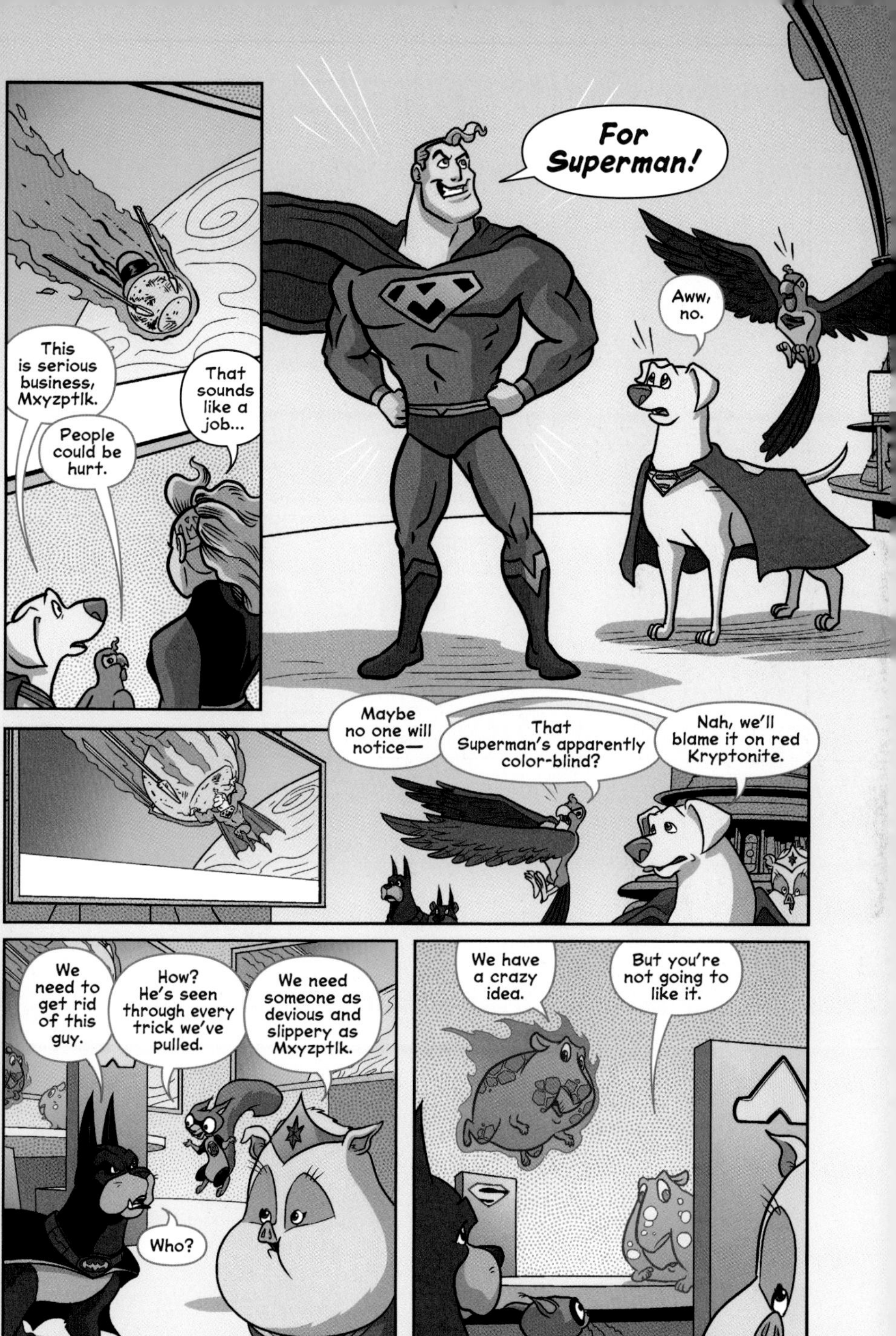
This is serious business, Mxyzptlk.
People could be hurt.
That sounds like a job...
For Superman!
Aww, no.
Maybe no one will notice—
That Superman's apparently color-blind?
Nah, we'll blame it on red Kryptonite.
We need to get rid of this guy.
How? He's seen through every trick we've pulled.
We need someone as devious and slippery as Mxyzptlk.
Who?
We have a crazy idea.
But you're not going to like it.

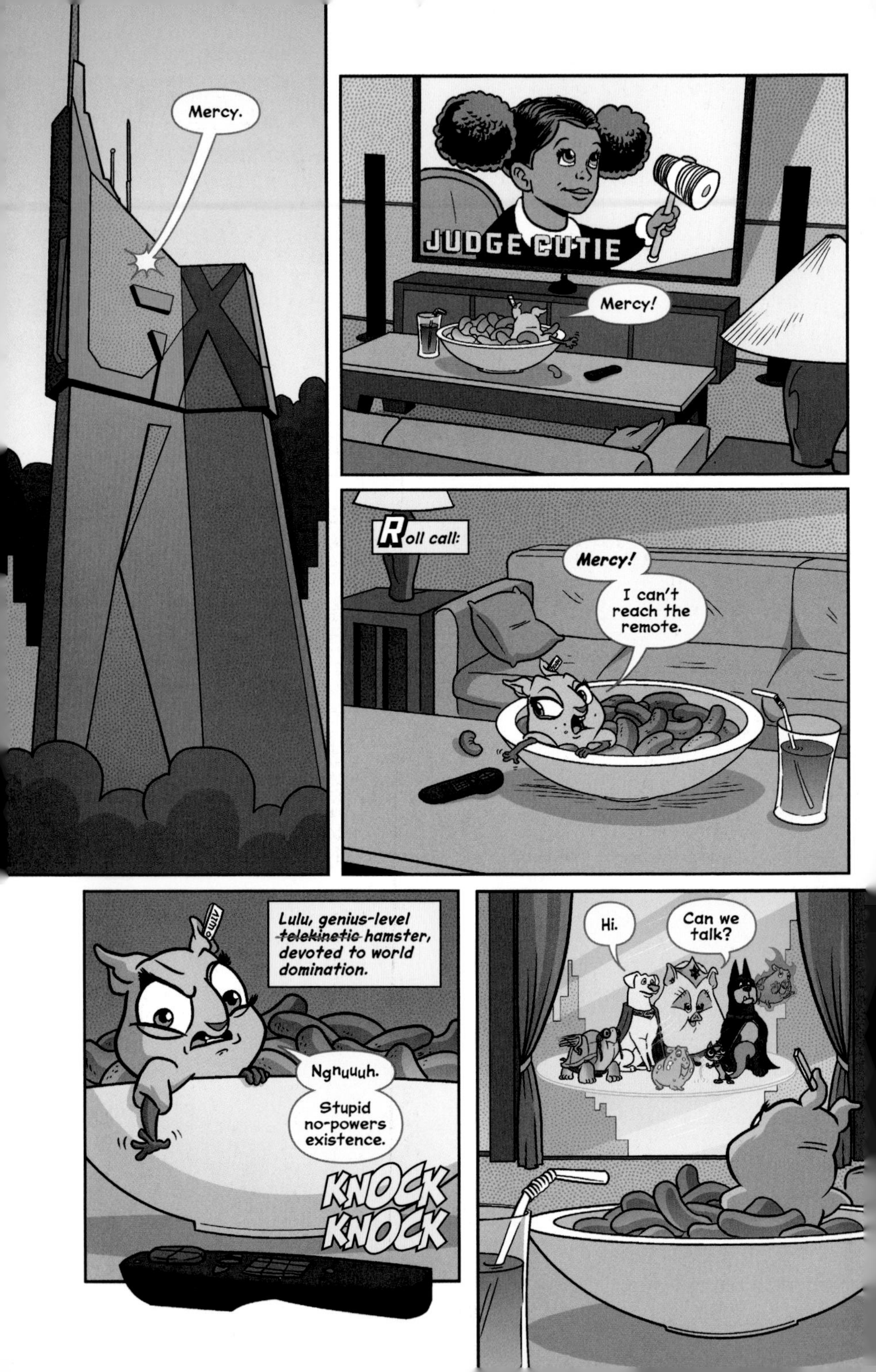
Mercy.
JUDGE CUTIE
Mercy!
Roll call:
Mercy!
I can't reach the remote.
Lulu, genius-level telekinetic hamster, devoted to world domination.
Ngnuuuh.
Stupid no-powers existence.
KNOCK KNOCK
Hi.
Can we talk?

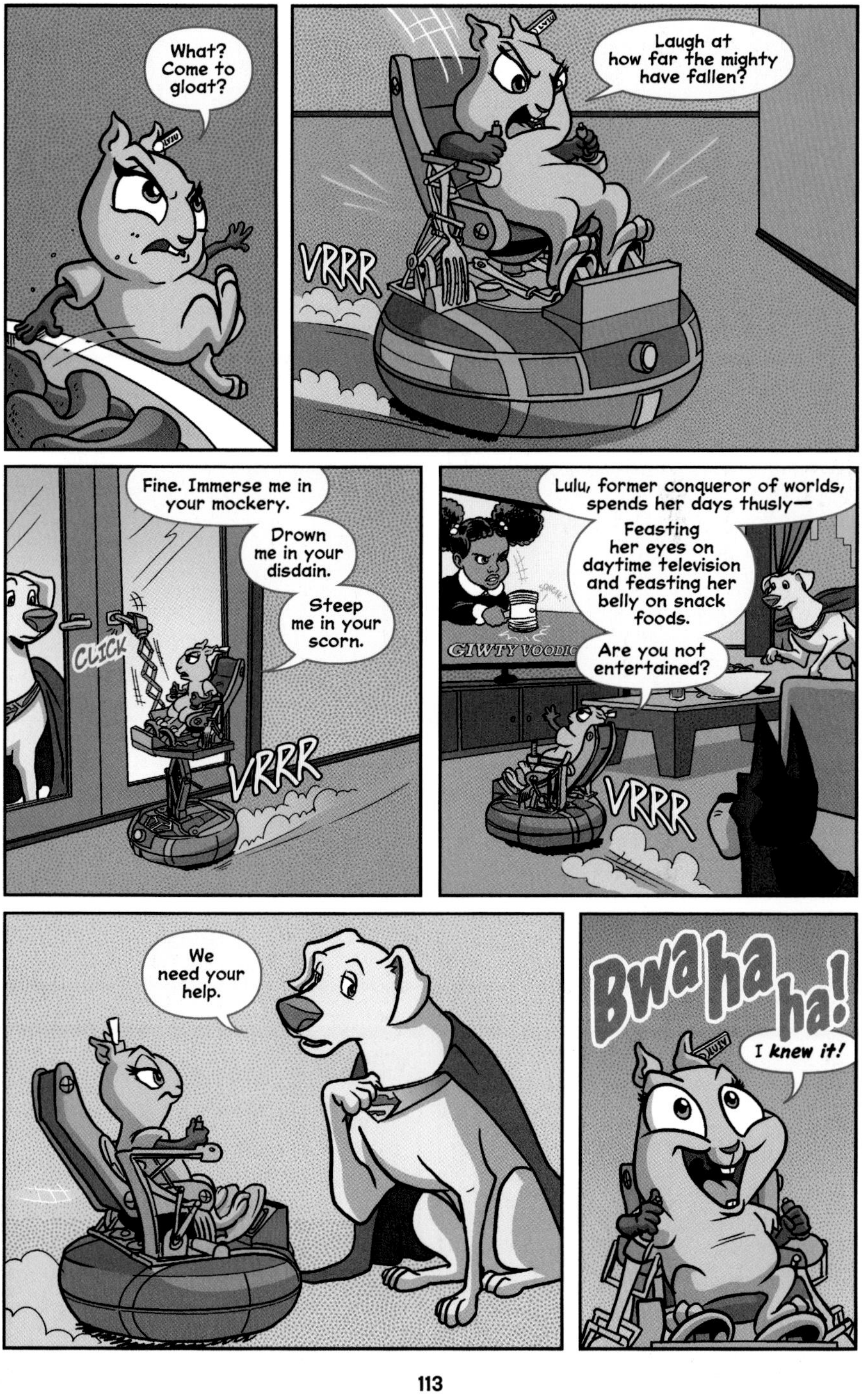
What? Come to gloat?
Laugh at how far the mighty have fallen?
VRRR
Fine. Immerse me in your mockery.
Drown me in your disdain.
Steep me in your scorn.
CLICK
VRRR
Lulu, former conqueror of worlds, spends her days thusly—
Feasting her eyes on daytime television and feasting her belly on snack foods.
Are you not entertained?
VRRR
We need your help.
Bwa ha ha!
I knew it!

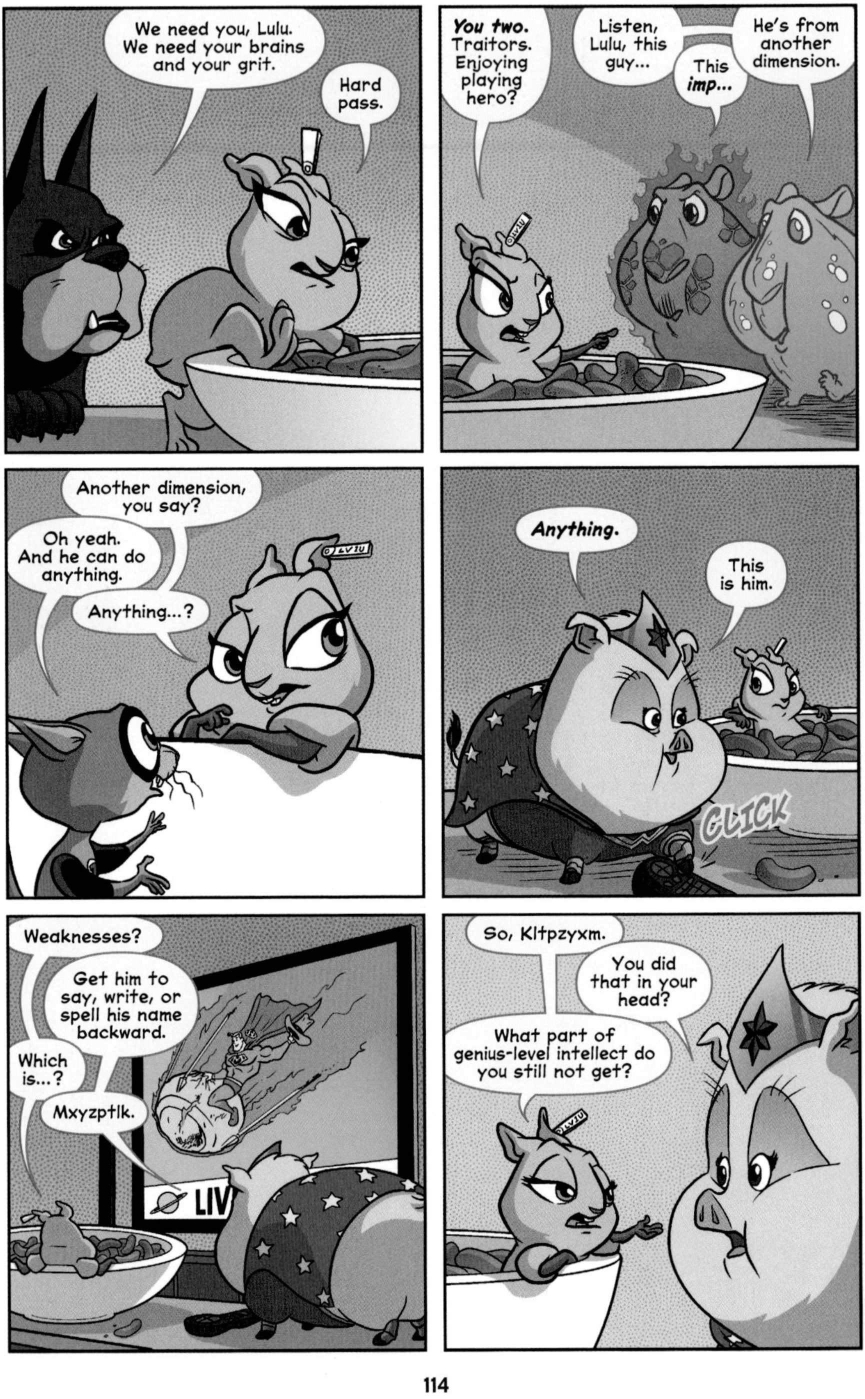
We need you, Lulu. We need your brains and your grit.
Hard pass.
You two. Traitors. Enjoying playing hero?
Listen, Lulu, this guy...
This imp...
He's from another dimension.
Another dimension, you say?
Oh yeah. And he can do anything.
Anything...?
Anything.
This is him.
CLICK
Weaknesses?
Get him to say, write, or spell his name backward.
Which is...?
Mxyzptlk.
LIV
So, Kltpzyxm.
You did that in your head?
What part of genius-level intellect do you still not get?

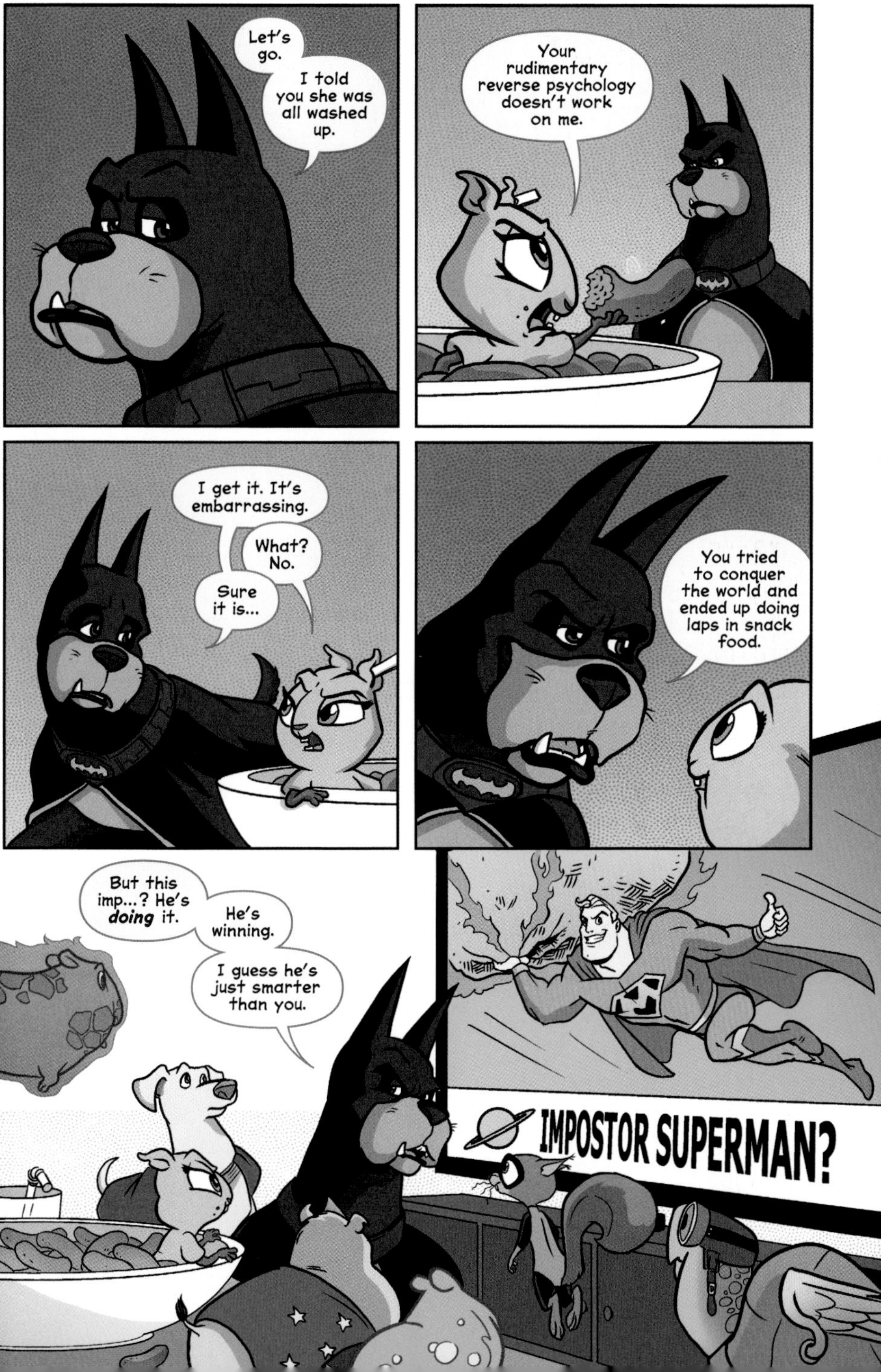
Let's go.
I told you she was all washed up.
Your rudimentary reverse psychology doesn't work on me.
I get it. It's embarrassing.
What? No.
Sure it is...
You tried to conquer the world and ended up doing laps in snack food.
But this imp...? He's *doing* it.
He's winning.
I guess he's just smarter than you.
IMPOSTOR SUPERMAN?

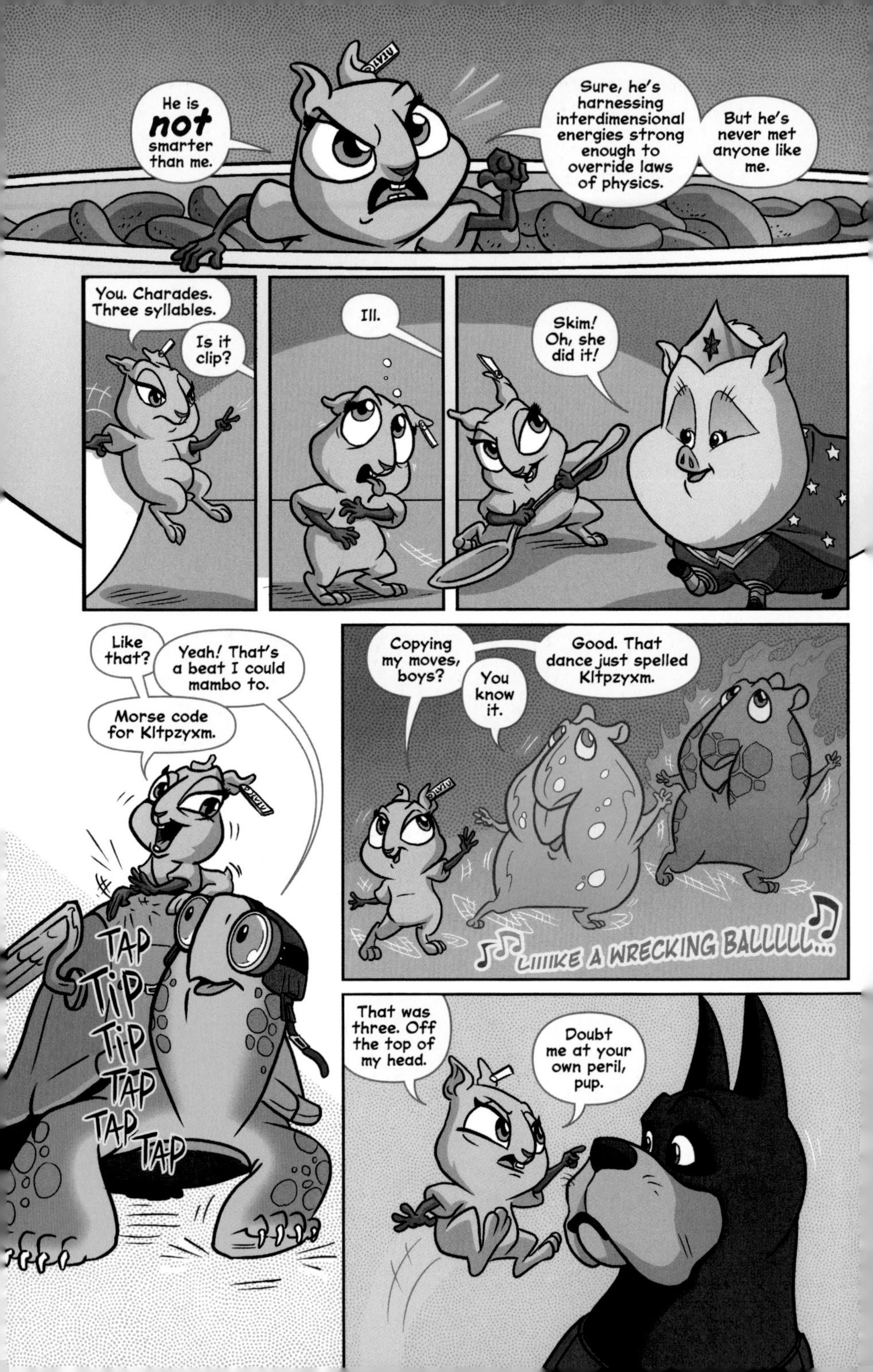

He is **not** smarter than me.
Sure, he's harnessing interdimensional energies strong enough to override laws of physics.
But he's never met anyone like me.
You. Charades. Three syllables.
Is it clip?
Ill.
Skim! Oh, she did it!
Like that?
Yeah! That's a beat I could mambo to.
Morse code for Kltpzyxm.
TAP TIP-TIP TAP TAP TAP
Copying my moves, boys?
You know it.
Good. That dance just spelled Kltpzyxm.
LIIIIKE A WRECKING BALLLLL...
That was three. Off the top of my head.
Doubt me at your own peril, pup.

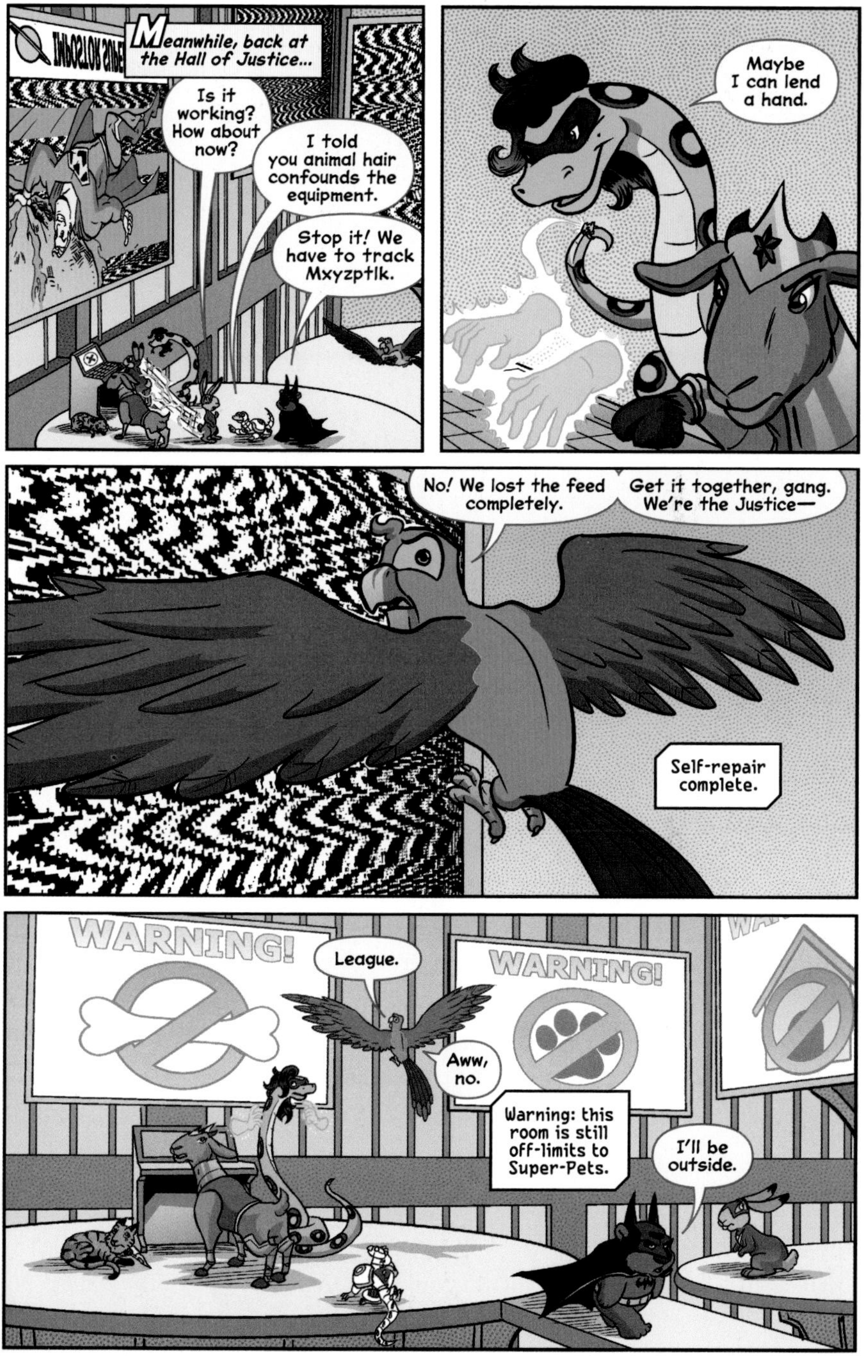
Meanwhile, back at the Hall of Justice...
Is it working? How about now?
I told you animal hair confounds the equipment.
Stop it! We have to track Mxyzptlk.
Maybe I can lend a hand.
No! We lost the feed completely.
Get it together, gang. We're the Justice—
Self-repair complete.
WARNING!
League.
WARNING!
Aww, no.
Warning: this room is still off-limits to Super-Pets.
I'll be outside.

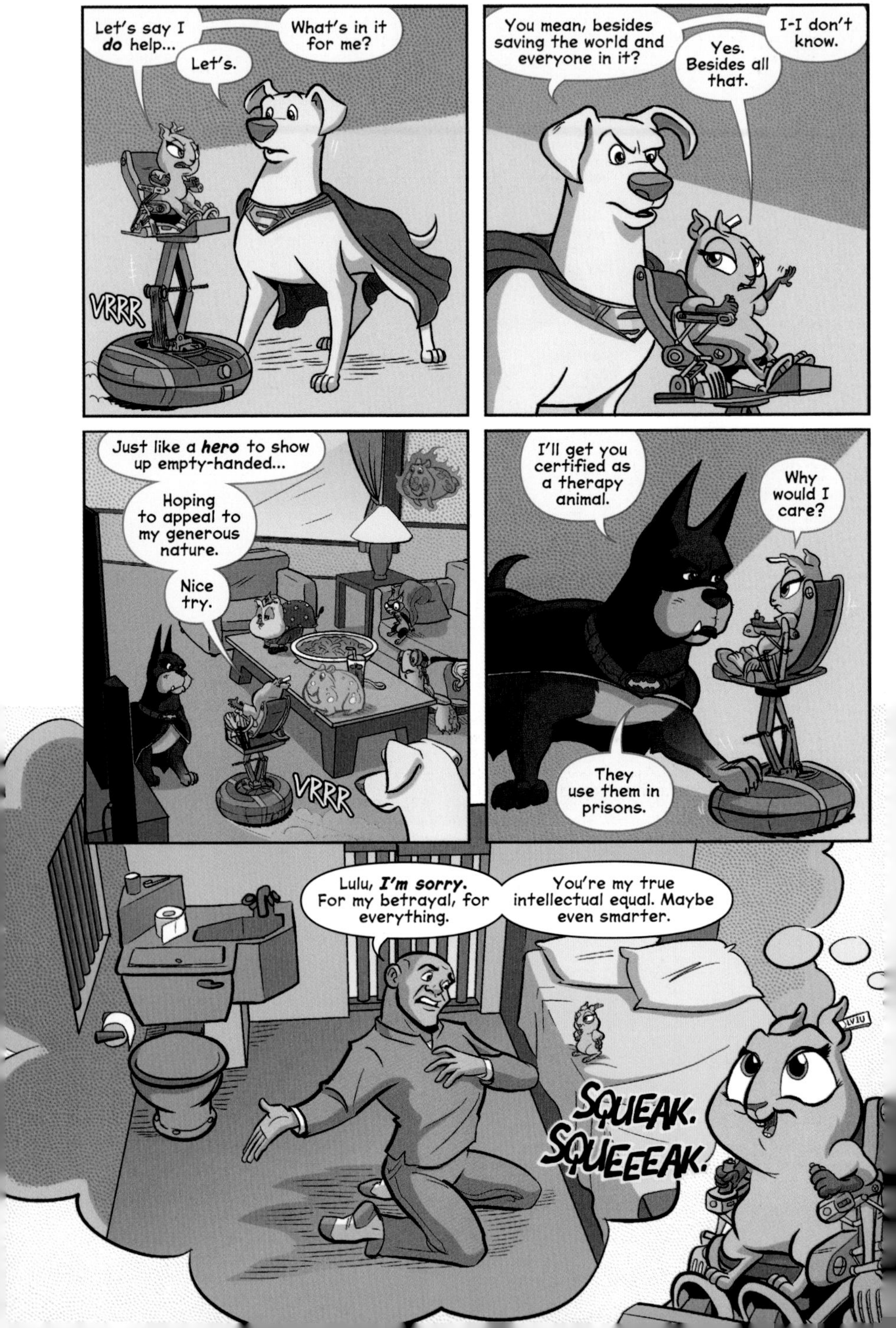
Let's say I do help...
Let's.
What's in it for me?
VRRR
You mean, besides saving the world and everyone in it?
Yes. Besides all that.
I-I don't know.
Just like a hero to show up empty-handed...
Hoping to appeal to my generous nature.
Nice try.
VRRR
I'll get you certified as a therapy animal.
Why would I care?
They use them in prisons.
Lulu, I'm sorry. For my betrayal, for everything.
You're my true intellectual equal. Maybe even smarter.
SQUEAK. SQUEEEEAK.

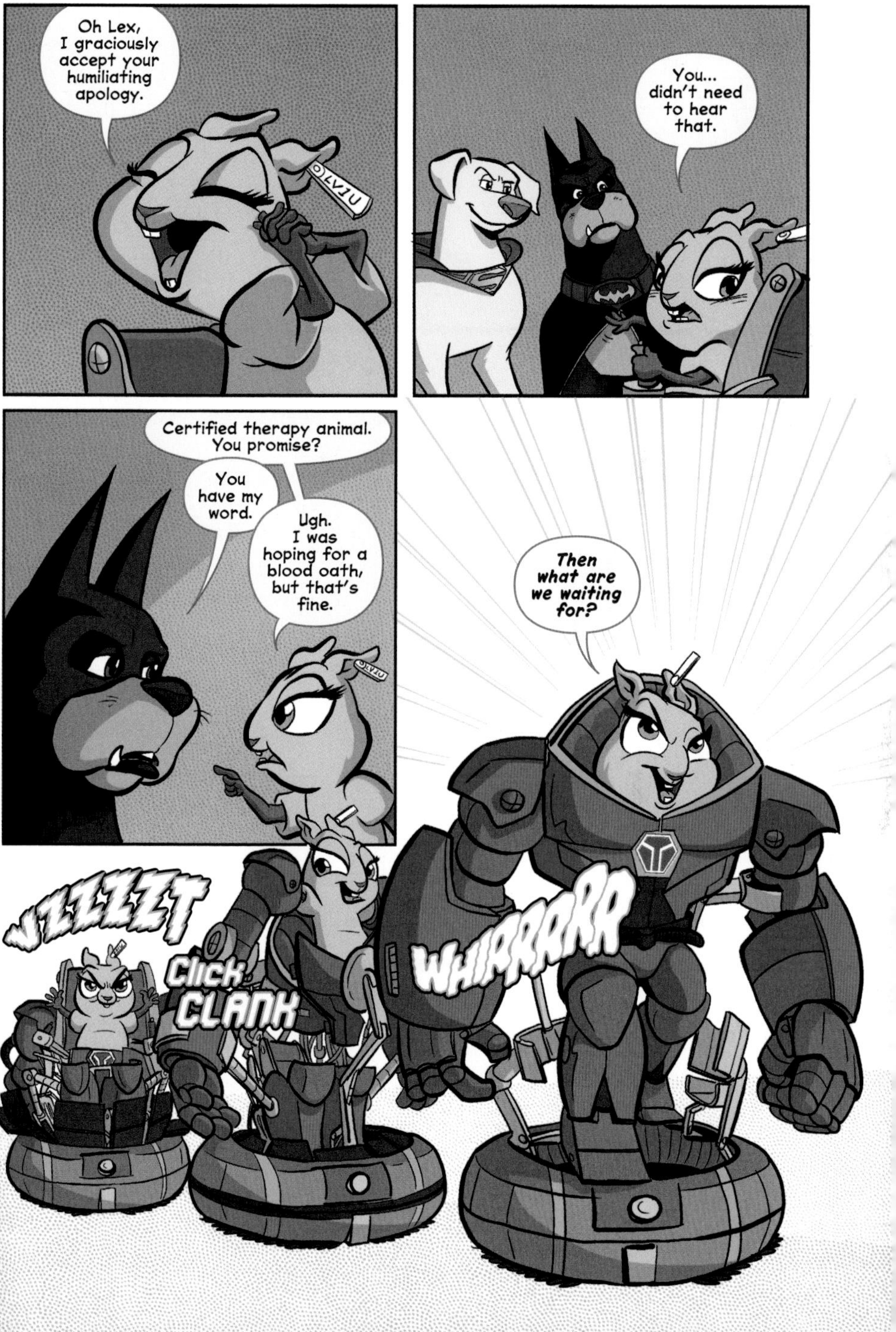

Oh Lex, I graciously accept your humiliating apology.
LVIU
You... didn't need to hear that.
Certified therapy animal. You promise?
You have my word.
Ugh. I was hoping for a blood oath, but that's fine.
Then what are we waiting for?
VZZZZZT
Click
CLANK
WHIRRRRRR

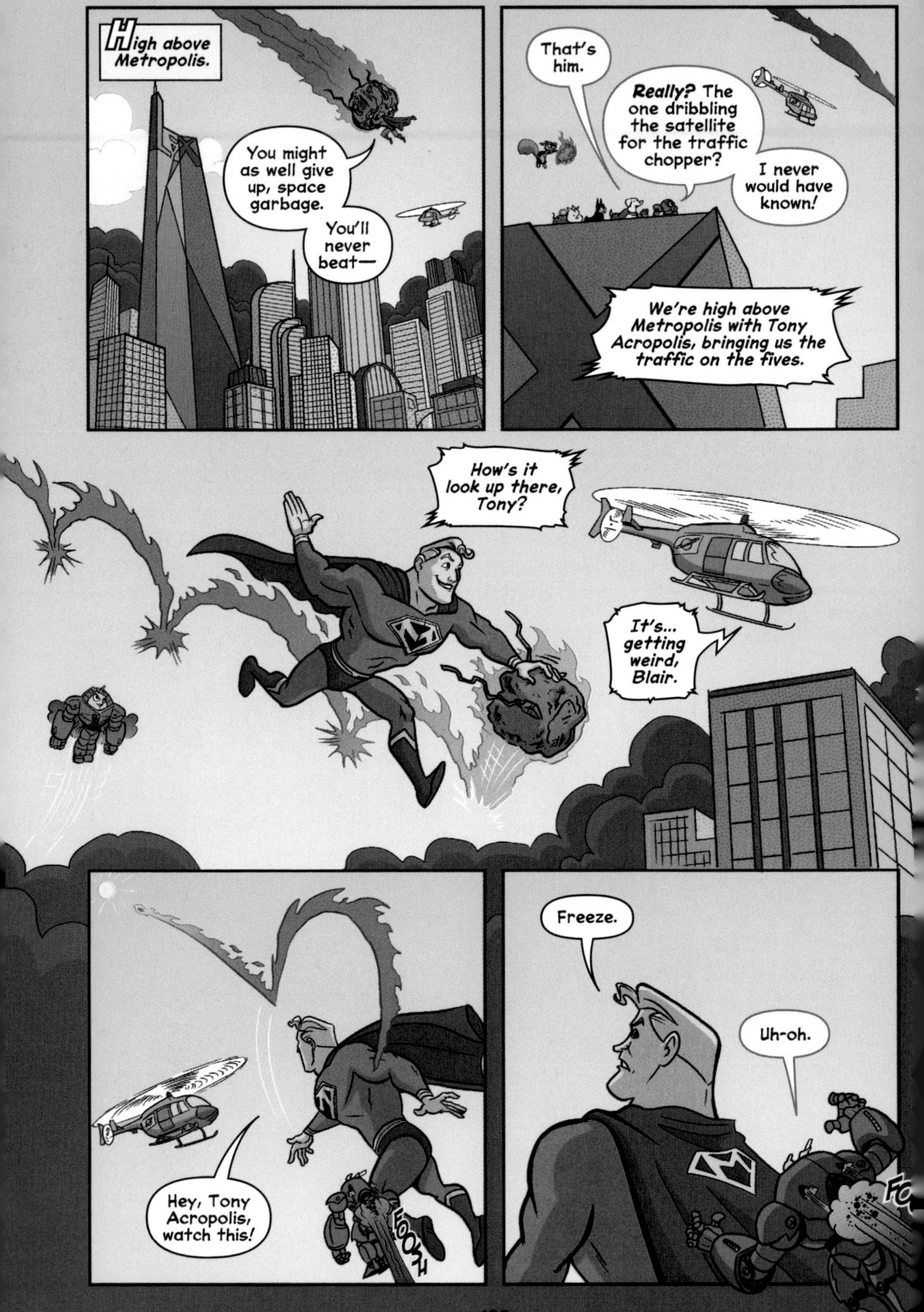
High above Metropolis.
You might as well give up, space garbage.
You'll never beat—
That's him.
Really? The one dribbling the satellite for the traffic chopper?
I never would have known!
We're high above Metropolis with Tony Acropolis, bringing us the traffic on the fives.
How's it look up there, Tony?
It's... getting weird, Blair.
Hey, Tony Acropolis, watch this!
Freeze.
Uh-oh.

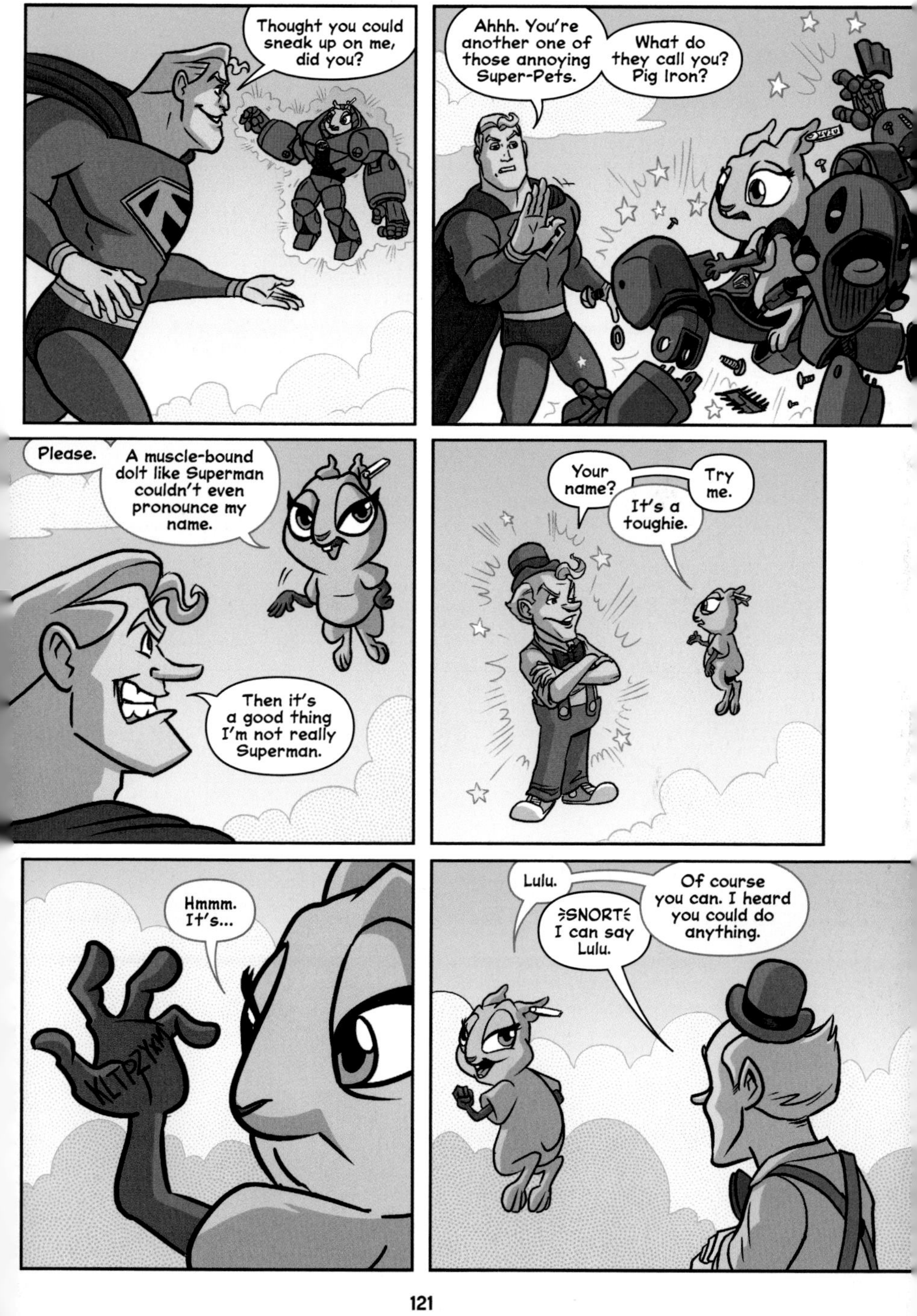
Thought you could sneak up on me, did you?
Ahhh. You're another one of those annoying Super-Pets.
What do they call you? Pig Iron?
Please.
A muscle-bound dolt like Superman couldn't even pronounce my name.
Then it's a good thing I'm not really Superman.
Your name?
Try me.
It's a toughie.
Hmmm. It's...
KLTPZYXM
Lulu.
≷SNORT≶ I can say Lulu.
Of course you can. I heard you could do anything.

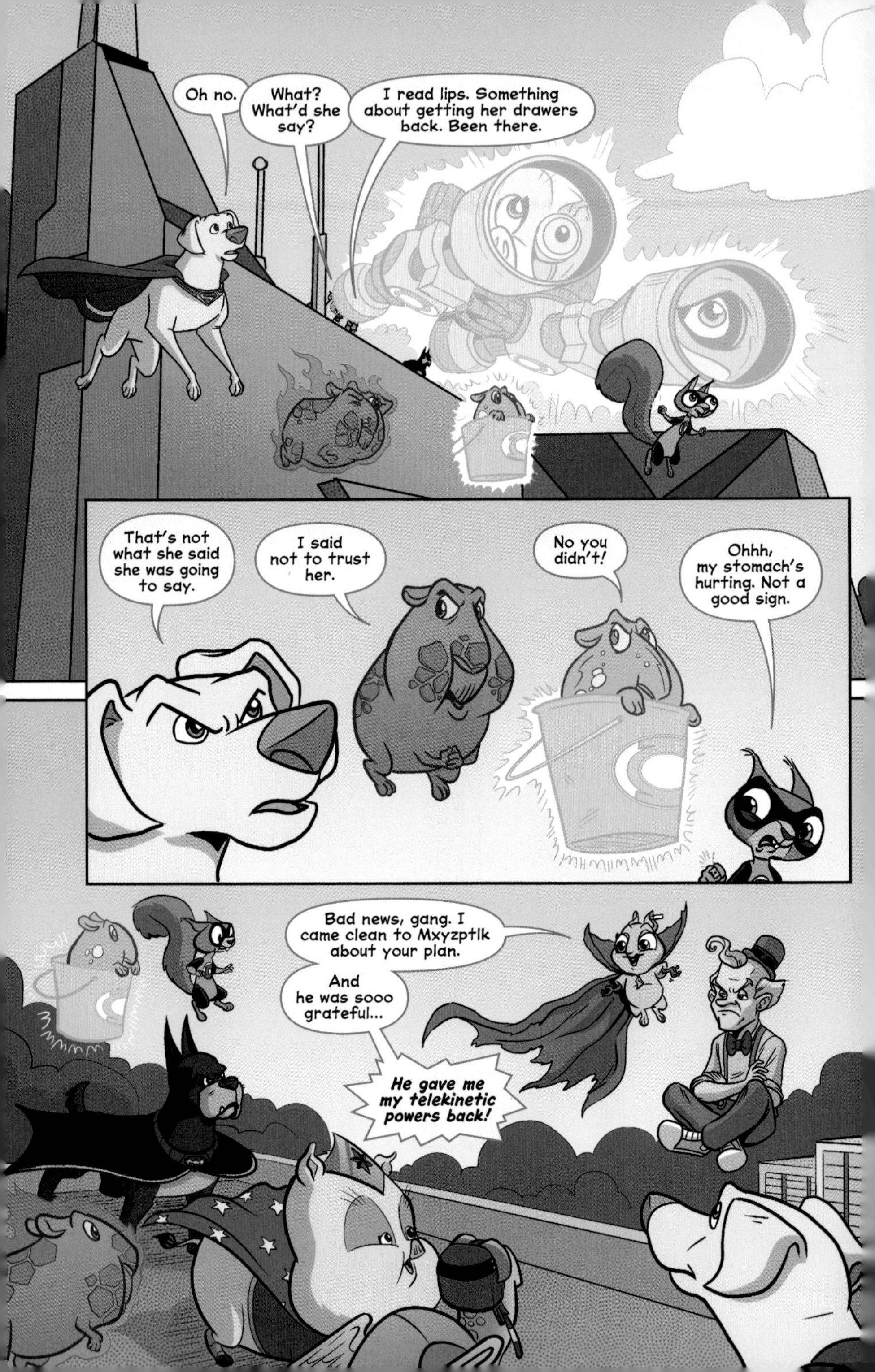
Oh no.
What? What'd she say?
I read lips. Something about getting her drawers back. Been there.
That's not what she said she was going to say.
I said not to trust her.
No you didn't!
Ohhh, my stomach's hurting. Not a good sign.
Bad news, gang. I came clean to Mxyzptlk about your plan.
And he was sooo grateful...
He gave me my telekinetic powers back!

CHAPTER 6

The Tortoise
and the Dare

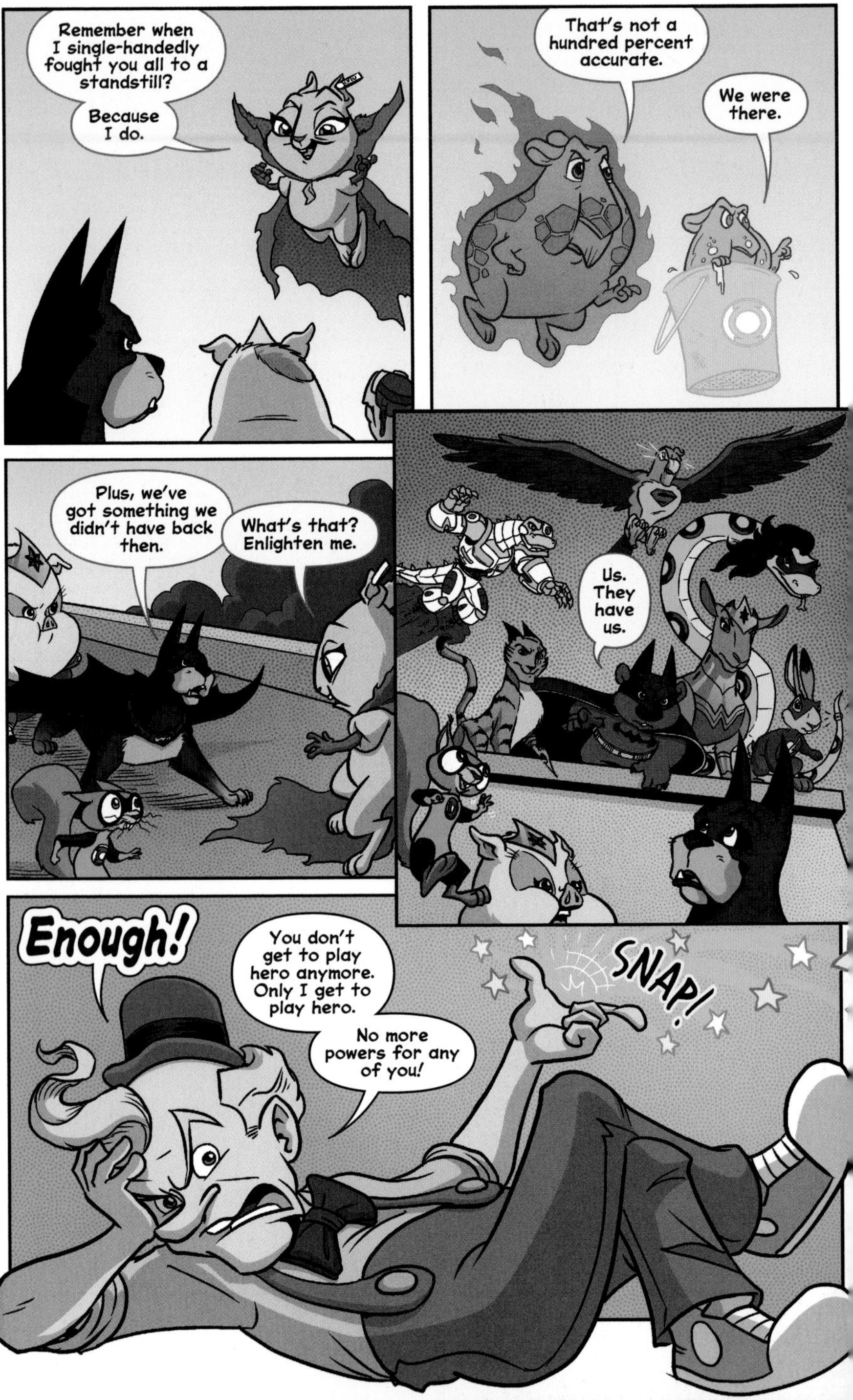
Remember when I single-handedly fought you all to a standstill?
Because I do.
That's not a hundred percent accurate.
We were there.
Plus, we've got something we didn't have back then.
What's that? Enlighten me.
Us. They have us.
Enough!
You don't get to play hero anymore. Only I get to play hero.
No more powers for any of you!
SNAP!

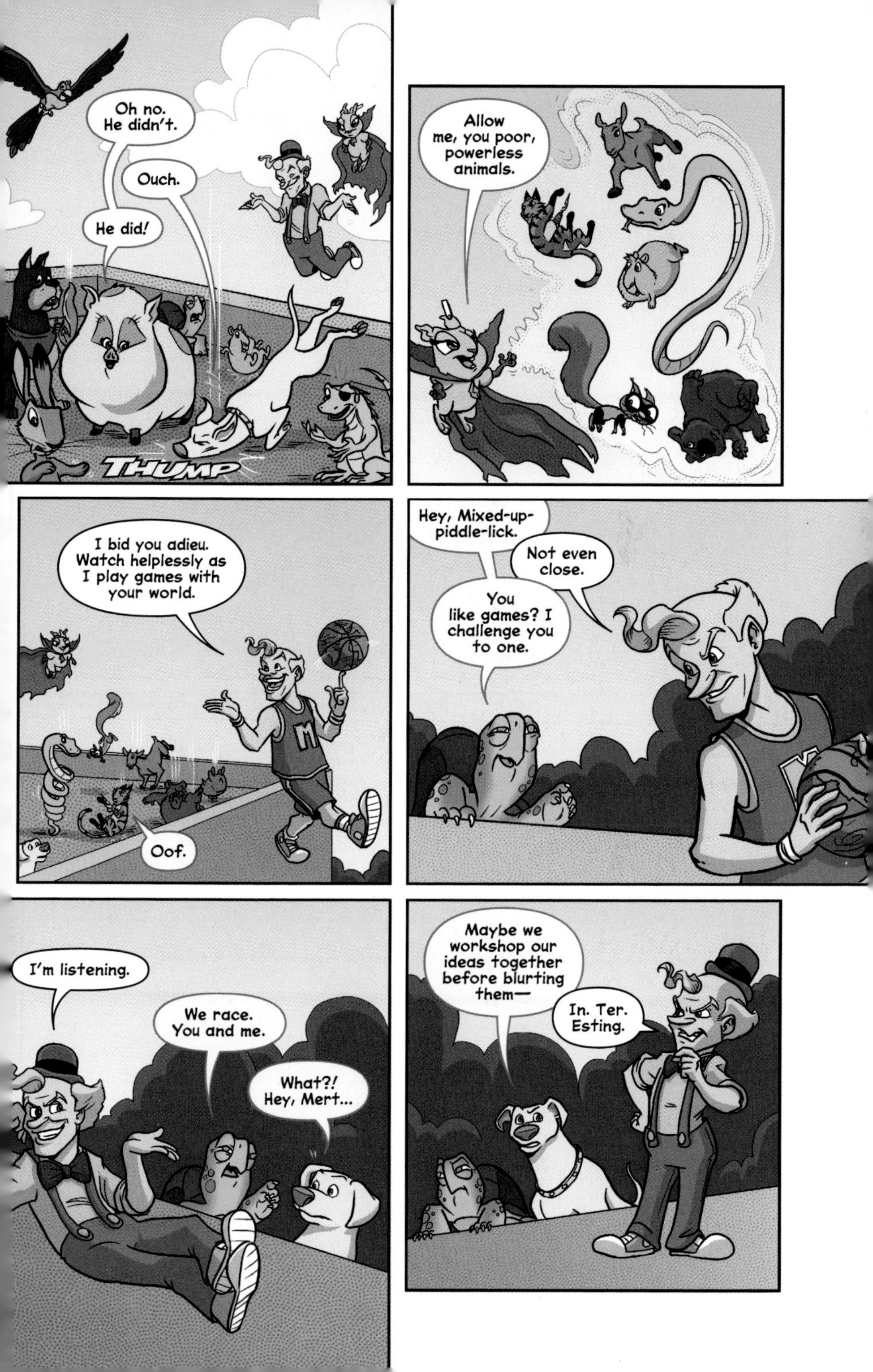
Oh no. He didn't.
Ouch.
He did!
THUMP
Allow me, you poor, powerless animals.
I bid you adieu. Watch helplessly as I play games with your world.
Oof.
Hey, Mixed-up-piddle-lick.
Not even close.
You like games? I challenge you to one.
I'm listening.
We race. You and me.
What?! Hey, Mert...
Maybe we workshop our ideas together before blurting them—
In. Ter. Esting.

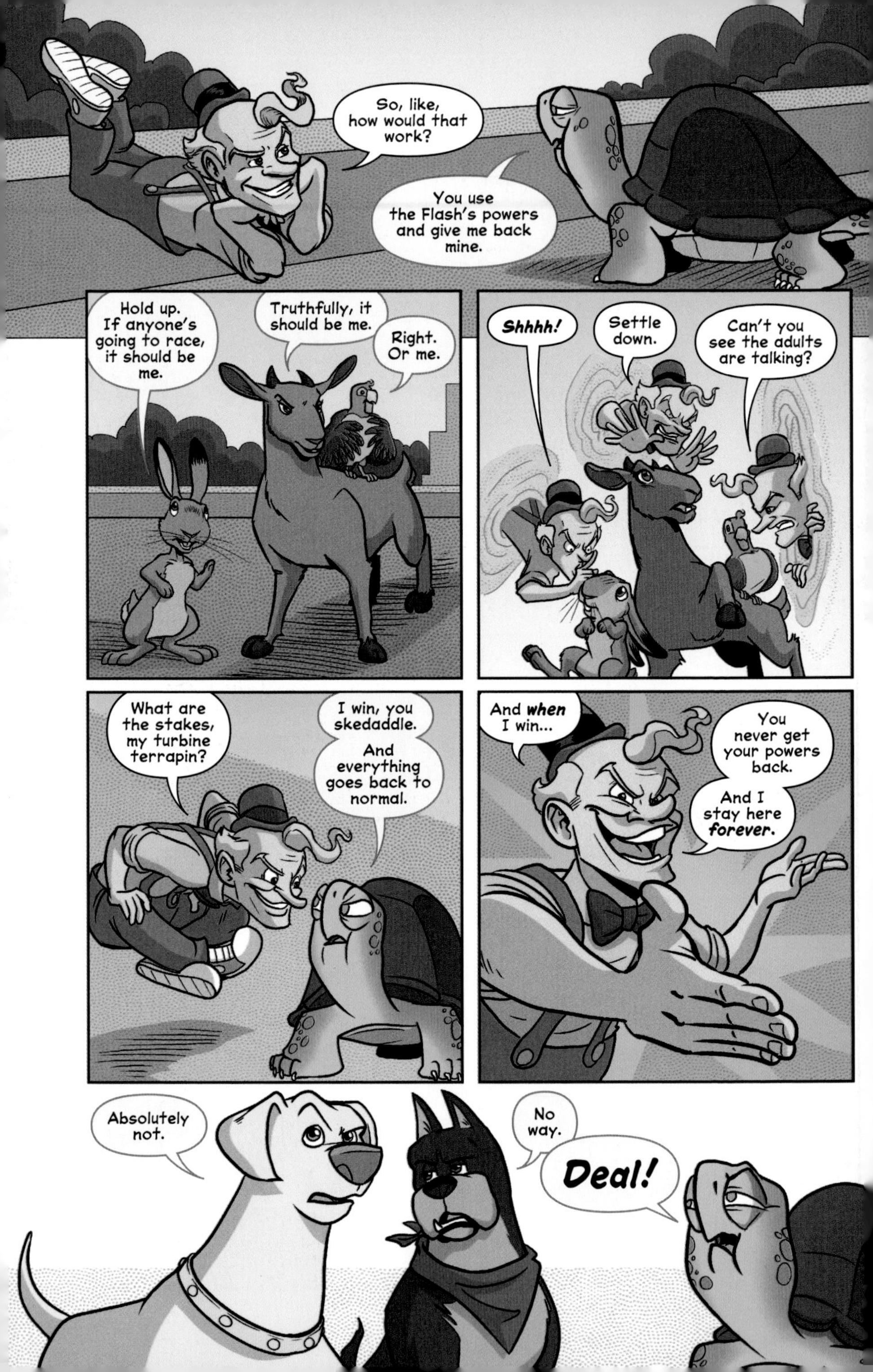
So, like, how would that work?
You use the Flash's powers and give me back mine.
Hold up. If anyone's going to race, it should be me.
Truthfully, it should be me.
Right. Or me.
Shhhh!
Settle down.
Can't you see the adults are talking?
What are the stakes, my turbine terrapin?
I win, you skedaddle.
And everything goes back to normal.
And when I win...
You never get your powers back.
And I stay here forever.
Absolutely not.
No way.
Deal!

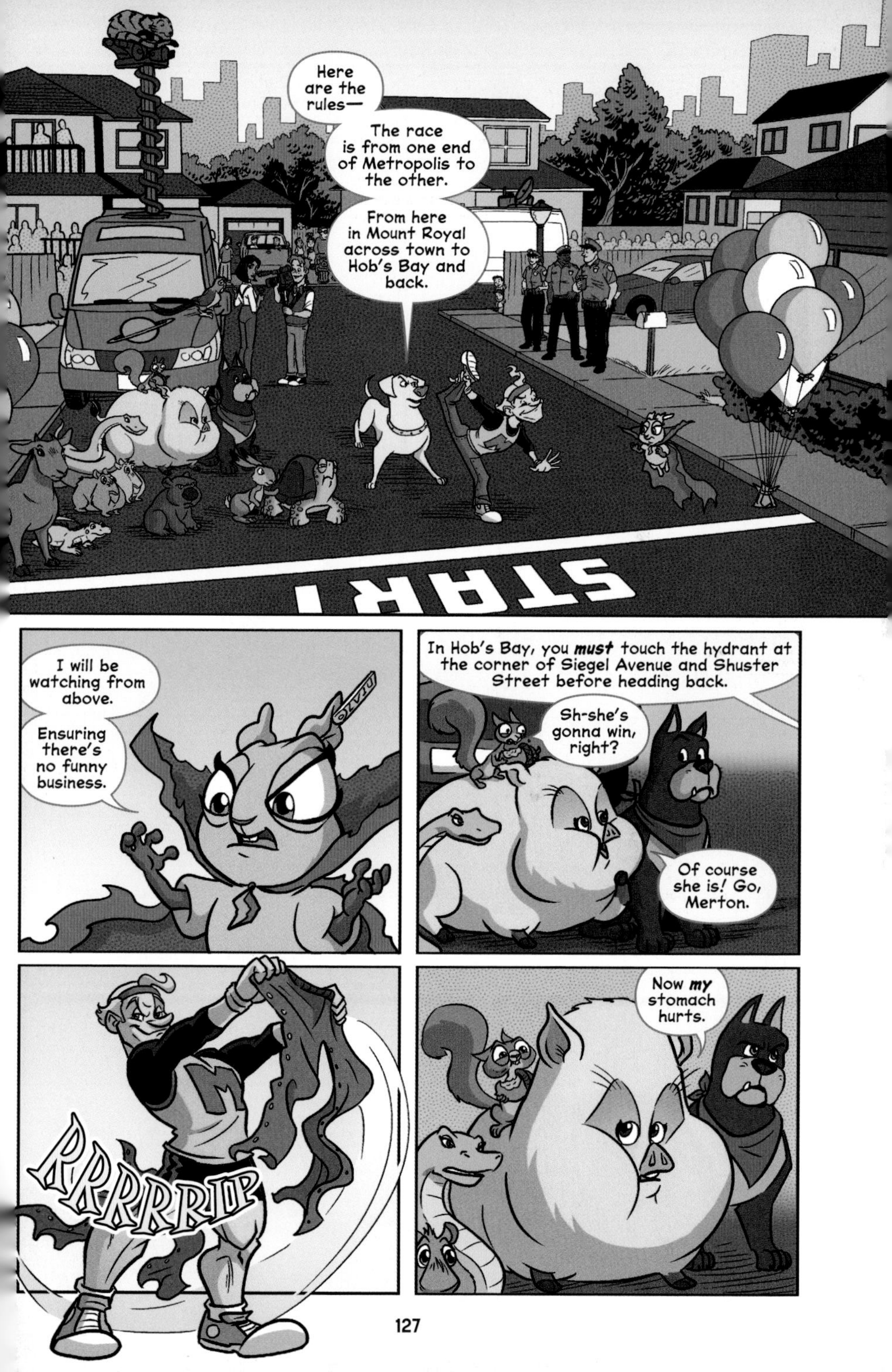
Here are the rules—
The race is from one end of Metropolis to the other.
From here in Mount Royal across town to Hob's Bay and back.
START
I will be watching from above.
Ensuring there's no funny business.
In Hob's Bay, you **must** touch the hydrant at the corner of Siegel Avenue and Shuster Street before heading back.
Sh-she's gonna win, right?
Of course she is! Go, Merton.
RRRRRIP
Now **my** stomach hurts.

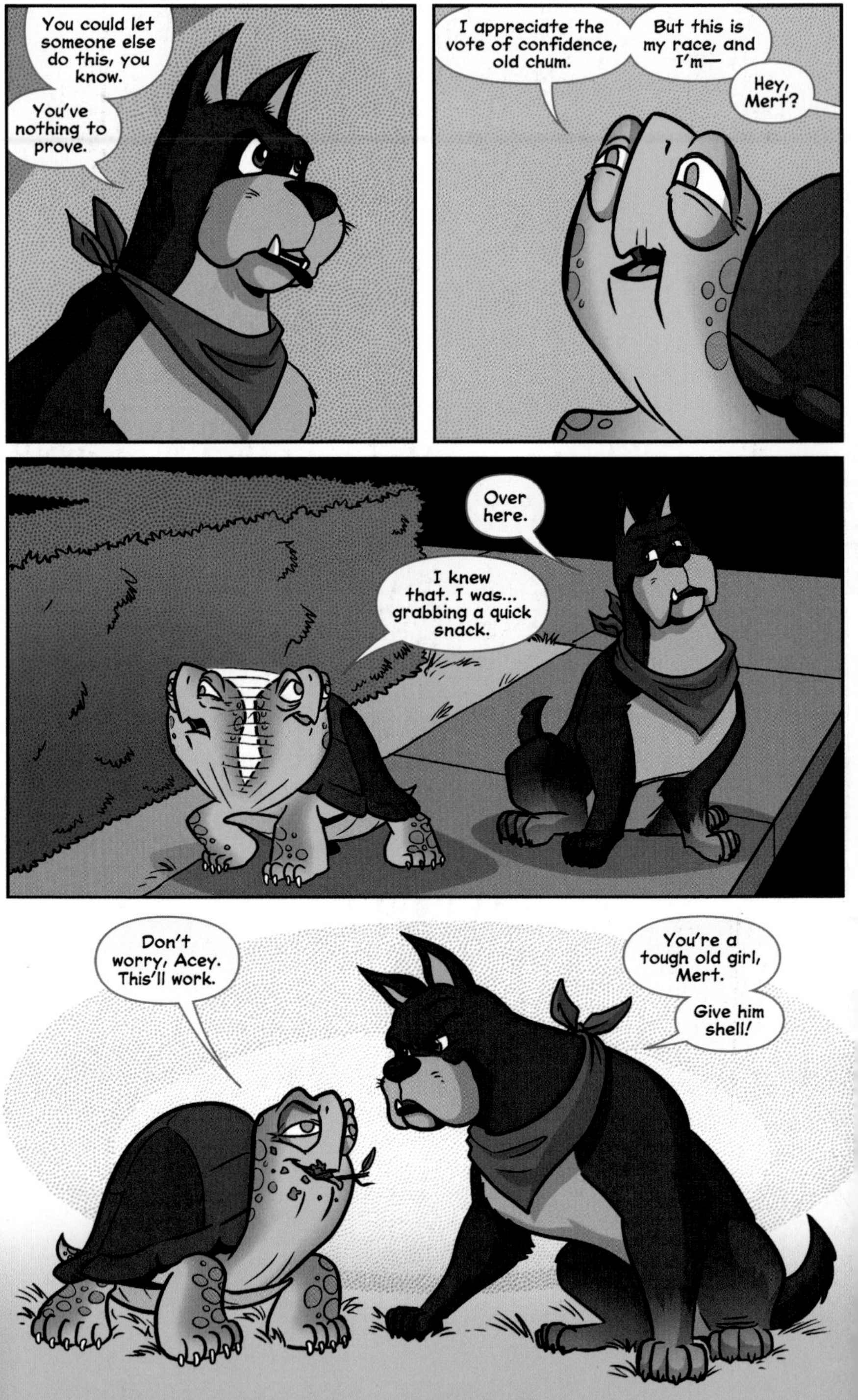
You could let someone else do this, you know.
You've nothing to prove.
I appreciate the vote of confidence, old chum.
But this is my race, and I'm—
Hey, Mert?
Over here.
I knew that. I was... grabbing a quick snack.
Don't worry, Acey. This'll work.
You're a tough old girl, Mert.
Give him shell!

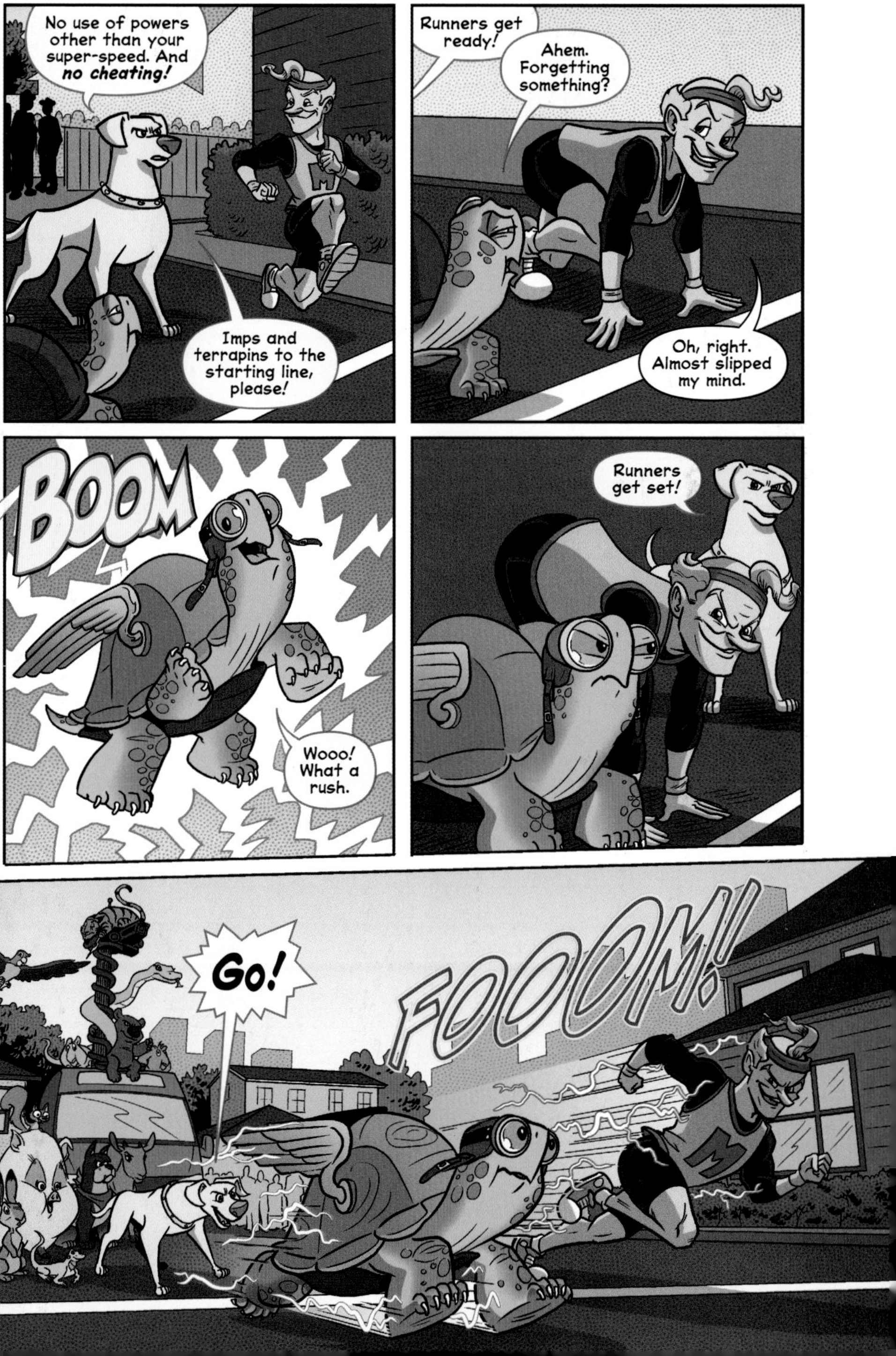
No use of powers other than your super-speed. And *no cheating!*
Imps and terrapins to the starting line, please!
Runners get ready!
Ahem. Forgetting something?
Oh, right. Almost slipped my mind.
BOOM
Wooo! What a rush.
Runners get set!
Go!
FOOOOM!

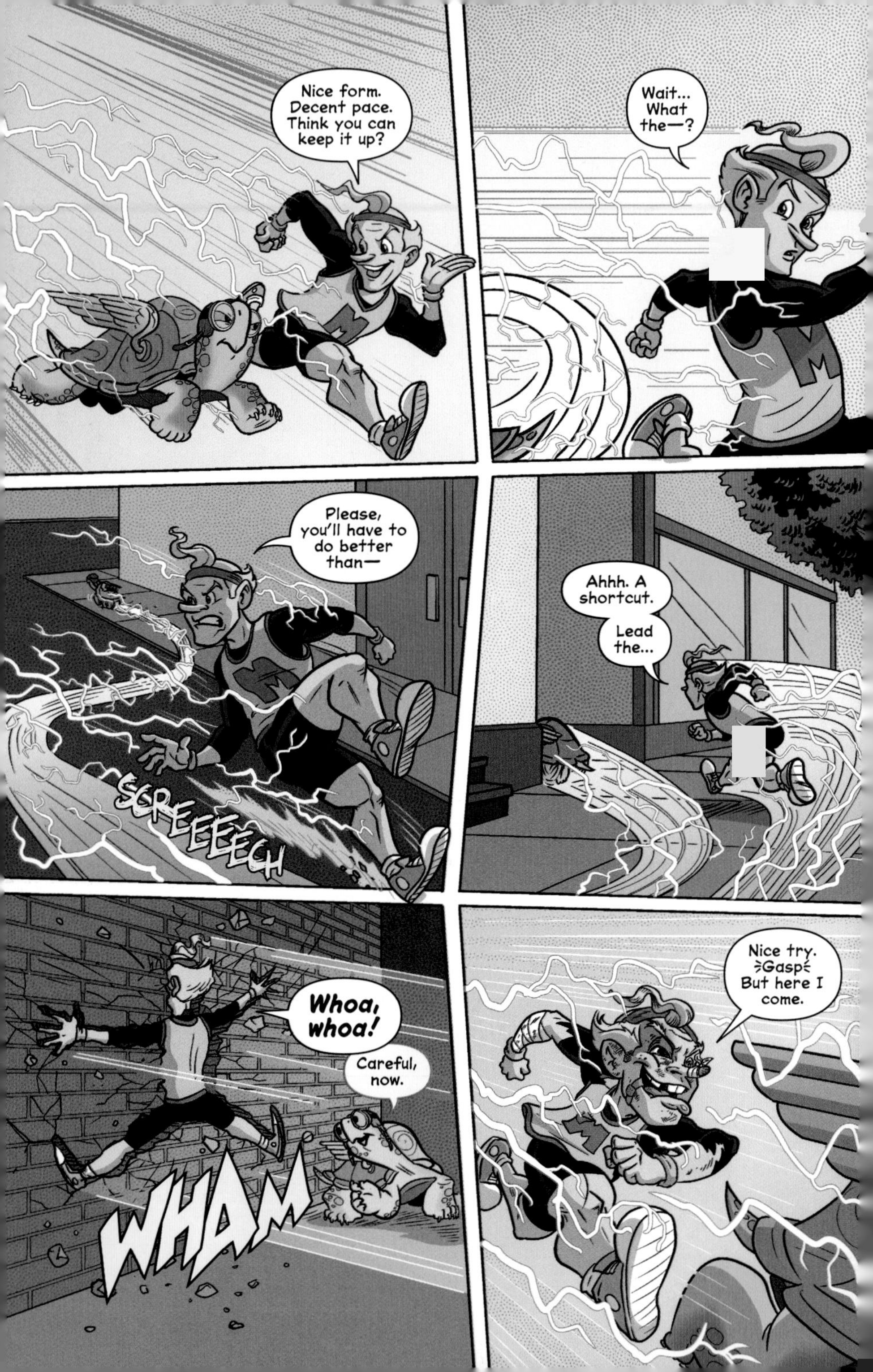
Nice form. Decent pace. Think you can keep it up?
Wait... What the—?
Please, you'll have to do better than—
SCREEEEECH
Ahhh. A shortcut.
Lead the...
Whoa, whoa!
Careful, now.
WHAM
Nice try. *Gasp* But here I come.

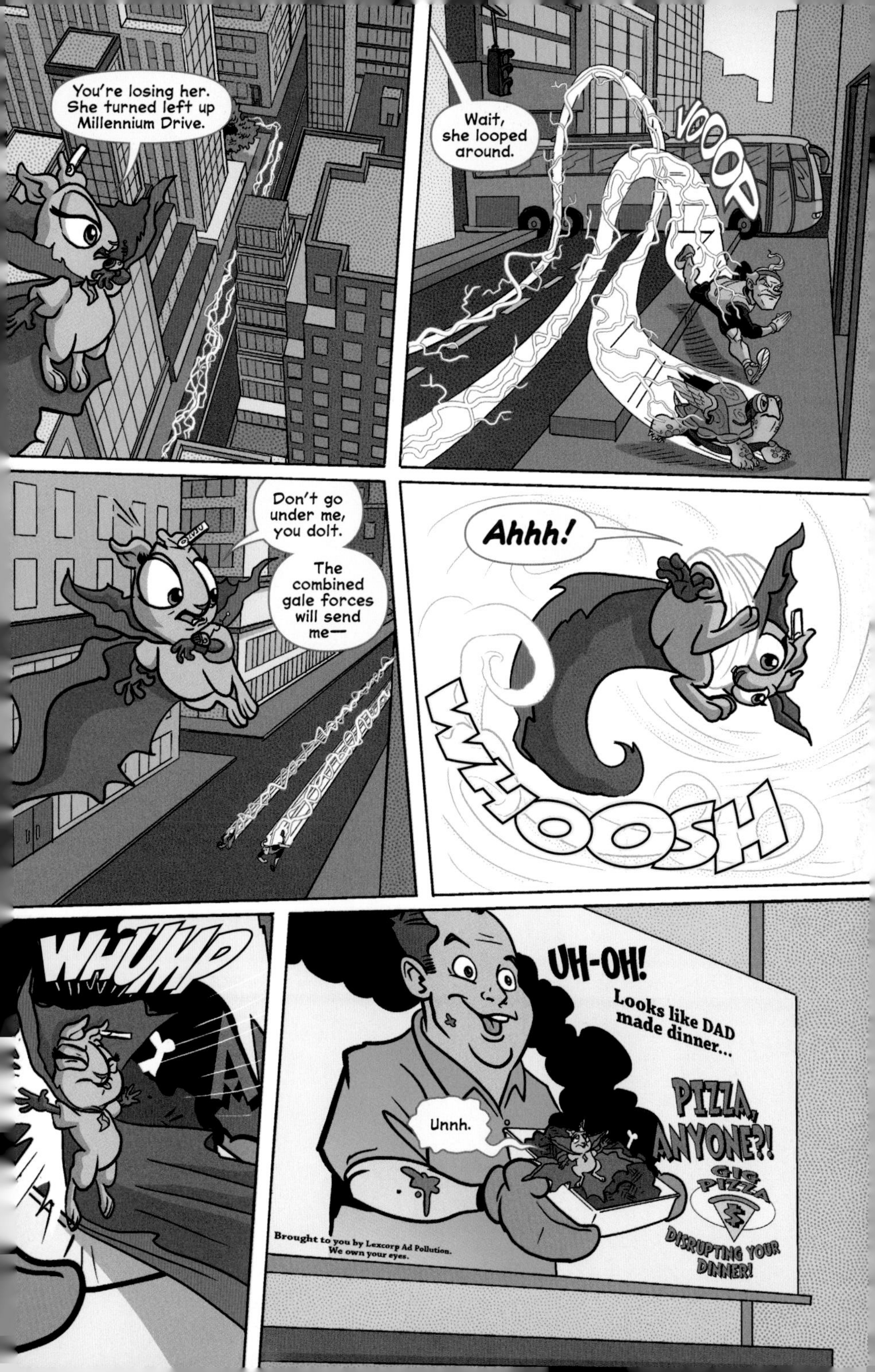
You're losing her. She turned left up Millennium Drive.
Wait, she looped around.
VOOOP
Don't go under me, you dolt.
The combined gale forces will send me—
Ahhh!
WHOOSH
WHUMP
UH-OH!
Looks like DAD made dinner...
Unnh.
PIZZA, ANYONE?!
GIG PIZZA
DISRUPTING YOUR DINNER!
Brought to you by Lexcorp Ad Pollution.
We own your eyes.

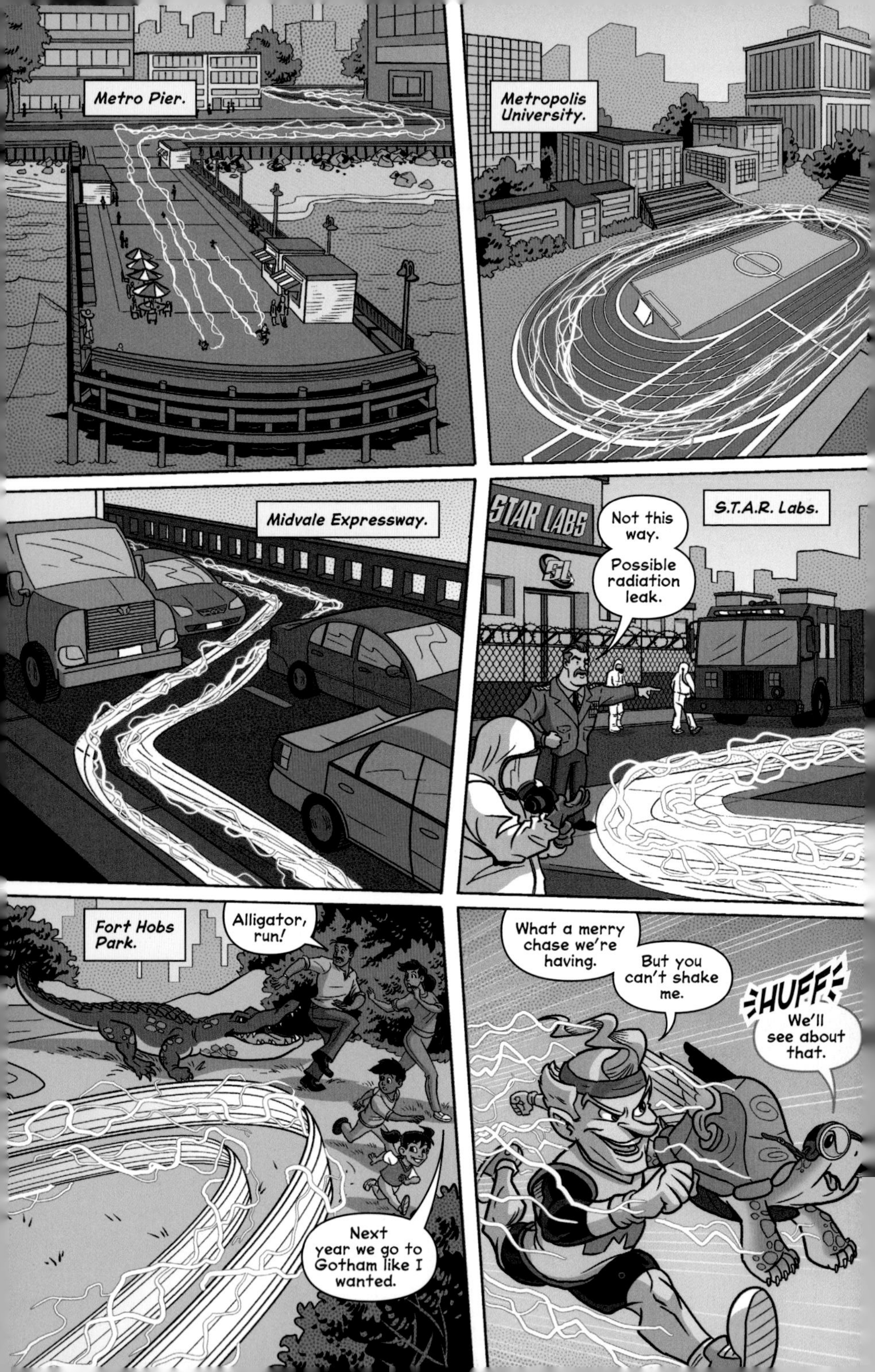
Metro Pier.
Metropolis University.
Midvale Expressway.
S.T.A.R. Labs.
STAR LABS
Not this way.
Possible radiation leak.
Fort Hobs Park.
Alligator, run!
Next year we go to Gotham like I wanted.
What a merry chase we're having.
But you can't shake me.
HUFF
We'll see about that.

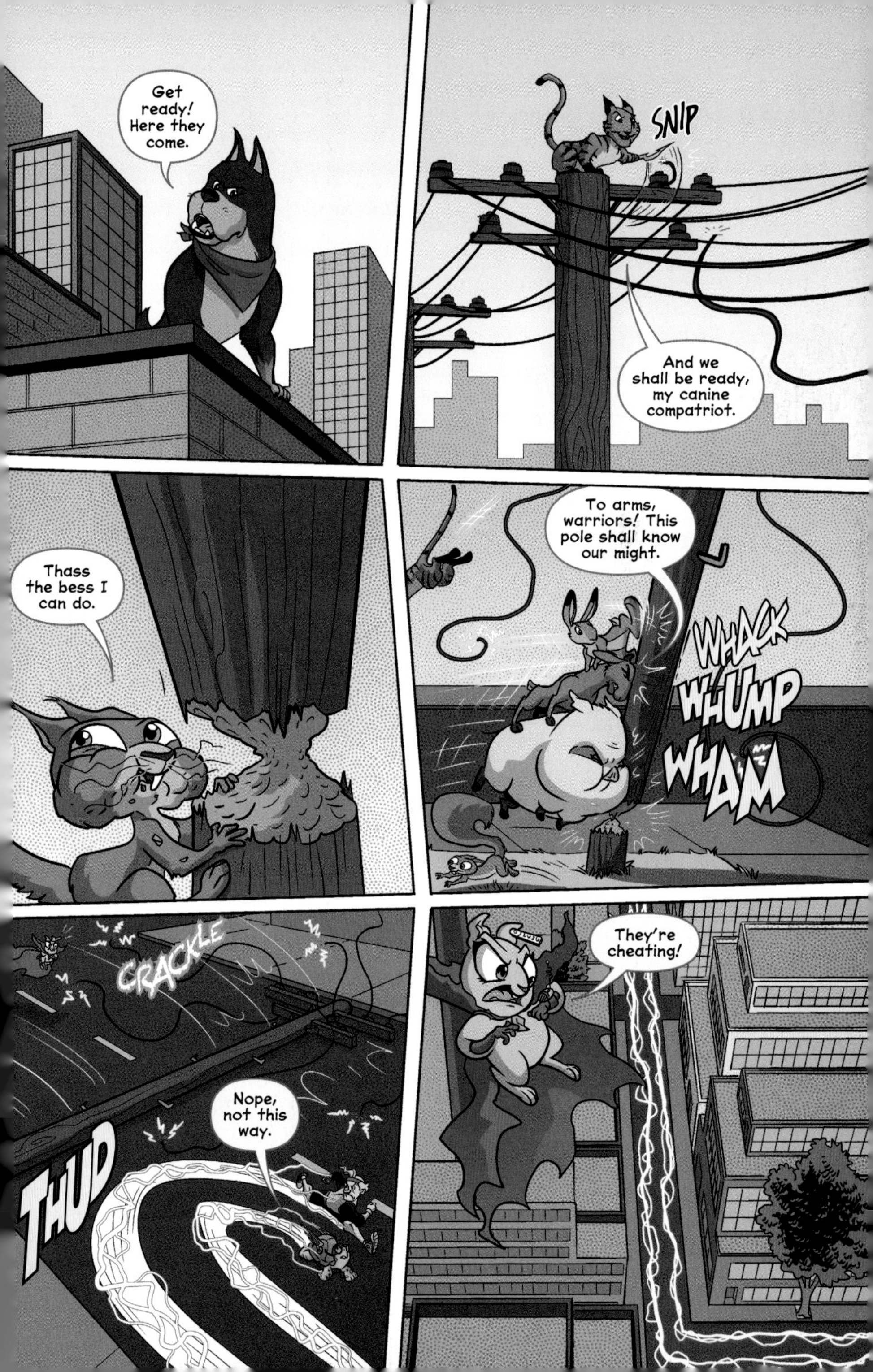
Get ready! Here they come.
SNIP
And we shall be ready, my canine compatriot.
Thass the bess I can do.
To arms, warriors! This pole shall know our might.
WHACK
WHUMP
WHAM
CRACKLE
THUD
Nope, not this way.
They're cheating!

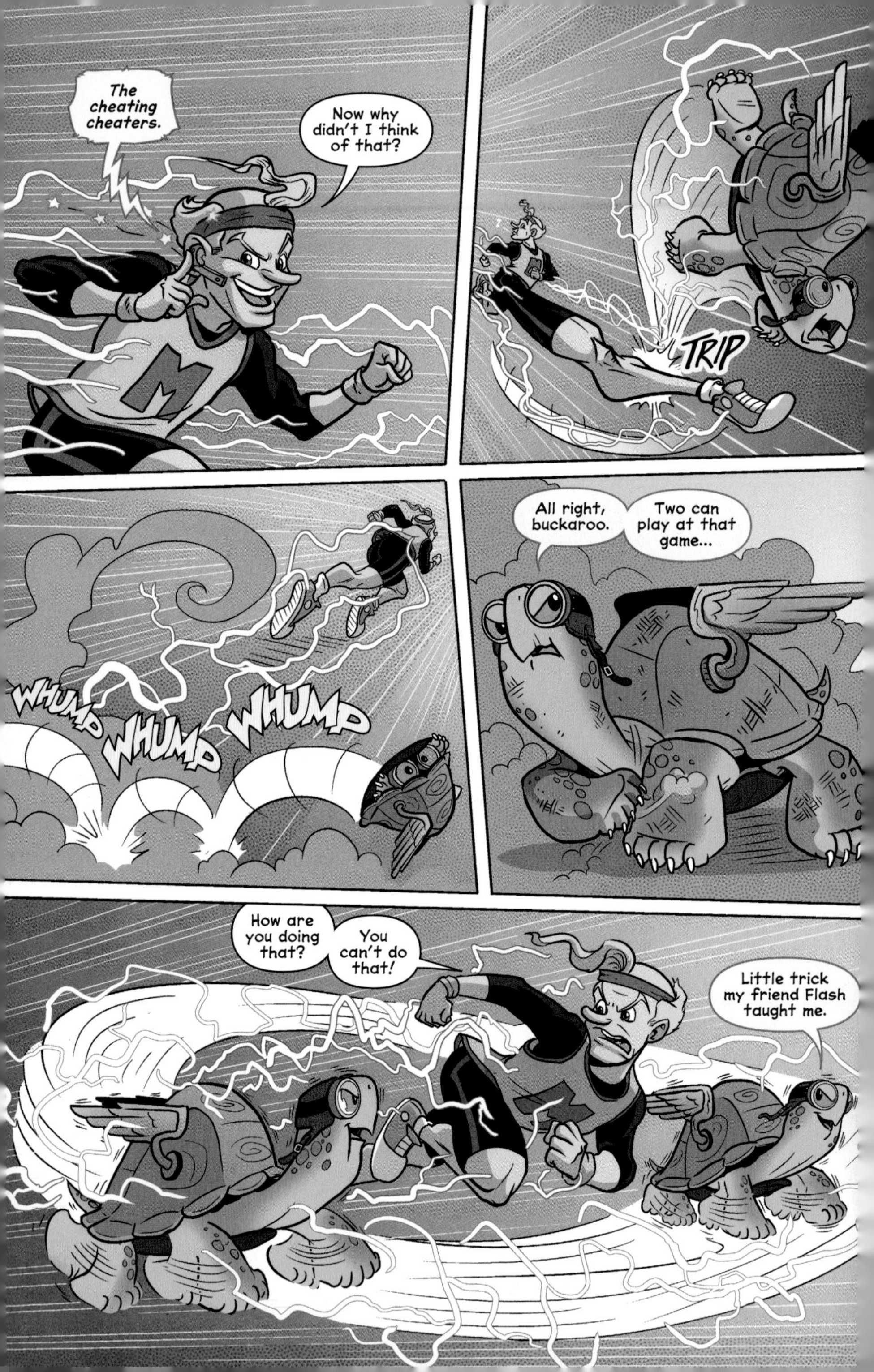
The cheating cheaters.
Now why didn't I think of that?
TRIP
WHUMP
WHUMP
WHUMP
All right, buckaroo.
Two can play at that game...
How are you doing that?
You can't do that!
Little trick my friend Flash taught me.

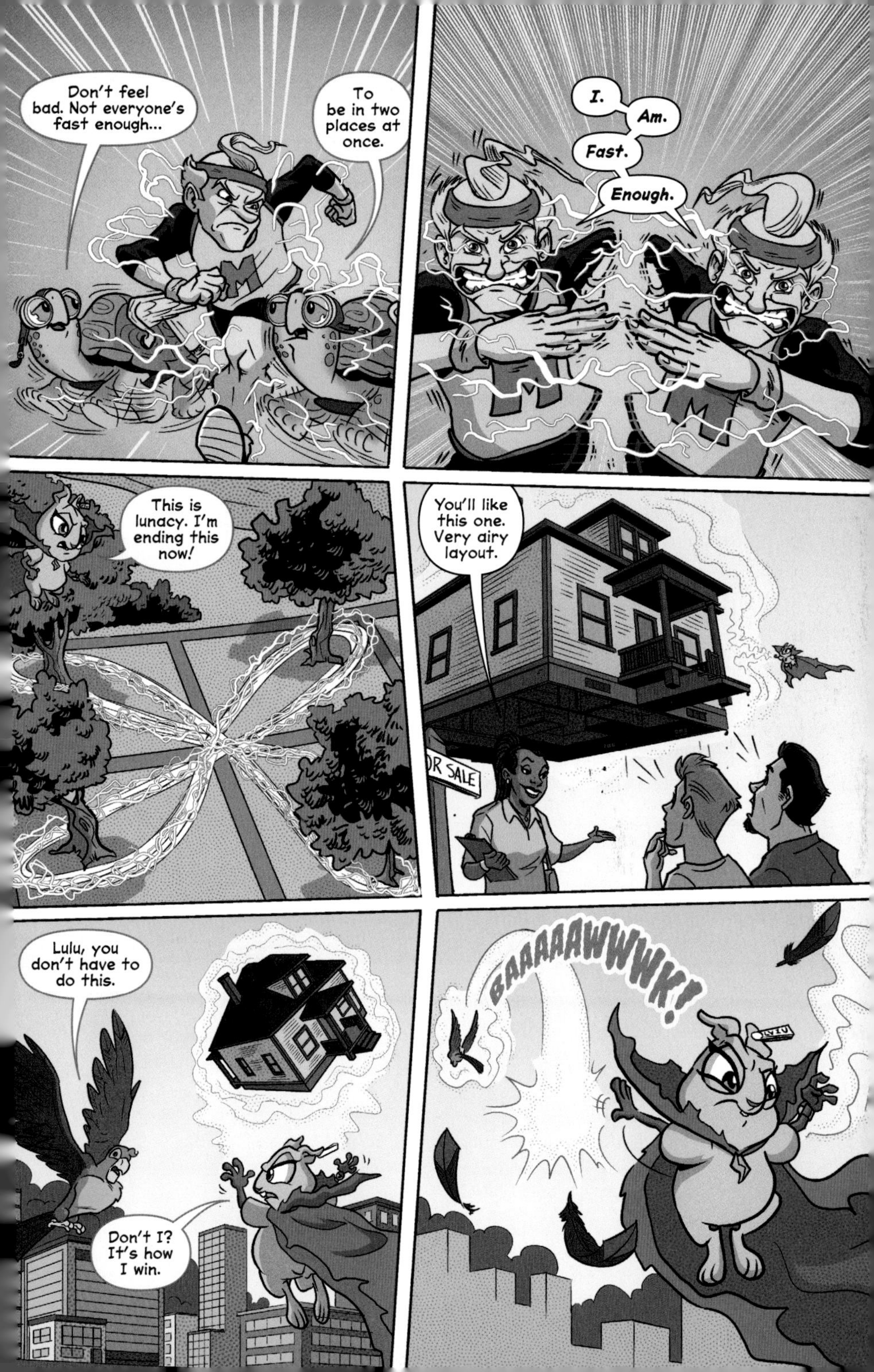

Don't feel bad. Not everyone's fast enough...
To be in two places at once.
I.
Am.
Fast.
Enough.
This is lunacy. I'm ending this now!
You'll like this one. Very airy layout.
OR SALE
Lulu, you don't have to do this.
Don't I? It's how I win.
BAAAAAWWWK!
LULU

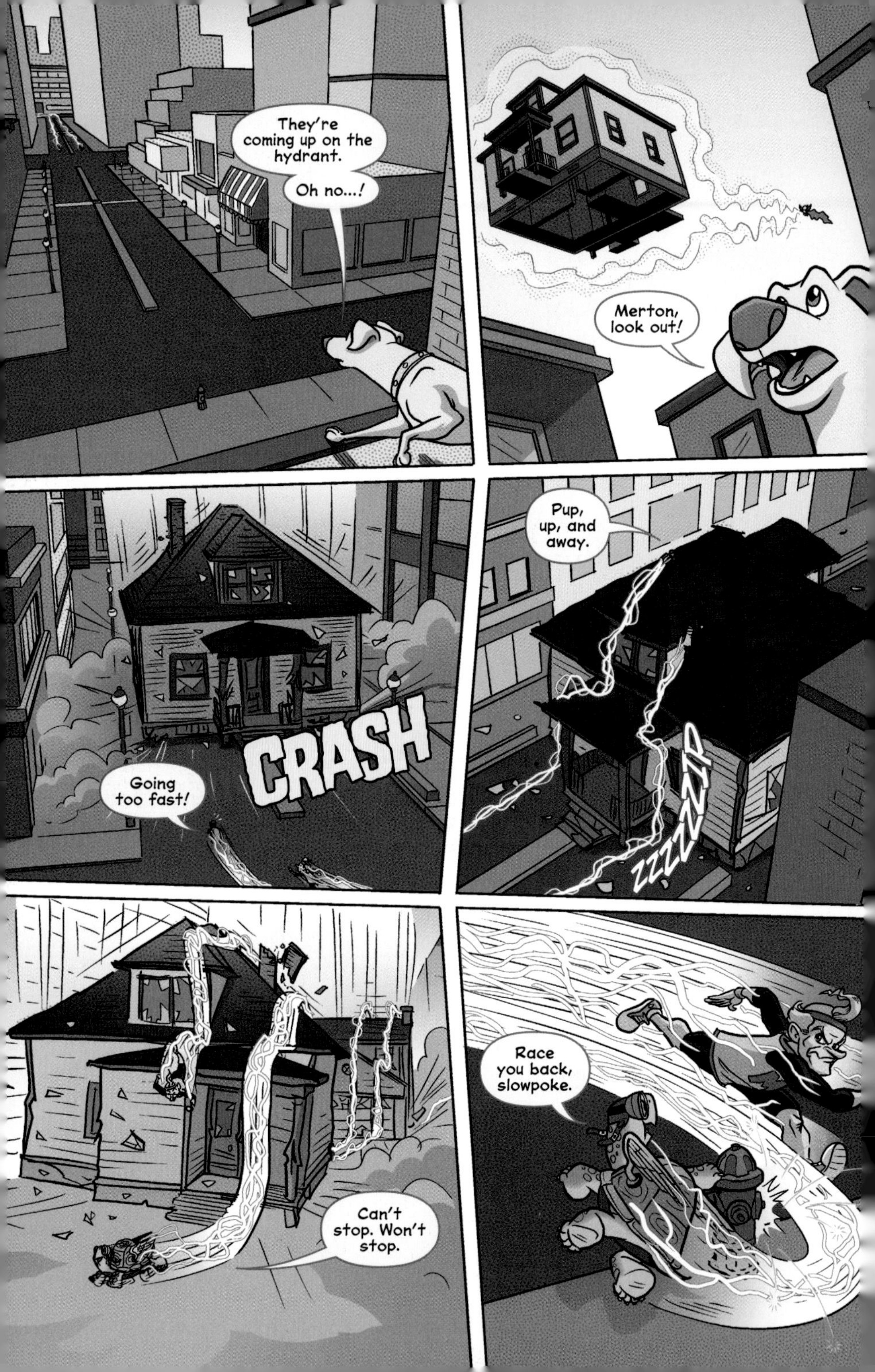
They're coming up on the hydrant.
Oh no...!
Merton, look out!
Going too fast!
CRASH
Pup, up, and away.
ZZZZZZIP
Can't stop. Won't stop.
Race you back, slowpoke.

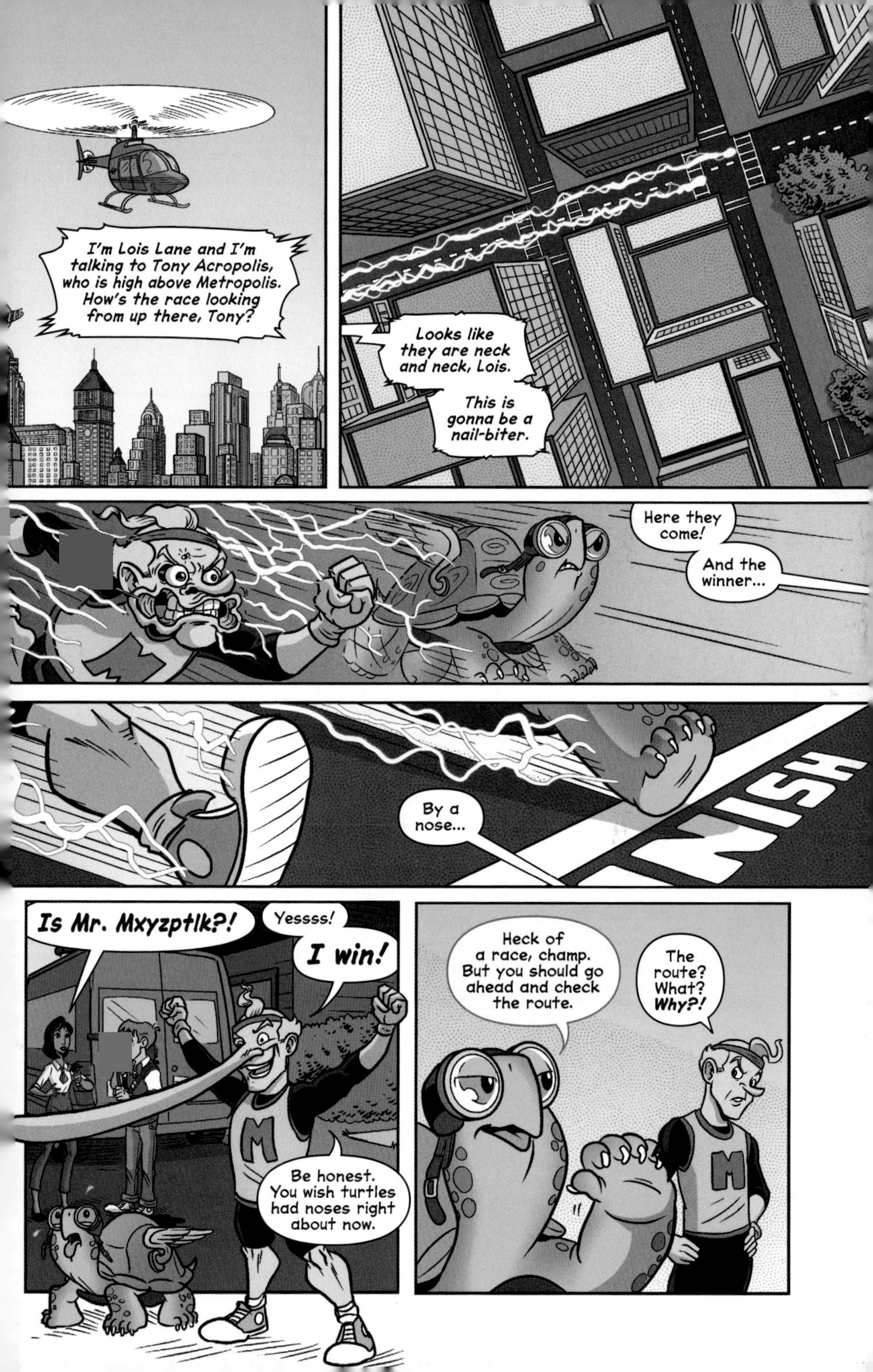
I'm Lois Lane and I'm talking to Tony Acropolis, who is high above Metropolis. How's the race looking from up there, Tony?
Looks like they are neck and neck, Lois.
This is gonna be a nail-biter.
Here they come!
And the winner...
By a nose...
NISH
Is Mr. Mxyzptlk?!
Yessss!
I win!
Be honest. You wish turtles had noses right about now.
Heck of a race, champ. But you should go ahead and check the route.
The route? What? Why?!

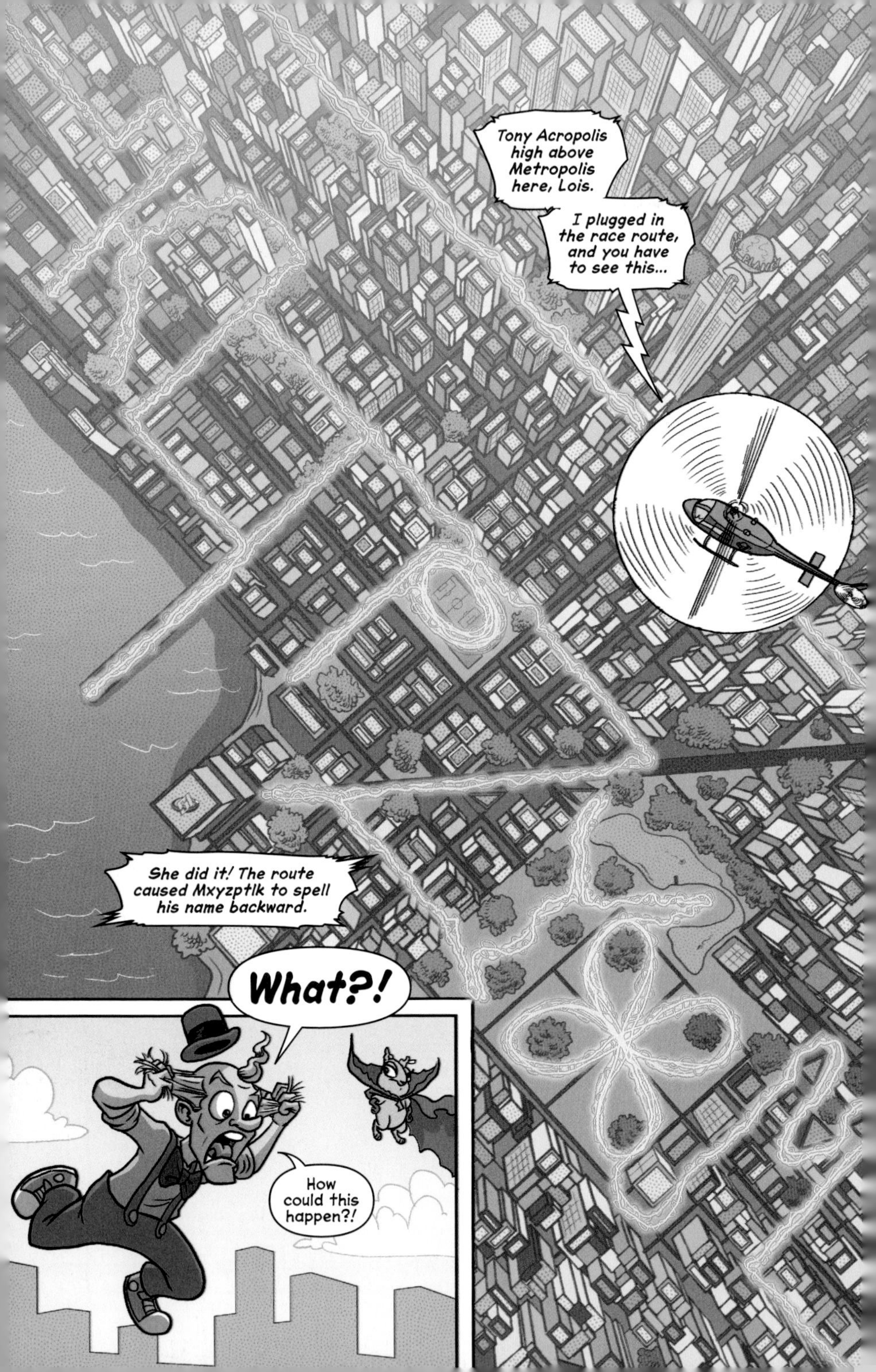
Tony Acropolis high above Metropolis here, Lois.
I plugged in the race route, and you have to see this...
She did it! The route caused Mxyzptlk to spell his name backward.
What?!
How could this happen?!

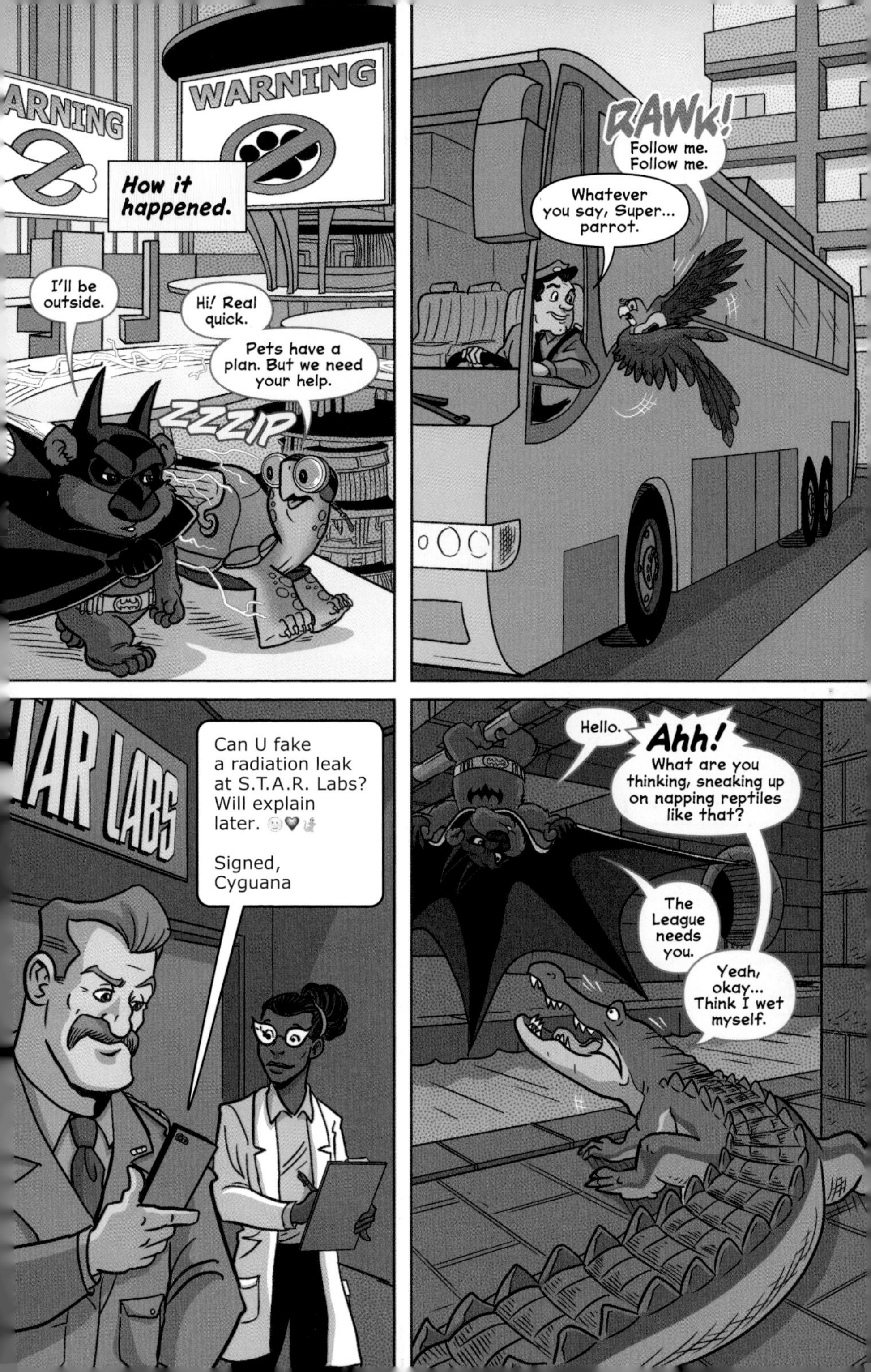
WARNING
WARNING
How it happened.
I'll be outside.
Hi! Real quick.
Pets have a plan. But we need your help.
ZZZIP
RAWK!
Follow me. Follow me.
Whatever you say, Super... parrot.
LABS
Can U fake a radiation leak at S.T.A.R. Labs? Will explain later.
Signed, Cyguana
Hello.
Ahh!
What are you thinking, sneaking up on napping reptiles like that?
The League needs you.
Yeah, okay... Think I wet myself.

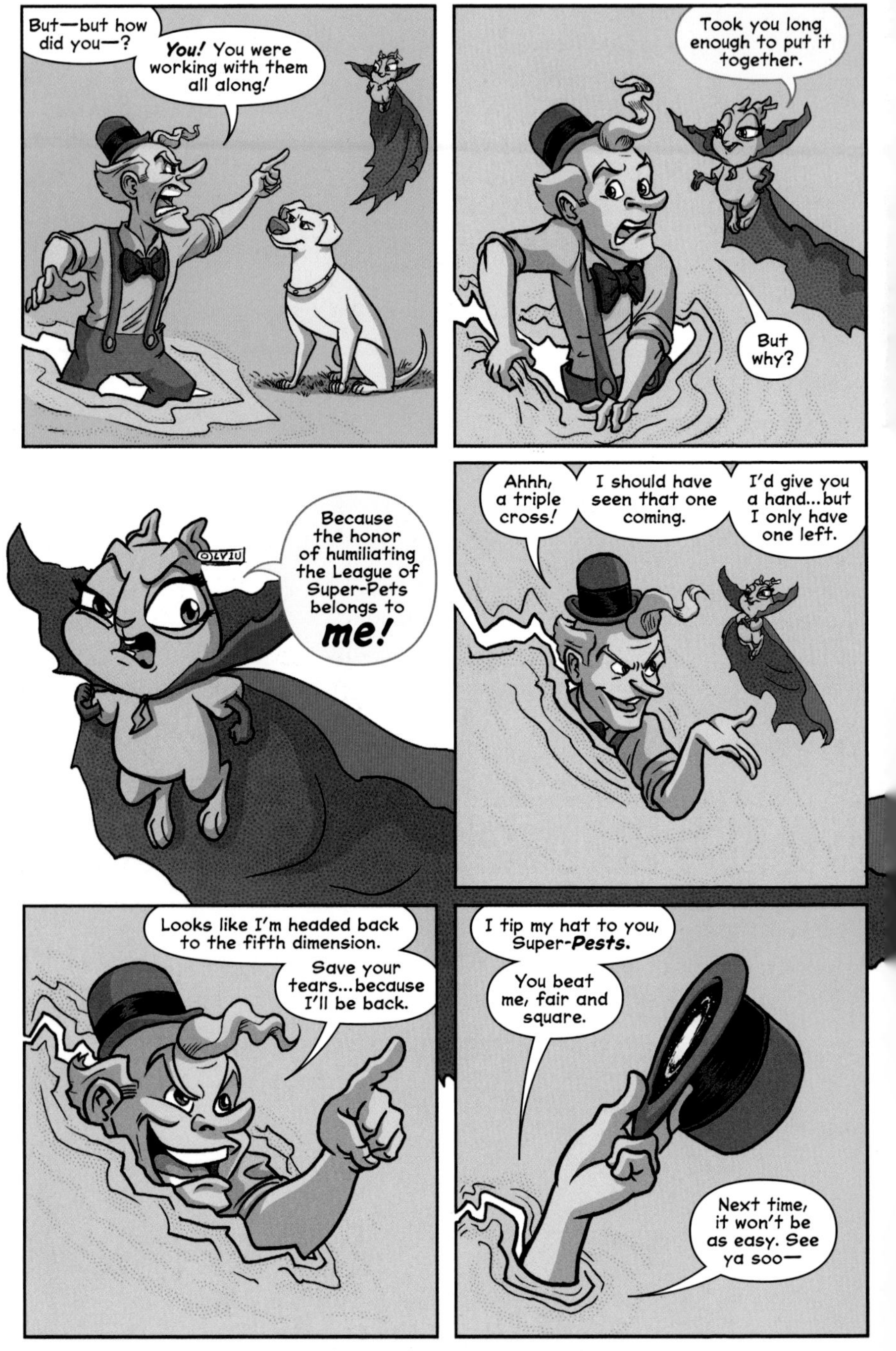

But—but how did you—?
You! You were working with them all along!
Took you long enough to put it together.
But why?
OLVIU
Because the honor of humiliating the League of Super-Pets belongs to me!
Ahhh, a triple cross!
I should have seen that one coming.
I'd give you a hand...but I only have one left.
Looks like I'm headed back to the fifth dimension.
Save your tears...because I'll be back.
I tip my hat to you, Super-Pests.
You beat me, fair and square.
Next time, it won't be as easy. See ya soo—

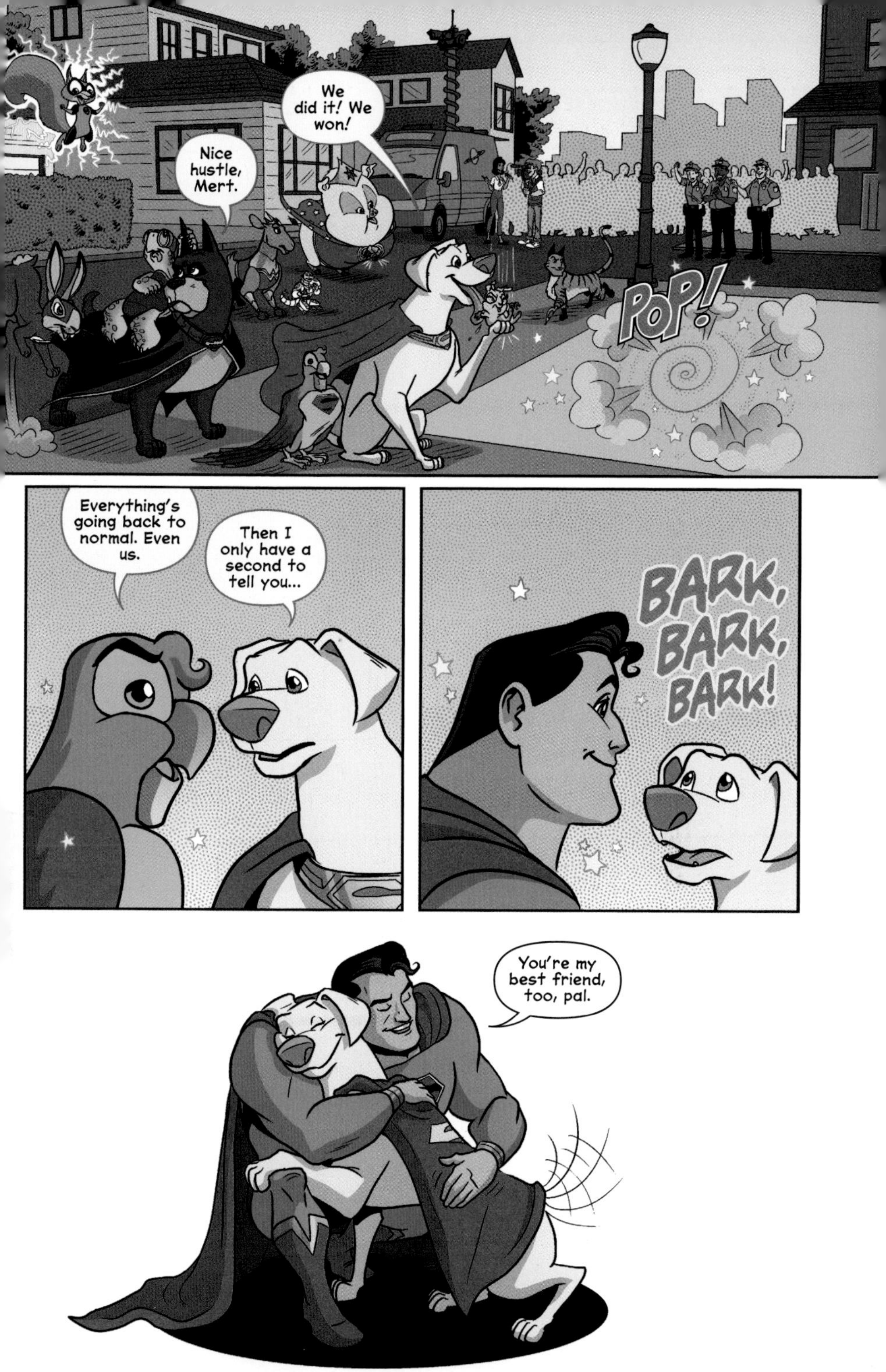
Nice hustle, Mert.
We did it! We won!
POP!
Everything's going back to normal. Even us.
Then I only have a second to tell you...
BARK, BARK, BARK!
You're my best friend, too, pal.

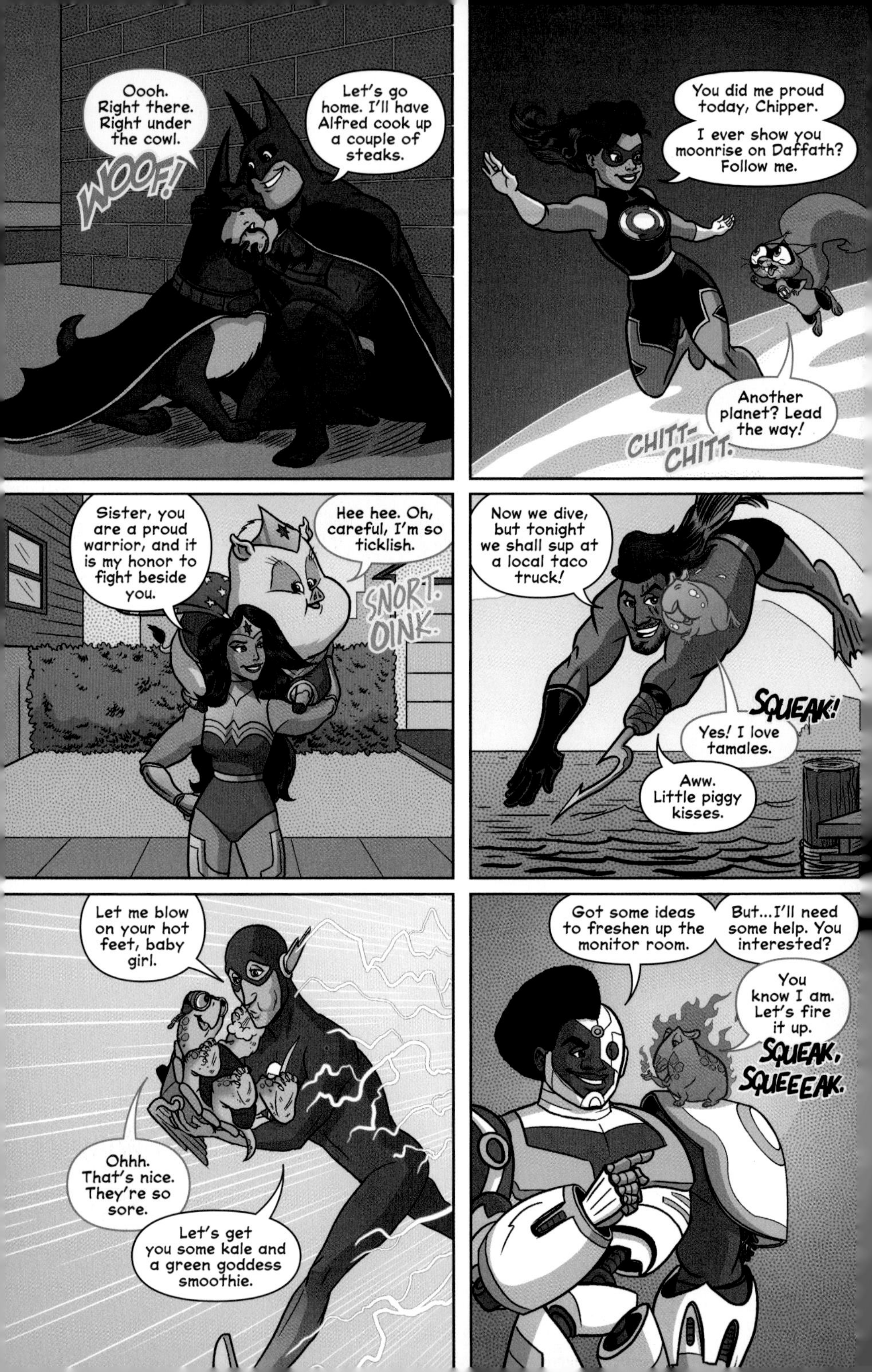
Oooh. Right there. Right under the cowl.
WOOF!
Let's go home. I'll have Alfred cook up a couple of steaks.
You did me proud today, Chipper.
I ever show you moonrise on Daffath? Follow me.
Another planet? Lead the way!
CHITT-CHITT.
Sister, you are a proud warrior, and it is my honor to fight beside you.
Hee hee. Oh, careful, I'm so ticklish.
SNORT. OINK.
Now we dive, but tonight we shall sup at a local taco truck!
SQUEAK!
Yes! I love tamales.
Aww. Little piggy kisses.
Let me blow on your hot feet, baby girl.
Ohhh. That's nice. They're so sore.
Let's get you some kale and a green goddess smoothie.
Got some ideas to freshen up the monitor room.
But...I'll need some help. You interested?
You know I am. Let's fire it up.
SQUEAK, SQUEEEAK.

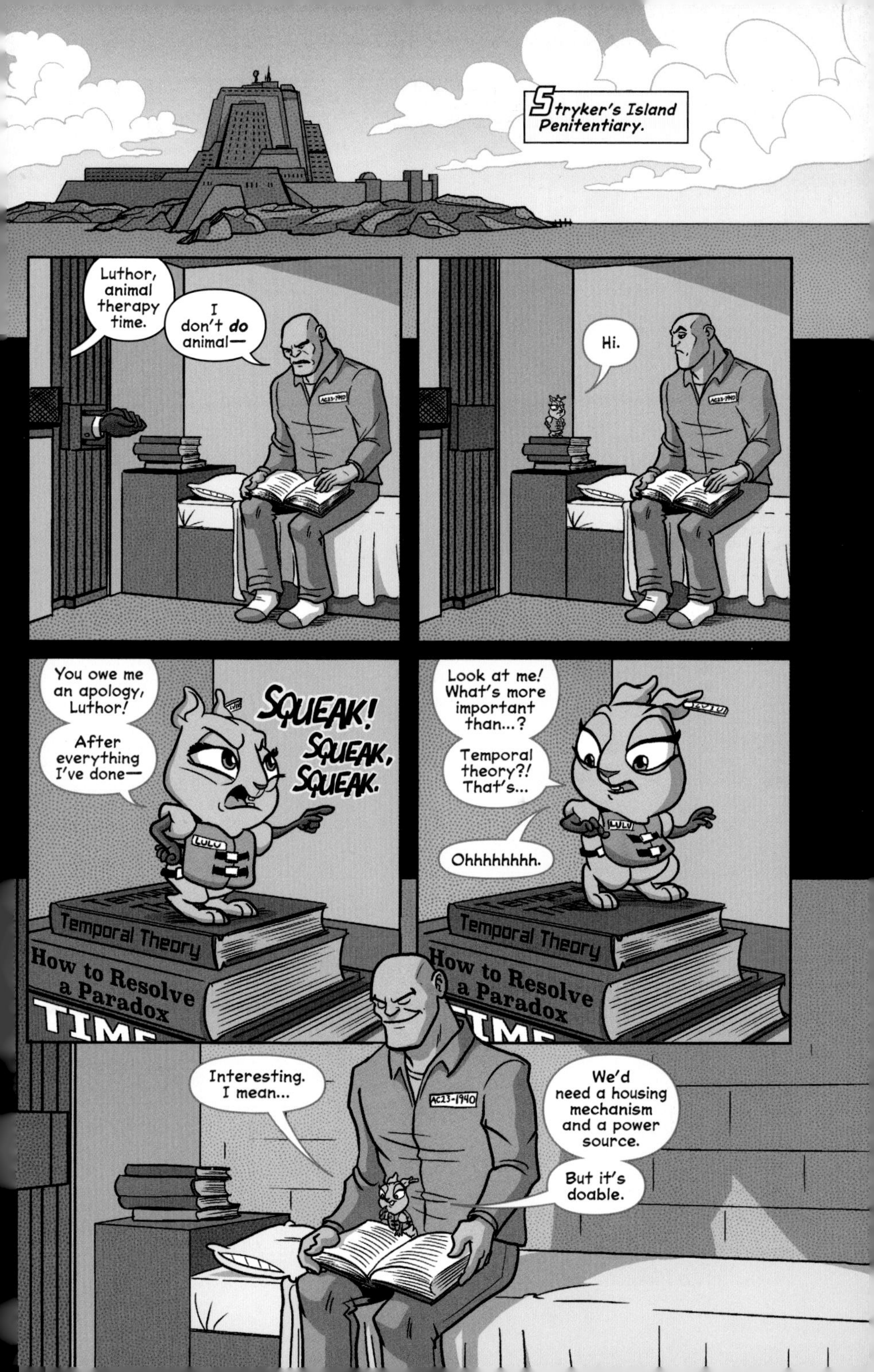
Stryker's Island Penitentiary.
Luthor, animal therapy time.
I don't *do* animal—
Hi.
You owe me an apology, Luthor!
After everything I've done—
SQUEAK! SQUEAK, SQUEAK.
LULU
Temporal Theory
How to Resolve a Paradox
Look at me! What's more important than...?
Temporal theory?! That's...
Ohhhhhhhh.
Interesting. I mean...
We'd need a housing mechanism and a power source.
But it's doable.
AC23-1940

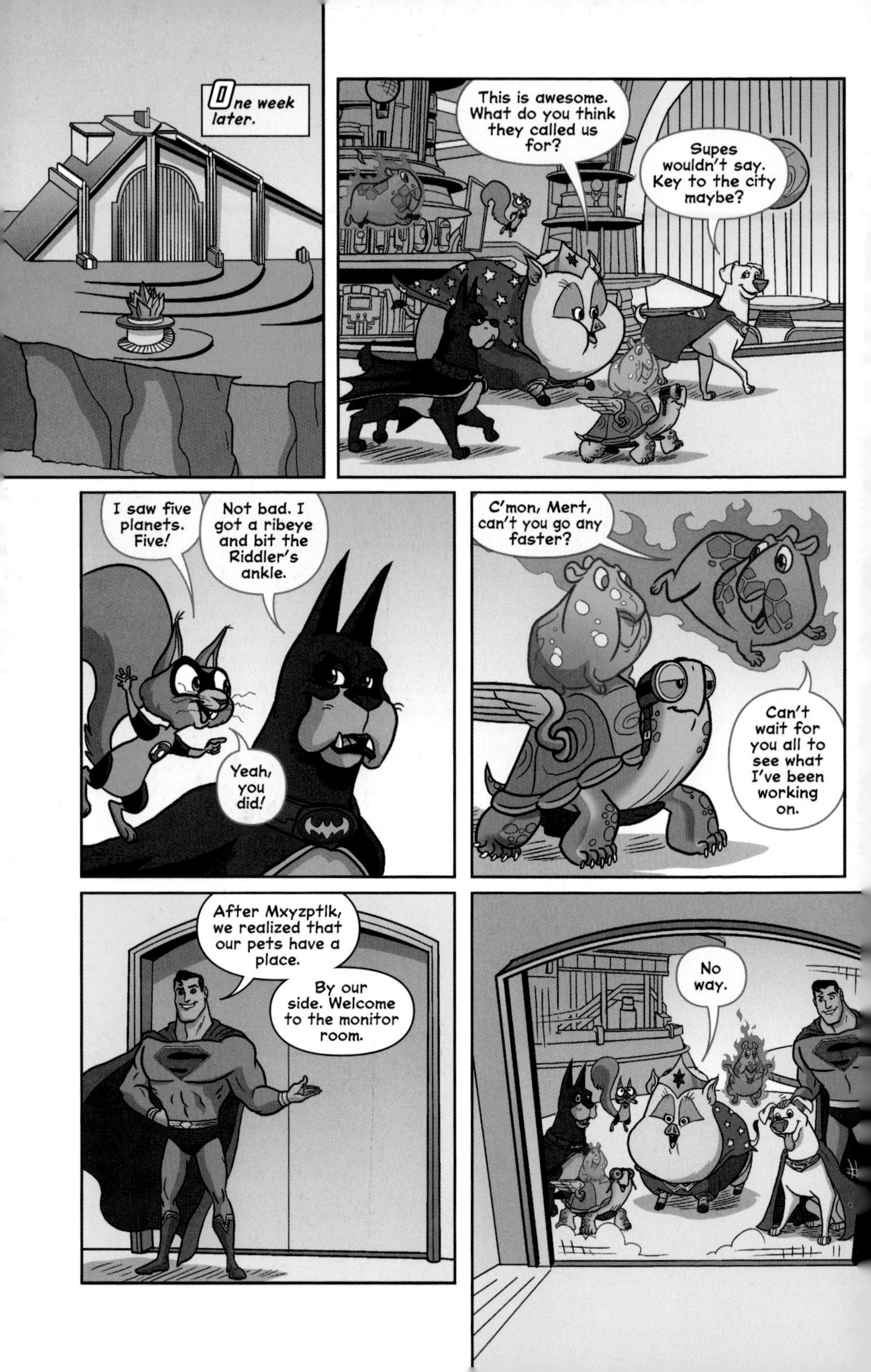
One week later.
This is awesome. What do you think they called us for?
Supes wouldn't say. Key to the city maybe?
I saw five planets. Five!
Not bad. I got a ribeye and bit the Riddler's ankle.
Yeah, you did!
C'mon, Mert, can't you go any faster?
Can't wait for you all to see what I've been working on.
After Mxyzptlk, we realized that our pets have a place.
By our side. Welcome to the monitor room.
No way.

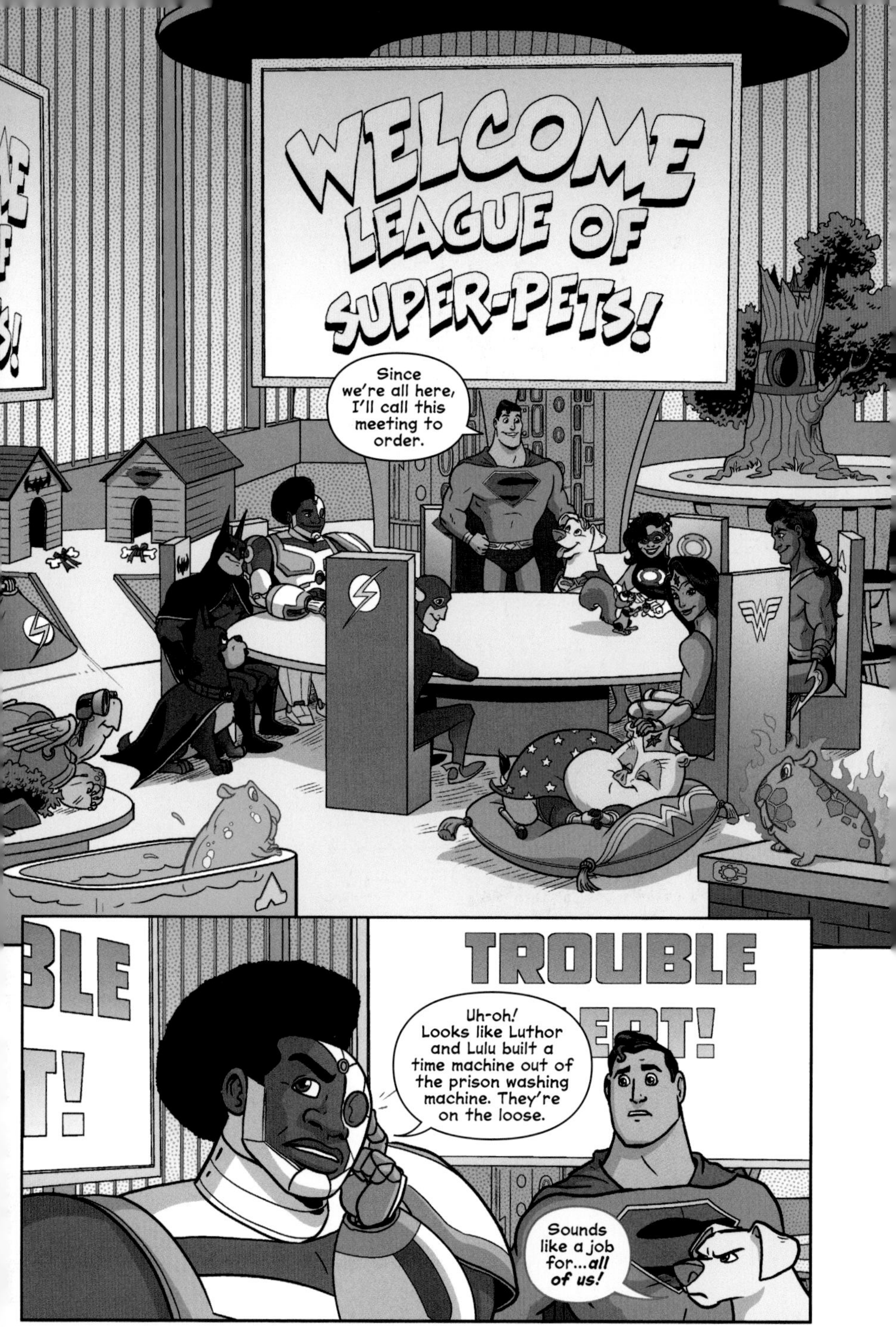
WELCOME LEAGUE OF SUPER-PETS!
Since we're all here, I'll call this meeting to order.
TROUBLE
Uh-oh! Looks like Luthor and Lulu built a time machine out of the prison washing machine. They're on the loose.
Sounds like a job for...*all of us!*

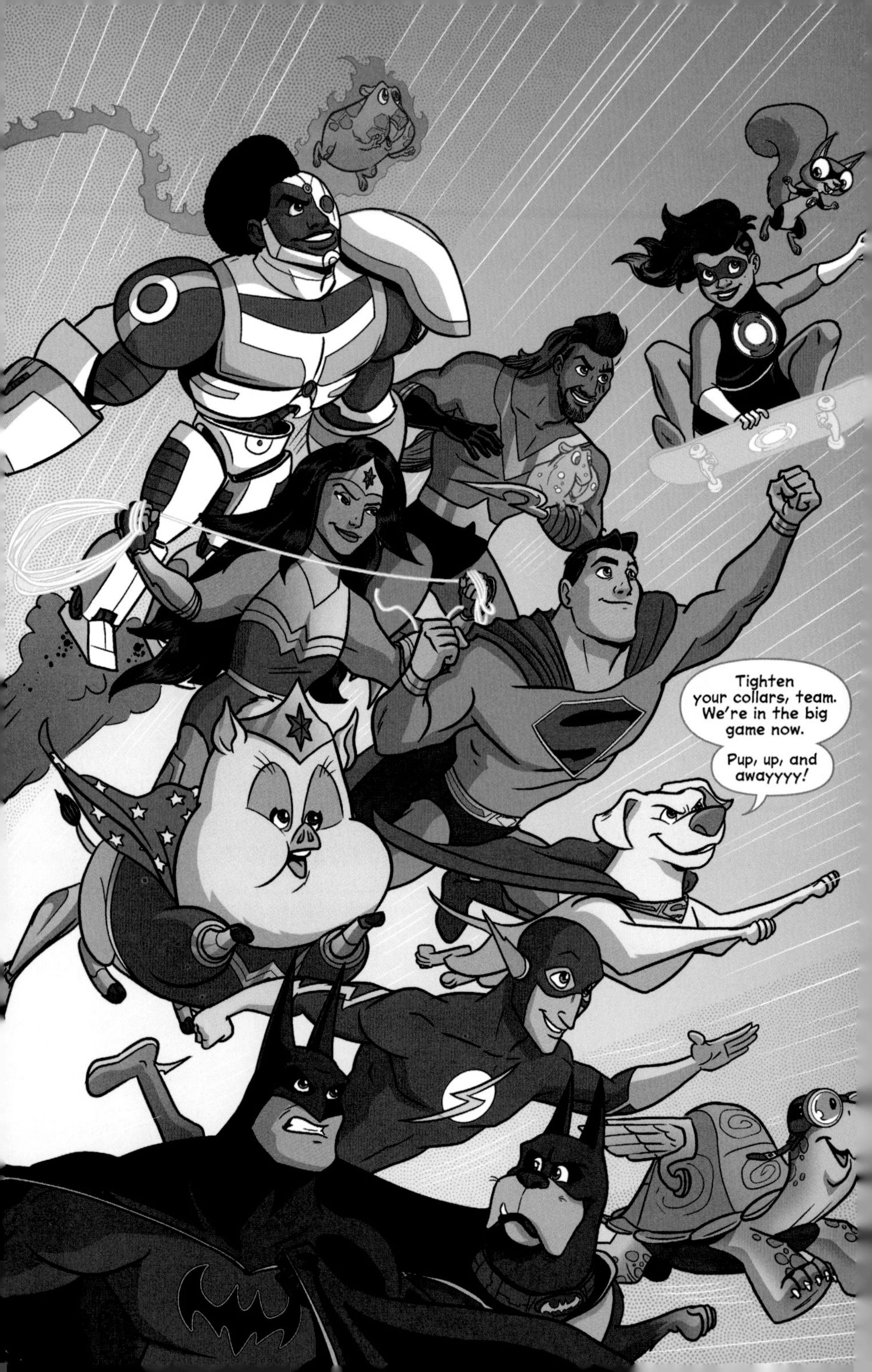
Tighten your collars, team. We're in the big game now.
Pup, up, and awayyyy!

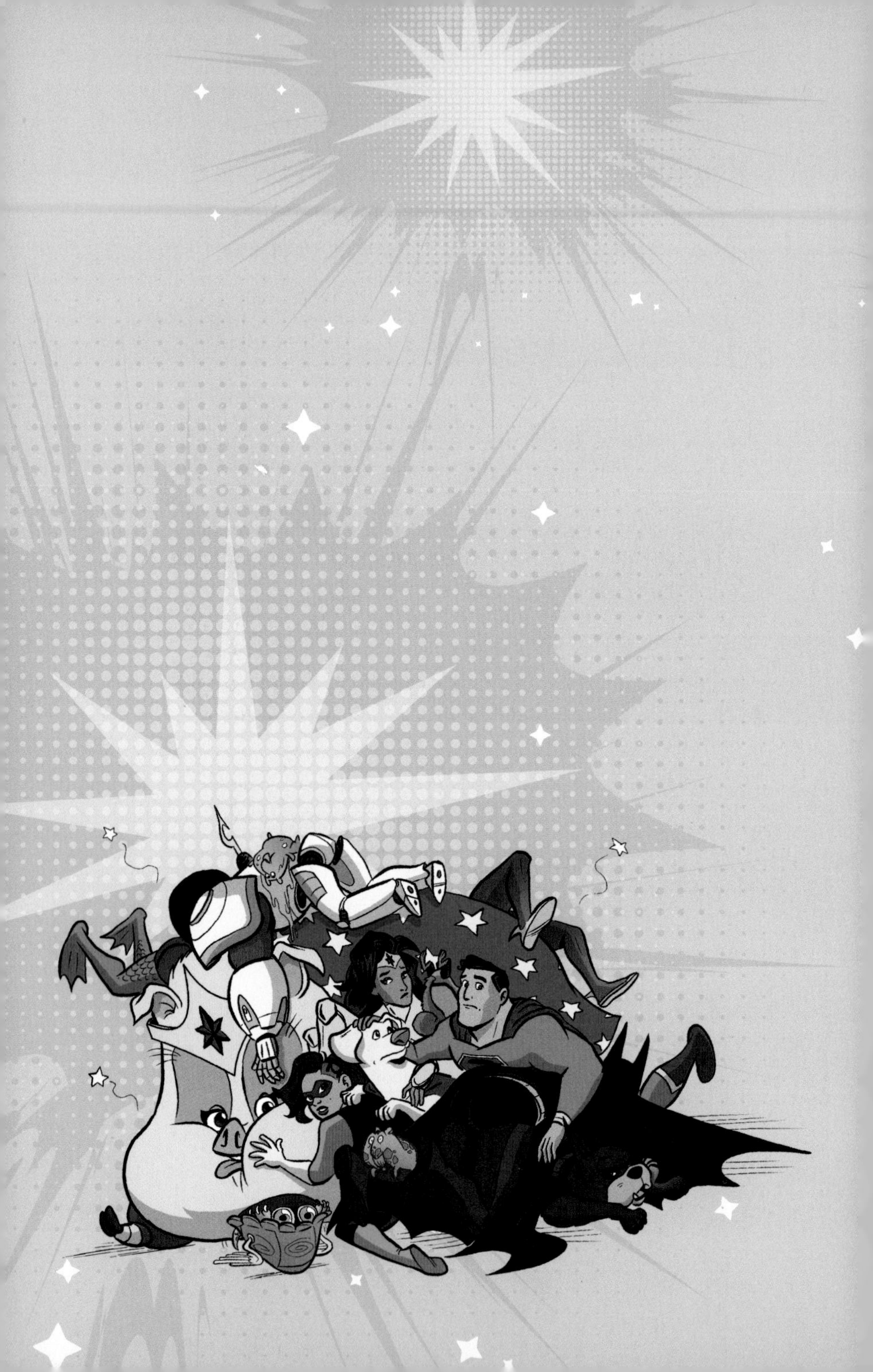

HEATH CORSON is a television writer (TNT's *Animal Kingdom*), a criminal mastermind, and an animal lover. He likes to think he has a black belt in superheroes since writing the *Bizarro* miniseries (*You am hate it!*) and *Blue and Gold*, *Detective Chimp*, and *Nightwing/Magilla Gorilla* stories for DC Comics as well as *Justice League: War*, *Batman: Assault on Arkham*, and about a dozen episodes of *Justice League Action* for Warner Bros. Animation. He would like to thank his rambunctious puppy, Moosie, for inspiring much of Krypto and Ace's behavior.

BOBBY TIMONY and his twin brother, Peter, created the multiple Harvey Award-nominated paranormal detective web series *The Night Owls* for DC Comics. Bobby has been an artist on *The Simpsons* and for Bongo Comics and was a featured artist on *The Sequels* for Fanbase Press. He is the creator of the original indie series *Goblin Hood*, and he recently illustrated a set of Disney trading cards for Topps.

Batman is a great detective, but he rarely works alone.
His sidekicks, Robin and Batgirl; his butler, Alfred; and the police of Gotham
City all play a role in helping him keep his city safe. You can too!

☑ **Look for clues!**
☑ **Analyze evidence!**
☑ **Solve riddles!**
☑ **Learn history!**

Help the Batman as he goes on his adventures and see if you can spot
the solutions to these mysteries before he logs them into his casebook.

ON SALE AUGUST 2022!

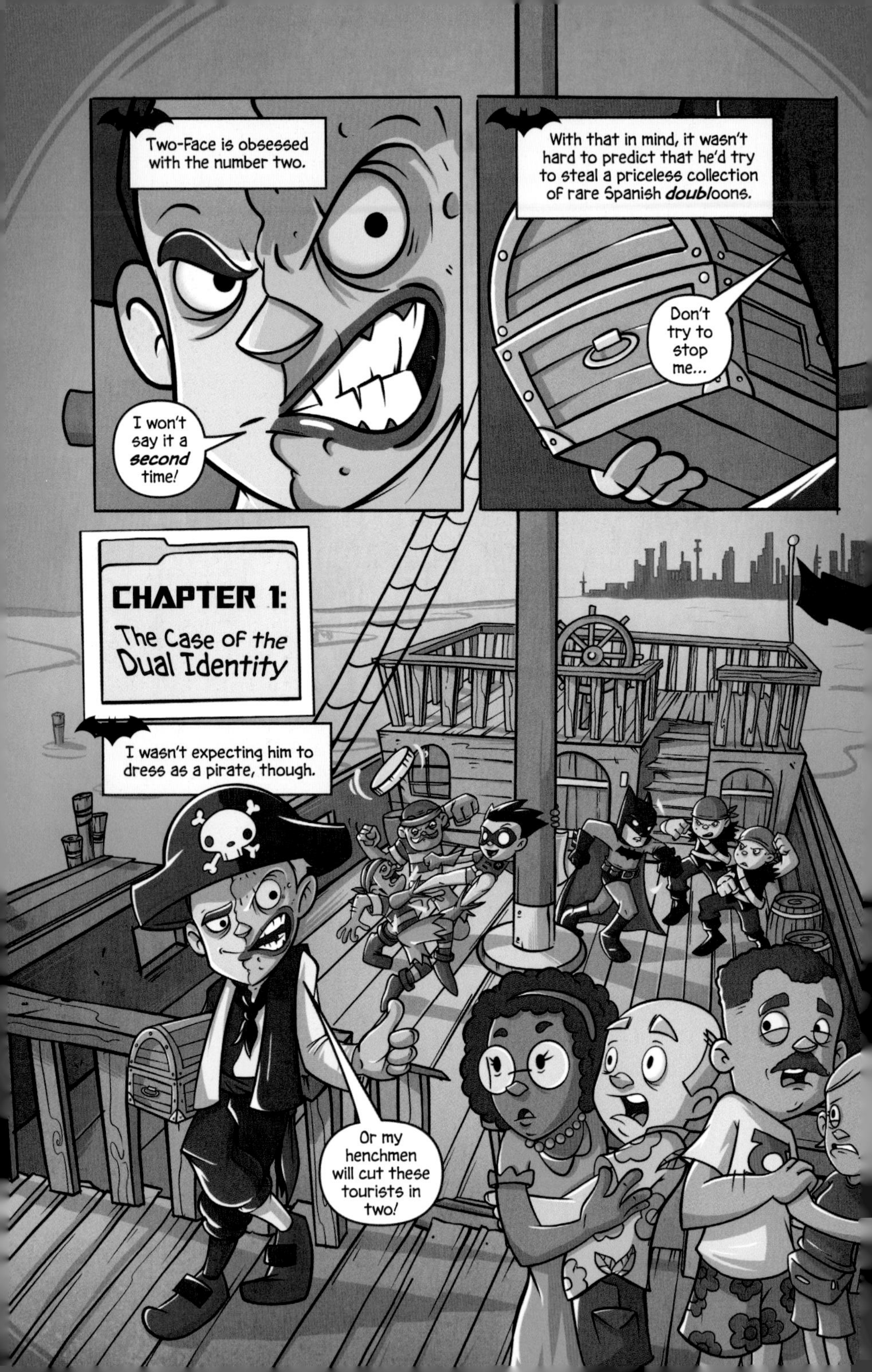
Two-Face is obsessed with the number two.
I won't say it a *second* time!
With that in mind, it wasn't hard to predict that he'd try to steal a priceless collection of rare Spanish ***doubl***oons.
Don't try to stop me...
CHAPTER 1:
The Case of the Dual Identity
I wasn't expecting him to dress as a pirate, though.
Or my henchmen will cut these tourists in two!

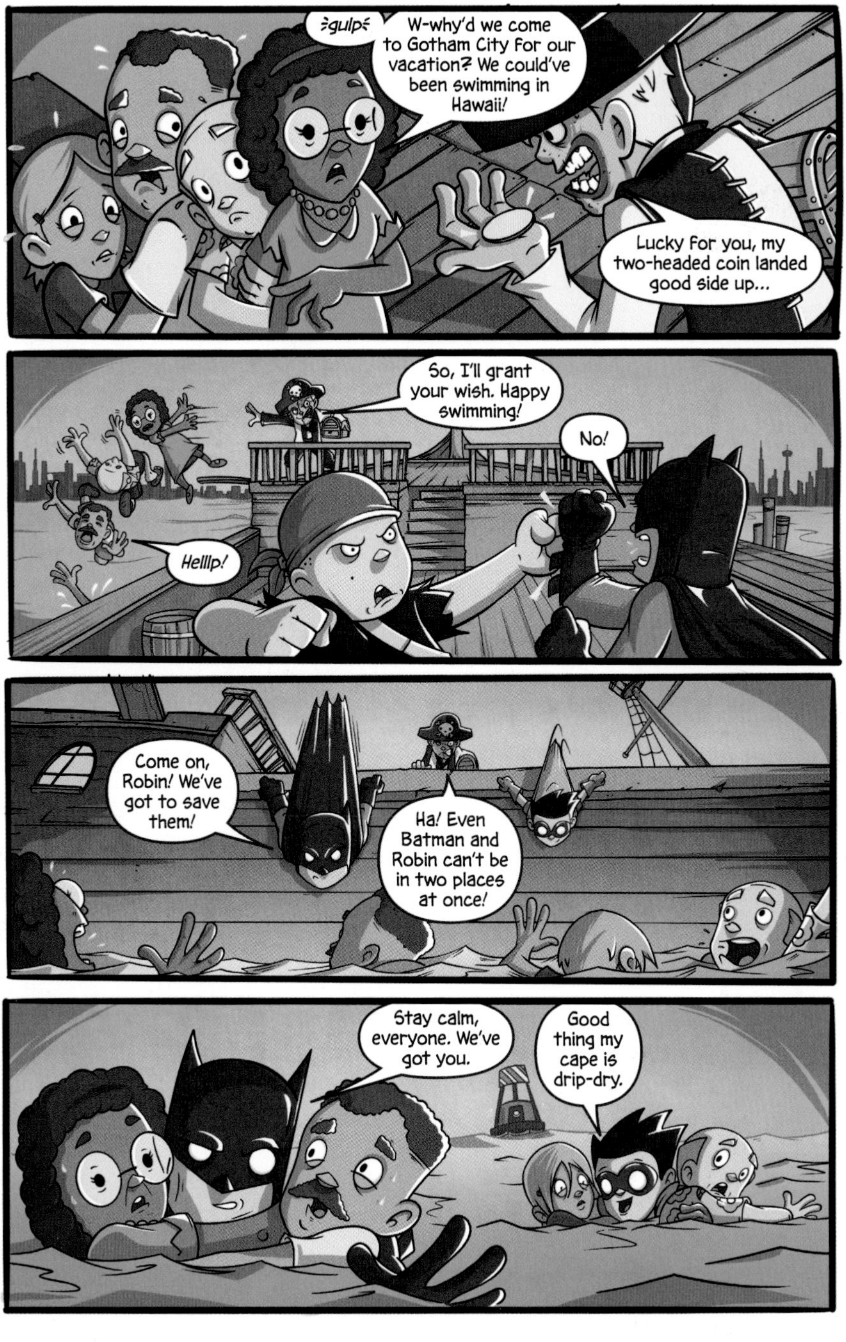
gulp
W-why'd we come to Gotham City for our vacation? We could've been swimming in Hawaii!
Lucky for you, my two-headed coin landed good side up...
So, I'll grant your wish. Happy swimming!
No!
Helllp!
Come on, Robin! We've got to save them!
Ha! Even Batman and Robin can't be in two places at once!
Stay calm, everyone. We've got you.
Good thing my cape is drip-dry.

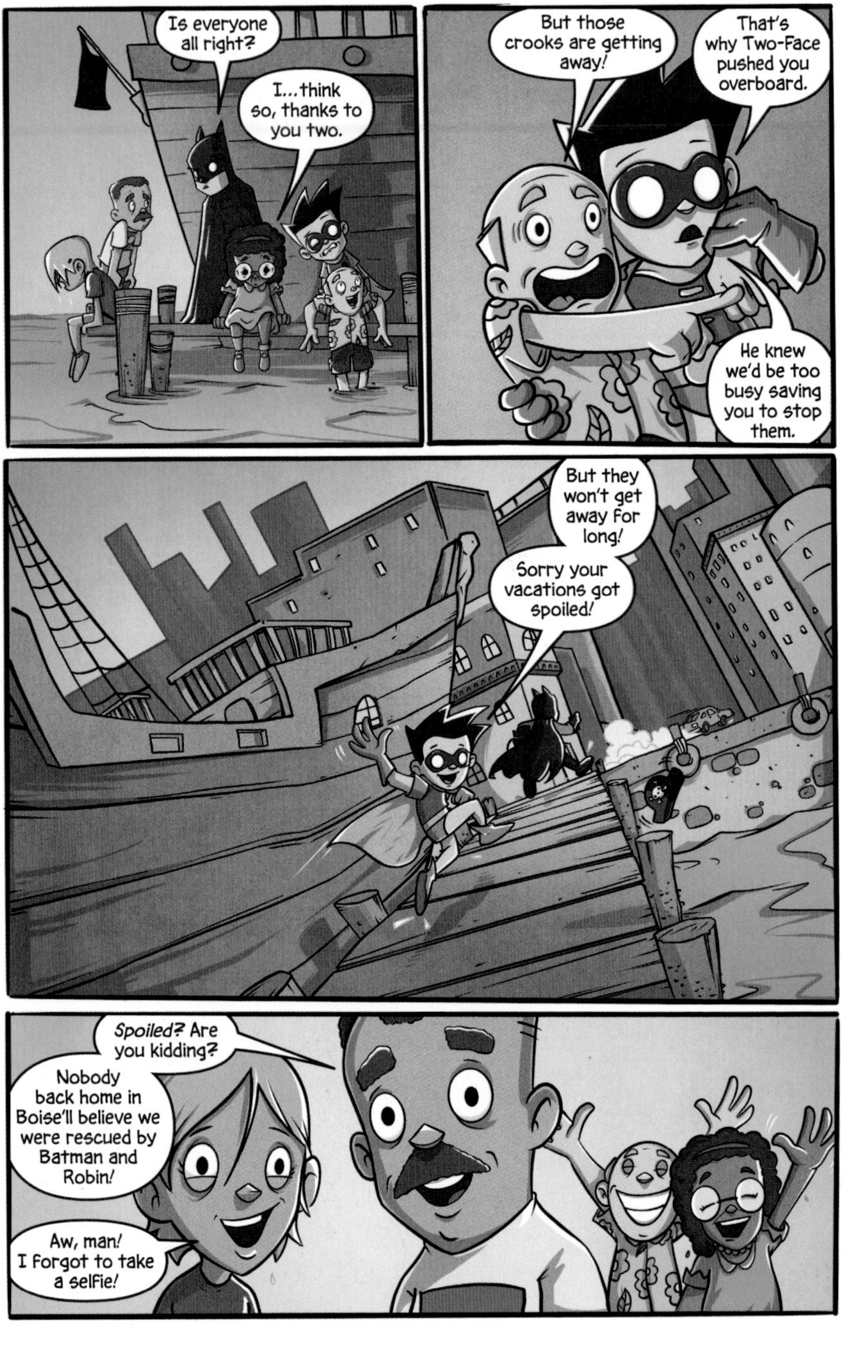
Is everyone all right?
I...think so, thanks to you two.
But those crooks are getting away!
That's why Two-Face pushed you overboard.
He knew we'd be too busy saving you to stop them.
But they won't get away for long!
Sorry your vacations got spoiled!
Spoiled? Are you kidding?
Nobody back home in Boise'll believe we were rescued by Batman and Robin!
Aw, man! I forgot to take a selfie!

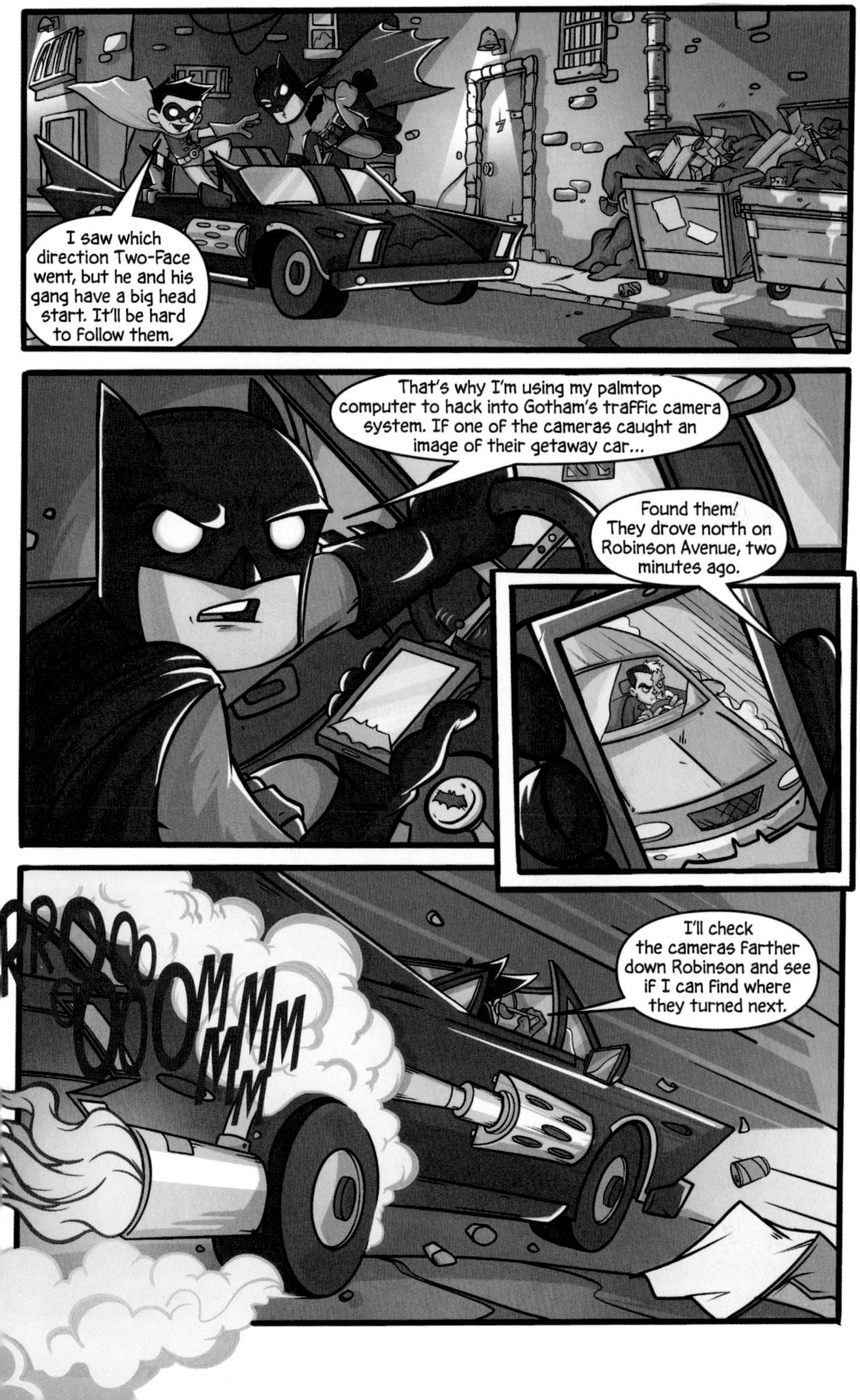
I saw which direction Two-Face went, but he and his gang have a big head start. It'll be hard to follow them.
That's why I'm using my palmtop computer to hack into Gotham's traffic camera system. If one of the cameras caught an image of their getaway car...
Found them! They drove north on Robinson Avenue, two minutes ago.
I'll check the cameras farther down Robinson and see if I can find where they turned next.

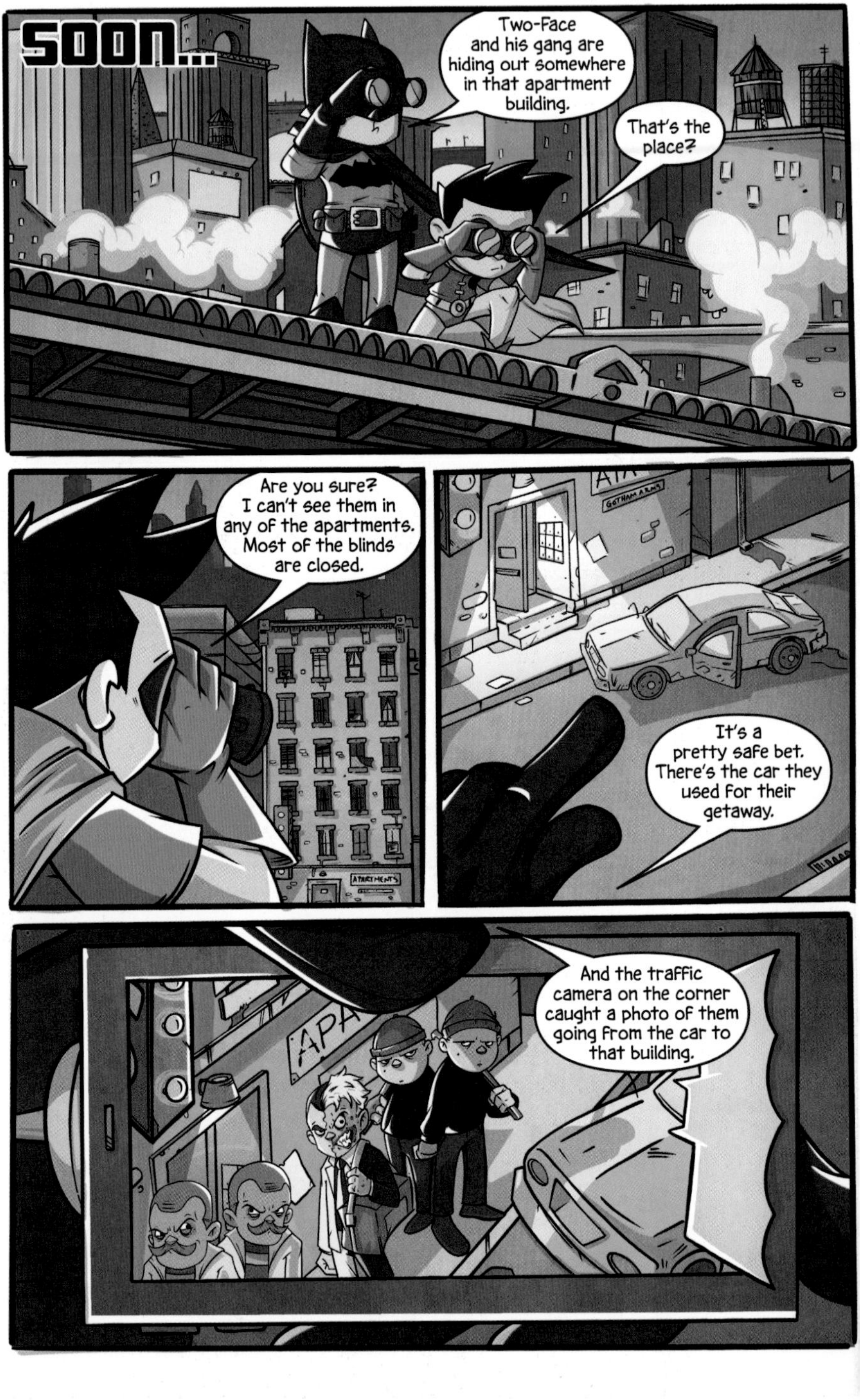
SOON...
Two-Face and his gang are hiding out somewhere in that apartment building.
That's the place?
Are you sure? I can't see them in any of the apartments. Most of the blinds are closed.
APARTMENTS
GOTHAM ARMS
It's a pretty safe bet. There's the car they used for their getaway.
And the traffic camera on the corner caught a photo of them going from the car to that building.
APA

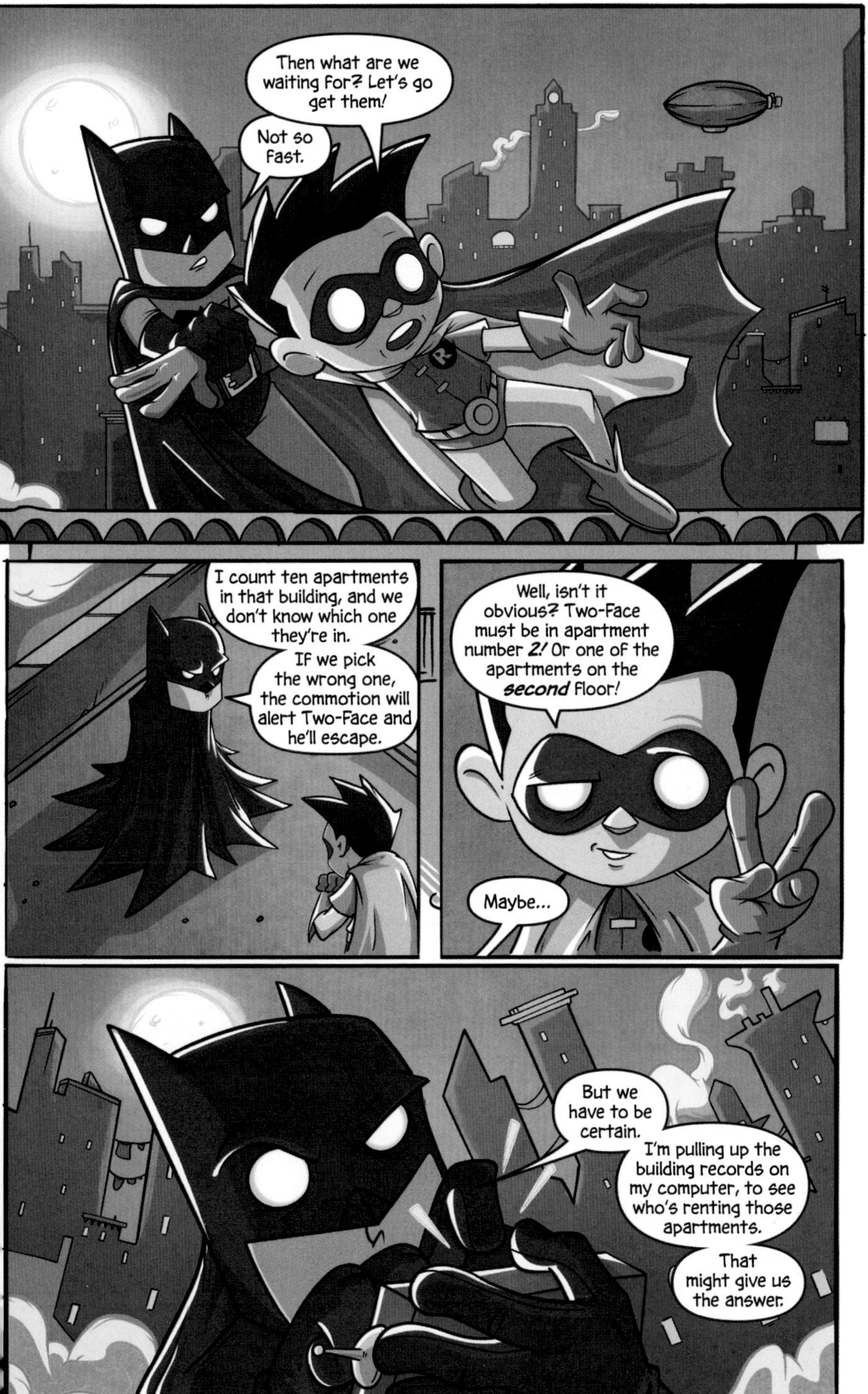
Then what are we waiting for? Let's go get them!
Not so fast.
I count ten apartments in that building, and we don't know which one they're in.
If we pick the wrong one, the commotion will alert Two-Face and he'll escape.
Well, isn't it obvious? Two-Face must be in apartment number 2! Or one of the apartments on the second floor!
Maybe...
But we have to be certain.
I'm pulling up the building records on my computer, to see who's renting those apartments.
That might give us the answer.

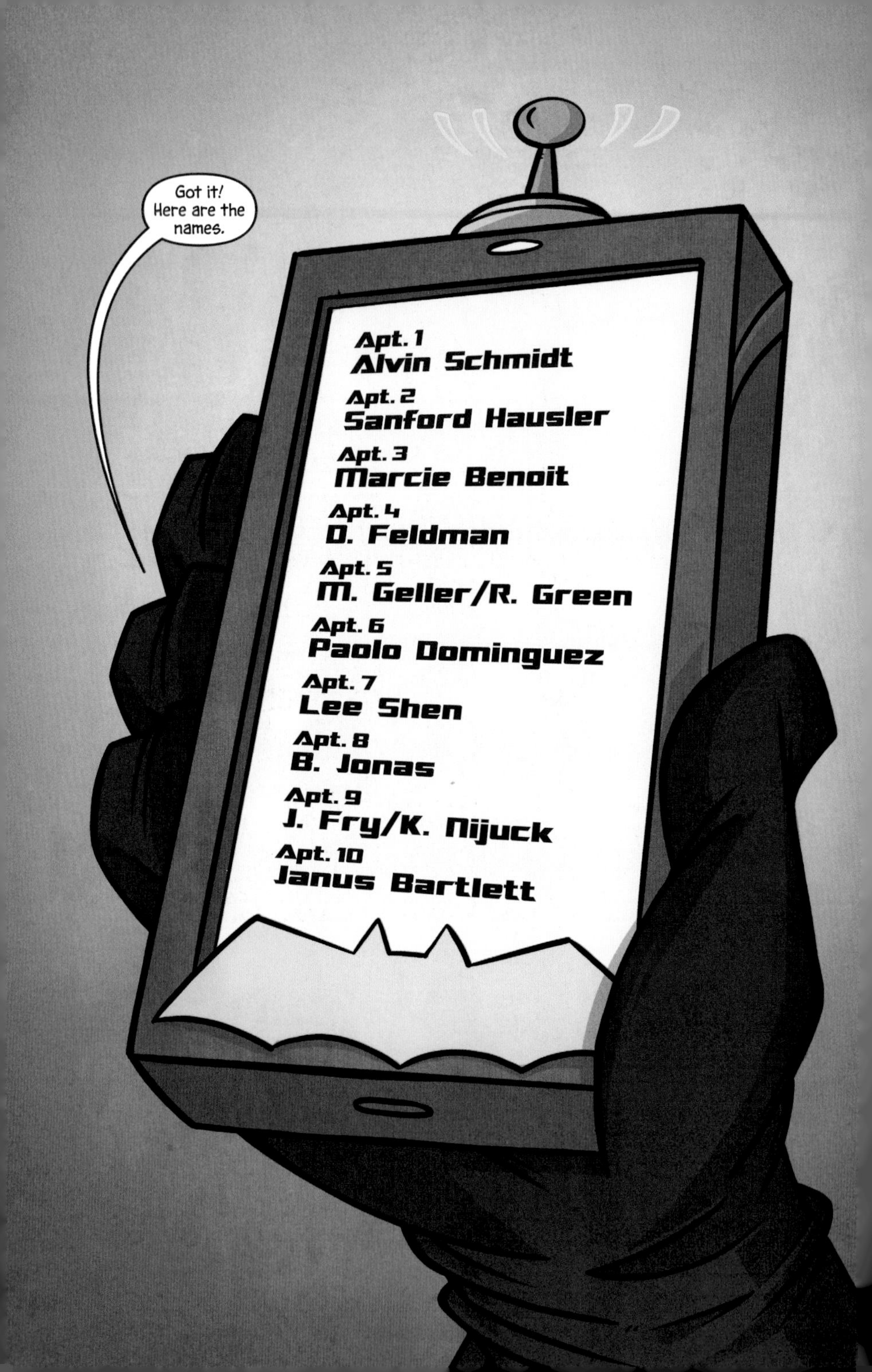
Got it! Here are the names.
Apt. 1
Alvin Schmidt
Apt. 2
Sanford Hausler
Apt. 3
Marcie Benoit
Apt. 4
D. Feldman
Apt. 5
M. Geller/R. Green
Apt. 6
Paolo Dominguez
Apt. 7
Lee Shen
Apt. 8
B. Jonas
Apt. 9
J. Fry/K. Nijuck
Apt. 10
Janus Bartlett

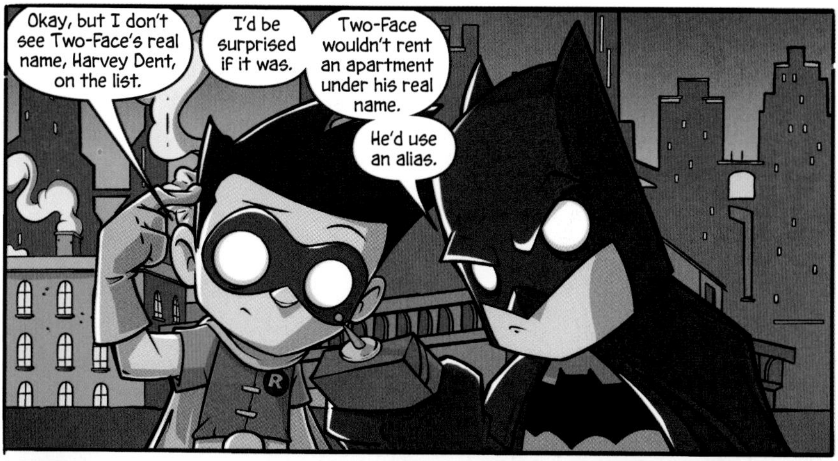
Okay, but I don't see Two-Face's real name, Harvey Dent, on the list.
I'd be surprised if it was.
Two-Face wouldn't rent an apartment under his real name.
He'd use an alias.

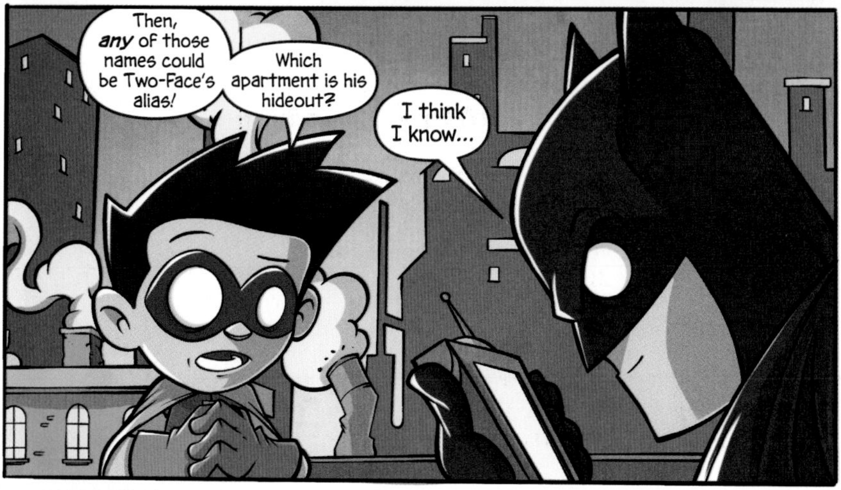
Then, *any* of those names could be Two-Face's alias!
Which apartment is his hideout?
I think I know...

STOP!

Do you know which apartment is Two-Face's hideout? Take another look at the clues and try to figure it out.

Think you have the answer? Find out in the ***Batman's Mystery Casebook*** original graphic novel!

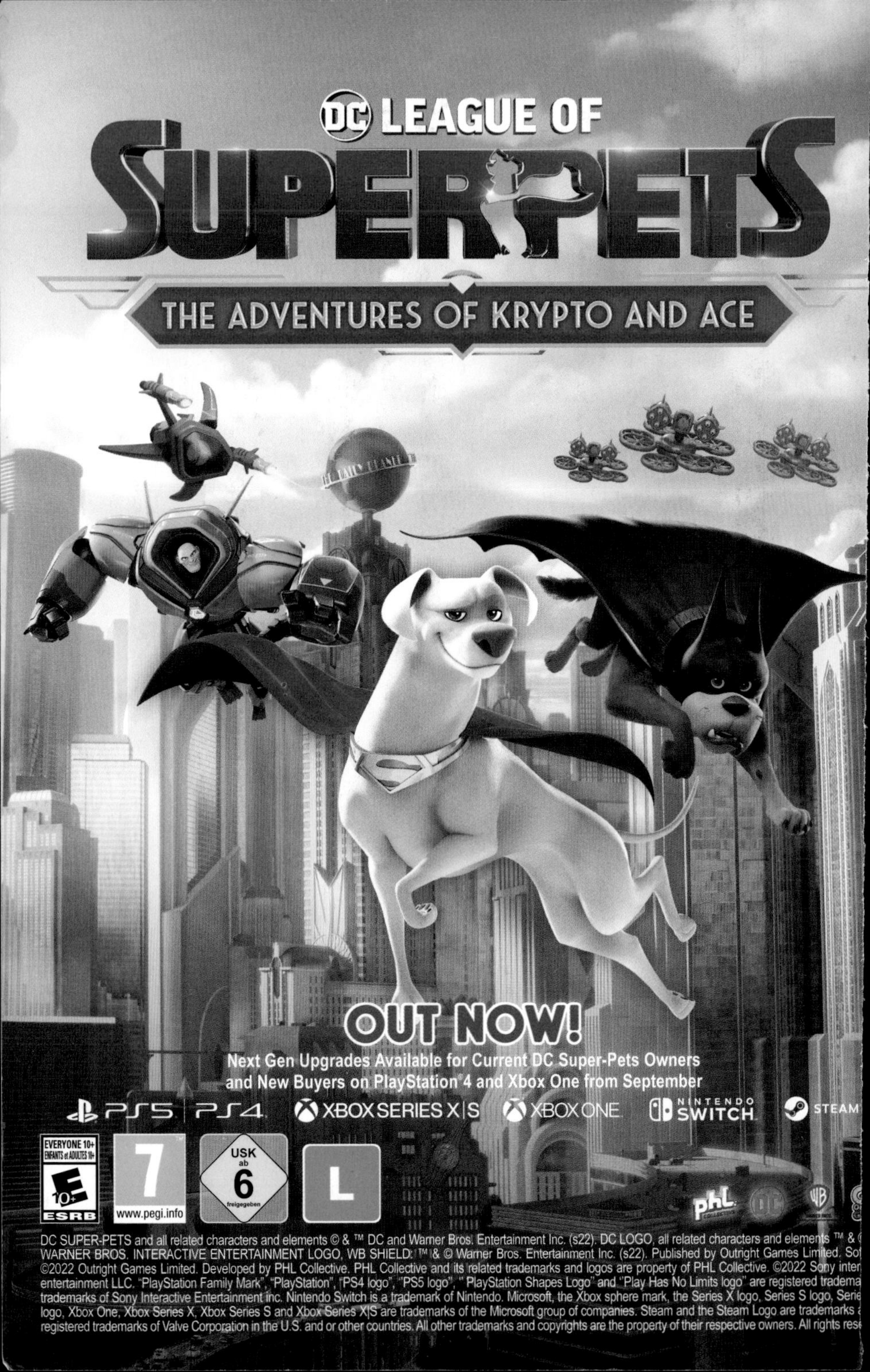

DC LEAGUE OF
SUPER-PETS
THE ADVENTURES OF KRYPTO AND ACE
OUT NOW!
Next Gen Upgrades Available for Current DC Super-Pets Owners
and New Buyers on PlayStation®4 and Xbox One from September
PS5 PS4 XBOX SERIES X|S XBOX ONE NINTENDO SWITCH STEAM
EVERYONE 10+ ENFANTS et ADULTES 10+ E 10+ ESRB
7 www.pegi.info
USK ab 6 freigegeben
L
DC SUPER-PETS and all related characters and elements © & ™ DC and Warner Bros. Entertainment Inc. (s22). DC LOGO, all related characters and elements ™ & ©
WARNER BROS. INTERACTIVE ENTERTAINMENT LOGO, WB SHIELD: ™ & © Warner Bros. Entertainment Inc. (s22). Published by Outright Games Limited. Sof
©2022 Outright Games Limited. Developed by PHL Collective. PHL Collective and its related trademarks and logos are property of PHL Collective. ©2022 Sony inter
entertainment LLC. "PlayStation Family Mark", "PlayStation", "PS4 logo", "PS5 logo", " PlayStation Shapes Logo" and "Play Has No Limits logo" are registered tradema
trademarks of Sony Interactive Entertainment inc. Nintendo Switch is a trademark of Nintendo. Microsoft, the Xbox sphere mark, the Series X logo, Series S logo, Serie
logo, Xbox One, Xbox Series X, Xbox Series S and Xbox Series X|S are trademarks of the Microsoft group of companies. Steam and the Steam Logo are trademarks a
registered trademarks of Valve Corporation in the U.S. and or other countries. All other trademarks and copyrights are the property of their respective owners. All rights rese